WIN
ARROW

A SINISTER FAIRY TALE

To: Becca

#BBBOS

USA TODAY BESTSELLING AUTHOR

LEXI C. FOSS

Winter's Arrow

Editing by: Outthink Editing, LLC

Proofreading by: Katie Schmahl, Julie Robertson, Jean Bachen & Barb Jack

Cover Design: Jay R. Villalobos with Covers by Juan

Cover Photography: CJC Photography

Cover Models: Jenna Elisabeth & Garrett Riley

Published by: Ninja Newt Publishing, LLC

Print Edition

ISBN: 978-1-950694-61-7

To Dee, for creating the Sinister Fairy Tales Collection and for giving me a reason to meet Kazek and Snow.

WINTER'S ARROW

X-Clan Series, Book Three

SINISTER FAIRY TALES COLLECTION

Once upon a time, a group of authors decided to play in the land of fairy tales and embark on a journey of sinister retellings.

Winter's Arrow is the result of that quest.

Enjoy xx

A SINISTER WORLD OF ALPHAS & THEIR CHOSEN OMEGAS

THERE WILL BE BITING...

PROLOGUE

KAZEK

"YOU'RE CORDIALLY INVITED TO ATTEND the celebration nuptials between Beta Snow, Princess of Winter Sector, and Alpha Enrique of Bariloche Sector on—" I stopped reading, the paper in my hand spoiling my mood. "What the fuck is this bullshit?"

"An engagement party," Ludvig replied dryly. "It seems Vanessa wishes to show off whatever enhancements she's made to Winter Sector. Because we both know this isn't for her 'stepdaughter.'"

I snorted. *Stepdaughter. Right.*

How the Betas of Winter Sector hadn't seen through the assassination plot and kingdom takeover was beyond me. It couldn't be a coincidence that Alpha Einar and his Omega mate died shortly after Vanessa joined their court as a mentor for their youngling. Yet everyone accepted the tale and welcomed the new female Alpha with open arms, particularly

1

I shuddered, my stomach twisting with the notion. *How?* I wondered for the thousandth time. *How* did he plan to force it? They never reached that part of the discussion. Or perhaps it'd been covered before I'd found them together in his quarters.

To think, I'd gone to him wanting a midnight kiss and instead... instead my world came crashing to a sudden halt.

I ran first to my quarters, then called a midnight meeting with my protective seven. The Beta circle had believed my tale without flinching, but their leader, Doc, told me to remain quiet and not tell another soul. Because while the kingdom adored my family birthright, the Queen of Mirrors had pulled shutters over all their eyes, her reign supreme in a land that should be mine.

Yet I was born a Beta. A rarity. Some might even claim it as an impossibility.

Hence the need for my wedding, to bring someone superior enough to rule at my side.

And he intended to kill me instead.

I lifted my wine, taking a big gulp of it, and flinched as Enrique's lips brushed my cheek. "Are you all right, Snow White?"

Ugh, that nickname.

An endearment that would haunt me for ages because I'd once revered that stupid set of words.

Until last night.

Last night changed everything.

"Sweetheart?" he pressed, his handsome face melting into a perfect visual of concern. He deserved a medal for his acting abilities, truly.

"I'm fine," I told him, my talents in the acting arena not nearly as gifted as his, but I forced a smile anyway. "Just nervous, you know, with all the visitors in Winter Sector."

"Ah, we have your queen to thank for that," he replied, sounding both amused and displeased—an intoxicating combination. Had he always been this puzzling to read? Or had my vision changed since the discovery of his treachery?

"What are you two whispering about over there?" Vanessa asked, her black eyes seeming to pin me down in that unerringly dominant way of hers.

Alpha.

I always submitted to her.

I couldn't help it.

Just holding her gaze for a second made my heart flutter in panic.

Her lips curled as my focus shifted downward, her pleasure at my constant capitulation evident. I suspected that was the real reason she refused to train me in the physical arts. She didn't want to give me any chance to best her in a fight. If she found out my protective seven had tutored me beneath her nose, she'd place all their heads on spikes at the sector gates.

Fortunately, Doc knew how to hide us all, and he played right into Vanessa's egotistical side.

She prided herself on being the most beautiful matron in the land, in addition to the strongest and most lethal. Enrique matched her in every way, his Alpha traits pairing beautifully with hers.

Ruling together made sense.

I just hadn't realized her intention until it was too late. Until I'd overheard—

"Alpha Kazek," Vanessa said suddenly, her voice sickly sweet. "I should have known Ludvig would send his infamous Huntsman instead of attending himself."

A grunt met her remark, drawing my gaze up to the Alpha male standing before us. "I haven't been called that in over a hundred years, Queen of Mirrors."

Amusement kissed the air in the form of a laugh, one I recognized from Vanessa as flirtatious. She adored males of all types, which was why she refused to take an Omega mate despite having three in her harem. "I see your conversational skills haven't improved with your genetic enhancement, hmm?"

The Alpha merely stared at her, his black eyes rimmed with flecks of sapphire blue, giving him a lethal appearance. *Huntsman,* I thought. *That's appropriate.* Danger oozed from him, as did an air of dominance that he maintained while Vanessa stared him down.

It both fascinated and sickened me.

This was her idea of foreplay, yet he seemed uninterested. Bored, even. Which I knew wouldn't end well. Queen Vanessa adored submission in all ways. He'd either heel for her or pay the price.

His focus shifted suddenly to me, his dark eyebrow arching upon finding me boldly studying his chiseled features. I nearly dropped my gaze, aware of his Alpha status. But I was a princess. The intended heir to the Winter Sector throne. Beta, yes, but powerful in my own right.

So I tilted my chin in defiance.

Which earned me a slight growl from the queen.

Normally, I'd take that as a warning and lessen my stance, but after overhearing last night's discussion, I felt a bit rebellious. So I remained ramrod straight, despite the increasing weight tugging at my spine in an effort to force my submission.

No, I thought. *No. I will not bow.*

I needed to be strong.

It was the only way I'd survive the night.

"You must be Princess Snow," Alpha Kazek mused.

"Did the tiara give me away?" I countered, the words falling from my lips before my brain could stop them.

Shit. I *never* spoke to Alphas like that. Only to members of my seven like Grum and Doc. *So much for playing it cool, Snow.*

Enrique's palm found my thigh, giving it a warning squeeze that made me wince. *That's going to leave a bruise.* It'd match the one he gave me the other night on the back of my neck when he'd lost his control during our kiss.

A kiss I now knew was a lie.

Because he intended to kill me tomorrow night.

"Forgive her," he said, a low growl accompanying those words. "She's had too much wine."

I nearly snorted. I'd indulged in a few sips.

No, it wasn't the alcohol. It was me finally opening my eyes and realizing the entire world had betrayed me.

I need to run.

And go where? some cynical part of me asked for the millionth time.

It doesn't matter. Away from here.

Alpha Kazek's jaw ticked, his blue-black eyes assessing me in a calculative manner. He'd be within his rights to make an example of me for blatantly challenging a male above my rank. But I was Princess Snow of Winter Sector. That should, in theory, afford me some leniency. At least from him.

Enrique and Vanessa would be another story entirely.

Yet another reason to escape.

However, I didn't regret my reaction. Rude, yes. But I was over all the theatrics of today. Everyone wanted to celebrate, and I was done playing the part of the good little princess.

My betrothed planned to assassinate me.

To take my throne.

To join a queen who was only here because my father had welcomed her all those years ago.

How had I been so blind as to accept the stories she'd spun? Why didn't anyone question her?

"You're the spitting image of your mother," Alpha Kazek finally said, ignoring Enrique's interference. Which was an insult of its own, really. He should be addressing the male at my side as his equal but instead chose to focus on me. "Dark hair, porcelain skin, slight frame. A breakable doll."

Breakable, I repeated to myself. *You have no idea.* I was weak for a Beta, something Vanessa harped on often. She gave me supplements that were supposed to help strengthen my muscles, but they did nothing for me. I took them because she made me.

Won't be doing that for much longer, I thought, adding yet another reason to my list to leave.

Now that I knew her true intentions, I wondered if she'd lied to me all these years. It was why I hadn't taken the pills last night or this morning. I didn't feel any different. Of course, my nerves were a tangled mess of insanity, so perhaps I wouldn't even notice.

Kazek arched a dark brow, indicating he wanted a response.

Typical Alpha.

Always in charge.

Always dominating.

Always controlling the scene.

And rather than react the way he expected—the way society dictated—I chose to follow my own path.

I forced a demure smile to form over my lips, one I knew he'd anticipate. Then I spoke my mind out loud. "I've been told I look just like her on the outside and have my father's heart on the inside."

Perhaps it was foolish to provoke him, this stranger known as the Huntsman. But I might as well enjoy myself on the way to death's door.

This is a great plan, Snow, I chastised myself. *The protective seven will be thrilled when you get your ass kicked on top of everything else.*

"Snow," Enrique hissed, his grip squeezing in warning and causing my bone to ache in response.

I swallowed my indignant yelp. Betrayal had altered my sense of focus and my ability to comply with the rules set forth around me.

It felt freeing and terrifying at the same time.

Enrique emitted a low growl, causing my heart to kickstart in my chest. *Here we go…*

But then something strange happened.

A flicker of respect caressed Alpha Kazek's features, giving me pause.

He couldn't possibly be amused by my antics. Alphas were prideful creatures, and I'd just delivered a verbal assault to his hypothetical balls. Which indicated I had a death wish. And maybe I did. Perhaps I wanted to inspire a deadly reaction from Alpha Kazek. If he beat me harshly enough, the wedding would have to be postponed, ruining Enrique's plans to fuck me to death.

Kazek cleared his throat, one eyebrow arching. "I hope that's true, Princess. Your father was a good wolf. My belated condolences on your loss." He held my gaze, his dominance swirling around me in a lingering threat—as if to warn me he could force me to kneel if he wanted to, but he *chose* not to.

I refused to acknowledge his concession, instead maintaining his stare in a way a Beta shouldn't. Vanessa would have my hide later. Good thing I didn't plan to stick around for her to punish me. I had no idea where I would go, but I couldn't stay here.

Another of those glimmers graced his gaze before he returned his attention to Vanessa. "I won't keep you all. Norse Sector congratulates the Winter Sector heiress on her joyous union. You must be thrilled, Vanessa." He canted his head just enough to demonstrate politeness without submitting, his irises flaring with power.

"I am," she agreed. "Thank you for coming."

What a strange Alpha male.

He should be raging and ripping me apart.

Instead, he seemed completely unbothered by my behavior. Not that I wanted him to react. Maybe.

Ugh, I didn't know.

I was a fucking mess.

I need to get out of here.

"Oh, Huntsman," Vanessa added just as Alpha Kazek shifted to walk away. "Be sure to send the young Mickelson son over. We've not yet had the pleasure of meeting."

The muscles along his jaw clenched, the motion defining his sturdy cheekbones. "Of course. But it would be unwise to challenge him. He's stronger than he appears."

Vanessa's excitement radiated around us. "Well, now that just sounds like a flirtatious invitation."

"The amusement will be all mine if you touch him inappropriately," Alpha Kazek replied, arching a brow, the clear challenge in his tone shocking the hell out of me. This male feared no one. Yet he let me disrespect him. *Who are you?* "Enjoy your evening, Queen of Mirrors."

The Huntsman took his leave, his broad shoulders shifting through the crowd with ease until he disappeared into one of the many shadows lurking inside the palace walls.

I'd been so focused on him that I hadn't noticed the penetrating stares prodding the side of my head.

"Where are your manners?" Vanessa hissed under her breath.

"Do you require a public demonstration of your place?" Enrique demanded, reprimand lining each word. "You might be my future wife, but that doesn't give you cause to speak to another Alpha in that manner." His grip turned to cement, my thigh screaming beneath his palm. "You yield, Snow. Always."

Vanessa cleared her throat, drawing our attention to the new guest approaching us.

Another Alpha.

This one, I didn't acknowledge or talk to.

I was too focused on fighting the instinct to weep beneath Enrique's death clutch on my leg. He refused to budge, his punishment severe.

Minutes passed. Maybe hours.

I held in my cries, swallowed the pain, and all the while, Enrique conversed with the guests without a care in the world.

He never let me go, to the point where I knew a shift would be required later to fix the damage. I'd be limping out of here tonight.

Which was why I nearly fainted when he leaned over and demanded a dance, one to appease the spectators. "And you will maintain your form," he added against my ear.

Meaning I wasn't allowed to limp.

A task that would be fucking hard with him having practically crushed my thigh for the last however many minutes or hours.

"Now, Snow," he bit out.

This behavior wasn't new.

He was an Alpha, after all. He adored dominance. They all did. Normally, his growly tones turned me on. Tonight, they just made me want to run.

Not yet.

Play along.

Smile.

Nod.

Dance.

Alpha Kazek caught my gaze from across the room, his expression emotionless as his eyes ran down my white dress to my right leg. A flicker of acknowledgment passed through his features. A punishment served. But he didn't appear to care either way even though he had to know it was because of how I spoke to him.

Enrique's grip on my hip hardened, drawing me into his muscular body as we took over the makeshift dance floor with less-than-fluid movements. I tried to keep pace with him, to shift the way he desired, but my leg continued to throb and my knee threatened to give out.

Vanessa would call me weak later, as she always did. She'd ask if I was taking my medicine as prescribed. Then she'd laugh and shake her head in false sadness, telling me again how I was never meant to lead.

No one saw that side of her except me.

And I supposed Enrique knew, too.

I'd been blinded by his charming dimples, his Alpha strength, and his intoxicating scent. But he was just like her— a monster with eyes set on what should be my kingdom.

Yet how could I lead in this state? I was barely even fit to be a Beta, let alone the Queen of Winter Sector.

Enrique dipped me backward, forcing me to balance on my bad leg, and gave me a wolfish smile. "Next time maybe you'll consider your manners before you speak, hmm?"

I wanted to bite him. And not in a good way.

Instead, I ducked my head in submission.

Which elicited a slight purr from him, his way of accepting my obedience with a reward. But I didn't desire to feel his purr right now. I hated him. I wanted him *dead*.

The vehemence behind my craving nearly set me on my ass.

To kill an Alpha broke so many laws. But why couldn't I slaughter him? He intended to do the same to me. It was only fair.

No. I'll lose that fight in a second.

I had to play this smart.

I needed time to plan.

Which was why I needed to follow through with Doc's idea to run. Oh, I hoped he'd found the right aircraft on which I could leave. He'd mentioned that some were supposedly heading out tonight. Others, tomorrow.

All I knew was that I couldn't risk staying here.

I needed to be on one of those ships.

And I needed to be on one of them *tonight*.

CHAPTER TWO

KAZEK

"THIS PLACE IS A FUCKING CIRCUS," Mick muttered under his breath as he returned to my side. He'd just finished paying his respects to Vanessa and Enrique, and his expression told me he wasn't at all impressed.

I snorted in unspoken agreement.

The Queen of Mirrors had put on an elegant show, but I sensed the deviant underworld lurking beneath her waves of superiority. Many of the Alphas were waiting, aware that the real show had yet to begin. Vanessa had promised us all a proper welcome, which I suspected would arrive in the form of naked slaves.

Not my thing.

I much preferred a bit of fight, like the challenge Princess Snow had leveled my way earlier. Her arrogance piqued my interest, mostly because I suspected she hadn't meant to

14

display it at all and then refused to back down. As if a regal bloodline could save her. Not in this world. Not when she possessed Beta traits that bordered on Omega strength levels.

And that was what captured my intrigue even more.

She hadn't submitted, yet I sensed her need to. Could practically taste her capitulation in the air even while she held my gaze.

An intoxicating conundrum, one that drew my focus to her once more.

She stood on the side of the dance floor, balancing on her left leg. I knew why. Alpha Enrique had put her in her place for the entire room to see, all by squeezing her right thigh.

Everyone had noticed.

Yet Snow Frost had barely flinched, demonstrating a remarkable pain tolerance. It made me wonder how much she could handle when properly dominated. Particularly, in the bedroom.

Which was exactly where my mind couldn't afford to go.

However, it kept wandering there anyway. And that alone irked me. I only fucked Betas out of necessity, not because I really wanted them. So what had me so enraptured by this very taken female? Her midnight eyes? Pert breasts? Long legs? Slender waist? The fact that she presented a forbidden challenge?

I stroked the stubble along my jaw, leaned against the stone-laden wall, and watched as her shoulders tensed from whatever Enrique whispered into her ear. It seemed her punishment was long from over. I couldn't blame him. He knew as well as I did that I could have broken her in front of the room for her outlandish behavior. The only reason I'd chosen not to was because I knew he'd handle it for me.

My version of a wedding gift, I supposed.

Except, now, I regretted it. Because I wanted to put my hands on her. Throttle her until she couldn't breathe. Make her beg for mercy. Then feed my cock between her plump red lips and fuck her while she cried.

And she would, too.

Because Betas weren't meant to take an Alpha's aggression.

It was why I rarely fucked them.

So why her? Why did I want to strip her bare and spank her pale ass until it displayed gorgeous crimson marks?

Those alluring obsidian eyes found mine from across the entertainment hall. She swallowed thickly and quickly glanced away. *Not so strong now, hmm?* I mused, cocking my head.

"You keep looking at her like that and Alpha Enrique is going to challenge you," Mick murmured.

I scoffed at that. "The idiot's not suicidal."

"But he is prideful."

Well, there is that. "It could be fun to take down a groom on the night before his wedding."

"Pretty sure that's not what Ludvig intended when he sent us here to represent Norse Sector."

I lifted a shoulder. "I told him I didn't want to go. He'd only have himself to blame."

Mick pulled out his ponytail and shook his long white-blond hair loose across his broad shoulders. "I'm ready to go when you are."

"I know." He hated this atmosphere as much as I did. Hence the reason I'd requested him as my backup. "But I'm curious to see what the queen intends to do to entice us to stay."

"If you're thinking she'll offer you that Beta princess, I'd say you're in for a rude awakening."

My lips curled. "There wouldn't be any fun in having her as a gift. I much prefer the chase."

He grunted. "Right. That's a tail you should leave alone."

"But it'd be so fun to tame, Mick. Where's your sense of adventure?"

"I left it back in Norse Sector. How about you come back with me and help me find it?"

I met his grinning blue eyes, his amusement palpable. "Tell me you're not eager to kick that Alpha's ass and show this court some real dominance."

"Not my circus, not my monkeys," he drawled.

"How twenty-first century of you."

"Hey, I learned that from your movie stash."

I chuckled at that. "I just bet you did." Fucker was always

16

getting into my stuff without permission. Somehow, the pup and I had become unlikely friends. He was about a hundred years younger than me, born in a time where zombies ruled the world, not humans, and had absolutely no understanding of my past or how I'd been accidentally turned into a wolf.

That innocence was probably why I allowed him to keep breathing.

Well, and his familial ties. Alpha Ludvig probably wouldn't appreciate me killing his youngest son.

My focus returned to my intended prey, her cheeks a dark pink in response to whatever Enrique told her now. He had a grip on her arm, his opposite hand on her hip. His body was angled toward hers in a way that suggested he wanted a favor of the oral variety.

Interesting.

Seemed I wasn't the only wolf thinking about her luscious mouth.

She nodded in response to whatever he said, and he released her.

Then she made quick work of the floor, heading in the direction of the back hall, while Enrique returned to Vanessa up on her throne. Her responding smile held a secret, one that intrigued my inner assassin.

What are you hiding, old Queen of Mirrors?

Murmurs went through the room. Several Betas were leaving, just like Snow.

Ah, it's time for our show.

Decisions, decisions.

I could stay and watch. Or I could hunt down the black-haired beauty.

The smart move would be to remain. But I wasn't into playing it safe. No, I preferred to indulge my darker proclivities, and that little vixen had engaged all my senses.

"Don't do it," Mick warned.

"Don't do what?" I countered, already stepping away. "I'm just going for a little jog. I'll be back in time to observe the party. Don't worry."

He muttered a curse under his breath and shook his head. However, unlike me, Mick was smart. Because he didn't try to stop me. That would have led to a dangerous outcome. Similar to what I was about to do.

I adored hazardous tasks for a reason—they made me feel alive.

And when I wanted something, I went for it.

That something tonight was in the form of a petite little Snow Frost.

I wasn't sure what I would do to her yet. I just knew I craved another verbal duel. Perhaps more. Perhaps less. I'd determine that when I found her.

Which required tracking her through this maze of a palace.

My nose twitched, her delectable scent a hint in the air. She reminded me of sunshine and warmth, something that didn't exist much in the Arctic Circle during this time of year. I inhaled deeply and followed her trail while staying close to the shadows.

If anyone asked my intentions for leaving the party, I'd say I required some fresh air. Not a lie. Darling Snow Frost appeared to be full of fresh—

An array of howls in the distance gave me pause, causing me to frown. They were coming from the entertainment hall.

And one of those howls belonged to Mick.

Fuck.

That was a mating call.

Which could only mean one thing—there was an aroused Omega somewhere in that room. I just hoped the female wasn't in the middle of a heat cycle.

Growling under my breath, I turned toward the chaos and inhaled through my mouth, not my nose. The right Omega in full estrus could knock even a male of my experience right off my feet.

Fortunately, patience was ingrained in my blood. Just like violence. It created a lethal combination that some said resulted in me lacking proper morals.

Perhaps they were right.

I froze at the entrance to the room, my focus narrowing on a petite blonde female locked inside a cage in the middle of the massive hall.

The translucent barrier rattled as Alphas and Betas tried to reach the whimpering Omega inside. One look confirmed she wasn't in heat, just turned on and perhaps nearing her cycle.

Chaos was imminent.

Vanessa observed from her throne, her expression intrigued, while Enrique paced beside her with veins bulging up and down his arms. He'd ripped off his suit jacket and shirt, the Alpha in him demanding he take the female the evil queen dangled before everyone like a tempting carrot.

Bitch.

A male flew across the room, the source of the throw belonging to Mick. He'd gone into protective mode. Typical. He'd see that poor creature as a broken being requiring help. But the collar around her neck marked her as a slave.

The cruel queen had probably shot the Omega up with a serum to force her sexual interest with the purpose of permeating the room with lust for tonight's festivities. I wouldn't put it past her to induce estrus, either. Which, from the looks of things, might actually be what she'd done. The girl just hadn't fallen into full heat yet.

Vanessa probably intended to give Enrique a taste of the whimpering Omega as some sort of bachelor gift. Hence his impatient strides and the reason he'd sent Snow to bed early. Or perhaps Vanessa only planned to let him watch.

Regardless, it was fucked up, and I wanted nothing to do with it.

In fact, I wanted out.

This place reeked of nightmares and dark intentions. I might have favored that in a past life, but not tonight.

I just had to corral Mick and force him to leave, which was going to be a problem. He stood in the middle of a pack of hungry visiting Alphas, all desiring the little Omega lamb in the cage. And Mick was stopping them all with his superior fighting skills.

Well, at least no one would question his birthright after this.

Fuck. Pinching the bridge of my nose, I blew out a breath and shook my head.

I had two options. Either I helped him or I seriously pissed him off by dominating him in front of the room.

19

The latter could be fun, but the former allowed for blood. I liked blood.

Especially when it came from other Alphas.

My lips curled as a blade fell into my hand. I always came prepared, and it seemed this occasion required my kind of party favor.

I'd wanted a way to work off my aggression and had planned to use Snow for that. But it seemed I'd be giving her a pass tonight.

A pity, really. I doubted she'd survive her first year with Enrique.

Perhaps we'll meet in another life, pretty Beta.

It's time to play.

CHAPTER THREE

SNOW

GOOSE BUMPS PEBBLED DOWN MY ARMS as howls reached every corner of the castle. Enrique had told me to leave, claiming that I needed my beauty rest for tomorrow's big day.

I snorted. *Bastard.*

Like I didn't recognize the mating call coming from the celebration hall. I wasn't a child. I might have spent many years hidden away in this castle, supposedly preparing for my future duty as a leader, but that didn't make me uneducated.

Vanessa's Beta brothels weren't a secret. I never approved of them. However, she argued that it provided a new source of income for the sector, one that supplied annual profit—unlike our fishing exports, which were only in the summer months.

I could practically hear my parents growling from their

graves.

It was one of the policies I'd intended to dismantle when I took over as queen. How naive I'd been to ever think that might happen.

I trusted you, I thought, my focus falling to one of the many mirrors lining the palace hallways. Vanessa was obsessed with them. *You were my mentor. My stepmother. My guardian. How could you?*

Except, I knew why. I'd suspected her true intentions for some time. Particularly after she chose my intended mate for me. But then I'd met Enrique and fell for his dimpled smile, wolfish charm, and intelligent mindset. And I'd forgotten all my misgivings, choosing to believe that perhaps Vanessa had my best interest at heart after all.

I'd been wrong.

So very, *very* wrong.

My jaw clenched, my hands fisting at my sides. *Stop wallowing and move*, I told myself, my dark eyes glimmering with resolve. *Run.*

I forced one foot to move in front of the other, my decision to flee bolstered by the uproarious sounds coming from the grand hall. Enrique was indulging in the games. The brothels. The willing females. That was the real reason he sent me to my quarters. He wanted to enjoy his last night of bachelorhood.

A growl worked its way up my throat, but I swallowed the rumble back down.

Jealousy didn't exist.

Neither did true love.

Or loyalty.

Or any other bullshit emotion I fancied once upon a time.

I knew better now. My mentor had betrayed me. So had my fiancé. They'd intended to *kill* me. To destroy the last of the Frost bloodline. I couldn't allow that to happen.

And what's your plan? that cynical part of me wondered for the thousandth time. *To run and hide in the woods? Go to another sector and beg them to help?*

It was laughable, really.

Oh, I sincerely hoped Doc had come through for me.

Because if he hadn't… I swallowed, shaking my head. *Don't think, Snow. Just move.*

My brain whirred in circles, all signs of logic lost. Failure and cowardice threatened my mind, but I refused to grant them entry. A coward would accept her fate and die. I chose to live, to fight another day when I had the appropriate resources and wherewithal to do so.

I couldn't allow myself to contemplate the notion that the time might never arrive.

It was too dangerous a consideration, one that could force me to remain.

And then what? Would I just lie down and take the knot? Die during sex? Fuck. That.

With a low growl, I entered my quarters and found Grum waiting for me. He was one of my trusted seven, a fellow Beta who had ensured I learned how to fight when Vanessa claimed I was too weak.

He remained silent, his silver-blue eyes glancing over my shoulder as if he expected someone to follow me inside. Perhaps Enrique. And wouldn't that be a fun confrontation? Of course, Enrique didn't know about the seven. Neither did Vanessa. It was an ancient Frost family secret. Only those in the line knew about the fealty of the protective circle. And it was created specifically for situations like this.

Grum's stance relaxed as I closed the door, and he opened his arms. "You look like you could use a hug, dove."

I ran into him headfirst, accepting his comfort and adoration. He and the others were my brothers. Not literally, but in spirit. I adored and cherished them as if they were my own blood. And I knew they felt the same about me.

He sighed into my hair, his palm a soothing caress against my back. "Doc found a way out."

My heart stopped. "Tonight?"

He nodded. "Yeah. He said to find you and take you through the tunnels. And… and he wants you to go alone." His tone told me how he felt about that idea, but I understood.

"Packs are easier to track down," I whispered. "It's… it's harder for a group to hide."

Grum's lips were in my hair, his arms tightening around me. "I don't like this, Snow."

"I know." *I don't either.* I didn't add that part, because it wouldn't fix the situation. "Which transport?"

"Norse Sector. Alpha Ludvig is known for his fairness. If anyone is going to help, it's him."

"Norse Sector?" I repeated, a slight squeak in my voice. *Norse Sector congratulates the Winter Sector heiress on her joyous union.* Alpha Kazek's deep voice played through my head, sending a shiver down my spine. "Are you certain that's the best place?"

He pulled back, his hands on my shoulders. "Alpha Ludvig and your father were friends. You know this."

Yeah, I did. But… "He sent an Alpha tonight to represent Norse Sector. I… I may have challenged him." I grimaced with the admission while Grum's eyebrows shot up.

"*What?*"

"He, well, I, I mean, I didn't *challenge* him; I just wasn't all that respectful?" It came out like a question, causing me to grimace once more. "It doesn't matter. I'll figure it out. Doc's right. Norse Sect—"

The doors to my quarters blew open as Ez and Leep charged inside, their matching expressions fierce.

Ez didn't waste a second. "We've gotta get her out of here. Now."

My brow came down. "Why? What's happened?"

The two Betas shook their heads as one, their matching flocks of brown hair hanging in their identical gray eyes. The male twins were always in sync with each other and rarely separated.

"No time, Princess. We need to move." That came from Leep, his rumbly voice just a hair deeper than his brother's. It was how I told them apart.

Grum took my arm, propelling me forward. "If they say we need to go, then we need to go." The three of them corralled me through the halls, peeking around corners to ensure no one saw us, before leading me down a narrow passage very few in the castle knew existed.

Danger hit my senses.

A lethal air coming from the main hall.

Something bad had happened, the stench of death reaching my nostrils and causing them to flare. I didn't ask what had happened, because I wasn't sure I wanted to know.

Doc met us at the exit, his bulky form hunched into the cramped space. He grunted as we approached, then his black irises met mine. Knowledge and experience radiated from him. He'd been my father's most trusted advisor and led the council of Betas who'd sworn fealty to my family's bloodline. Vanessa thought they worked for her and were enamored with her beauty and strength, but they only tolerated her to remain close to me—the only heir.

These men were my teachers. My family. My trusted brothers.

Without them, I wouldn't be *me*.

And now… now I had to leave them.

"Come," Doc said, the male not known for many words.

We followed and met three more Betas—Opy, Happa, and Bash—rounding out my seven protectors.

They maintained a fierce facade, but I caught the underlying worry in their scents. We all liked to plan, and this had been thrown together at the last minute.

"You're sending her on a jet with a notorious assassin," Bash muttered. "He's taken down half the fucking room already."

I trembled at the image his words stirred because I knew whom he meant. *Alpha Kazek.*

Doc ignored the disgruntled male and handed me a necklace. "Wear this. Alpha Ludvig will recognize it."

I eyed the paw print symbol at the end of the chain, then pulled it over my head.

"And you're going to have to put those on." He gestured to a pile of clothes—jeans and a sweater. "They'll mask your scent."

My brow furrowed, then I sniffed the air and cringed. *Dead fish.*

"Yeah. It's not pleasant," Bash agreed, his lip curling in a snarl. "But it matches the import in their cargo." Meaning he'd found whatever wedding gift Norse Sector had sent and rubbed the clothing against it. Smart.

I took a step toward it, my stomach churning. It'd been doing that all evening, my nerves running a riot through my system.

"We don't have much time," Doc pressed, the Beta's alpha-like personality shining through.

Bash snorted. "Yeah. Because the infamous Huntsman is on a murderous rampage, and oh, you want to send our Snow back in his plane. Good plan, that. Fully support the idea, mate."

"Which sector would you recommend?" Leep asked, arching a brown brow, his tone holding a touch of irritation.

"Yeah, which one?" His twin echoed that tone.

"I've already said we need to leave together, protect her as a pack," Bash said, his green eyes gleaming. "It's the best way."

Leep scoffed at that. "Until the Queen of Mirrors tracks us down."

"Let her try." Opy cracked his neck, his pale hair reminding me of the moonlight overhead.

With a shake of my head, I walked over to the clothes with Grum at my side. He unzipped my dress without me having to ask, and I let it fall to the ground. Nudity wasn't something any of us cared much about. We were wolves. We frequently roamed around naked.

Happa, the shortest of the group, lifted his hands, his demeanor calm and collected as he said, "Guys, we already decided—"

"No, *he* decided," Bash cut in, stabbing his finger against Doc's chest and stirring a growl from the much older Beta.

Doc wrapped his hand around Bash's wrist, squeezing. "Watch it."

"You *watch* it, old man," Bash seethed, trying to poke him again.

Ah, hell, I thought, pulling the foul-smelling sweater over my head. My stomach twisted in revulsion. *Ugh, yuck.*

"This isn't helping the situation," Leep pointed out, his expression bored while he observed Bash and Doc's nonverbal standoff.

"Not at all," his twin agreed.

"Oh, will you two shut it?" Opy snapped, stepping up to Bash's side to demonstrate his allegiance. The two males always had each other's backs. Which I typically adored about them, but right now, I needed a show of solidarity.

I started pulling on the putrid jeans. "Guys—"

"This is a horrible plan," Bash said, interrupting me. "At least let one of us go with her."

I worked up the zipper and buttoned the top of my pants. "Seriously, guys—"

Leep sliced his hand through the air. "If one of us goes with her, we all go with her."

"Yeah. We're a team." Of course Ez agreed. "We all go."

"Guys! Listen—"

"Now you're speaking my language." It was like Bash and the others couldn't fucking hear me. They just kept cutting me off. "Let's go into the woods and formulate a better plan."

"And risk the queen sending all her guard mutts after us? Yeah, that sounds brilliant." Doc folded his muscular arms, his dark skin blending into the night. "This is the best way to give Snow a fighting chance at survival."

I opened my mouth to point out that I was capable of making my own decisions, but my stomach clenched sharply, causing a wave of dizziness to swim across my mind. *Oh...* I grabbed Grum's arm on instinct, needing something to keep me upright.

"What is it?" he asked me softly while the others continued their argument, their voices low but angry. I wanted to tell them to be quiet and listen to me, but I couldn't speak, the air whooshing from my lungs as another spasm knocked my insides.

"Snow." Grum turned me toward him. "What is it?"

My lips parted, words hanging on my tongue, when suddenly all the hairs along the back of my neck shot up on end.

Everyone froze.

Then a piercing howl startled the night, the source of it a furious Alpha Queen demanding the attention of her subjects.

My knees threatened to buckle, submission yanking on every fiber of my being and demanding my capitulation.

But Grum kept me upright, his own jaw clenched as he fought the call to kneel.

"*Fuck*," Doc muttered, his voice gruff. "You need to get on the plane right now."

No one argued.

Bash walked over, knelt before me, and helped put on my shoes. I hadn't even seen them on the ground. My vision swam with emotions, my brain blinking in and out of understanding. All the while, my insides spasmed.

I squeezed Grum's arm, a groan building in my throat. But I swallowed it down. *It's just the smell. I'll be fine. It's going to be fine.*

"Snow?"

I shook my head. "I'm fine." I had to be.

Doc stepped forward, holding out a device. "This is fully charged. Don't turn it on until you're ready to contact us."

A satellite phone.

These were rare. "Where did you—"

"Don't worry about that. Take these, too." Doc handed me three knives, my second-favorite weapon. "A bow is too bulky."

Yeah. He was right. I quickly stowed the items, then cringed as the howls started up once more. Whatever justice Vanessa had just dispensed must have pleased the crowd.

"That's where you need to go." Doc pointed to a higher-tech plane parked beside a set of stairs about twenty feet away. "It's already unlocked. Go directly to the cargo area. There's a bunch of boxes to hide in."

"You've been on the plane?"

He nodded.

"But they'll smell that you were there." And then maybe check the plane for a stowaway. "Doc—"

"All the planes were swept by Vanessa's guards. That's why they're unlocked. Trust me, they won't think anything of it, other than knowing it was part of the sector security measures." His lips curled into one of his fatherly smiles. "I've thought through all the angles. This is your best solution. Go to Alpha Ludvig. Tell him what's happened. He'll help us. I know he will."

I wished I shared his optimism. I'd never met the Alpha of Norse Sector. But his Huntsman had certainly left a strange impression. "What if he doesn't?" I asked, my insides protesting once more. "What if…?"

"That's what the phone is for," he replied, pulling me into a hug despite my filthy clothes. "You're going to be okay, sweetheart."

The others began to mumble, their bodies pressing in for a group embrace. Lips caressed my hair and neck; a few brushed my cheeks.

My brothers.

My family.

Tears prickled my eyes. "I'm going to miss—"

Another howl pierced the night, this one closer and victorious. I didn't recognize the owner, but the dominance in it forced my knees to bend. Had the males not been holding me up, I would have fallen in immediate submission.

Whoever owned that howl was *strong*. Terrifyingly so.

The males held me as if I weighed nothing. Which, really, compared to them, I didn't. I'd always been small for a Beta, something my pills—

"Oh!" My eyes went wide. "Should I take my—"

Another howl had my protective seven releasing me to Doc's arms alone. "You must go. Anything you forgot can be replaced."

"I don't—"

"Now, Snow!" He pushed me into Grum's taller frame. "Get her on the fucking plane, Grum."

There was so much to say, but the increasing howls made it impossible for me to speak. We wouldn't be alone out here for long, and if someone saw me now, we would all be as good as dead. Vanessa would not take kindly to this situation, especially after what I learned last night. And the others in the sector would see me as a defector, a traitor, an unworthy royal blood.

I swallowed. *They'll see me that way regardless.*

"We'll figure this out," Doc called after me softly as Grum carried me off toward the plane, seeing my indecision. "It's going to be okay."

29

I wasn't so sure about that, but what choice did I have? He was right. This was the best option.

"Be good, sweet girl," Grum whispered, hugging me close. "We love you." He didn't give me a chance to reply, his hands tightening around my hips as he pushed me up the stairs. My hand shook as I tried to open the door, my heart beating wildly when I found it unlocked, just like Doc had said.

I glanced over my shoulder to see Grum standing guard, the others having dispersed to the shadows, but I could feel their eyes on me.

"Go," Grum growled. "*Now.*"

I hated leaving him.

Hated all of this.

Hated Vanessa, Queen of Mirrors.

She had to pay for what she'd done. One way or another, I'd find vengeance, even if it was in the afterlife.

I twisted the handle and stepped through the threshold, gave Grum one final glance, and then closed myself inside the plane.

Time to hide.

CHAPTER FOUR

KAZEK

I LOVED THE SCENT OF BLOOD. It came second to sex. Both were arousing as hell, but there wasn't a single female here I wanted to fuck.

Well, maybe little Snow Frost.

However, that most certainly wasn't going to happen, not with Vanessa shooting daggers at me with her eyes. What had she expected when she started that riot?

I winked at the angry Alpha. "Amazing party, Queen of Mirrors."

She growled. "Leave."

"Now, is that any way to reward your victor?" I drawled. "I mean, that was the point, yes? Battle for the pretty Omega in the cage?"

"She's not on the market."

"Then why advertise her as such?" I asked, arching a brow.

"Do I need to break the glass to make a point?" It wouldn't be hard. I had a pistol tucked into my boot that would do the trick just fine.

"She's a gift for Alpha Enrique, and you're walking a fine line, Alpha Kazek."

My lips twitched. "A fine line indeed. And what a magnificent gift to bestow upon your *stepdaughter's* betrothed." I knew that'd been her intention all along, but that didn't mean I'd allow her to get away with it.

Black flames danced in the wicked queen's eyes. "It was customary for the groom to enjoy a bachelor party in your former culture, yes? Consider this his."

Mick radiated fury at my side. I knew what he wanted. I just wasn't sure if I desired this battle. The female was pretty, with her long blonde hair, supple breasts, and shaved sex, but her scent oddly didn't allure me the way Snow Frost's had. Fortunately, the female wasn't in heat at all, just forcibly turned on by the stimulators on her clit and nipples.

Clever.

Twisted.

Cruel.

"I want the Omega," I said, folding my arms. "I'm happy to fight Alpha Enrique for her."

Some of Mick's tension seemed to abate, his approval evident. He probably would have issued the challenge if I hadn't, and while he'd taken on the room with expert skill, I wasn't sure how he'd fare against Alpha Enrique. Something told me the older male fought dirty, and Alpha Ludvig would not be pleased if I lost his youngest son to this mess.

"As I said, she's not on the market." If Vanessa could breathe fire, I suspected the room would be burning.

"A good hostess doesn't advertise a product and take it away when a victor proves himself. That can lead to a war, *Alpha*." I glanced casually at Mick. "How do you think your father will feel about it?"

"Not great, Kaz. Not great at all."

"Yeah, that's my thought, too. I mean, truly, we'd be doing her a favor by taking the female. It'd prevent a lot of death." I glanced around the carnage in the room. "Well, more death, anyway."

"She's sterile," Vanessa hissed. "A worthless cunt for you to knot. Why bother?"

"Pleasure," I replied, giving her a wolfish smile. "Isn't that the point?" Fear permeated the air, the girl in the cage not appreciating my statement at all.

I'd deal with that later.

Or let Mick do it.

This was for him, after all. Not me. I saw the way he looked at her. He wanted the female. We'd fought for her. Now we'd take her.

"What's it going to be, Queen of Mirrors? Will you dishonor my fight by retracting what was clearly an offer to the room? Or will you cut your losses and give me the girl? It's not like you can do much with her *cunt*, right?"

Vanessa snarled, her howl shooting up into the night once more and causing me to yawn. She could demand my submission all night. I'd never give it to her.

Which only infuriated her more.

Alpha Enrique raged behind her, his lip bloody from the punch I'd landed across his jaw.

"Is your pride worth that much to you?" I asked Vanessa softly. "To risk a war over this misunderstanding?" I tsked. "What kind of *queen* does that make you?"

If looks could kill, I'd be a dead wolf.

Fortunately, murder required skills, and mine trumped hers.

"Fine," she bit out. "Take her for the night."

My brows rose. "Oh, no. We'll take her for every night. You'll transfer rights of her to Norse Sector. Or I'll go home and tell Alpha Ludvig about tonight's events. Your choice."

I had her backed against a wall, and she knew it.

Mick and I had just made an enemy for life, but as I had no intention of ever returning to this godforsaken sector, it worked for me. Besides, enemies were fun, and it'd been so long since I'd had the opportunity to make one.

Her jaw ticked.

Alpha Enrique growled.

And then Vanessa's lips curled, an idea forming and

activating with merciless precision. "All right. She's yours." Her gaze twinkled and she lifted a hand. "Release the girl."

Ah, fuck.

The glass began to rise, causing a fresh wave of Omega lust to rush the crowd. Mick snarled and went right for the female. He picked her up and cradled her petite form against his chest, leaving me with the work of fighting off the ravenous wolves stirring in the crowd.

Vanessa had created the perfect conditions to inspire rutting instincts in the weaker Betas and Alphas.

"Well played," I muttered at the bitch who stood smirking beside her throne. "Run," I told Mick. "I'll be right behind you."

And the dance began.

More blood.

Bites.

Scratches.

Howls.

Chaos.

I adored it all, my growl loud as I cut off all those in pursuit of Mick. We'd done some serious damage already, making this a rather easy situation to handle. Most of the wolves had remained in a submissive form. Only the idiots controlled by their libidos tried to trail after Mick. Everyone else bowed.

Bet you just love that, I thought at Vanessa, giving her a wink from the doorway. Her lip curled up into a snarl. I hadn't exactly issued her a challenge, but I'd certainly disrespected her. She would be within her rights to formally request a duel. I sort of hoped she would. It'd be fun to make her bleed.

Mick was already halfway to the airfield by the time I reached the exterior of the archaic castle-like structure. It was one of those old European fortresses with the stone walls and torches.

Winter Sector lacked updated technology, something that had been evident in the cool interior where they relied mostly on fire to keep themselves warm. At least they had all the plumbing issues worked out and had access to fresh water. Otherwise, they'd be no better off than living in the Ice Age.

"The Omega passed out as soon as I removed the

stimulators," Mick informed me as I met him at the stairs leading up to our plane. The males lost to the rut were somewhere behind us, their hungry growls painting the night in violent passion.

Mick responded to their irrelevant claims with a snort and threw the sensual clamps onto the ground. Apparently, Winter Sector could afford sexual technology, but not a proper working furnace. *And how do your wolves feel about your prioritization skills, hmm, Queen of Mirrors?*

Alas, I wouldn't be sticking around to ask her.

"Fucking collar." Mick eyed the metal contraption, searching for a clasp. Finding none, he took the steel between his thumb and finger and used his strength to create his own release mechanism.

"Here." I grasped the ends with both hands and carefully widened the gap, something he couldn't do one-handed.

"Thanks." He gently removed the device from her neck, then hissed at the purple bruising beneath. "*Fuck.*"

"No time," I said, hearing the approach of boots. "Inside." I pushed open the door, my nose curling at the stench inside the main cabin. "Damn it. Those idiots must have brought our gift through here."

Mick grunted in reply, slamming the door with his heel and turning to throw the lock. That'd keep the others out, at least temporarily. He glanced around and frowned. "They've been through our stuff."

"I told you they would do that." There were very few sectors we could visit without going through ample security sweeps, and Winter Sector was not among those locations. "Here. Give me the Omega. I'll secure her somewhere back here while you get us ready to go." Because there were more howls coming and I really didn't want any claw marks in Ludvig's precious plane.

Mick considered me for a minute before he begrudgingly passed over the sleeping Omega. I didn't tease him for it, even though a few choice comments rolled through my mind. Alphas were innately enamored by Omegas. They were rare among our kind and specifically bred to carry our seed. It meant we could fuck them the way we truly desired and not risk breaking them.

Most sectors treasured their Omegas, while some treated them as slaves. And if Vanessa spoke the truth about this female's inability to procreate, then the girl fell into the latter class. Because without the ability to breed, she'd be good for only one thing—taking the knot.

But that didn't make it right to torture the poor thing through sensual technology. Ludvig would probably use her to appease some of the unmated males in Norse Sector. Males like me and Mick. However, unlike Winter Sector, we'd ensure her health and care in return for her services. The bruising along her frail form told me that had not been the case with Vanessa.

Poor little lamb.

I moved a lock of her hair and tucked it behind her ear. She was beautiful, with a pert nose and full lips, but it did nothing for me. Another mouth taunted my mind, one painted in dark red and framed by porcelain skin. Two obsidian eyes graced my vision, the challenge in their depths an aphrodisiac to my wolf.

Oh, how I longed to make that adorable Beta submit.

How strange that Snow Frost remained at the forefront of my hungry thoughts while I held an overstimulated Omega in my arms. I could swear, even now, that her scent surrounded me.

Maybe I'd picture her later while I knotted this darling Omega.

Hmm, perhaps not. That'd be rather hard with their opposing physical traits.

Shaking my head, I focused on finding something to cover up the shivering female in my arms. I grabbed a thick wool blanket from one of the overhead bins, swaddled her in it, and buckled her into one of the chairs.

She wasn't mine to make any decisions about right now. Ludvig would have that honor because anything I won technically belonged to him as the Alpha of Norse Sector. Besides, Mick should be able to taste her first. It'd been his unspoken idea to go after the damsel.

Which left me craving the one I couldn't have.

Sighing, I walked away from the female to tend to my destroyed wardrobe. The plane had a shower, but we wouldn't be in the air long enough for me to fully appreciate it, so I just traded my bloody clothes for a fresh pair of jeans and a sweater from my overnight bag.

"Buckle up," Mick demanded as I entered the cockpit. He'd changed as well but had discarded his clothes in a pile just beyond the doorway. I kicked them backward and took the seat beside him. He seemed surprised by my choice. "What if she wakes up?"

I lifted a shoulder. "What can she do? She's on a plane."

His blue eyes slid sideways to mine. "Sometimes I wonder how well you understand women."

I scoffed. "What's there to understand? She moves, I growl, she submits. Done."

Mick chuckled under his breath and did something with the controls to skyrocket us forward. The air fleet Ludvig had acquired from his oldest son in Andorra Sector functioned more like rockets than the planes of my youth.

A feminine yelp from the back told me the Omega had awoken as a result. "You're fine, little one," I told her. "Just don't move. We'll be in Norse Sector in about an hour."

She didn't reply. I hoped that meant she intended to comply.

I closed my eyes, a female with dark eyes and ruby lips gracing my mind. Oh, what I would do if she were strapped back there instead of the blonde. She wouldn't have been given a blanket because I'd have kept her naked. If she wanted to be warmed up, I'd make her ask for my hands and mouth. And then she'd repay my kindness by sucking my cock.

Mmm, yes, I liked that fantasy.

I allowed it to play out in my mind over and over while Mick concentrated on navigating the dark skies. All the while, her scent taunted my nostrils as if she were on the plane with us. I still didn't understand that part. The Omega should be overpowering me with her addictive perfume, but something about Snow Frost had stayed with me.

Did I make a mistake leaving her behind?

I frowned at the thought.

No, of course not. How could it possibly be a mistake? I didn't even know the woman. I only wanted her because I hadn't handled her challenge the way I should have—by dominating her before the entire kingdom.

It didn't matter. I'd made my point later by taking down all those hungry Betas and Alphas and stealing Alpha Enrique's bachelor party gift.

I smirked, pleased with the outcome, and let myself doze the rest of the way home.

* * *

MY NOSE TWITCHED again as we landed, Snow Frost's delectable scent still calling to the predator within me. *What is it with you, little wolf?*

I shook my head to clear it. This temporary fascination needed to end. She'd probably be dead in the coming months, as I couldn't imagine the Queen of Mirrors would allow the Beta to rule long. Her Alpha instincts would demand submission in every way.

"How do you want to handle the precious cargo?" I asked, forcing all thoughts of the alluring female from my mind.

Mick unbuckled his seat belt after throwing all his controls into the right gears and pinned me with a serious gaze. "Am I going to have to fight you for her?"

I frowned, uncertain of whom he meant for a moment. *Stop thinking about Snow, dumbass.* "You want to fight for the Omega? Why?"

Both of his eyebrows shot up. "Did you not smell her?"

Yeah, I had, but another scent had piqued my interest more. And still was. *Why? How? She's not even here.*

"Why are you giving me that look?" Mick demanded. "I get that she's sterile, but she's still an Omega. There are only three of age in Norse Sector, and none of them have called to me like this one did in that cage."

"That was your protective instincts, Mick."

"Maybe. But now I want her. Are you going to fight me on it?" A flicker of determination glimmered in his blue irises, one that told me he was deadly serious.

"You wouldn't win."

"I know."

"So why are you challenging me?"

"I'm not. I just want to know if I need to prepare to issue the challenge."

I looked him up and down, my brain temporarily short-circuiting. "What the hell is wrong with you?"

"Answer me, Kazek. Are you going to fight me for her?"

Jesus. The kid had lost his damn mind. I mean, yeah, he was one hell of an Alpha. But way too young to be trying to claim an Omega. That usually happened when Alphas reached my age, not the ripe year of twenty-five. I almost admired his determination.

"You always were a cocky son of a bitch," I mused, my lips twitching.

Mick didn't share my amusement. Instead, he stared, his wolf lurking in his gaze.

"Shit, you've got it bad, man. You don't even know the girl." Of course, the same could be said about Snow Frost, and here I was, moping over my missed opportunity to track her down. Maybe Winter Sector had drugged us? I wouldn't put it past the Queen of Mirrors to spike the drinks with some sort of lust potion. *Wicked bitch.*

Mick didn't reply, his wolf continuing to watch me, waiting for a response.

I blew out a breath and sighed, "Your funeral, Mickelson." I rarely used his full last name, preferring to call him Mick, but the situation seemed appropriate. "I won't challenge you for her. However, others likely will."

"I disagree. We won her from Winter Sector. If you're not going to take her, then I can lay claim."

"That's not how it works. Anything I win belongs to your father."

"Not her," he replied, not backing down.

Stubborn wolf. "You'll have to take that up with…" I trailed off, my nose twitching once more with a fresh wave of Snow's scent.

I slowly turned toward the main cabin, taking in every

detail and finding nothing out of place, just a timid Omega female listening to our every word with wide blue eyes. When I met her gaze, she dropped her focus to the ground in instant submission, and Mick growled a low warning.

"Shh," I hushed him, listening and scenting the air. Something wasn't right. Snow Frost's scent shouldn't be trailing after me like this. Unless I'd gone and lost my mind. "Get the girl off the plane," I told him softly. "Take her to Ludvig. He'll want to know what happened."

"Isn't that your job?"

"Do you want the girl or not?" I snapped, irritated that he'd ignored my command. If it meant taking the female from him, I'd do it. *After* I figured out why Snow's perfume seemed to be suffocating the air inside this plane.

"She's mine," he replied, the Alpha coming through in his tone.

"Then do what I said. Now." I met his gaze and held it. "You want her, then you fight the Alpha of Norse Sector for her. I won't do it for you."

Understanding seemed to finally register in his expression. I'd pretty much just handed him a gift in the form of a pretty blonde Omega. If he presented her to Ludvig as our prize without me by his side, then it meant I'd given up all rights to her.

An insane move on my part, considering the treasure between her thighs, but I was far too consumed with Snow and her fucking enchantment over my senses.

Mick didn't thank me with words; he thanked me by acting.

He approached the trembling female, unbuckled her, and scooped her up into his arms. She whined at the contact, and he purred in response, surprising the shit out of me.

Alphas only purred for their intended mates.

How could he possibly want to mate a broken Omega?

There really had to be something in the damn water in Winter Sector. Neither of us was acting right. I'd have to follow up with the sector physician in the morning.

For now, I had a scent to hunt.

I stood absolutely still just outside the cockpit near a

shadowed space in the main cabin.

Mick opened the main door and left with the female in his arms, taking the Omega's scent with them. Something sweet remained behind. A perfume that reminded me of apples baking in the sun. Very specific. Intoxicating. And far too present to be a coincidence.

Either Snow Frost had been part of the inspection crew earlier—something I highly doubted—or she'd snuck onto our aircraft as a stowaway.

This could all be a figment of my imagination, a dream I desired to act upon, but I indulged it anyway because I was too fascinated not to.

I had two options: find her hiding place or grab her as she exited the plane.

Tapping my jaw, I considered and opted for the latter. It'd be much more fun to spy on her every move. Where would she go? What would she do?

Because I was absolutely certain of her presence now. This couldn't be in my head. Her intoxicating scent had filled every inch of the main cabin. I should have caught it before, but the Omega and the adrenaline from the fight had clouded my judgment. I'd also thought it was just a fantasy playing in my mind.

But no.

Snow Frost was here.

I could *taste* her in the air. Her fear. Her pain. Her hope.

Ah, it seemed I'd be able to play with her after all.

She'd traveled here without permission. That gave her no rights. No safety. No protection. I could do whatever the fuck I wanted with her, and no one would be able to hold me accountable.

A beautiful invitation.

And a fantastic end to a very long day.

All right, little wolf, I thought as I disembarked and went to lean against a nearby tree, my body cloaked in the natural surrounding shadows. *Let me know when you're ready to begin. I'll be waiting for you outside.*

CHAPTER FIVE

SNOW

MY HEART BEAT WILDLY AGAINST MY RIBS. For a minute there, I'd thought Alpha Kazek had found me. But then he'd left, whistling some tune I didn't recognize.

I collapsed onto my side, my stomach churning with the nerves from our flight. We'd taken off so fast that I'd yelped. Fortunately, Kazek had thought it had come from Kari. She'd not said anything to contradict him, but she had glanced around to search for the noise. It'd only be a matter of time before she told the others someone else had been on the plane with them.

Or maybe she wouldn't.

How did they steal her from Vanessa? I wondered for the thousandth time since they brought her on board. Kari was one of the gifts Bariloche Sector sent with Enrique, their way of expressing gratitude to Vanessa for arranging the courtship between me and Alpha Enrique. I didn't know the Omega, had only seen her during the exchange, and I'd suspected the real reason for her presence was to satisfy Enrique's knot. So I hadn't expressed much interest in getting to know the female who would clearly be my husband's mistress.

Except the collar signifying her servitude had been missing from her neck. Strange.

With a shake of my head, I forced myself to stand. I could worry about Kari later. Right now, I needed to be more concerned with my own fate. Like where I planned to go once I got off the plane.

Could I go directly to Ludvig? Show him the necklace and beg for his help? What if the other wolves of this sector found me first?

I frowned. *This really wasn't well thought out.*

But I did have a few blades and a satellite phone.

My lips twisted to the side. Standing here wasn't going to help anything. I'd just peek outside, look around, and decide where to go from there.

Maybe I could find a tree to sleep under outside of the sector to regain some strength. All the stress had weakened my limbs, leaving a quake behind that continued to curl in my lower abdomen.

I felt… sick.

Impossible.

It was probably just withdrawal from the strength drugs Vanessa force-fed me, coupled with the insanity of the last twenty-four hours.

Shaking it off, I crept forward to peek out the windows across from the door. The ocean stared back at me with a crystal-clear reflection of the moon overhead. My lips parted at the sight. I knew Norse Sector bordered the Baltic Sea but didn't realize their airfield sat beside it. Vanessa hadn't allowed me to travel, stating I was too weak to put myself in that position. This had been my first trip on an aircraft, which I could honestly say I wasn't a fan of at all. My ears still hadn't acclimated to being back on the ground. Maybe that was why I felt ill? Motion sickness. How peculiar.

I snuck over to the other side of the plane to find

landscaped trees and hills in the distance, with subtle glows creeping up the nearby mountainside. *Where's their castle?* Maybe it was hidden behind the mountain. That'd make for quite a hike.

I can do this, I coached myself. *There's no other option.*

Blowing out a breath, I gripped the handle and toggled it gently to release the door as slowly as possible. When nothing happened other than a hiss of air tousling my strands, I jerked it the rest of the way and glanced around.

Dried leaves rustled in the night, still clinging to their snow covered branches. The temperature reminded me of home, as did the white landscape. But everything else felt different. Energy hummed in the air here, tickling the hairs along the back of my neck. The scents were unique, too. No ash or embers on the wind, just the sweet scent of pine and ocean. It reminded me of the summer in Winter Sector.

I inhaled, then cringed as my stomach convulsed.

Maybe it's my clothes. They still reeked of fish guts.

Forcing one foot in front of the other, I somehow made it down to the ground without falling. "Ow," I moaned, my knees threatening to buckle. I clutched my midsection as a wave of dizziness forced me back into the stair railing.

Something's wrong.

I whimpered, my legs giving out beneath me. The icy cement chilled my limbs, providing unexpected relief. A groan caught in my throat as I sprawled out along the tarmac at the bottom of the stairs, craving more of the cold pavement.

My skin burned beneath my clothes. "Too hot," I whispered, writhing. My wolf urged me to disrobe, only a pair of hands caught my wrists before I could rip the sweater over my head.

I yelped, shocked by the sudden touch, my gaze flying upward to meet a pair of smoldering blue-black irises. *Alpha Kazek.* My heart skipped a beat at the intensity of his expression. "What are you?" he demanded, his words underlined by a low growl that had my thighs clenching in response.

Oh Gods… "Don't do that," I begged, the sound too much. *What the hell is wrong with me?* My limbs quivered almost violently, and this sweater really had to go! I tried to pull my hands away from him, to rip the fabric from my body, but he held me with the ease of a much stronger wolf.

He pressed his nose to my neck and inhaled, a low rumble vibrating his chest.

I groaned in response, a wave of wetness caressing my core. My legs tensed, embarrassment hitting me at the same time another spasm shot through my insides. I cried out in surprise and pain, my knees tucking into my abdomen as I shuddered around the convulsion.

What's happening to me?

Maybe Vanessa had poisoned me at dinner. Did she know I overheard her conversation? Was this her secondary plan to ensure I died?

Tears fell from my eyes, followed by another yelp as Alpha Kazek grabbed my chin. He'd been saying something, his low, masculine voice making it impossible to concentrate. I leaned into his touch, my mind failing to comprehend the desire warming my veins. His touch soothed me, intrigued me, subdued me.

Yes…

He muttered something about suppressants, causing my brain to flicker back into action. My brow furrowed. "Suppressants," I repeated, a sultry note caressing the word. "Mmm, no. Strength pills. Forgot. Home." Why couldn't I form proper sentences? Ohhh, and why did his touch feel so good?

I practically melted into him. It didn't matter that I barely knew him. He radiated dominance, and I wanted to bathe in the power he offered. Little sounds left my mouth, betraying my interest. It should have mortified me, but I couldn't hold them back, nor could I feel any remorse for allowing them to escape.

This wasn't like me.

It felt as if I'd been drugged.

So suddenly, too.

No, not really. It started… hours ago. With the cramps.

"Snow," Alpha Kazek snapped, drawing me back to him. He'd been talking again. I had no idea what he'd said or why.

But, my, he had the most beautiful eyes. Strong jaw. Mmm, that mouth.

I traced a finger across his lower lip, intrigued by the fullness. He nipped at my touch, making me swoon. *Strong. Alpha. Male. Yes, please.*

I pressed into him, wanting more, craving *him*.

Ugh, but I needed the clothes off. "Hot," I complained, again trying to free my wrists.

Alpha Kazek growled, his annoyance palpable, yet all that sound did was make me even wetter. Oh, that was weird. Why had I wet myself? Another reason to undress. And wow, did I need a shower.

No, I needed *him*.

I pressed my lips to his neck, tasting his skin with my tongue and moaning at the divine essence coating his being.

We started moving.

Or maybe the earth did.

Everything spun, reminding me of the dizzy spells from earlier. Some logical part of my mind screamed at me to focus, but it was so hard to pay attention when the sky disappeared beneath a gorgeous array of evergreens and snow.

Beautiful, I breathed, lost to the scents and sounds of the forest. The air helped cool my heated skin as well, my body coated in a sheen of sweat and grime. "Shower," I managed to say, my throat dry. "Please."

Alpha Kazek grunted. He said something about suppressants again, his tone radiating disapproval. I whimpered in reply, sad that I'd somehow displeased him. Which was odd. I'd purposely challenged him earlier.

I should fear this male, I realized. A whiff of his delicious scent calmed me before I could react to the thought, and I sighed instead. His strength wrapped me in a warm blanket of security, one I never wanted to leave.

Somewhere in my mind, I recognized the absurdity of this. But my wolf seemed to be in charge now. I liked my wolf. She was reliable. I often listened to her.

So I allowed her to stretch to the surface and control my instincts.

"You and I are going to have a very long discussion after

I finish fucking you," Alpha Kazek informed me. "You've been a very bad little wolf."

I blinked. "Fucking?" I'd done that a few times. But I never enjoyed it. I could never react the way females should. However, his words ignited another spell of warmth between my legs that suggested this time might be very different.

How?

Why?

Vanessa must have done something to me. Did she spike my drink with some of those seductive pills she favored? The ones that supposedly enhanced sensual experiences. I'd never been allowed to indulge in them before. Why would tonight be any different?

Because she wants to kill you, I thought dizzily. *Yes. Right. That's why I'm here!* "I need Alpha Ludvig," I said in a rush to explain myself. I fumbled for my necklace, my hands suddenly free. "This. Show him this."

"What you need is a good knotting," Alpha Kazek replied.

My brow furrowed. "No." *Knotting?* Understanding slapped me across the face as an ice pick jolted my heart. "No!" That was how Alpha Enrique intended to kill me. "No, please. No. I don't… I can't… Vanessa—"

Frozen water hit my forehead, shocking me into a scream as my back met a hard, tiled surface. I sputtered, my hands flailing as I tried to protect my face from the assault of chilly pellets. "Calm down. It'll warm up in a minute," Alpha Kazek said, his warm body still holding mine.

He'd walked us under a waterfall of sorts.

No, a shower.

Wait… when did we get inside?

We were surrounded by glass and black marble, the masculine tones highlighted by a low light in the ceiling. My eyes widened at the colossal bathroom surrounding us. Not only had he taken us into a building, but it was one with modern technology I'd only seen in magazines from the past.

I gaped at the room, then at him, my senses temporarily returning. "What are you doing?"

"Washing the stench off you. Did you bathe in a pile of rotten fish before you got on my plane?" He snorted and ripped off my sweater to reveal my bare breasts. We both froze, me in shock, him in clear appreciation of the view.

"Kazek," I whispered.

"Shh," he hushed, his breath minty and addicting and drawing my focus to his mouth. What was this pull between us? Why did I want to thread my fingers through his hair and kiss him? No, not just kiss. *Devour.*

My thighs clenched, causing me to gasp as I realized they were wrapped around his hips. When had all this happened? How was I losing time? His hard length pulsated against my drenched sex, our pants the only barrier between us.

I shook my head, trying to clear it, my mind caught in a web of arousal I didn't understand. "What's happening to me?" I asked, another harsh pang curling inside my lower belly. It ripped through me, shooting off stars behind my eyes that blinded me to the room once more.

"You're going into heat." He yanked on my jeans, his movements furious and terrifying, and I was helpless to stop him. One minute, I was clamped around his waist, partially clothed, and the next, he had me naked and up against the wall again.

"I-I don't understand."

"You've been taking suppressants."

I shook my head. "N-no."

"Yes. And they've worn off at the most inopportune time for you. No wonder your scent seduced me." He dipped his head to my neck once more, his lips skimming my thundering pulse. "I have no idea why you snuck onto our plane, and right now, I don't care."

I whimpered, my limbs trembling as another shock of fire flooded my veins. "L-Ludvig," I managed to say. "I-I need Alpha Ludvig."

"Not happening, little wolf. Not in your current condition." He drew his mouth up to my ear. "If I let you loose, the entire sector will be on your tail. You have no rights here. You're an intruder. And you're an Omega in heat. It won't end well for you, darling."

"B-Beta," I corrected him. "Can't knot me." *It'll kill me.*

"Ah, but I can," he murmured, pressing his impressive

erection to my stomach. When had he lost his clothes? Why couldn't I focus for longer than a few minutes at a time?

And *how* did he plan to knot me?

"Y-you'll kill me," I breathed, arching into him. It was like my body refused to listen to my mind. "D-drugs," I added, hoping he would understand. *I've been drugged.*

"Oh, no, little wolf. No more suppressants for you."

Ugh. He didn't understand! "Not… supp… ressants." I swallowed a moan as he rocked against my body, the water warm as it flowed overhead. It was confusing my senses, both pulling me back into a state of awareness while simultaneously drowning me in lust. "Vanessa w-wants to kill me. Tried, maybe. Drugs."

That gave him pause. "Say that again."

I shook my head, unable to focus long enough for so many words. "Help," I begged instead. "Need… help."

He frowned at me. "You're going into estrus, Snow. I'm planning to help you."

I shook my head, a whine catching in my throat. He didn't understand. "No knot." I couldn't accept it. This had to be part of Vanessa's plan, to make an Alpha think he could fuck me fully.

She'd planned to entice Enrique with this spell, to force him to knot me.

That was what she'd meant by having methods to induce the sensations. She'd cast some wicked enchantment that convinced Alphas I could handle them in a rut.

Tears collected in my eyes.

I'd escaped her clutches, only to fall into the hands of someone so much worse—an Alpha driven by need.

She'd won.

After all that… she'd still won.

I crumpled against him, sobbing beneath the crushing emotions of betrayal and defeat. And worse, arousal.

Because I wanted him.

My thighs slicked with the desire for him to fuck me. But once he did, he'd kill me. "You'll kill me," I whispered, the words on repeat in my mind and out loud. "I'm a Beta. I'm a Beta. I'm a Beta."

CHAPTER SIX

KAZEK

"YOU'RE NOT A BETA." And I was fucking tired of her trying to convince me otherwise. I could smell her true nature now. An Omega hidden beneath a cloud of suppressants. It was disgusting, and it pissed me off. "You know it's illegal in our sector to hide your true form?"

Just another crime to add to her very long record.

"P-please," she begged, causing me to growl in annoyance. I hated this pitiful presentation. What happened to the strong female who challenged me unnecessarily? Why had she crumpled into this pathetic being?

It had to be her heat cycle. "Is this your first estrus?" I wondered out loud, then frowned. "No, that's not possible. You're at least twenty."

She shook her head back and forth, repeating her mantra about how I was going to kill her. Some would argue I was within my rights, considering all the crimes she'd committed tonight. But assassinating an Omega, especially one as beautiful as her, would be wrong on so many levels.

"Why would Enrique ever let you out of his sight?" I asked, my thumb drawing across her cheekbone. "You're stunning. And you smell divine." I pressed my nose to her neck once more, inhaling her perfume of sunshine and apples. *Mmm.* "I want to taste you, Snow. I want to dine on the slick pouring between your thighs. Then I'll knot you."

A moan slipped from her lips, followed by a cry of pain as she buckled over once more.

My lips curled down.

I'd seen Omegas in heat before. This was not how they acted. It had to be the suppressants. There was a reason we outlawed them in Norse Sector. They tended to harm more than help the estrus situation.

I guided her to the bench in the corner of my walk-in shower, then lathered her petite form in soap to help remove the grime and residual stench from her clothes. Those offensive items would be going in the trash as soon as we finished here.

Her nipples pebbled as I brushed her breasts, and her thighs squeezed together in obvious want, and all the while, agonized sounds left her lips. She kept repeating her words, claiming to be a Beta, begging me to help her, and muttering things about Vanessa's plan to kill her.

It all jumbled together into a slurred speech of nonsense that started to sound more like excuses than the truth. But I couldn't deny that her reactions were all wrong.

She wept and moaned in sequence, her slick permeating the air with a desire that didn't match her expression.

The convoluted mess of it all had me hard as a fucking rock.

"Do you know why they call me the Huntsman?" I asked her softly while I lathered her thick, dark hair with shampoo. I crouched before her, trying to capture her gaze. "Because I was an assassin before Ludvig turned me into a wolf. The Huntsman was my code name."

She didn't react.

I rinsed the suds from her black strands, then squatted before her once more. "I enjoy punishing others for their crimes," I informed her quietly, my finger wrapping around a luscious lock of her damp hair. "Usually, I kill them for their sins. Some more harshly than others. And while you've certainly earned a strong reprimand, you've not done anything worthy of a dance with death." I gave her curl a little tug. "Now spread your legs."

She clamped them together instead.

My lips twitched, amused at her reluctance. "Are you denying me, little Snow?"

"I can't... It'll... kill me."

That pretty much answered my question about whether or not she'd ever gone into heat before. Because if she had, she'd know that she could handle my size. Would it hurt at first? Yeah. But her cunt would acclimate, then she'd be begging me for my knot. That was how this worked.

I stood to finish my own shower and smirked when I found her gaping at my dick. "I'm taking that look as a compliment, sweets." I liked that it intimidated her. I'd like it even more when she screamed out in fear-induced pleasure as I drove inside her.

But, clearly, we had a few things to work out before that happened.

She appeared to be fighting her cycle, probably with the assistance of whatever remained of her suppressants. Her sexual perfume told me she had maybe another hour before that resistance crumbled.

I turned off the water and grabbed a towel. She hissed as I wrapped it around her, quickly shrugging off the material as if it burned her. Frowning, I repeated the action on myself and found the fabric to be soft and acceptable.

"You can't knot me," she said, her voice suddenly sturdy.

I arched a brow and met her gaze. "Do you prefer I let you run off on your own to find another Alpha to sate your needs?"

Her eyes widened. "No."

"Then you'll let me knot you."

"No," she repeated. "It'll kill me."

I towered over her and decided to use her position to my advantage. "Open your mouth."

"What?"

"Open." I cupped her cheek. "Your." I pressed my thumb to her chin. "Mouth." I pressed down to unhinge her jaw. "Wider."

Fear-tinged arousal graced the air, her tongue snaking out to dampen that plump bottom lip in unspoken anticipation. Omegas were made to take Alpha cock, something her body seemed to understand while her mind did not.

Fortunately, it was her wolf that stared at me now, the animal smoldering in her irises as she did exactly as I requested. "Beautiful," I praised, shifting forward to press the head of my cock to the welcome opening. More of that alluring slick saturated my senses, her cunt preparing for the rut ahead. However, I was still very much in control of my actions. To prove it, I slowly entered the cavern of her mouth while watching her response closely.

Terror melted into intrigue, followed swiftly by lust.

I smiled. "You like that."

She responded by swirling her tongue over the tip of my cock. Oh, I didn't know who taught her to do that, but I thoroughly approved. My eyes fell closed as she took me deeper, her mouth heaven around my—

"Fuck!" I shouted, yanking backward as her teeth clamped down on my shaft. I growled when she didn't release me, the pain screaming up my spine. Thank God she wasn't able to shift, or my cock would have been split in two between her wolf's jaws. "Let go," I demanded, my tone all Alpha.

She immediately complied, but rather than submit, she dove for her clothes.

And grabbed her knives.

Yeah, I'd felt those when I'd undressed her. Along with her phone.

I narrowed my gaze. "You want to play, baby? Because I adore a good round of violent foreplay."

"Don't touch me." Her voice was stronger now, her backbone clearly enabled.

Fascinating. An Omega this close to her heat cycle should

be a weeping mess, just as she was moments ago. But she'd found some form of reserves tucked away within her spirit, and damn if that didn't turn me on even more.

She took on a fighter's stance, causing one of my eyebrows to rise. "You realize this is only arousing me, right?" My cock bobbed in agreement, her bite already forgotten. "I'm addicted to pain, Snow."

Her thighs visibly clenched, her slick an intoxicating perfume that only excited the moment. I took a step back, leading us toward my bedroom.

"Come and get me, sweetheart," I coaxed, continuing my momentum in the direction I wished for her to follow. She moved exactly where I wanted her to, her two knives tucked expertly against her palms.

Someone had taught her how to spar.

I very much approved.

Most Alphas enjoyed submission. I preferred to have to work for it. Maybe that was the human male in me. Or perhaps it stemmed from my life experiences. Regardless, a feisty female always intrigued me. I adored the art of convincing a strong woman to go to her knees to serve me. It required skill and patience, two attributes I possessed in spades.

"I'll give you the first shot," I told her.

Her lip curled in response, defiance radiating through her and accompanied by a palpable wince.

"I suggest you move quickly," I added. "You won't be able to continue this fight for much longer, little Omega. Your estrus is coming."

"I'm not an Omega," she replied, her voice holding an edge to it. "I'm a Beta."

"Your scent says otherwise."

"My scent has been altered," she growled.

I snorted. "Suppressants only work for so long."

"I'm not on suppressants!" She lunged for me, her blade almost nicking my pectoral muscle, but I caught her wrist just in time. An adorable little yelp fell from her lips as I twisted her into my arms, effectively capturing her with my chest to her back.

"Want to try again?" I asked her conversationally.

She growled.

I gave her one back just for fun and smiled when it caused her to whimper. "Definitely an Omega," I mused, then shoved her away from me. "I'll give you another opportunity, but I suggest—"

A flash of silver was my only warning as she threw the dagger with perfect aim toward my heart. I caught the knife by the sharp side, my eyebrows kicking up in surprise.

"Nice aim," I praised, then held the dagger out for her once more, the metal glistening with my blood. "Let's go for round three."

Rage poured off her, the scent an aphrodisiac when paired with her lust.

She roared and came after me, her hand releasing her weapon while her other batted the second knife from my palm to land unceremoniously on the ground.

What the hell? That move made absolutely no sense. Neither did her decision to jump on me.

I caught her by the hips and allowed her nails to dig into my chest for a brief moment before I tossed her onto the bed. A howl ripped from her throat and she attempted to come at me again, but I had her pinned to the mattress in a second flat.

She shrieked as I captured both her wrists in one of my hands above her head, my opposite hand grasping her hip to hold her where I wanted her beneath me.

Shock seemed to knock some much-needed sense into her. "H-how?"

"What do you mean, 'how'? You just dropped your only defense onto my wood floors and tried to scrape me up with your very feminine nails." *Crazy Omega*, I added. I was no longer impressed by her training. What a stupid move on her part. If she were my student, I'd teach her one hell of a lesson for that reaction. Ridiculous.

"I-I can't shift," she said, the stench of terror altering the scents of the room.

I frowned at her. "Of course you can't. You're about to go into heat."

She shook her head. "I'm not an Omega."

"That phrase is growing tiresome," I drawled. "Your suppressants are no longer doing their job, little wolf. I'm not sure how else to convince you of that."

"Not suppressants," she snapped, sounding exasperated. "I only take strength pills."

Strength pills? I repeated to myself, incredulous. *Is that what they call them in Winter Sector?*

"Vanessa gave them to me," she added, her voice breaking as her shoulders slumped in defeat. "They were supposed to make me a stronger Beta. Clearly, they didn't."

I blinked. *Wait...* "How long have you been taking these, uh, 'strength pills'?" I asked slowly, a realization simmering on the surface of my thoughts.

"Always." She cleared her throat. "For as long as I can remember."

"Every day?" I pressed.

She nodded. "Yes. Until last night." She flinched with the admission. "And again today."

I studied her, searching for any sign of a lie and finding none. It was my job to read people well, and this female resembled an open book. "Vanessa told you they were meant to make you a stronger Beta."

She nodded again, her jaw clenching. "And now she's given me something to make me smell like an Omega. It was meant for Enrique, so he could knot me to death."

What? "Enrique was going to...?" I couldn't finish it because the phrase didn't make sense. How could an Alpha knot an Omega to the point of death? Unless he intended to starve her? But why would he do that? Hell, why would he let her out of his fucking sight? Alphas were extremely protective of their chosen mates. Yet he'd chosen to play at the party instead of with Snow.

"Tomorrow," she whispered, replying to the question I couldn't finish. "After the wedding. But whatever she did must have started early. Or maybe she knew I overheard them." She shook her head. "I'm not an Omega."

"On the contrary, sweetheart, you are very much an Omega. No drug could make you smell this sweet." Although, her suppressants had hidden it well earlier. Mostly. Yet I'd still been intrigued by her. And now I completely understood why.

"Ugh, you're not listening to me."

"Oh, I'm listening to you. You're just not realizing the truth."

Vanessa had convinced her and everyone else that Snow Frost was a Beta.

She'd used suppressants to hide Snow's true nature.

All to, what, maintain the throne? That had to be it. So why did she allow Enrique to court her? He must not have known she was an Omega. Except he'd intended to knot her… to death? "Why do you think Enrique was going to kill you?"

"Because I overheard their plan," she mumbled, sounding broken. "Vanessa said… it would be my fault… for being a Beta. That the kingdom would understand. She'd *make* them understand."

"That doesn't make any sense. If he knotted you, he could mate you and take over Winter Sector with you as his queen."

"*I'm not an Omega,*" she repeated for the thousandth time.

"Yes. You are."

She grumbled a curse, adding, "Stubborn wolf," to the end.

"You'll see very soon that I'm right," I promised her.

Her lower lip trembled, and she shook her head back and forth. "You're going to kill me."

"No, darling, I'm going to fuck you. And you're going to thank me for it."

She started to cry. "I… I hate you."

"Doesn't change what's about to happen, sweet wolf." I nuzzled her throat, drawing my lips up to her ear. "Don't worry. I'll make sure you enjoy it, even if you don't quite deserve it." She'd broken a lot of rules, after all. Although, I'd keep the suppressants off her list. That appeared to be Vanessa's fault more than Snow's.

The other items, however, she'd answer for.

In time.

CHAPTER SEVEN

SNOW

SOMETHING STRANGE HAD HAPPENED when he put his cock in my mouth. For a second, I'd been lost in the bliss of his scent and taste. Then his precum had hit my tongue, shooting clarity through my mind for the briefest of moments.

And now… now it was disappearing again.

The pain had risen once more, causing me to tremble so hard that I couldn't hear whatever he was saying to me. Something about his intention to fuck me.

I wanted to scream and beg him not to, but he refused to listen. Whatever potion Vanessa had woven into me was working.

A tear fell from my eye.

This wasn't me. I didn't give up. But I felt weak and broken beneath him. I could hardly even breathe beyond the pain in my chest.

"Ludvig," I mumbled. "Necklace." It sounded like gibberish to my ears, the thudding of my heart reverberating so loudly through my mind that I could barely concentrate.

Kazek trailed his lips down my neck to my breasts, scattering goose bumps up and down my arms. *Ohhh, yesss,* I thought, my fingers weaving through his thick, dark hair. Part of me registered how wrong it was to indulge him. But I couldn't stop myself from reacting, nor could I swallow the guttural moan his touch evoked.

He gazed up at me knowingly, deadly intent lurking in his blue-black orbs as he sealed his mouth around my stiff nipple. I bowed up off the bed, the sensation intense and stealing the breath from my lungs.

"I… I…" There were no words. No more air. Just his tongue trailing fire across my skin. He suckled my opposite breast, his teeth dragging along my sensitive skin.

Why do I like this? I wondered, flabbergasted. *I never like this.*

Enrique had tried.

My body just… didn't respond.

But now I had enough wetness between my thighs to accommodate an army of horny wolves.

"Wrong," I managed to bite out. "Something's. Wrong."

"Shh," he hushed. "Just relax and enjoy. I'll see you through your heat, then we'll talk."

I shook my head, a whine catching in my throat. There would be no heat. Just death. He didn't understand. He'd kill me if he kept—

My back bowed off the bed again at whatever he'd just done between my thighs with his tongue. I couldn't even process how he'd moved so quickly, my brain fracturing beneath the onslaught of sensation he awoke with his mouth against my clit. He nibbled, sucked, groaned, and growled, all the motions collecting as one inside my broken mind.

This was so wrong.

I didn't know him.

I'd challenged him.

Tried to stab him.

Fought him.

And now it felt as if I couldn't live without him.

"Kazek…" His name felt foreign on my tongue, a dark whisper I was never meant to utter, yet I did it again and again as he tortured my damp flesh.

I wanted him to stop.

The word "no" bubbled onto my tongue a hundred times but never passed through my lips. Everything burned. My blood. My heart. My soul. The world around me. *So hot.* Too hot.

Hurts.

"Come," he demanded.

I couldn't. It was impossible. Enrique had tried many times in a similar manner, but I could never find release. He'd never tried fucking me, claiming to want to wait until our wedding night. Yet others had graced my bed. None of them fulfilling. Always the male seeking his own release while I remained dry and uncomfortable.

Oh, but this was different.

Kazek's mouth coaxed a river of want to flow in open welcome.

My body *wept* for him.

How?

Why?

The spell, I reminded myself, shaking my head once more to clear it. "Hurts," I forced out, the word not adequate to describe the pleasurable agony filling my veins. Every breath took effort. As did general thought.

I'm dying.

This is my end.

I've failed everyone.

No.

I couldn't afford to think that way. I had to… had to… *something.* I groaned in frustration, my chest aching from the exquisite *pain.*

"Something isn't right," Kazek said, his strong, muscular form stretched out on top of me again. I admired the tattoos down his left arm, my focus shifting between reality and a dreamland where his embrace solved all my worries.

How is he tattooed? I wondered dumbly. *Mmm, he feels nice.*

His body seemed to absorb my heat, pulling parts of me into him and sharing the burden of my torment. I sighed, nuzzling him. A rumbling purr met my touch, the sound soothing and perfect and oh-so beautiful.

"More," I begged, craving the temporary peace of his embrace.

What's happening to me?

My thighs were parted.

His cock—

"No!" I screamed as he entered me in a swift pump of his hips.

But it didn't burn the way I expected.

Instead… instead I felt *complete*. I trembled beneath him, my nails digging into his strong shoulders to both push him away and hold him closer.

He whispered a foreign praise into my hair, his massive form taking mine in a sweep of emotions and strength that I didn't understand.

And then he was moving.

I shuddered, moaned, and cried all at once.

The conflict left me dizzy, my vision coming in and out as Kazek tried to provoke the necessary responses from my body.

Not Omega, I thought at him, crying inside my mind.

He stilled as if he understood me, his dark eyes meeting mine and a flicker of concern painting his depths. I suspected that was a rare reaction for this male. Alpha Kazek struck me as the type that took what he wanted when he wanted it. Yet he gazed at me with an intelligence I couldn't help but admire.

"The suppressants are impacting your cycle," he said, his expression momentarily pained. "This won't be enjoyable for you. Not yet."

I whimpered in response, unable to say more.

Not that he'd listen.

I wanted to tell him the real reason I wouldn't enjoy this was because I wasn't made for it.

But he started to move again, his hands on my hips to hold them where he wanted them.

"My seed will help," he whispered against my neck.

"Without it, you'll be in incredible agony."

I'm already in agony! I tried to scream at him, but my mouth opened on a groan instead.

Animalistic.

Rough.

Torture.

All the while, I gushed for him, my body broken beneath his dominance. I couldn't fight him. Couldn't even rebuke him. I merely held on and let him destroy me in what should have been beautiful, passionate bliss.

I hated Vanessa more than I'd ever hated an individual before. I blamed her for every thrust. Every grunt. Every agonized cry for more. Because *she* did this to me. As much as I wanted to despise Kazek for accepting the opportunity, I sensed that, deep down, he thought this would help me.

Or maybe that was my naive hope, that perhaps Alpha Kazek harbored at least a sliver of humanity.

His mouth found my ear, his body slick with sweat. "Stay with me," he demanded. "Stay with me, Snow."

Where else would I go? I wanted to ask him, delirious from the pounding inside my lower body and my head. The room kept fading in and out of darkness, his light source finicky and out of focus.

How strange.

I swore it was a dull, constant orb moments ago.

I blinked.

Darkness.

Light.

Darkness.

Light.

Sweat.

Sex.

Hot Alpha male.

Seed.

Oh, no...

His chest vibrated against mine, the impending roar a call for my inevitable doom.

And then a fire erupted in my lower abdomen. The knot taking form.

Ripping through my uterus and stomach.
Killing me.
Filling me with fluid.
Blood.
Death.
My death.

CHAPTER EIGHT

KAZEK

"FUCK!" I shouted, trying to pull Snow back to reality.

She'd fallen into some sort of sleeping spell, her eyes half-closed, her lips parted on a scream she never released. All the while, our bodies spasmed together in joint climax below.

The suppressants were killing her.

She must have been on a heavy dose of them to hide her true nature, and that nature was ripping through her with a force that seemed to be dismantling her from the inside out. I'd tried to fill her with my seed to trigger her full cycle, but all it'd done was make her convulse without pleasure.

I couldn't pull out of her without risking a severe tear to her insides, one that might just destroy her in this state. She couldn't shift. She couldn't fall into her estrus as expected. She was hardly even breathing.

"Snow," I said, trying futilely to pull her back to me.

Nothing.

She'd been fading fast when I started fucking her, my goal having been to wake her the hell up.

That'd clearly backfired.

I couldn't even enjoy what should have been the most amazing orgasm of my life because the female beneath me was fucking dying on me.

Think. Think. Think. I had to do something. I couldn't just let her float off into whatever state the drugs decided to take her. There had to be a way around this. A method to bring her back. To *save* her.

I didn't play protector often. I wasn't a hero or a prince or a knight in shining armor. My playground courted death. Give me a rifle and a target, and I was in my zone. Saving this darling damsel was so far outside my comfort zone. I *took* lives, not saved them.

She began to quiver again, this time with sharp, raspy breaths that ripped through my chest.

How could Vanessa be so cruel? Hiding Snow's identity, and now this? And how had this become my problem?

Because you wanted her, I reminded myself. *You waited outside that plane with every intention of taking her. And now you have your wish.*

Except my plans hadn't involved Snow turning into an Omega.

A fertile, yet broken, little wolf.

I could force her to shift. But that might cause more damage. Omegas were meant to remain human during estrus, their animal at the forefront of their need and thoughts without actually making an appearance. It was how they mated.

However, her scent told me she couldn't breed like this, much less survive.

An Alpha's growling command couldn't be ignored, not by an Omega. She'd phase even if it killed her.

I shook my head, denying the option. It was a risk I didn't want to take. There had to be another way.

Strength pills, I thought, considering the term. Norse Sector didn't believe in suppressants or genetic alterations. Science, yes. Dismantling the true nature of our wolves, no. But I didn't have time to consult anyone about a medical remedy. Not with Snow's slowing heart rate.

Her body refused to recover, too weakened by the toxins in her blood. This was precisely why Omegas weren't meant to suppress their natural instincts.

This shouldn't be happening.

My seed should have *fixed* that issue. Yes, I'd had to tear her a little to work myself inside her, and her womb wasn't used to accepting a knot. Yet she'd accepted it. I'd *felt* the connection. Her body didn't reject mine, nor did I do permanent damage.

Still, she wasn't healing. She hadn't fallen into the throes of passion the way an Omega should. Was it a result of her mind convincing her body not to accept her true nature? Or something more?

There was only one method left for me to prove to Snow that she wasn't a Beta.

I had to mate her.

My head fell to her neck, my lips hovering over her waning pulse.

"You're not supposed to be mine," I whispered, cringing. Made wolves were commonly considered inferior to born wolves in our society. Ludvig never treated me as such, but others frequently tried. I always proved them wrong, yet it didn't stop them from testing my skills. They saw me as inferior plainly because of my human origin.

Although, that wasn't the primary reason that kept me from claiming a female. It was the baggage that came with a bonding of souls. It just didn't suit my profession. And as such, I'd never truly craved an Omega mate.

Yet my wolf desired this female. So much so that I'd forgone all protocol and taken her as my own already.

A claim couldn't be undone. Our souls would be married as one, our wolves forever destined for the other. My strength would become hers, her heart and body mine to possess and protect, and only death could rip us apart.

Snow gasped, her full red lips parting with the motion, and then nothing followed.

No exhale.

No more inhales.

Her pulse sputtering to a chaotic rhythm.

Fuck this. The dominant predator inside me took over, my teeth sinking into her neck before I could further consider our options. *Mine.*

I'd claimed her from the moment our eyes met. That feisty, stubborn Beta with her disregard for manners and submission had captured my focus and held on. I'd almost broken a dozen decorum rules myself by pursuing her. Vanessa's party favor had been my only deterrent, my instinct to help Mick overpowering my desire to follow Snow. Yet she'd chased after me anyway.

Well, not exactly.

She wanted help.

And that was exactly what I intended to do now.

Her eyes flew open as our connection locked into place, her chest inhaling a much-needed breath. If she didn't believe she was an Omega before, she knew for sure now. Because Alphas couldn't mate Betas, and my wolf had definitely just claimed her as his.

"No," she whispered, her irises flaring with understanding.

"Yes," I countered, a low growl accompanying my words.

She arched into me in response, her pupils dilating with overpowering *need.* Slick pooled between her legs, bathing my still-hard cock in warm welcome.

"Much better," I praised softly, kissing the mark on her neck. "Now we can begin."

Her arms came around my neck, her nails digging into my shoulders. "*More.*" She accompanied the command with an adorable little growl that had me chuckling against her throat.

"Oh, sweet Snow. You're not in a position to demand anything from me." I laved the blood that pooled from my bite wound, eliciting a violent shiver from her. "But fortunately for you, I want to give you more. A hell of a lot more."

She mewled as I began to move, my knot finally drawing back into my shaft to ready me for round two. This would be a proper fucking. Normally, I preferred to draw out the moment, to torment the female and force her to beg, but Snow had already been through enough.

Tonight, I'd please her.

Tomorrow, we'd play.

"Wrap your legs around me," I told her.

She complied, her thighs hugging me as her ankles locked at the base of my back.

"Now hold on, baby." I didn't wait for her to acknowledge my demand, my hips pistoning in and out of her in a way that would break a Beta. But Snow accepted the pounding with a half-pained moan that quickly turned into a chant of acceptance and adoration.

Each thrust pushed her deeper into her heat cycle until the female beneath me was a writhing bundle of passion. She came alive in my arms, her wolf shining in her gaze as she openly submitted to the Alpha dominating her.

A beautiful sight.

Addictive.

One of the most amazing experiences of my existence.

I'd heard about the pleasures of taking an Omega in the throes of estrus, but I'd never indulged in the activity until tonight.

And now I wasn't sure I'd ever crave a normal female again. Because *fuck*.

Snow's slick sheath hugged my shaft, squeezing me in protest while quivering in violent acceptance of my size. An intoxicating combination that left me near the edge faster than I ever could have considered possible.

My palm slid between us, down her flat abdomen to her hairless mound. One stroke of my thumb against her clit had her shrieking with pleasure, her orgasm rippling around my cock and driving me to follow her into oblivion.

"*Fuck*," I breathed, this time for an entirely different reason than before. My knot shot into her again, pulsating with a release that rocked every inch of my body and forced her into another spiraling climax.

She milked every drop I possessed, her little body accepting it greedily and immediately demanding more. Her mouth moved over the words, her commands a chant to my senses. I grinned and huffed out a laugh. "Not yet."

Snow released a protest, one that she'd probably be embarrassed about later, but it entertained me immensely. I could feel her mounting need like a violent flame through my veins.

Slipping my hand downward to the place where we joined, I scooped up some of our mingled arousals and brought the dessert to her lips. She groaned as I fed her the sensual fluid, her tongue wrapping around my fingers in a quiet request for more.

So I did it again.

And again.

Brushing her clit each time I went down, painting her nipples as I stroked upward, and tracing her full lips before letting her suck me clean. "You're going to do that to my cock soon," I promised her.

"Yesss," she hissed, bowing off the bed in expectation.

"Insatiable," I mused, aware this was only the beginning.

She yelped as I rolled us, placing me on my back and her on top. We were still locked together, my knot pulsing deep inside and refusing to release. But that didn't mean she couldn't have a little fun.

"Ride me, Snow. Use my cock and come again." I wanted to admire the show. And oh, what a show it was with her tits bouncing in time with her eager thrusts. She chased after her pleasure with sensual movements, her small hand sliding to her cunt to thrum her clit. Yet no matter what she did, she seemed unable to fall apart.

Tears streamed down her face, her passionate moans turning to pained cries, as she begged me to help her, to give her what she needed.

It seemed games weren't needed at all.

This little wolf longed to submit.

So I decided to indulge her inclinations.

I grabbed her hips as my knot receded, then pulled her off my shaft. "Hands and knees, Snow. Now."

She presented herself to me, her thighs glistening with her arousal as she spread her legs in eager welcome. I palmed her ass, adoring the sweetheart shape and beautiful fullness of each cheek.

Hmm, fucking her there later would be fun.

But I decided to reward her eager supplication by kneeling behind her and positioning my head at her sopping entrance. Her pussy fluttered around me as I surged forward, her resulting scream likely awakening the entire fucking sector.

I didn't care.

I gave her what she desired and more, driving so deep into her that she cried.

I'd never taken a female like this, so harshly and thoroughly and completely. And rather than beg me to stop, she urged me to continue.

Fucking oblivion.

Perfection.

A dream I wasn't entirely sure resembled reality.

And then we were coming again, my seed claiming her insides, marking her as mine for eternity. I bent over her, my lips finding my mark once more as my chest covered her back.

She whispered something unintelligible, but whatever it was, my wolf reacted and I bit her all over again.

She shrieked, her body spasming in some convoluted mixture of enjoyment and agony. All the while, my wolf chanted the same word on repeat, engraving my future in Snow's name and securing our destiny together as one.

Mine.

Mine.

Mine.

CHAPTER NINE

SNOW

EVERYTHING ACHED. My limbs. My breasts. My ass. The sensitive space between my legs.

I squirmed, seeking relief, requiring more of the sexy beast who kissed my bruises away and fucked me to utter completion. He was somewhere nearby. Outside the cloud of softness. I searched for him, my hands roaming the mounds of quilted bliss until I reached the edge of my safe space and hissed at the cool air.

A male chuckle caused me to freeze, my senses searching madly for the source of that sound. It belonged to the male I'd rutted with for days on end, the male I now craved more than air.

"Let me finish this, then I'll come feed you."

I growled. Food wasn't what I wanted. He kept forcing water down my throat, most of which I spat back at him. I liked that game because he always made me lick it off him afterward. Mmm, and sometimes he fed me with his cock. When I ate enough, he let me suck him dry for dessert.

Who am I?

Oh, I don't care.

This is heaven.

Because I'd clearly died. Which sucked, but at least my beast had followed me.

Alpha Kazek, I purred to myself. *Yes, yes.*

"Here," he said warmly, walking into my view. I lunged for the hardness between his legs, only to have my wrist caught in one of his much stronger hands. "No."

I growled at him.

He growled back, the sound causing me to whine as dampness flooded my thighs. Rather than alleviate my pain, he set a plate on the bed beside my head. "Eat that and I'll give you my cock."

My eyes narrowed at the sandwich. *Not hungry.*

"Eat," he said again, this time with a harsher tone. "Or I won't let you come again for hours."

I gnashed my teeth together, my stomach cramping at the thought of not being able to find any relief. The last time we went through this dance, I'd played with myself while he'd watched with amusement in his gaze. After several agonizing minutes, I realized I couldn't come on my own. Something he'd known. So I'd eaten the food, and he'd rewarded me by taking my ass.

I never thought I'd like that.

But with him, I did.

I liked *everything* Kazek did to me. Minus the feeding times.

"Now, Snow," he said as if sensing my disobedience.

I grumbled at him but picked up the sandwich and took a bite. My eyebrows flew upward at the taste, my wolf immediately perking up.

He'd seasoned it.

With his cum.

I devoured the sustenance with a moan of approval, eliciting a deep laugh from him. "That's a first," he mused. "I might need to keep you in this state for eternity."

He prowled forward, his palms balancing on the mattress as he leaned into my nest of blankets. His expression radiated approval at whatever he saw in my eyes. He took the plate, set it off to the side, and joined me beneath the sheets, his muscular legs twining with mine as he threaded his fingers through my tangled strands. "You probably need a shower," he whispered. "But I really like you marked up and saturated in my scent."

I drew my nails up his strong arms, scratching his skin along the way and leaving rivulets of blood in my wake. He shivered, his pupils flaring.

"Are you claiming me, little Omega?"

I dug my claws into his shoulders in response, daring him to rip away from me.

But all he did was smile at my possessive hold. "Mmm, I'm going to miss you in this state."

I snorted, unsure of what the hell he meant. "Fuck me," I said, my voice hoarse from days of screaming his name. I was a shell of my former self, my body and mind no longer belonging to the female known to the world as *Snow Frost*.

Whoever I'd become was bolder. Sexier. Animalistic. *Starving.*

I tried to pull him to me, but the damn male remained in control, his expression gleaming with masculine pride. "You have no idea what it means to be mine, but you will." He pressed his mouth to my jaw and gently nipped my skin. "Soon, Snow. Very soon. Hmm, but you've been so good for me. I think I'll indulge you until you tell me to stop."

He pulled my thigh over his hip and slid inside me once more, the blissful union immediately sating the ache growing inside me.

Slow.
Slick.
Warm.

I moaned, needing more. He responded by pushing me to my back, his hips settling between mine. "Grab the bars, sweetheart."

My hands moved on autopilot, my body his to command. I wrapped my fingers around the dark wooden poles decorating his headboard and sighed in content. His palms traced my sides, his alluring gaze capturing and holding mine.

I knew what would come next, could see it written in the intensity of his expression and feel it in the direction of his touch.

He grasped my hips, angling me to his desire, and drove deep inside. Some part of me wondered how he hadn't killed me with these assaulting thrusts, while the other part reveled in his roughness.

There were no emotions between us.

Just hard, violent need tinged with possession.

Our animals thrived in the passion, taking us to heights I didn't know existed. Each thrust forward made me scream, my grip on the bars tightening to hold myself in place. I should be begging him to stop. Instead, I urged him on, demanding more and groaning in wanton approval.

His lips skimmed my throat, my jaw, but never my mouth. He breathed words in my ear, praising me for taking his cock, for giving him my body and my trust. Mmm, that last word sent goose bumps across my skin.

Trust.

Was that what this meant? Did I trust him? The lethality lurking beneath his skin terrified me. I felt his savage desires in every caress and in the way his body harshly claimed mine. Trust seemed impossible. But my wolf willingly gave him everything. How strange. Since when did she make all the decisions?

His cock hit a particularly painful spot inside that rippled pleasant waves through my form. Such a strange reaction. Who knew I favored a bit of agony with my ecstasy?

"Come for me," he whispered, his teeth catching my earlobe.

My body complied, my inner walls clutching his thick shaft as he forced me over the edge with those three words. I chanted his name, begged him for more, and he rewarded me in kind with another of those deep, penetrative strokes.

"Fuck," he breathed, his lower half clenching as he followed me into oblivion once more, his knot tying us together for what felt like eternity.

It hurt.

But I liked it.

Another of those bizarre conundrums my mind couldn't seem to process.

Maybe I would spend forever in this state.

Happy.

Sated.

Claimed.

Mmm.

My eyes drifted shut, sleep taking me under into euphoric unconsciousness.

CHAPTER TEN

SNOW

UGH, OW.

Soreness taunted me to awareness, my body protesting as I burrowed deeper into the blankets surrounding me. There had to be over a dozen sheets on this bed. I frowned at them, my focus falling to the shirts and boxer shorts used to decorate what appeared to be a nest of some sort.

Nest, I thought, my mind hazy. *Why am I in a nest?*

I sat up and stretched, the scents of the room swirling around me in a mix of cedar, peppermint, and virile male wolf. My thighs clenched, causing me to shudder at the delicious ache awakening inside me.

"Ohh," I moaned, falling back into the pillows. My wolf wanted to roll around in the perfume of sex and musk and *man*. So good. I wrapped my body around the clothes, reveling in the addictive cologne. It didn't matter that I hurt all over. *This* was my cure.

A masculine chuckle rolled across my skin, causing my head to pop out of the blankets. I looked sharply to the left to find Alpha Kazek leaning against a dresser with a cup of coffee in one hand. He gave me a wicked smile that made all my memories rush in with a flourish.

Sex.

So. Much. Sex.

And biting.

Oh, by the gods… My eyebrows flew upward. "You claimed me."

"I did."

"I… I…" I couldn't speak. How was that even possible? Alphas didn't bond with…

Wait…

I studied the formation of blankets and dirty clothes around me, took in the state of my bruised hips and thighs, and felt my jaw unhinge. "I'm… No. That's… that's impossible."

He grunted and set his coffee mug down, then sauntered over to me in a pair of jeans that sat far too low on his hips. I didn't need that wall of muscle to come any closer. Not with the residual spasms shooting off between my legs.

Oh, but he smelled good. My wolf practically purred in welcome as he settled his palms on the bed, his much larger body pushing me to my back. He bathed me in his masculine warmth, his chest resembling fire against mine.

"Kazek," I whispered, uncertain of his intentions. The abrasive fabric of his jeans pushed against my heated sex, driving a groan from my throat that was part pain, part pleasure. "I'm sore."

"I know." He nuzzled my neck, his lips sealing over my thundering pulse. "But if you claim not to be an Omega one more time, I'm going to knot you until you forget how to speak, Snow. Do you understand?"

A shudder went through my body. "But—"

"I won't warn you again," he replied, his teeth skimming my jaw as he settled onto his elbows on either side of my head.

His blue-black irises flickered with power, his dominant air shivering across my skin.

"I don't understand," I admitted in a choked whisper.

"You just went through a very short heat cycle," he explained, his voice soft and not matching the violence radiating from his eyes. "Only four days. You were unable to conceive as a result, which I suspect is tied to the suppressants Vanessa has kept you on all these years."

"Suppressants," I repeated, my mind recalling the word well. We'd argued quite a bit about that term.

"Yes, your strength pills."

I started to shake my head but stopped at his arched eyebrow. "W-why? I mean, how?"

"What was your relationship like with Vanessa?" he countered, his expression curious. "It's rumored she raised you as her own, but given that she hid your Omega bloodline from everyone, including you, I suspect she wasn't the kindest of stepmothers."

A lump formed in my throat from his words, my childhood sheltering taking on a whole new meaning inside my head. "She rarely let me out to see the people, claiming I was too weak a Beta for them to respect. It was why she encouraged me to take the pills. She said they were helping me." I felt so naive and stupid for believing her, but what was I supposed to do? "I trusted her."

He considered me for a long moment, no hint of emotion in his gaze. "If the sectors knew you were an Omega, you would have had Alphas coming from all over to express their interest in mating with you. It would have been an unprecedented challenge and situation because of how royalty works in Winter Sector. Whoever won you would win Vanessa's prized position as Alpha, too. So she kept you a secret instead."

I swallowed, his deduction one I never would have considered in a million years. But the proof of her betrayal rested between us now, in the claim he'd laid on my neck and inside my body.

"What I can't figure out is Enrique," Kazek continued thoughtfully. "How did he not sense your Omega traits? And why would Vanessa ever risk the two of you meeting and mating?"

"Sh-she intended to have him kill me."

"Yeah, you mentioned that. But I don't understand how. Your body can obviously take a good knotting." Approval gleamed in his blue-black irises, causing my legs to tense at the memory of his cock deep inside. It had hurt, but I'd enjoyed the resulting sensations.

And I kind of wanted to feel them again... right now.

His lips curled at whatever he read from my facial response, his mouth brushing a kiss against my cheek. "Don't worry, sweet Omega. I'll knot you again soon. After I deal with the items I've ignored for the last few days. Fortunately, Ludvig's been a bit preoccupied with Mick, and the pack knows better than to bother me out here."

Alpha Ludvig. My eyes widened. "He needs to see my necklace."

"Who does?"

"Alpha Ludvig," I whispered, shaking my head to clear the jumbling words swimming through my brain. *Omega. Heat. Claimed.*

Never in my wildest dreams could I have anticipated any of this happening. Because a week ago, I believed I was a Beta. A weak, petite... *Beta.*

"How did she...? But why? And how could I...?" The thoughts all came out in a muddled assortment of questions that made no sense, not even to me. Because this was insane. Vanessa had convinced me I was a Beta, and I'd believed her. Even while the truth stared me right in the face. "Alphas and Omegas never create Betas." I knew that. Everyone had told me how strange my existence was, and rather than analyze it, I'd felt like a failure because of it.

Yet all along, I was an Omega.

A rightful heir to the throne with an Alpha mate.

One I had been meant to choose.

But Vanessa took that away from me.

"You claimed me," I said, repeating my words from earlier. "Why would you do that?" He had to know it was wrong. Winter Sector would never approve of him taking liberties with their princess.

"To save your life," he replied. "For which, by the way, you're welcome."

You're welcome? I repeated in my head, causing a laugh to burst out of me unbidden. "Are you fucking kidding me? *You're welcome?* So I should be thankful you claimed me during a moment of weakness?"

"Yes. Because had I not done so, you would have died."

Ice slithered through my veins, followed swiftly by a flame of rebuttal. "Maybe you should have let me die," I seethed, fully aware that had it been my choice, I would have preferred to live. But that wasn't the point. "You had no right to take me."

"*No right,* hmm? Now there's an interesting choice of phrases," he replied, darkness painting his features in lethal edges.

This male was not one I should be talking back to, let alone disrespecting. And deep down, I knew he wasn't even the one I should be hating. Vanessa earned that title.

However, she wasn't here.

He was.

I growled at him the same way I would at her, my fury rising to the surface. "Get. Off. Of. Me."

His eyebrows shot up. "Oh, you don't want to do this, Snow. Trust me."

"Or what? You'll mark me?" I demanded, pointing at my neck. "Too late. You took me against my will! I never consented!"

"So you would have rather died, is that it?"

"It wasn't your decision to make!" I raged, my emotions all rising to the surface at once. He took everything from me. No, Vanessa did. Ugh, what did it matter? No one consulted me. No one requested my opinion. All these choices had been made without a single care in the world about me or what I might want.

Suppressants.

How the fuck had I been so blind?

"It was precisely my decision to make," Kazek replied, his calm tone holding an edge to it that caused my belly to flip. "You're an Omega, Snow Frost. You have no rights. Not here. Not when you stowed away on a plane without permission and infiltrated *my* territory. You're lucky I'm the one who found you when I did. My bite is why you're still breathing. You should be thanking me for saving you, little Omega, not throwing a bratty tantrum."

"Fuck you!" I snarled, hating him as much as I hated Vanessa. "Get off me!"

He growled, the sound hypnotizing me momentarily, my body reacting to the call of an Alpha. *Oh, dear Gods. I really am an Omega.*

How had Vanessa hidden this from me?

Enrique's growls never did this to me.

Sucking his cock never made me wet. Sex with other Betas had *hurt*. Yet Kazek had awoken things in me that shouldn't exist. What if Vanessa had drugged me? What if—

"Get on your hands and knees," Kazek demanded, his palms on my thighs. He'd lost his jeans, leaving him proud and ready between my splayed legs.

"No!" We were not having sex. Not right now. Not when I couldn't even process the insanity that had befallen my life.

His eyebrow lifted. "What part about your lack of rights didn't you understand?" The words were said in a tone that brooked no argument.

A smart wolf would have cowered.

I bared my teeth instead, not having anything else to lose. "You do not own me."

"On the contrary, I very much do," he replied, his hand covering my mound. "This is mine to fuck whenever I damn well please. And it's up to me whether you enjoy it or not." He pinched my clit to drive his point home, causing me to yowl in pain.

"I didn't choose you!" I screamed at him.

"And you think I wanted to choose you?" he countered, fury deepening his tone to a savage level. "I saved your life by taking you under my control. Now you're mine, and I will not tolerate such disrespect from *my* Omega."

He grabbed my hips and flipped me as if I weighed nothing, and to him, I probably didn't.

I squirmed under him, trying to escape, but he pinned me with ease, one palm on the back of my neck, the other on my hip. "Submit or I'll take you in the ass and ensure you feel every inch of it without pleasure."

"I hate you," I muttered into the pillow beneath my face.

"Regardless, you'll respect me and *thank me* for saving you. I could have left you out there to be fucked to death by the other Alphas and Betas in the sector. Instead, I chose to bring you here, even after your behavior back at Winter Sector." His grip tightened painfully on my hip. "Decide, Omega. Pain or pleasure?"

I screamed into the cotton, refusing to answer him.

This can't be happening! He was worse than Enrique. Worse than Vanessa. The worst Alpha I'd ever met. I wanted to kill him. To slice him with a blade and plunge it deep into his chest. Use him as bow practice. Destroy him with my claws.

I blinked. *Yes. I can shift!*

I called upon my wolf, her response immediate, only to be halted by a growl of fury from the Alpha above me. The sound instantly stopped me, sending pricks of pain through every fiber of my being as he *forced* me to submit. Made me remain in human form.

Energy hummed over my skin from the shift he'd denied me, reminding me of needles pricking my insides.

I cried out in agony and anger, astonished and appalled that he could do this to me.

Betas don't submit this way. Omegas do.

My entire world had been overturned in the matter of a week, and I didn't know how to accept this new reality.

And the pain of being denied my shift left me crippled and unable to move.

"Oh, Snow," Kazek said, those two words causing goose bumps to pebble up and down my arms as my wolf retreated beneath his command. "Your disobedience cannot continue, not if you want to survive in Norse Sector. I'm second in command for a reason, and if I can't keep an errant little

Omega under my control, you'll risk my status. Which I can't allow."

The world shifted as he pulled me across his lap, my rump in the air and my head hanging off the bed. *What the hell?*

"Count," he demanded.

Count wh— I yelped as his palm came down over my ass, the slap shooting fire across my skin. "Ow!"

"That's not a number," he informed me, his voice like ice. "*Count.*"

His palm sliced through the air, hitting my other cheek and causing me to curse instead.

He tsked. "I won't be repeating myself, Omega. If you don't obey, I will have no choice but to make this hurt."

"It already hurts!"

He chuckled, the sound infuriating me. "No, sweet wolf. This is foreplay." His next smack sent a shock up my spine. "*That* is proper punishment. You want a choice so badly? *Choose.*"

He repeated the action, causing me to bite my lip to keep from crying out. What the hell did he have in his hand? Spikes? What the fuck was this? He was spanking me like a damn child!

The next slap had tears prickling behind my eyes. "Please! Stop!"

"*Count,*" he snarled, his hand connecting with the sensitive space between my thigh and cheek.

"One. Six. I don't fucking know!"

"You'll start at one," he replied, his palm smoothing over my skin and exciting every fiber in his wake.

Why does that feel good? I marveled, completely lost to the sensation and momentarily forgetting about our situation.

But his hand soon reminded me, except it lacked the momentum of the one before it. "Snow?"

"Two," I bit out, hating him.

"Good girl," he praised, rubbing my cheeks again, warming the tenderized skin. "Your ass is gorgeous with my handprints decorating your pale skin."

A low purr came from him as he said the words, confusing my instincts. It made me relax just in time to receive another slap. Only, this one seemed concentrated near my thighs again, sending a jolt upward into my hot center.

"Three," I said, my voice breathy from the conflicting sensations.

More petting.

Seductive growls mingling with purrs.

Another open-handed slap to my ass that caused electricity to zip up and down my spine.

"Four."

"Five."

"Six."

I kept counting, but each increased number seemed to be leading to a climax that I didn't understand. Somehow this had turned me on. It'd gone from punishing to *arousing*. I shivered, perplexed by the change, my core thrumming with *need* as he connected with my backside once more.

A whimper left my lips, earning me an amused chuckle from the Alpha.

It was degrading and wrong.

I hated him.

He'd proven my weakness, forced me to submit, and my body was openly weeping for him, eager to thank him in a manner my mind failed to comprehend.

"Why?" I moaned, my face soaked in the tears of my shame and frustration. "*Why?*" I broke on a sob, my body and mind playing on two opposite fields and my heart trapped between the two.

Kazek pulled me up into his arms, cradling me against his chest as one would a small child. Only then did I realize just how much bigger he was compared to me. It hadn't registered during the heat cycle, but he was massive, even larger than Enrique. And his left arm was covered in intricate tattoos.

"Shh," he murmured, his purr vibrating my side as he hugged me close. "It's going to be okay, little wolf."

I shook my head, not believing him at all. "She wanted to kill me. And now… now I'm…" I couldn't finish the words, unable to define my new existence. "She killed me," I whispered more to myself. "Snow… no longer exists."

He held me for a long moment, his lips in my hair as I repeated words about my death, my mind lost to a delirious state of nonexistence.

Doc's plan had failed.

I'd turned into an Omega, been claimed by an Alpha I barely knew, and lost all sense of my identity in the process.

Because I liked that spanking. Who the hell was I to enjoy something so belittling? Even now, I wanted him to fuck me. My thighs were slick with my arousal, something no male in Winter Sector had ever been able to accomplish. Maybe because of the pills.

Oh Gods. Had I just kept taking them… *No.* No, that wasn't an option at all. I still would have ended up in this situation, or worse. Because Kazek was right. His claim had saved my life. That hadn't been a normal heat cycle but an urgent correction my body had forced upon me after the drugs had cleared my system.

But only in twenty-four hours?

Did it really work that quickly? Or had Vanessa set me up prior to that? What if she'd been secretly weening me off of them? I tried to recall the last time she provided my pills, but Kazek's steady purr interrupted my thoughts.

"Choose a new name," he whispered.

My brow furrowed. "Wh-what?"

His fingers trailed up my bare arm to my shoulder, traced the column of my neck to my jaw, and settled on my chin. He applied subtle pressure to tilt my head back, forcing my eyes to meet his. "Pick a new name."

I stared at him, his handsome features distorted by my blurry vision. "I don't understand."

"You said Snow is dead, that Vanessa killed her. I agree. You've been reborn with a new opportunity, and with that comes a new identity. So who do you want to be?"

His question repeated in my thoughts. *Who do you want to be?* "I…" I frowned, my wolf peeking up at me with intrigue.

A new identity.

Who do you want to be?

"No one has ever asked me that before," I admitted softly. "I've always been destined for the throne."

"And is it the throne you still want?" he asked, his dark brow lifting in question.

"It's mine," I answered automatically.

"But do you want it?"

"Yes." I didn't need to think about that. "Vanessa stole it from me. From my family. She put me in this situation. I should have had a choice. I should be allowed to mate who I want to mate."

He didn't react to my rising tone; he merely studied me intently. "You won't be able to change the past. *I* am your mate. You'll accept that. And then you'll tell me what you want."

"What if what I want is to be able to choose?"

"Then I'll put you back over my knee and remind you that you're mine. Fate already dealt our hand." He paused as if to give me a chance to argue with him, but I really didn't want the reminder he mentioned, so I remained quiet. "Good girl. Now I'm asking you, who do you want to be? What gift would you have me give you as your mate? What identity shall we assume together?"

"A name," I replied, trying to understand what he meant.

"We can start there, yes."

"I'm Snow Frost."

"But Snow is dead," he reminded me gently. "So who are you now?"

"An Omega slave to an asshole Alpha," I muttered.

Both his eyebrows came up. "Are you trying to goad me again, little wolf? Because I promise the second time won't be nearly as kind as the first."

"That was kind?"

He snorted. "I'm the Huntsman, *Omega*. That was *very* kind."

I swallowed, his expression resembling stone. Danger lurked in his gaze, the black orbs rimmed in a dark sapphire blue that blazed with deadly intent. This male was a killer, his irises allowing me a glimpse into his black spirit. "You're a killer."

"Yes. An assassin. And I enjoy my job very much."

"You won't kill me."

He smiled. "No, darling Omega, I won't. But I will punish you to a point where you'll beg me to kill you instead."

I shivered at the promise in his words. "You'll break me."

He shook his head, his thumb drifting from my chin up to my jaw and back down. "Never. Your feistiness is an aphrodisiac. But you need to learn your place. It's the only way I can keep both of us safe." He pressed his lips to my cheek, his nose nuzzling mine. "I have a lot of enemies, sweet girl. They'll use you against me if they can."

My stomach clenched at the admission. "Vanessa is my enemy."

Kazek pulled back to study me once more. "Would you like me to kill her for you?" A serious question, one that had me gasping.

"You'd kill her?"

He didn't hesitate. "Yes."

"W-why?"

"She hurt what's mine," he replied simply. "That can't go unpunished. But I need to know what you want. Snow is dead. So who are you now? What will you become? What do you desire?"

"Revenge," I whispered.

It was the right answer because his eyes gleamed. "Yes. What else?"

"I want my kingdom back."

He considered me for a long moment. "That might be harder to achieve."

"Why? It's *my* kingdom. She stole it from me, hid me away, made me think I was a worthless Beta for two decades, and planned to kill me with Enrique's knot." By the time I finished, I was shaking with the need for vengeance. "She destroyed my life. And she's destroying my kingdom, too. I want it back. I want her gone. *Winter Sector is mine.*"

CHAPTER ELEVEN

KAZEK

THERE'S MY FEISTY FEMALE, I mused, happy to see her return.

I didn't mind her strength when she focused her anger on the right target, but when she started disrespecting me, we had a problem. I meant what I'd said—her behavior reflected directly on me. If she was rude to me like that in public around the other wolves, we would have a serious problem on our hands. Omegas were born to submit to their Alphas, not question them or shout obscenities at them.

Had I taken her without consent? Sure. But it'd saved her life. Alphas made decisions every day that protected weaker wolves. I'd made the best one for her situation, and she needed to accept that rather than shout at me about it.

Besides, we both knew it wasn't me she hated right now. It was Vanessa, and rightly so.

"Your wolves might not accept me as their Alpha," I told her now, referring to her wish to retake Winter Sector. "I'm a turned wolf, not a born one. And you said yourself that you didn't *choose* me." Until we worked through that detail, there would be no revenge. I couldn't afford to fight on her behalf without mutual respect and trust between us. And that would take time to develop.

Lust was easy.

The other stuff, not so much.

"A turned wolf?" she repeated, her gaze falling to my arm. "That's why you're colorful." Her fingers stroked my forearm, her touch feather-soft. "How were you turned?"

That was a very personal question, but I allowed it under the circumstances. Had she been anyone else, I'd have growled and either struck out in reprimand or walked away.

She must have realized the insult, because she froze, her shoulders tensing as she whispered, "I'm sorry. You don't—"

"Ludvig turned me after I killed another Alpha," I replied, cutting her off. "It was back when humans didn't know about supernaturals. I didn't even know, but I figured it out quickly when my rifle wasn't enough to take the bastard down. We ended up in hand-to-hand combat because he shifted and sniffed me out. I nearly died. Ludvig shot me up with some remedy that should have healed me, but instead… I turned."

She gaped me. "Against your will."

"It saved my life. I thanked him for it." The words were pointed and made her flinch. Because yeah, I understood what it was like to have a choice taken from me. But had I been in the right frame of mind at the time, I'd have accepted his option. So what was the point in hating him for the opportunity?

Her jaw ticked as she ground her teeth together. "I'm not ready to thank you yet," she finally admitted. "I… This is a lot for me to accept."

That was fair. I conceded with a nod. "So who are you now?" I asked her, guiding her in the direction of acceptance. "Snow is dead. You want to avenge her. How will you do that? *Who* will do that?"

"Arrow," she whispered, her brow furrowing. "Doc always called me Winter's Arrow because I never miss a shot."

"Who's Doc?" I asked, my wolf pacing inside my mind, not at all appreciating the mention of another male inside the sanctuary of my bedroom.

"One of my seven," she replied, her eyes darting to the bathroom. "I need to call them, to tell them what's happened. I need—"

I tightened my hold around her, securing her in place as she tried to escape my lap. "One of your seven?" I repeated through my teeth. "Seven what?"

She blinked, her eyes coming back to mine on a wince. She immediately looked down, her wolf submitting as a result of whatever she saw in my expression. Probably fury. *Possessive* fury.

"I can't tell you," she whispered, causing my eyebrows to shoot up in incredulity.

"The fuck you can't. You're *mine*. What or who are the seven?" I laced a demand with my tone, one I knew the Omega couldn't ignore.

"A family secret." Pain touched each word, causing me to frown.

"I'm your mate, which… makes me family." Such a strange concept. I hadn't experienced the obligations of a family in over a century. My parents and siblings were long dead, their offspring, too. The world went to hell too fast for me to help them. By the time I returned to my childhood home, they were all already dead.

"I don't even know you," she bit out, her expression strained. "I *can't*."

Fascinating. She was fighting my control, not wanting to give me more than she already had. Because she didn't trust me. Whatever secret she harbored meant a great deal to her and her *family*. I might have claimed her as my own, but she didn't consider me hers.

We were sexually mated, not emotionally bonded. I'd never been one for emotions or to embrace the concept of love. However, something told me that was what this female expected.

It would take time for us to develop any sort of true relationship. If I tried to force it now, she'd hate me. While I could live with that, I suspected she couldn't.

"All right," I said softly, purring to lessen the previous command. "But if you're sleeping with Doc or any of the others, that ends now. I don't share."

Her eyes rounded. "Sleeping with Doc?" She blanched. "*No*. He's like my big brother."

Well, that reaction made me feel a little better. "Good. As I said, I don't share." I wanted her to acknowledge that part.

"Then I don't share, either," she countered, arching a brow as if daring me to argue.

"Fine." The little Omega was more than satisfying. I saw no reason to take another.

"Fine."

I waited for her to say more, our gazes locked in some sort of battle. She seemed to be testing my resolve. "I won't bow to you, little wolf. And if you want to challenge me in the privacy of my own home, I'll allow it. But try this in public and I will discipline you for it. I can't afford to be seen as weak, and as my mate, you can't afford it either. I'm sure you know what happens when an Alpha loses a challenge to another Alpha."

She considered for a moment before saying, "He gains rights to anything the Alpha owns."

"Including the Alpha's Omega," I replied.

But she didn't appear to be focusing on that, her eyes flickering with unexpected excitement. "And their territory."

"Yes, if the Alpha owns territory."

"Like Winter Sector."

Ah. "You want me to challenge Vanessa."

She shook her head. "No. *I* want to challenge her. It's my kingdom. She stole it. I want it back."

I gaped at her. "You wouldn't stand a chance against a Sector Alpha." It wasn't meant as an insult, just the truth.

She bristled. "You don't know anything about me or my skills."

"Yeah?" I held her closer, drawing her focus to the fact that she still sat in my lap. "Your little dagger show was impressive for an Omega, but I could have subdued you in less than five seconds."

"I was going into heat."

At least she seemed to be accepting her Omega status. "Doesn't matter. I could do it again right now, without your estrus as a barrier."

"You haven't seen me with a bow."

And now that she mentioned it again, I really wanted to see it. But that was beside the point. "You're not trained to take down an Alpha. Especially not one as strong as Vanessa. It's impossible."

"Then train me."

My jaw actually dropped. She couldn't be serious. "You're mine to protect, not train."

Her eyes narrowed. "Afraid of the challenge?"

Shit. This female was going to be the death of me. "I'm not afraid of anything."

"Prove it."

Jesus Christ. "You're an Omega."

"And you're an Alpha," she countered. "An assassin. A turned wolf. You have a lot of enemies, right? So training me would be in your best interest. Then I can use the skills to take down Vanessa and reclaim my throne."

Right. My mate was delusional. It had to be the drugs. "In no fantasyland will that ever happen." However, yeah, I did have a penchant for pissing off other wolves, mostly because I enjoyed asserting my dominance and position. So it did make sense to ensure she was properly trained in the event that someone chose to use her against me. But letting her take on Vanessa? No. Absolutely not. "I won't risk you against Vanessa."

She still hadn't dropped my gaze, her strength admirable. "Then help me defeat her."

"Why?"

"To reclaim my kingdom. Then you can rule at my side."

I arched a brow. "Is that supposed to be my reward? To rule at your side?"

"Not a reward, just a fact. I'm the heir by our laws. My mate, chosen or otherwise, is the rightful King of Winter

Sector."

Which was precisely what made her valuable.

Snow Frost resembled a priceless gem other wolves might try to steal from me. My death would allow her to take another mate, and that mate would rule in my stead.

My teeth clenched at the thought. I didn't particularly fancy dying or having another price on my head. But here we were.

"Pick a name," I said, bringing us back to the original topic. "You can't exist here as Snow." Very few would be allowed to know her true name, Ludvig being among them.

Fuck, this was a mess.

I hadn't considered all the repercussions of saving her, my wolf acting on instinct alone.

Damn animalistic nature.

Now I was stuck with a princess who wanted to take back her kingdom without any regard to the impossibilities of that request. I could train her day and night and she still wouldn't be a match for Vanessa. Omegas just weren't built to withstand battle. They were petite, fragile, and meant to bear children, not go to war.

But she was right about needing to be trained. No mate of mine could be seen as delicate or weak. I needed her properly prepared to handle my enemies lest one of them chose to hurt her as a way of harming me.

An Alpha's value included his handling of his mate, both in protection and in behavior. I couldn't afford for her to be seen disrespecting me in front of the others, just as I couldn't afford for her to be perceived as an easy target.

Fuck.

This was not the life I desired.

I sighed. I could dwell all day and night on the outcomes of our fated meeting, or I could do something about it. "Pick a name," I repeated. "Now."

"But what about—"

"We'll talk about the rest later. I need you to pick a name so I know what to call you when others ask me about you." Because they would soon. I had to talk to Ludvig, and her scent was wrapped all around me, marking her as mine. While

I could tell him her true identity, the others needed to remain ignorant. "If anyone asks, I found you during my last mission. That's all you're allowed to say."

She frowned. "You don't want them to know who I am."

"No. And you don't either, if you value your life."

That raised the hairs along her neck and arms. "Are you threatening me?" A haughty tone for such a little wolf.

This female was absolutely going to cause trouble.

I shook my head, irritated all over again. "If others realize who you are, they'll be more inclined to issue a challenge. You're not just a fertile Omega but also a wolf with status. Removing me opens you up to be taken, along with your kingdom."

She frowned, considering. "Oh."

"Yeah. Oh." I cupped her cheek, the tips of my fingers touching her matted hair. "Your name, Omega. What shall I call you to the others?"

Her pupils dilated, her wolf reacting to my softer tone. Gentleness wasn't my strength, but for her, I would try. "Winter," she whispered. "Call me Winter."

While it definitely linked back to her heritage, I couldn't deny the appropriateness of the name. Her pale skin reminded me of wintry landscapes, while her dark hair and matching eyes were reminiscent of the constant night during the long winter months. It was a tribute to her kingdom as well and suited the passion inside her heart.

"Winter," I repeated, tasting the name. "I approve." I pressed a kiss to her cheek once more, my nose inhaling her sweet scent tinged with my seed. *Mine. All mine.* My forehead rolled against hers, our breaths mingling between us. "Go shower, Winter. We need to meet with Ludvig."

I'd ignored his summons for the better part of four days. While he frequently allowed me my space as his second-in-command, he wouldn't be happy about me pushing him off. If I did it much longer, he'd show up, and that would be a very bad day indeed.

I brushed a kiss near the edge of *Winter's* lips before pulling back to capture her focus once more. "Do us both a favor, sweetheart, and behave today. Ludvig's the Alpha of Norse

Sector for a reason, and he won't hesitate to put you in your place."

She nodded, a hint of uncertainty gracing her features.

"He's a good Alpha," I assured her. "But he *is* an Alpha. I've been very lenient with you, Winter." She had to know that. I'd been within my rights to punish her several times over, and instead I chose to spank her, which led to her enjoying the experience. "He won't show you the same leniency."

I lifted her off my lap before she could reply, then gave her rump a little tap that had her jolting forward. "Go bathe yourself. I'll be here waiting." Mostly because if I joined her, I'd end up fucking her again. While I'd enjoy it, I didn't think she would. I recognized her need for space, and I gave it to her.

A temporary gift.

One I doubted she understood or appreciated.

This little wolf required training on so many levels. I flexed my palm and smiled at the handprints decorating her ass. Mmm, yes, we'd find ways to make our lessons together fun. I almost looked forward to her disobedience. *Almost.*

CHAPTER TWELVE

WINTER

"Snow Frost is dead," I said, staring at myself in the mirror. "Snow *White* no longer exists." I couldn't help my bitter tone, the pathetic pet name belonging to Enrique. My former betrothed. My betrayer.

However, it was Vanessa I hated most.

My eyes narrowed at the thought of the *Queen of Mirrors*.

I would have my vengeance.

She would pay.

"You'll call me Winter," I decided out loud, wrapping a towel around myself for warmth.

Kazek's shower had felt like heaven against my skin, the knobs somehow controlling the temperature and flow. I'd have to ask him about it later. In Winter Sector, we used fire to warm our baths. No one had showers. So it'd taken me a moment to understand how to properly use his bathing facilities, as he didn't have a bathtub.

I rolled my shoulders, content, and picked up a comb to run it through my hair. His conditioning liquid had worked wonders on my tangled strands, leaving them clean and soft.

Kazek entered with a knock, a bundle of clothes in his hands. "Here." He set them on the marble counter. "They might be a little big, but they'll suit for today. I'll order you a new wardrobe this afternoon."

I picked up the sweater on top and sniffed it, frowning. "This smells like Alpha female."

"Yeah, they belong to Alana."

"Alana?" I repeated, arching a brow. The easy way he said it told me he and *Alana* were close. "What happened to 'I don't share'?"

His eyes narrowed. "I don't. But I wasn't a saint before I met you. Alana and I saw to each other's needs on occasion."

My jaw clenched at the thought of him inviting another female into the nest. "And you want me to wear her clothes?" Did he have any idea how insulting that was?

"You weren't a virgin, Omega. And someone taught you how to suck cock like a champ, so I don't want to hear it, princess. Get dressed." He turned away with that lovely demand, expecting me to cooperate.

"No," I snapped at his back. "Give me something else to wear."

He rotated slowly, the predator flexing beneath the ample muscles on display. I really did want to explore his tattoos later, preferably with my tongue.

Which was entirely *not* the point.

"Oh, I'll give you something to wear," he said, prowling forward, his hands finding my hips and lifting me onto the counter. "Spread your legs."

"What? No."

His grip shifted to my thighs, yanking them apart and stepping between them before I could snap them back together. "You want something to wear? I'll cover you in my seed, then march you naked through the fucking sector."

I gasped. "Kaz—"

"We're done discussing it, little wolf. I told you that I

require obedience, and you've done nothing but disrespect me from the moment you woke up. We—"

"Disrespect you?" I cut in, my nails grabbing his shoulders and digging in to draw blood. "You want me to wear your whore's clothes!"

"Whore?" he repeated, fury claiming his features. "Alana is an Alpha. *Your* superior. She's not a fucking whore."

That was so not the point. "How would you feel if I gave you Grum's pants to wear?" I demanded.

"Who the fuck is Grum?"

"The Beta I gave my virginity to," I retorted before I could think about the words coming out of my mouth. *Oh...*

"Are you trying to earn a punishment fuck?" Kazek asked, his wolf dancing in his dark eyes. "Is that what this is about? You want me to mark you up for the sector to see? Because I'll happily lay claim to your ass again."

I shivered at the thought, my brain short-circuiting at the feel of his growing arousal between my thighs. He still wore his jeans, but that didn't stop his impressive length from pulsating against my still-sore sex.

"Kazek," I whispered, my claws retracting from his skin. "I... I can't wear her clothes." It undermined me as his desired mate. "It's akin to dressing me in your mistress's wardrobe."

He gaped at me. "I don't have a mistress. We've already reviewed the 'no sharing' policy."

My forehead fell to his chest on a sigh. He didn't understand. And I wasn't naive enough to bring up Grum again. Besides, that'd been a matter of convenience, and neither of us had enjoyed it.

I grimaced. Based on the stories I knew about my parents, my father never would have done this to my mother.

Of course, she'd chosen her mate.

I didn't.

I hadn't even known I could have one... until it was too late and the decision was made for me.

Kazek's palm slid up my side, his touch soft and sure as he passed my neck to grip my chin. He seemed to enjoy doing that. With a little tug, he forced my gaze back to his, but the fury I'd witnessed before was gone and replaced by something akin to curiosity. "Would you prefer to wear something of mine?"

I would rather procure my own wardrobe, but that was clearly impossible right now. However, donning his clothes would be a close-second preference. "Yes, please."

His expression softened considerably. "Okay."

"Okay?" I repeated. *That's it?*

"I'm not entirely disagreeable, Winter," he replied, pulling me off the counter. "Let's see what of mine will fit you."

My arm brushed Alana's clothing on our way out of the room, and I flinched. He glanced over and picked up the sweater and jeans, then led me to the fireplace in his room and tossed the garments inside. "Better?"

I blinked, shocked by his change in behavior. "I… Yes. Thank you."

He brushed his lips against my temple, then led me to his closet. "Everything in here is mine. I promise. The only reason I had her clothes was because she often runs off in wolf form after…" He trailed off, and I scowled at the implied activity that followed his statement.

The idea of Kazek with another female enraged my wolf.

Which made no sense because I didn't know him at all. However, she'd claimed him during my heat cycle, and now I couldn't seem to push the possessive instinct away.

It wasn't like me at all. Enrique had intended to take Kari as a mistress, something everyone knew, and while I hadn't been thrilled by the idea, I'd accepted it. He was an Alpha. He had needs I couldn't satisfy as a Beta. Why wouldn't he take an infertile Omega as a mistress? Yet the idea of Kazek even looking at another female had my hackles rising.

He kissed the back of my neck. "Shh," he hushed. "It won't happen again. After today, everyone will know I'm yours."

My wolf calmed at his words, my shoulders relaxing as he pulled me into his arms from behind. I really loved the way his chest felt against my back, but the towel kept me from the full experience. Part of me wanted to shred the fabric between us and melt into him.

"How do I feel so attached to you?" I mused out loud. "I know nothing about you. Not really."

He pressed his nose into my hair, his arms tightening around me. "Our wolves rely on instincts and senses that we can't comprehend in our human form. But I learned long ago to trust my animal spirit."

"How can I trust mine when she's been hidden from me all my life?" I whispered, my heart breaking inside. "I feel like I don't even know myself right now." All my inclinations were foreign, including the one that urged me to trust the male behind me. "Who am I?"

"You're Winter of Norse Sector," he replied, pressing his lips to my neck, near the mark he'd left embedded in my skin. "You're my mate, and your future is yet to be determined." He gently turned me in his arms, his hands locking against my lower back. "Let's get through today. Then we'll continue discovering who you really are, Winter Flor."

"Flor?"

He smiled. "Yes. That's my surname."

I frowned at him. "But you're not a Sector Alpha." Only Sector Alphas were permitted last names, unless the territory hierarchy allowed for royalty, like Winter Sector.

"I'm a turned wolf," he reminded me. "I had a last name before my first shift, and I chose to keep it."

"You can do that?" I didn't know much about human-turned-wolf politics. They were uncommon.

"I think you'll find that I do what I want," he replied, winking at me.

"How does Alpha Ludvig feel about that?" I wondered out loud.

Kazek shrugged. "He uses it to his advantage when the opportunity suits. I know when to show respect and when to push for my own path." He gave me a pointed look as if silently adding, *A distinction you need to learn.* "Now let's find you some clothes." He walked me backward with his hands on my hips, stopping when I bumped the rack of clothes at the back of his closet.

Cedar and man surrounded my senses, causing my wolf to purr in delight. She liked the way her Alpha smelled. I begrudgingly had to agree. I also really enjoyed the way his muscles flexed as he released me and began pulling items from the shelves.

A fine Alpha wolf indeed, I thought, admiring his strong back, tapered waist, and finely sculpted ass.

"Keep checking me out like that and we're never going to leave my cabin," he replied without turning around.

I had no idea how he knew, but suspected it was a change in my scent.

A week ago, I couldn't even produce natural lubricant. Now I couldn't seem to stop.

I clenched my thighs together, hating this change in my body's chemistry. It felt foreign and wrong, but I couldn't deny it'd made things rather enjoyable these last few days.

I'd gone into heat.

Sort of.

Kazek claimed it was short, only lasting four days. Most Omegas went into estrus for at least a week, and they often came back pregnant. But not me. I pressed my palm to my flat belly, uncertain of how to feel about that.

Continuing the Frost line was the biggest task of my existence. What if Vanessa's drugs had left me sterile? What if the royal bloodline ended with me?

My heart skipped a beat at the thought, my eyes closing on instinct. *Stop. Don't even consider that.* Kazek had called me a fertile Omega. "My cycle was off because of the strength pills, right?" I lifted my eyelids to find Kazek watching me, a shirt and black pants in his hands.

"Yes. That's my theory." He held out the clothes. "We'll ask Ludvig if he has a better one. His son is the Alpha of Andorra Sector. They're pretty savvy in X-Clan genetics."

Ander Cain, I thought, familiar with the familial line.

I nodded and put on the soft gray shirt, which reached my knees. Kazek had at least twelve inches on my five-foot-two height, so that was to be expected. I pulled the pants on next, then realized they were actually shorts with a string to cinch the waist.

Kazek's lips twitched as I finished, his amusement palpable.

"I know. I look ridiculous." I didn't need a mirror to confirm that.

"On the contrary, princess." His gaze danced over me with unfettered interest. "You look like you belong to me, and I rather like it." He found a sweater to pull over his athletic torso.

My wolf nearly whined in response, disapproving of him hiding all that smooth, tan skin. That had to be his natural coloring because no one in this area of the world possessed that sun-kissed shade during this time of year.

He reached over my head to pull down a pair of shoes and dropped them by my feet. "Socks are in the dresser in the corner." He gestured with his chin. Something about that small action paired with his words felt intimate. Real. A firm awakening that this had become my life.

I'm an Omega.

I have a mate.

My name is no longer Snow. It's Winter.

Winter of Norse Sector.

I mulled over the thoughts as I found a pair of wool socks and stuffed my feet into shoes that were way too big to function as practical. It only further proved my Omega status when compared to the massive Alpha beside me.

Yet I didn't feel small so much as secure.

"Ready?" he asked, his own feet clad in a pair of boots. He pulled a jacket off the rack to drape over my shoulders, further claiming me as his own.

I started to nod, then paused. "I need my necklace." Alpha Ludvig had to see it. That was what Doc had said.

Kazek pulled it out of his pocket and dangled the paw print charm before my eyes. "This one?"

"Yes."

"What's the significance of it?" he asked as he moved my hair off to one side. "A family mark?" He clasped the chain behind my neck, his gaze intent.

"I-I don't know. But Doc was adamant that I show it to Alpha Ludvig. He said he would recognize it."

Kazek gave me another one of those intense looks, the kind that told me very few details ever escaped his notice.

Definitely a killer. I suspected he rarely felt remorse, choosing logic over emotion at all costs. I wasn't sure how that would work out for me and our new mating. Probably badly.

Eventually, he conceded with a single dip of his head, his expression giving nothing away. "All right. Let's go."

CHAPTER THIRTEEN

KAZEK

LUDVIG SAT AT HIS DESK, his jaw ticking in time with the clock hanging from the wall behind him. He wore a suit—his preferred wardrobe—without the tie. A good thing because I suspected that tie would be strangling his neck right about now, given the muscles bulging there.

To say he was pissed would be an understatement.

Winter clearly felt it, her small frame shrinking into the chair beside me. She'd behaved appropriately so far, allowing me to do all the talking as I detailed my visit to Winter Sector and the aftermath of her stowing away on the plane.

I didn't apologize for claiming her. Mostly because it wouldn't hold value. I wasn't sorry. I wanted her. I took her. Therefore, she was now mine. End of discussion.

Would the other Alphas be furious by my claim? Probably. But I couldn't give two fucks what the world thought of me, and Ludvig knew that better than anyone.

"Well." Ludvig paused, that tick still going strong. "It seems you and Sven had an interesting visit in Winter Sector."

His use of his son's first name told me just how he felt about our *interesting visit*. "Yes, it was certainly eventful," I admitted.

Ludvig snorted. "At least now I know why you didn't challenge for the girl. You already had your own Omega to play with."

I couldn't argue that point. I'd sent Mick home with the Omega slave as soon as I realized Winter was on the plane.

So yeah, I'd chosen the dark-haired vixen over the petite blonde.

"I don't regret it," I told him honestly.

"I bet you don't," he replied. "Did anyone see her on your way here?"

"No. But as I said, she's chosen the name Winter to hide her true identity. That's how I intend to introduce her to the others."

More ticking.

More silence.

Then he shook his head. "Hiding her identity isn't going to work. Not in Norse Sector. She looks just like her mother. Hell, she even *smells* like her."

Winter flinched, while I frowned.

He had a point, one I hadn't really considered when we spoke about her new name. Wolves lived for hundreds to thousands of years, our species being incredibly hard to kill. Hence our immunity to the virus that had infected ninety percent of the human population.

But with that longevity came long memories.

I myself had even said she was the spitting image of her mother.

Which meant changing her name wouldn't do a damn thing to hide her true identity.

"Fuck," I muttered, annoyed both at myself and our situation.

"Yeah. *Fuck*," Ludvig agreed. "You realize this is cause for war, yes? You stole a prized commodity. Fucked her. Claimed her. And now have rights to a throne in another kingdom. Which now makes you a direct threat to my position as Sector Alpha. How do you want me to react to that, Kazek?"

"It doesn't matter what I want, Ludvig. You'll react however you want to react."

Normally, a comment like that would have earned me a smile. Not today. The bags under his eyes told me he hadn't slept much. I wondered if it was related to Mick. He'd exuded some strong possessive Alpha urges with the other Omega that had shocked me at the time. If he'd continued that behavior with his father, well, that couldn't have ended well.

Ludvig would never want the girl for himself, but his position put him in charge of her fate. It was his job as Sector Alpha to protect all the wolves in his territory, and that included acquired property from other domains.

He held my gaze, his dominance thick in the air between us. Most in my position would yield. But not me. I didn't bow to anyone, including my maker.

"We both know I won't challenge you for your territory," I said. "I'm your Second because I choose not to lead."

"Yet the circumstances have now changed."

"Either I asserted my claim or I let her die, Ludvig." He had to understand that much. Making her mine came with the baggage of her inherited property, a consequence I hadn't considered at the time. Not that it would have changed my mind. Complications didn't bother me. If I had to take Winter Sector as a result of my choice, then so be it. But Winter would be properly trained in the art of defense first.

More silence.

More ticks.

His expression giving nothing away other than his profound annoyance at the situation.

I knew better than to push for a verdict. We'd danced through enough issues together over our century of acquaintance that I knew what to expect. His reputation for being a fair and wise leader was well known, even outside Norse Sector.

Winter squirmed in the chair beside me. I reached over to wrap a palm around her nape, silently telling her to remain steady and calm. The action drew Ludvig's attention to her, his nostrils flaring as he took in her Omega scent.

"I can understand your actions, Kazek," he finally said. "What I fail to comprehend is hers. What were you thinking boarding that plane, little one? Do you have any concept of how dangerous that was for you and my men?"

"I had no choice," she replied, causing Ludvig's white-blond eyebrows to shoot upward. He'd meant the questions rhetorically and wasn't expecting her to speak. She emboldened the move by lifting her chin and meeting his gaze, similar to how she'd addressed me the other night in her court. "Vanessa planned to kill me and end the Frost family bloodline. I ran here after being told you were an honorable Alpha who would help me. Were my advisors wrong?"

The haughty note in her tone was not lost on me or Ludvig.

He glanced at me to convey his shock before pinning her with a dark look. "You dare to address me in that manner after sneaking into my sector and nearly causing a riot in the process?"

"No, I—"

"I'm not done," he interjected harshly. "You snuck into my territory as an unmated Omega and went into estrus within my borders soon after. Had Alpha Kazek not found you and taken you when he did, your heat cycle would have ended violently and at the cost of *my* men. While I'm not pleased with the overall outcome, I can forgive Kazek's claim, as he acted in your best interest. But your behavior is not so easily forgiven."

"My behavior?" she repeated, sounding incredulous. "I didn't know I was an Omega until after it all happened, because Vanessa *suppressed* my true identity. She's the one you should blame. She's the one who shouldn't be so 'easily forgiven.'" Winter's ire grew with each statement, causing me to shake my head by the end.

This was not going to end well.

"You forget your place, Omega," Ludvig said.

"Maybe because I didn't know I was an Omega until recently," she retorted.

107

"Winter." I tightened my grip on her nape in warning. Not enough to hurt her, just enough to snag her attention. "You're being disrespectful."

She snorted. "He's acting like I meant for this to happen. I didn't choose to be an Omega or to be lied to my entire life. Vanessa did that. She also planned to kill me. And she's clearly stolen my kingdom. So why am I being ridiculed?"

"Because you snuck into my sector without permission," Ludwig replied, his anger causing his cheekbones to protrude slightly more than normal. "Your actions have consequences, something you seem to be ignoring. Or maybe you're too selfish to care. Is that it? You consider yourself more important than the wolves living in Norse Sector?"

"No, I—"

"You put all their lives at risk by coming here, and not just because you're an Omega. You abandoned your people without a word. They won't know you escaped. Hell, they might think Alpha Kazek kidnapped you. And what then? What am I to do when Alpha Vanessa and her wolves come to claim you? Shall I fight on your behalf? Or hand you over to your fate?"

She stilled, her pulse racing in her neck. "I... I didn't think—"

"That's precisely my point," he snapped, interrupting her. "*You didn't think.* The only reason I haven't already put your bratty ass on a plane back to Winter Sector is because you mated my second-in-command. And that complicates things."

The growl in his tone elicited a fear-driven shiver from Winter. A foreign part of me wanted to pull her into my arms and hold her.

She'd been through hell these last few days.

I recognized that.

But Ludwig was right.

Winter had put the entire sector in jeopardy when she boarded that plane.

Vanessa would be well within her rights to start a war over this. The others might not believe Winter, even if she claimed to have left of her own accord. I appeared just as guilty, especially with the way I'd openly pursued her in the palace after she left. All it would take was one person to have seen me, and the rest would assume I'd kidnapped her.

After my display with Vanessa, she'd openly use that as a reason to act.

And as Ludvig said, Norse Sector would pay.

"It's partly my fault," I said, locking gazes with him once more. "I antagonized Vanessa by taking her Omega slave. She'll look for any reason to attack us now, something Winter could never have anticipated. Don't punish her for that."

He scoffed. "Sven already told me it was his idea. I know why you participated."

"I enjoyed the bloodbath."

"Of course you did. But we both know that's still not the real reason you jumped into the fight. And it had nothing to do with the girl." He held my gaze, daring me to claim otherwise. We both knew I considered Mick a close friend and would do almost anything to protect him. But that didn't mean I'd admit it out loud.

I lifted a shoulder. "He's the best pilot in the world. Can't afford to lose that."

"Right." He sighed and glanced at a contrite-looking Winter. Her shoulders had caved inward, her gaze on her knees instead of on the Alpha in front of her. "That all said, I still have to punish her. She entered my territory without permission and nearly incited a riot. That's unacceptable."

I knew better than to fight him on this decision. Because he was right. Winter needed to acknowledge the consequences of her action, and while I understood her desire to flee, she'd gone about it the wrong way. At a minimum, she should have made her presence known on the plane.

And I still didn't know what she'd intended to do upon landing. Hide in the woods? Run to the nearest zombie-infested city? Did she even have a plan beyond showing Ludvig the necklace?

All those uncertainties only created more concern.

What if she did something reckless like that again? It wouldn't just be her life put in jeopardy, but mine as well. Our mating tied us together. My instinct to protect her was resolute. If something happened to her, I'd have no choice but to fight on her behalf.

Yet another reason to ensure her training.

"May I speak?" she asked in a whisper-soft tone, her shoulders still caved inward in a broken way I longed to fix.

I shared a gaze with Ludvig, and he gave a slight nod, giving his permission. Not that I necessarily needed it, but I didn't want her to risk a harsher punishment than whatever he already had in mind.

"Yes, little wolf," I told her. "You may speak."

She cleared her throat, her hands twisting in her lap. "What will be done about Winter Sector? It's my kingdom. She stole it from me. I want it back."

Ludvig considered her for a moment, his forefinger and thumb stroking the full ash-blond beard at his jaw. "Your mate and I will need to discuss that further before I can provide a clear answer."

He leaned forward to clasp his hands on his massive oak desk, his shoulders stretching the black fitted jacket across his muscular frame. Ludvig was the only Alpha in Norse Sector who could best me, and a lot of it was due to his solid mass. He was an intimidating motherfucker when he wanted to be.

"I know why you came to me, Omega. Your father and I were good friends, and he would be furious if he knew what had become of his kingdom. I'm not saying I won't help you, but I do need to make an example of your behavior. To be too lenient in this situation would not benefit any of us."

She bit her lip and nodded. "I understand."

I drew my thumb up and down the column of her neck, conflicted. Part of me was pleased by her submission. Yet I also hated seeing this shattered side of her. She appeared to have given up hope, and I despised that.

"He's not going to hurt you," I promised her. "That's not Ludvig's style."

She swallowed and nodded again. "I realize my actions have consequences. But I didn't expect to go into estrus. I never could have anticipated that."

"And I'll take that into consideration while I determine your punishment," Ludvig replied. He glanced at me. "Have you given any thought as to how you want to announce her presence to the sector?"

I released Winter and leaned forward to rest my forearms on my splayed thighs. "The moment they realize who she is, I'll be challenged."

"Yes," he agreed. "You will." He didn't flinch, his gaze knowing.

And suddenly I understood why. *Ah, fuck.* "You bastard. That's my punishment, isn't it? Fending off challengers?"

He lifted a shoulder. "Seems appropriate. You claimed a valuable Omega. While I know you acted in her best interest, the others won't be as accepting of that excuse. And they deserve their battle. It's the only way to keep the peace. You know that as well as I do."

Yeah, that didn't mean I liked it, though.

A string of curses filtered through my mind as I shook my head in heavy acceptance. "I fucking hate you."

"Good," he replied, a hint of amusement finally entering his tone. "That means I've done my job appropriately."

"I might kill some of them," I warned him.

"Only if they fail to yield, in which case, that will be their fault, not yours."

Damn right. I rolled my neck and shook my head again. "You're a right bastard, Ludvig."

"So you've already said." His lips quirked. "But it's the only way the pack will respect your claim. And once they do, they'll also accept the Omega as one of theirs. At which point, should she choose to become Winter of Norse Sector, she may, and they will protect her as their own."

I stared at him, the realization of his intention causing my chest to burn with a foreign emotion. He'd just offered me loyalty on a silver platter. If I convinced the others of my claim, they'd acknowledge Winter as part of the pack while also respecting me as a superior.

Which meant they would be much more accepting of the pending war. They might even fight for us.

I fell back into my chair, the weight of understanding making me uncomfortable. Normally, Ludvig requested a favor and I carried it through. Never did I request payment of any kind, choosing to follow him out of loyalty rather than need. And he was officially repaying my service with an opportunity disguised as a punishment.

"You never fail to impress me, Ludvig."

"That's why I'm Alpha of Norse Sector."

My chin dipped in consent, not enough to show submission, but a payment of respect all the same. "I'll announce our mating this afternoon. However, I ask that the violence leveled against me count as part of her punishment." Because we both knew pretty much every unmated Alpha in Norse Sector was going to challenge me. They'd be too prideful not to.

And when word eventually spread to other sectors, I'd face even more challenges.

It was the nature of being a turned wolf. No one saw me as worthy until they faced me in the arena. Only then did they bow.

He shook his head. "No. Her punishment will be having to listen to the trials from the high-rise. She won't know if you've won or lost. And she won't be permitted to help you heal."

My jaw clenched. "Separating a newly mated pair. That's cruel."

"On the contrary. I consider it a growth exercise." He pressed a button on the comm screen hovering in the air above his desk.

"Yes, Alpha Ludvig?" a feminine voice asked.

Alana.

Fuck.

Ludvig looked at me as he said, "I need you to escort our new Omega asset to the holding suite."

"Of course, sir," she replied.

I glared at him. "Seriously?" We both knew he'd called Alana on purpose. My sexual relationship with the pretty Alpha female was well known. She wouldn't really care that I'd taken an Omega mate, but Winter would absolutely care about being *escorted* by my former lover to a cell.

Victory danced in Ludvig's features. The dick was actually proud of his punishment choice. When I finished this asinine trial, I'd punch him in the face. Just for good measure.

"As I said," he drawled, "it's a growth exercise."

"Yeah." *Asshole*. I ignored him in favor of Winter, going to my knees in front of her. "I've sparred with these idiots several times over, and I never lose. Just… don't lose your faith in me. Okay?"

Her big obsidian eyes met mine, fear evident in their depth. "What if…?"

"Don't think like that. I need your faith, not your doubt. Do you understand?"

She swallowed and slowly nodded. "O-okay."

Yeah, that wasn't a vote of confidence at all. Not that I could blame her. She barely knew me.

Right.

I blew out a breath and stood, my palm gliding over my face to the cluster of hair that dotted my chin. It'd been too many days since I'd enjoyed a proper shave. And it'd probably be a few more before I could again.

This was not going to be a fun afternoon, and knowing she expected me to lose only burned me more.

"If I'm defeated, Alpha Ludvig will ensure you're properly cared for," I muttered, effectively ending the conversation. There wasn't much else for me to say.

I had to go fight for a female who harbored no belief or trust in me at all, despite having saved her life. Not a great realization, but I could only handle one problem at a time.

So I'd assert my dominance among the Alphas.

Then I'd work on my mate's misgivings.

How the fuck has this become my life?

CHAPTER FOURTEEN

WINTER

MY HANDS REFUSED TO STOP SHAKING. Being in this room, accompanied by two male Alphas, had set all my nerves on edge. I could almost taste their testosterone.

Ludvig was the larger of the two, his blond hair framing a face frozen at the age of thirty. But I caught the experience lurking in his blue eyes the few times I was brave enough to gaze at him.

Old, my wolf whispered each time. *So old.*

He had to be near five or six hundred years old, at a minimum. Experience weighed heavily on his shoulders, his muscular frame boasting strength and confidence.

It left me submitting on instinct and only afforded me spare moments of conviction where I voiced my opinion and almost immediately regretted it.

But my response to Kazek was the one I mourned the

most.

He asked for my faith.

I gave him a pitiful response that betrayed my concern.

A stupid reaction. His wolf's skill and prowess were evident in every move he made. He practically wore his resilience as a shield. Two decades by Vanessa's side and I never felt anywhere near the same sort of lethality as I did in Kazek's presence. He put Alpha Enrique to shame as well.

So why had I doubted him?

I reached for him now, wanting to apologize, but the door opened just as I began to move. A new scent blasted through the room, one that caused all the hairs along the back of my neck to stand up and take notice.

Competitor, my wolf growled.

Kazek wrapped his palm around the back of my neck, causing me to realize the rumbling sound hadn't just been in my head but in my throat as well. "Calm down," he demanded.

Calm down? I repeated, incredulous. *Calm down?!*

His Alpha whore had just entered the room. I would not fucking *calm down.* Instead, I stood and wrapped my arms around him, claiming my male and glaring sharply over my shoulder at the wide-eyed blonde standing in the doorway.

I challenged her with my gaze, not giving a damn about her status or the fact that she boasted a similar energy level as Vanessa.

Alpha females were rare.

The only one I'd ever met was Vanessa, and she hadn't exactly provided the best example of leadership.

"Did that Omega just challenge me?" the female asked, both her light-colored eyebrows in her hairline.

Seriously, we couldn't be any more opposite.

She was all legs and torso, putting her at least seven or eight inches taller than me. Her hair glittered like the sun, while mine resembled the night. We were both pale, but her cheeks held a pink tone that mine lacked. Slender hips, curvy chest, toned arms. Very pretty face. Full mouth.

I hated her on sight.

Kazek's fingers threaded through my hair, his other palm

splaying across my shoulder blade. I rubbed against him in response, pleased with his clear claim. "I made the mistake of trying to give her some of your clothes earlier," he replied. "We're both very new to our current situation."

The Alpha bitch snorted. "New indeed. Where the hell did she come from?" She sniffed the air again, her brow furrowing. "Wait, is that…?"

"She's Sofie and Einar's daughter," Ludvig confirmed. There was a hint of some sort of emotion in his voice, one I couldn't identify. Mostly because I was too wrapped up in Kazek's strength to pay attention to much else. He'd enveloped me in a blanket of certainty, a slight purr caressing my ear. I melted into him, my wolf caving to the sensations before my mind could comprehend what it meant.

"Oh, hell," the female breathed, interrupting my serenity.

I growled at her in response.

And she growled back, the sound sending a chill down my spine. That sound told me there would be no competition between us. But my wolf refused to back down, my hackles rising at the perceived threat in the room.

"Winter," Kazek cautioned softly.

"It's okay," the female answered for me, causing me to snarl in response. "I'm not going to fight your little mate, just showing her that I also know how to growl." Amusement touched her tone, which only pissed me off more.

Kazek sighed, his arms folding around me as if he feared I might lunge at the other woman. Which, yeah, I sort of wanted to. *Bitch.* "Winter," he repeated, his lips near my ear. "She's not a threat." He lowered his mouth to the semi-healed bite mark on my neck, nibbling it gently. "You wear my claim. Not her."

"How the hell did this happen?" I heard the female ask, her voice pitched low.

"Alpha Kazek will explain this afternoon during the battle ceremony," Ludvig replied.

"Battle ceremony?" she repeated.

"My punishment," Kazek replied. "I will announce that I've taken a mate, acknowledge I did so without approval from the sector, and allow challengers to fight my claim, if they so desire." He lifted his head while he spoke, his gaze capturing mine as he added, "And I will win each battle."

I felt the certainty in that statement.

He wasn't saying it to pacify himself, but me. Because I'd doubted him. And the flicker of annoyance in his dark irises told me he hadn't appreciated that one bit.

I nodded, accepting his belief. This male oozed danger and dominance. He might be a turned wolf, but he was all Alpha.

"You're preparing him to take Winter Sector," Alana said. "Get all the wolves behind him so he can claim the throne."

"Is that what I'm doing?" Ludvig asked, a note of innocence in his tone that didn't quite ring true. "Well, he has to win first. Let's see how the cards unfold as we go."

Kazek's lips twitched. "Sure. We'll see how it unfolds." He cupped my face and drew his thumb across my lower lip. "You need to go with Alana and do what she says. I'll come find you after this is all over, assuming Ludvig allows it."

"We'll discuss it after the ceremony," he replied.

Kazek slanted a look sideways at him and grunted at whatever he saw in the Sector Alpha's expression. Then he refocused on me, his dark eyes flaring with possession and something else. Something *lethal*. Yet it seemed to soften the longer he held my gaze, his pupils slowly shrinking to allow more of the blue to come through.

The human behind the wolf, I realized, fascinated by the display and his willingness to allow me to hold his gaze when most would have required my submission by now.

This Alpha male was nothing like the ones I grew up hearing about. Strong and dominant, yes. But he regarded me with a kinder side I didn't know Alphas possessed.

"I'm doing this for you, Winter," he said, his voice lower and underlined with a subtle warning. "I need you to be respectful to Alana for me. Okay?"

I gritted my teeth at his choice of phrasing, talking to me like some sort of child. However, he was right about this all being because of me. His Alpha wanted him to stand on ceremony before the entire sector and face challengers as a result of him claiming me.

Something that wouldn't have happened had I not snuck

on that plane.

Yet I couldn't bring myself to fully regret it because had I not chosen that path, I'd probably be dead right now.

Or worse. Claimed by Enrique.

Did he know? I wondered, frowning. No. He couldn't have had any idea. But how did Vanessa expect his knot to kill me? She knew I was an Omega. Had she played us both?

"Winter," Kazek murmured, drawing my focus back to him. "Can you cooperate with Alana for me?"

"I'm an adult, Kazek," I replied, irritated by his phrasing all over again.

His gaze slowly dipped downward, a smirk playing over his luscious mouth. "I'm very aware of your adultlike status, baby." His dark eyes glistened with amusement as he drew his focus upward once more. "I'm asking you not to challenge Alpha Alana. You've already won me. Fighting her won't change a damn thing."

I pressed my palm to his chest, my wolf satisfied with his statement. "I'll do my best not to growl at her, but I expect you to win today." My inner beast felt strongly about him being the victor. She wouldn't accept any other outcome.

"It won't even be a competition," he promised. "Now I need to prepare what I'm going to say, and I want to run it by Ludvig first." He brushed his lips across my forehead. "Don't bite Alana."

I considered his demand and glanced at the female in question. She seemed more entertained than angry. Vanessa would have dished out a swift and harsh punishment by now for my behavior, but Alana didn't appear all that bothered. Even Ludvig wore an amused expression.

Well, one thing was clear—these Alphas were nothing like the one I grew up with.

"I'll bite back," Alana warned, but there was humor in her tone.

The instinct to snarl at her remained, but I swallowed it and refrained from speaking. Kazek rewarded me with a kiss against my temple, sending a shiver of delight down my spine.

Who am I? I wondered, mystified by how much had changed in my reality over the last week. *Since when do I claim males?* Enrique had intended to take a mistress, something I knew and had accepted. Sure, I hadn't been thrilled by the knowledge, but I'd kept my mouth shut.

Yet somehow the idea of this stranger—*my mate*—being with another female made me want to draw blood. I'd never been a violent female before, only training so I knew how to protect myself. And right now I very much wanted to use my strengths and skills to take this Alpha female down. The very thought defied all logic.

"I'll see you soon, Winter." Kazek smiled, his dark eyes conveying pride as he released me.

Pride because I was behaving? Or pride because I'd staked my claim?

I suspected the latter. The mating bond had to make him just as territorial, if not more so, as an Alpha.

I never understood why Vanessa's male Omegas craved her mating bite. But now I sort of did. It was the possession and security that helped the wolf feel safe and complete. They had to be miserable without that comfort. So why hadn't Vanessa taken one of them as her own? Was she that selfish that she couldn't claim another?

"Let's go, Princess Snow," Alana said, interrupting my thoughts. "I'm looking forward to watching your new *Prince Charming* hand the entire sector their asses this afternoon."

Kazek grunted. "I'm no prince. Nor am I a fucking hero. So don't go putting wishes in her head."

"Right. Terrifying assassin. Got it." Alana gave him a mock salute that had me rethinking my opinion of her. She didn't appear afraid of him at all, not even when he growled in response. "Terrifying," she deadpanned, then switched focus to me. "Come on, Omega. I'll escort you up to the holding suite."

I glanced at Kazek and he gave me a nod, encouraging me to follow her. "Try not to miss me too much, mate," he said.

"Then don't take too long," I tossed back at him, surprised by how easily we fell into this familiar camaraderie. Maybe something could be said about fated mates. Except I never in my wildest dreams would have anticipated *him* to be mine.

And something told me he felt the same.

119

I took a step toward Alpha Alana after a final look at Kazek. He seemed completely at ease by the situation, his acceptance calming my nerves.

At least until I made the mistake of looking at Alpha Ludvig. His semi-friendly candor of minutes ago was long gone, that same stern expression back on his face. I shivered and darted out the door to where Alana waited patiently in the hallway.

I said nothing as she led me down a windowless hall. It was the opposite direction from which I'd arrived with Kazek. A knot formed in my stomach, only to grow as she turned down another corridor that ended in a massive open space decorated with windows.

The sun peeked overhead, telling me midday would be here soon. From what I understood, this area of the world shared a similar daylight path to my home sector.

Alana pressed a button, which caused two metal slats to open before us.

An elevator, I marveled, intrigued by the advanced technology. We didn't have these in Winter Sector.

The female Alpha selected a series of keys, causing the doors to close and the interior box to whir to life. My palm hit the wall as we shot upward, my stomach disappearing into the ground below. It reminded me of the plane, my insides immediately nauseated by the unfamiliar motion.

"He'll be fine," Alana promised softly, shocking the hell out of me. "Alpha Ludvig would never design a challenge Kaz couldn't win."

I wondered if she was saying that for my benefit or her own, because I could smell the concern wafting off her.

Did she think Kazek might lose?

Kaz, I thought, frowning. *She called him Kaz.*

"Ludvig's only doing this to prove Kaz is worthy of the Sector Alpha position," she added, but that note of worry stung the air.

"Do you really believe that?" I asked softly, swallowing the bitter note of her discomfort. Was it because of our close proximity or the topic of Kazek's duel?

A ding sounded before she could reply, the metal slats

opening to reveal a white wall.

"Left," Alana advised, cocking her head in the direction in case I didn't know what that meant. The increased uncertainty in her scent didn't help put me at ease in the slightest. That, coupled with the pangs of the foreign motions, I felt on the verge of expelling the contents of my stomach.

Which, I was pretty sure, included a healthy dose of Kazek's cum.

I flattened my palms against my stomach as if to hold my contents in place and carefully stepped onto the marble-floored hallway. Light shone in from the skylights above, indicating we were at the top of the building but not giving away how high up we were. There were only two doors, one at each end.

"The door's unlocked," Alana said from the elevator. "You're free to explore either suite on this floor, but the elevators on this level only work with authorized retinal scans. So don't think about trying to leave. Food will be brought up for your comfort at meal intervals. Oh, and there's a forest area that ties the two suites together. For your wolf."

"You're not…?" I trailed off as the doors began to close.

Alana didn't say anything else, leaving me alone in the cold corridor.

I swallowed. "Great. Thanks."

Not only had she left me questioning Kazek's fate, but she'd also abandoned me up here. Perhaps that was her own way of punishing me.

Alphas really didn't appreciate it when Betas or Omegas questioned their authority.

Sighing, I ventured left and twisted the knob.

Only to freeze on the threshold at the growl emanating from inside.

All the hairs on my neck rose as a second one followed, this one sharper. Louder. And distinctly Alpha.

I darted backward into the hallway, running for the other door.

"*Stop.*" The command sliced through the air, halting my forward progression and causing my blood to run cold. "What the fuck are you doing here?"

CHAPTER FIFTEEN

KAZEK

I STUDIED LUDVIG, waiting for him to speak. He'd gone silent after Alana and Winter left, his expression one of deep concentration as he settled back into his chair, his air of intimidation long gone.

I took his stance as an invitation to sit again, my ankle over my opposite knee, my hands splayed across the armrests.

He had something to say. Some sort of speech. It wouldn't be a vote of confidence but a warning. Claiming Snow Frost meant I'd technically just become a Sector Alpha. The world didn't know it yet, but he did, and that left him in a particularly tough political position.

I respected that.

And I had no idea what we were going to do about it.

His idea for the challenge suited because it would help me assert my dominance over Norse Sector and garner support for a future invasion of Winter Sector, should I choose to take it. I just wasn't sure if that route was one I wanted to take or not. My mate absolutely wanted to reclaim her throne, but was she ready to lead? She'd been a shadow to Vanessa her whole life, brought up to believe herself a Beta, and had no idea what being an Omega truly entailed as a result.

She was vulnerable.

Not necessarily weak, but not trained properly either.

And very much mine to protect.

I wouldn't infiltrate Winter Sector until I felt confident about her abilities, and I had no idea how long it would take to convince myself of that. I wasn't exactly known for my leniency, especially when it came to physical combat training.

"You're going to have your hands full with that one," Ludvig finally said, breaking the silence. "She was clearly raised with a Beta mentality and a rebellious streak."

I inclined my head in agreement. "She thought her suppressants were strength pills." I'd already given him the brief synopsis, but it was worth repeating.

"Fucking Vanessa." He ran a hand over his face, sighing. "She'll need to be dealt with."

"I know."

"By you," he added.

"I know," I repeated.

"But your little Omega wants to handle it herself." Not a question, but an observation.

I confirmed it for him anyway. "She does."

He shook his head, a smirk playing over his lips. "Well, I can appreciate her resolve, just as I'm sure my Mila will, too. But you're going to need to ensure you're both ready for the trial ahead. Today's only a warm-up. Alphas from sectors all over the world are going to challenge you for her. The only way to combat it is with one hell of a statement."

"By making an appropriate entrance as the new Sector Alpha," I translated.

"Exactly."

I palmed the back of my neck, giving it a squeeze while blowing out a long breath. "I've never desired a leadership position. You practically had to blackmail me into being your

Second."

The bastard had threatened to kick me out, saying if I couldn't fall in line beneath him in an orderly fashion, he'd have no choice but to declare me a lone wolf. I didn't appreciate authority as a human, and I certainly didn't as a shifter either.

I preferred to work alone.

Hence my assassin career choice.

"I'm not a leader."

"Perhaps not," he agreed. "But Snow Frost was born one. That'll be her strength in your relationship, just as your enforcer-like proclivities will be yours. Just because an Omega isn't seen as the one in charge doesn't mean she's not advising from the shadows."

It was a popular opinion among Alphas that Omegas were cherished, vulnerable creatures meant to be put on a pedestal and worshiped. However, Ludvig had never maintained that position. Neither had his son Ander. And I suspected Mick would turn out similarly because their mother, Omega Mila, had a backbone. While she submitted when required, Ludvig made it very clear that her opinion mattered. And he shared it frequently.

"She's stubborn, and she's handy with a knife," I admitted, thinking of how Winter had tried to use her little daggers on me in my cabin. "Someone's trained her in combat. At least elementarily."

"Well, then it's a good thing the Alpha who claimed her has a century of paramilitary experience." He arched a brow. "You ready to apply that knowledge this afternoon?"

"You realize this is going to be a bloodbath, right? They only respect me because you made me your second-in-command, and now they're going to use this as an opportunity to prove you wrong about me." They wouldn't succeed, of course. But they'd try. And I'd have to hurt a lot of them to prove a point.

"It's a good thing I'm rarely wrong," he replied, the dimple in his cheek appearing and giving him a younger appearance that belied his true age. He shoved back from his desk and stood, his palms running down the lapels of his jacket. "I need to go have a word with Mila before the ceremony, and I assume you need a bit to prepare. Whatever you plan to say, I approve."

I gaped at him. "Since when?" He hated when I spoke my mind to the troops because I usually ended up calling them a bunch of ignorant assholes.

"Since you became a Sector Alpha," he replied, flashing me another of those grins. "Let's see how well you wear the leadership hat, hmm?"

I clenched my teeth to keep from growling at him. "Bastard. This is another punishment." He knew I hated speeches. This was fucking torture. "The challenge isn't enough for you?" I wondered out loud. "I did the honorable thing and you know it."

He glanced back at me. "Yes, I agree it was the right thing to do where Snow Frost was concerned. However, this punishment is for helping my son bring back a broken Omega. He's completely lost his mind over her, and you're part of the reason he was able to keep her." He arched a brow, daring me to deny it.

"You'd have preferred I let him handle that room of wolves on his own?"

"Yes. Because similar to you, he needs to learn his place in our society, not rely on others to help him lead."

"Similar to me?" I repeated. "I'm well aware of my place, Ludvig." The other Alphas rarely let me forget it.

"Are you?" he countered. "Because just moments ago, you stated that the Alphas of my sector only respect you because of my favor."

"They do."

He tilted his head, his shrewd gaze pinning me in place in the only way an Alpha of his standing could do. "We have a very different opinion on that, Kazek. Perhaps later today you'll understand."

Ludvig didn't give me a chance to respond, his broad shoulders already disappearing through the door.

Fuck. I ran my fingers through my hair. *Fuck.*

CHAPTER SIXTEEN

WINTER

THE BLOND MALE IN THE DOORWAY was the spitting image of Alpha Ludvig. I recognized his face and scent as the pilot from the other night, but I couldn't remember his name.

"Well?" he demanded, arching a single eyebrow. "What the fuck are you doing here, Snow?"

I cleared my throat, my focus falling to my hands as I strove for an explanation. Alana said nothing about there being anyone else up here, let alone a pissed-off Alpha male.

"Why do you smell like an Omega?" he asked, the warmth of his body singeing mine as he entered my personal space. He grasped my chin between his thumb and forefinger, then bent his head to my neck to inhale. "*Kazek?*"

He released me as if I'd burned him, stumbling back a step. I swallowed, uncertain of how to reply.

"Shit. *How?* Did he go back for you?" He shook his head,

not waiting for an answer as he began to pace. "Oh, that fucking idiot. I told him to leave you alone, but of course he didn't listen. When Kazek wants something, he goes after it. Including invaluable females who are strictly off-limits, apparently."

He appeared in front of me again, moving with a speed that indicated his power and strength. This male was definitely his father's son.

"Did he hurt you?" he asked.

I blinked, frowning. I didn't quite meet his gaze as I questioned, "Alpha Kazek?"

"Yes."

"No." Well, not really, anyway. He was a bit rough, but my wolf seemed to like that. My cheeks burned as memories of the last few days swam through my thoughts, each of them more wanton than the next. Gods, I had no idea who I was anymore.

"Good," the Alpha replied, backing off once more. "Why are you up here?"

"Alpha Ludvig sent me up here," I replied, clearing my throat again. "I'm… He's…"

Get it together.
You're Winter now.
Choose who you want to be.

Except that was hard to do with a virile male before me. One who I could tell from his scent was unmated. However, something sweet clung to his skin. My nose twitched as I took a tentative sniff. Then my eyes went wide as the familiar Omega perfume registered.

"Kari." I glanced around him sharply, concerned. "Is she here?"

He bristled at my tone. "Tell me why you're here, Omega. Now."

I flinched at the commanding growl of his words, hating that my first instinct was to kneel. That'd always been my primary reaction, something I thought marked me as an inferior Beta. It made so much more sense now that I knew my true nature.

Omegas submitted.

Always.

"Punishment," I replied, the response grinding over my teeth. "For sneaking onto your plane."

I could feel his shock, the energy in the air buzzing all around us. "*What?*"

"Alpha Vanessa was going to kill me, so I… I hid in the back of the plane. Then I almost died anyway by going into estrus unexpectedly. And, uh, Alpha Kazek mated me." That was the abridged version. But it conveyed the general events. "Alpha Ludvig… isn't happy."

The male fell silent. So silent that I wondered if he was even breathing.

Then he broke out in a fit of deep laughter that caused me to grimace. "I'm telling the truth," I promised him.

"Oh, I don't doubt you are," he drawled, chuckling with each word. "That's why he let me leave with Kari. He sensed you on the plane."

My eyes were still on the ground, but I heard his hair moving as he shook his head. From the glimpse I'd taken of his face, the strands hit him just below his ears. He didn't have a beard like his father but had clearly missed a few days with his razor.

"Well, welcome to Norse Sector, *Omega* Snow. I imagine my father is busy planning for a war now?"

"Winter," I whispered. "I'm no longer known as Snow, but as Winter."

"Was that Kaz's idea?"

I considered the inquiry, torn on how to respond. While Kazek had encouraged it, I'd welcomed the notion. I didn't feel like Beta Snow any longer. She died with the strength pills.

"I prefer Winter," I said, glancing up at his bright blue eyes before immediately returning my focus to the ground.

"Winter it is," he replied, his demeanor shifting slightly. "Where's Kaz? I'd like to congratulate him on breaking a dozen or so laws."

"Alpha Ludvig has demanded that Kazek announce our mating to the sector and accept challengers this afternoon." Just saying it out loud had my stomach churning all over again. I'd almost forgotten about the pain from the elevator, but now it was back and only made worse by the stench of dismay coming from the male in the hallway.

"Oh, fuck…," he breathed, his concern mounting by the moment. "That's… that's not good."

I twisted my hands in front of me, my earlier confidence completely gone. If this Alpha and Alpha Alana were worried, then I should be, too.

"Shit. I need to…" He trailed off, then turned for the door without a word.

A growl came from the room, matching the one I'd heard when I first arrived.

"We're not done with this conversation," the Alpha said, his voice stern. "Consider this a gift of time, Omega. You now have at least two hours to fix your attitude."

A snort was the reply, suggesting he was talking to someone in wolf form. I sniffed the air, noting Kari's familiar scent again, and crept forward out of curiosity.

"You will eat while I'm gone," he continued.

The sound of gnashing teeth met that demand. She sounded pissed.

"Starving yourself isn't an option," he snapped. "I will force-feed you just like I did yesterday. Your choice, Omega."

I glanced into the room to find a blonde wolf sitting on a pile of torn-up cushions. She boldly glowered at the Alpha while he stood before her with his hands on his hips, his size much larger than her own.

"Two hours," he said. "Eat, bathe, and be human when I return."

Her grunt told me she had no intention of complying.

He squatted slowly, holding her gaze the entire time. "I've been lenient because of your situation. That will end when I return, and this behavior will be sternly corrected."

She didn't even flinch, shocking the hell out of me.

I'd only met Kari in passing the one time, but she'd struck me as terrified and meek. This wolf was neither of those things and had me wondering if she possessed a death wish.

Of course, I'd spoken similarly to Kazek.

Sort of.

The Alpha spun on his heel, causing me to jump back in

129

the hallway as he all but charged through the door. "Talk some sense into her, will you?" He stalked over to the elevator bank, pressed his thumb to some sort of panel, and huffed out a sigh as the doors opened. "I need to go make sure Kazek doesn't kill half the fucking sector."

I gaped at him, a litany of questions lining my tongue, but none of them escaped fast enough, the doors already closing.

What did he mean by that?

He had broadcast concern. Was it not for Kazek? Had he worried about the others?

A crash from inside had me jumping, the blonde wolf skidding to a halt in the foyer inside as she eyed me with annoyance. Everything in her stance said she was measuring me up for a potential fight.

When she snarled, I snarled right back.

"I'm not in the mood, Kari," I told her. "But I'm glad to see you're all right."

If wolves could lift their eyebrows, I'd suspect that was her expression right now.

Ignoring her, I prowled into the room to see if I could find a window somewhere. Alpha Ludvig had said I'd be able to hear Kazek but not see him. So there had to be a vent or something.

Blackout curtains met my view throughout what I suspected used to be an elegantly decorated room. It seemed Kari had redecorated, perhaps with her Alpha's help. A tray of food sat on the kitchen bar, the open space beyond it immaculately clean and showcasing technology that gave me momentary pause.

Two ovens.

A microwave.

An entire refrigerator and, holy crap, a freezer, too?

"Wow," I breathed, having only seen these items in magazines. Winter Sector used fire, wood, and the natural elements to keep our food cold. This explained my distaste for Kazek's food this week. He'd been feeding me things using these means, not just roasting a fish over the fire.

With a shake of my head, I moved through the dining area, noted the claw marks on the table, and continued into a thoroughly destroyed bedroom. Sheets, blankets, mattress pieces, clothes… "Okay." I turned back around and nearly ran into Kari.

She'd shifted back into her human form, her blue eyes narrowed. "What are you doing?"

"Trying to find the outside area Alana mentioned," I said.

"Oh." Kari nodded her head and led me back through the chaos of the room to a door I would have thought was a closet. She opened it to reveal an outdoor area littered with trees and real grass and encased in glass windows. "It's a greenhouse. I suppose it's all right for a glorified prison cell."

She shrugged and stepped out to pick a flower from one of the plants, then tucked it behind her ear before padding naked over to the windows.

They overlooked the ocean, not the land, and had a vent at the top that allowed fresh air to infiltrate into the room. My wolf purred in approval, urging me to shift, but I denied her. *Later.*

"Why did you sneak onto their plane?" Kari asked softly.

"Why didn't you tell them I was there?" I countered. It was clear from Alpha Ludvig's reaction today that he had no idea I'd snuck into his sector. And the Alpha she'd been doing, uh, whatever, with was surprised as well.

"I wasn't sure if you were real or not," she whispered, her fingers trailing up and down the glass. "I'm still not convinced *this* is real." She turned, her blue eyes flashing with her wolf as she looked me up and down. "They're not good men, you know. *He* continues to lie. To trick me. But I know better. All Alphas do is seek and destroy, and I won't let him destroy me." Her chin wobbled a little, betraying the conviction in her tone.

She swallowed and took a step, only to freeze as a series of howls blistered through the air. Her knees gave out beneath her as she crumpled to the floor, her palms covering her ears as she began to rock back and forth. Terror filled my nostrils, her keening sound piercing my heart.

Gods, what had they done to her?

"What can I do?" I asked, startled into movement. "How can I help?"

She didn't reply, and outside, the howls only grew louder.

"I… I'm so sorry," I said, falling before her. I knew better than to touch her but hoped my presence would help at least a little. Maybe if I spoke to her? Answered her question about the plane? Told her about my situation?

I wasn't sure, but I gave in to the impulse and started with the night I overheard Enrique talking to Vanessa. By the time I got to the part about Kazek finding me in Norse Sector, her shaking had subsided. And when I spoke about his claim and how terrified I'd been, she'd stilled completely.

I ended my explanation by telling her about Alpha Ludvig's punishment and added, "I think that's why they're howling. He said I'd be able to hear it but not see him."

She said nothing, her even breathing the only sound in the room apart from the chaos erupting outside.

Goose bumps pebbled my arms as Kazek's voice echoed up to my ears. We had to be at least forty stories in the air, but it was hard to tell with only the ocean below. My wolf tuned into him, picking up each word on the wind in broken order.

He stated his name.

His position.

Announced he'd broken the claiming laws.

And then informed the crowd whom he had taken.

Snow Frost of Winter Sector.

A series of snarls erupted after that announcement. Followed by the words I dreaded hearing him say: "I stand before you all, ready to accept challenges from those who wish to protest my claim. However, be advised, I will duel to the death before I ever submit. So come forward. I welcome your blood on my hands."

Kari trembled. "*That's* your mate?"

I swallowed, my stomach twisting as growls met his announcement. "Uh, yeah. That's Alpha Kazek."

"He sounds terrifying."

He is, I thought. Except at some point, his lethality had worn off on me. He didn't frighten me at all. Yet he probably should.

As the sounds of a brawl reached my ears, my heart dropped to my stomach.

I had no way of knowing who was winning, Kazek's growl foreign to my senses. It drove home how new and fragile our mating truly was.

"What happens to you if he loses?" Kari asked softly.

"I'm claimed by a new Alpha." Just the notion of it sent a chill down my spine.

"But if he dies, the shattered link will destroy you." Her blue eyes gazed up at me remorsefully. "The bonds are supposed to be unbreakable."

"Unbreakable?" I didn't know much about the tradition because there hadn't been any Alpha-Omega pairs in Winter Sector. And Vanessa refused to take one of her harem members as a mate.

Kari nodded solemnly. "Yes. I used to believe my father ruining me was a blessing because Alphas won't claim a broken Omega. Not bonding means my soul will never be connected to another, you see. But I found out the hard way that Alphas can destroy me in an entirely different manner."

"Your father ruin—"

A sharp jab to my chest cut off my statement, sending me to the floor on a cry of agony as something cracked inside my heart. *Kazek!* I screamed in my mind, the blow knocking the wind from my lungs and cascading darkness over my vision.

I couldn't breathe, my body on fire from sensations I didn't understand.

Until Kari's words replayed in my head.

The shattered link will destroy you.

No…

No!

CHAPTER SEVENTEEN

KAZEK

FUCKING JOEL!

I snarled at him, urging him to submit, but the arrogant prick wouldn't give.

He snapped his jaws, doing absolutely nothing of consequence. I had him pinned to the ground with my teeth wrapped around his throat.

We were harder to kill in our wolf form, something he seemed to be relying on in our current situation. He seemed oblivious to the fact that I had the advantage, lost to his blood rage and the desire to claim an Omega that didn't belong to him.

I understood why Ludvig had sent Winter upstairs. It served as a punishment while also protecting her. If the Alphas smelled her, this battle would be a lot more gruesome. As it was, my first two contenders went down in less than a minute each.

But Joel seemed hell-bent on making this last.

They all chose to fight as wolves because they erroneously thought it was my weaker form. I used it to my advantage, moving with an agility I'd honed both as a human and an animal. And decades of sparring familiarized me with all their weakness, allowing me to exploit each one. Which was how I'd pinned Joel so quickly. However, I should have known it wouldn't be that easy. It never was with him.

This really had nothing to do with Winter and everything to do with taking me down. He was the loudest in the pack about my unworthy position at the top of the hierarchy. I'd known before this even started that he'd be one of my contenders. Although, I'd expected a lot more protests. Only four had stepped forward, with him being third in line. The rest had all bowed in acknowledgment, respecting my claim.

Ludvig hadn't seemed too surprised at all, and I suspected that was the real lesson here. He wanted me to see that I'd won my position through respect.

Unfortunately, Joel didn't possess a respectful bone in his body. The idiot would probably challenge Ludvig someday for Sector Alpha. Assuming he lived through this fight.

Submit, I urged with a low growl.

Joel growled back, refusing, his claws attempting to dig into the ground for leverage. His strength and skill were no match for mine; he just failed to realize that.

I idly wondered what his blood would taste like, the sensual notion causing my heart to beat in anticipation.

Moments such as this dismantled the small grasp I had on humanity, leaving me thirsty for violence and completely in tune with my wolf.

That was my secret. The reason I always excelled. So many of my kind mistook my mortal upbringing as a weakness. They failed to realize that I had always been an animal. Ludvig's turning me just made me an even stronger one.

My jaw clenched, causing my deadly incisors to pierce the fur and threaten the fragile skin beneath.

A little more, the darker part of my heart whispered. *Yes, just like that.*

Blood.
Delicious.
Sweet.
Victorious.

My mind submitted to the savagery of my existence, my need to do damage rising to the forefront of my thoughts.

This male had challenged me. Threatened me. Thought he could best me. Such lunacy could not be ignored. He needed to be punished, to pay for the sins of his arrogance.

Fury boiled through my veins, loosening my grip on reality and pushing me into a plane of existence where violence thrived. *Time to dance, asshole.*

My jaw tensed, ready to end the miserable existence beneath me, when something tugged on my conscious. A delicate thread, a honed-in foreign energy. It piqued the curiosity of my wolf, dividing my focus.

At least until fear permeated the air.

The sweet scent drew my predator out to play, my craving for death driving my instincts, calling me to *finish it.*

Joel didn't submit when he had the chance.

Now it was—

A screaming howl bit my ears, causing me to flinch.

Feminine.

Familiar.

Mine.

I released my hold on the jackass and spun toward the sound, my heart beating wildly in my chest. *Where?* my wolf demanded, searching for the source of anguish. It struck me through the chest, driving me forward several steps, only to be reminded of my reality in the makeshift arena outside.

Snow blanketed the field. Wolves and shifters in human form dotted the sidelines, all of them watching me with a keen sense of awareness.

And then their gazes drifted to the challengers.

All four were bowing in submission. Including Joel, his lacerated neck on full display.

And the howling scream ceased.

What just happened?

I blinked at the contenders, confused by the sight and

distracted by my animalistic need to find Winter. This new sense of responsibility weighed on me. She'd become the most important being in my life in less than a fucking week, all because of the mating claim.

Hurting her was unacceptable, and something had harmed her in the last few minutes. I just didn't understand what had caused that agonized cry. She was quiet now, the thread tying us together thrumming with life.

"She pulled you back," Ludvig explained softly as he approached me. "That's what a good bond does. It balances the wolf."

He casually and purposefully took in the crowd, noting their stances of submission, some more prominent than others.

"Is there anyone else who wishes to challenge Alpha Kazek on his claim?" he asked, his voice quiet yet powerful.

Silence.

Only three? I thought, baffled. I expected at least a dozen.

"A good choice," Ludvig continued. "I think it's rather evident how strong his claim is, yes?"

I glanced up at him, unsure of what he meant by that. Because I felt her pull? Her pain? Wasn't that normal for a mating bond? As I'd never experienced one, I didn't really know. And it hadn't exactly been a situation I'd spent much time looking into.

"As is customary in Norse Sector, the challenge period will remain open for the requisite seventy-two hours. However, if today's demonstration is anything to go by, I'd say the chances aren't great for anyone who chooses to participate. But at least you know he'll refrain from killing you, even if he falls into one of his infamous rages."

I grunted at his chosen phrase. *Infamous rages*. I liked to kill. No need for a romanticized view of it. But it was interesting that I'd been able to pull back. I rarely denied my inner beast when he craved blood.

Yet Winter had managed to pull me out of my mindset.

That had definitely never happened to me before. I wondered if Joel realized just how lucky he'd been today. I'd wanted to scatter the grounds with his intestines, just to make a point. Shit, I still wanted to. But as long as he continued to submit, I didn't have cause to shred him apart.

"Once the trials are over, we'll host a celebration for our newest additions to Norse Sector and formalize Kazek's claim." His focus fell to Mick on the sidelines, who stood with a scowl on his face.

Newest additions. Plural. Meaning Ludvig wanted to introduce the slave Omega as well. Mick's gaze told me just how he felt about that.

What is it with the female that had him so obsessed? I wondered. Then I thought of Winter and my initial inclination to punish her and take her at Winter Sector. Perhaps it hadn't been part of the atmosphere at all, just the females themselves.

Alpha Alana approached and tossed me a rare slab of beef. I caught it with my teeth, the juices immediately calling to the hunger inside. I'd barely eaten in the last few days while tending to Winter's estrus. It wasn't an ideal way to fight, but I'd been through worse.

"Congrats on the mating," Alana said, giving me a knowing smile. "She's a feisty one."

I snorted. *Feisty* seemed lacking.

Winter had a fire in her that I couldn't help but admire and a sense for survival that I understood. She just lacked the execution. With some training, she'd become formidable, and that made her perfect for me. Meek wasn't attractive. I preferred strength and a backbone.

Alana gave me a nod and turned away, her gesture one that several of the wolves noticed. She approved of my claim, which meant a great deal in Norse Sector. Being a rare Alpha female granted her a certain status, one she strengthened by her natural leadership skills.

I ripped into the steak with gratitude while the others began to disperse.

I had a long three days ahead of me. Waiting in this field for potential challengers would prove exhausting and exhilarating at the same time. My wolf paced in excitement, the raw meat on my tongue an aphrodisiac to the desired fight.

Winter was already mine.

As well as Winter Sector, if I wanted it.

The lack of competitors today had me rethinking what I thought I knew about my position of power. Having self-confidence was very different from seeing the respect and confidence come from others. That was what had happened today. Almost the entire sector had acknowledged my dominance without question.

Would Winter Sector do the same? They were Betas, so I suspected they would. But what about other sectors?

Would my life become a constant battle for the throne as Alphas from all over tried to take the territory from me?

No one challenged Vanessa. Maybe they wouldn't come for me either.

I shook my head, swallowed the last bite of meat, and licked my jaw clean before taking a seat on my rump.

Determining the future required Winter's input. I also needed her absolute trust and physical preparedness for such a task of leadership. We were nowhere near ready.

So I'd follow the steps.

The first being to win this challenge without question.

Then we'd go from there.

CHAPTER EIGHTEEN

WINTER

I CURLED INTO A BALL on the floor as the pain subsided, my wolf shaking inside. Whatever I'd just felt was bleak and devastating, like my very soul had detached from my body to venture somewhere dark and cold.

I shivered, my throat dry from the sensation.

"Snow?" Kari asked, panic in her tone. "A-are you…?"

"I'm okay," I rasped, my voice destroyed from the howls that had forced their way through my mouth moments ago. Or had a longer period passed already? I couldn't tell, my grasp on reality wavering beneath a frozen wave.

Did I just feel Kazek leave me? Was that the bond shattering? My mind whirred, my heart thumping wildly in my chest. *I… I still feel him. I think. Maybe.*

A whimper escaped my lips, my adrenaline spiking as I tried to sort truth from fiction. What if I only thought the bond remained? Like a hopeful part of me lost in a perpetual spiral of dreams that no longer existed?

I shook my head and immediately regretted it as the world spun around me.

Something wasn't right.

Something had definitely fractured.

Unless that was the residual pain I felt cracking along my rib cage?

Kari growled suddenly, drawing my gaze upward to catch her in mid-shift. I frowned, not understanding her reaction.

Then I felt it—the change in atmosphere that announced an approaching Alpha. And not just any Alpha, but a powerful one.

Ludvig.

I recognized his essence from our initial meeting, that intoxicating cloud of dominance swirling around him like a riptide, threatening to take down anyone in his path.

I curled into myself on instinct, needing to hide. He'd caught me in a moment of weakness, my heart uncertain of my fate.

Kari snarled at him as he entered the room, earning a sharp growl in return that sent her skidding into a corner with her tail between her legs.

"Don't make your punishment worse than it already is, Omega," he said to her, the warning in his voice one that had me shrinking into the wall and he wasn't even talking to me. He stared her down, waiting for her reaction. When she didn't move or utter another sound, he switched focus, his blue eyes blazing with power as he took in my quivering position.

He sighed, ran his fingers through his hair, and made a rumbling sound that made all the hairs along my arms stand on end. I inhaled sharply as he increased the deepness of the reverberation, my wolf perking up inside and releasing a subtle sigh of her own.

What is that? I wondered, glancing at Kari. She hadn't moved, but I sensed her unease and distrust.

Ludvig increased the volume, causing my lips to part with realization. *He's purring.* That sound was meant for mates. My blood went cold at the realization, which caused him to rumble louder.

My wolf bowed to his superiority, bathing in the soothing relief his purr evoked. But my mind refused to submit. "W-why?" I asked, unable to say anything more. *Why did you kill Kazek?*

"It's my duty as Sector Alpha to provide relief to those who need it," he replied, crouching before me, that rumble still radiating from his chest and causing me to flinch. "Don't worry. This isn't a mating purr, little one. That's reserved for my Mila."

I frowned. *There's a difference?*

"I suppose you wouldn't be as familiar having grown up in a Beta colony, and I doubt Alpha Vanessa purrs often," he explained as if he'd heard my unspoken question. Ludvig reached out to cup my jaw, drawing my gaze up to his. "Why are you distressed? Is it because you felt Kazek pull away?"

My lips moved, but words failed me. All the confidence I felt earlier had fled, leaving me a shell of a female I barely recognized. I'd stood up to this Alpha with Kazek at my side, but now I felt alone and exposed. *Weak.* I hated this sensation. I wasn't this woman. *I'm royalty. The heir to the Winter Sector throne.*

Maybe a new identity was a bad idea.

I needed Snow to return.

No. She was just as fragile. A doll used as a pawn without ever knowing the truth.

Until Kazek.

Had he not intervened when he did, I would have died. I swallowed, my heart thumping against my rib cage in a chaotic pattern. *Not true. I* did *die, and I came back as an Omega.*

"It's not wise to ignore an Alpha's direct question," Ludvig said, his tone conveying a hint of patience. "Did you feel the threat to your connection with Kazek?"

I swallowed the ball in my throat and nodded. "Yes." It came out on a rasp, my vocal cords still not healed from my howls.

He seemed pleased by my response. "I imagine it hurt to feel him slipping away, but you called him back." He released my jaw but remained crouched before me. "Kazek switches off his emotions when he falls into a rage. It's his one weakness. But I think he's about to strengthen it through his bond with you."

Ludvig stood, his thick thighs bulging through the fabric of his dress pants.

"In seventy-one hours, you'll be released from holding. Use this time to consider what the separation feels like and try to remember it going forward. Perhaps it will dissuade you from future reckless activity, such as secretly boarding a plane to escape fate. Because the agony you're about to undergo is nothing compared to how it would feel if you or Kazek departed this world for good."

This is the real punishment, I realized.

Ludvig wanted me to know what it would be like to exist without my Alpha. And as Kazek already pointed out, it was cruel to separate a newly mated pair. I didn't fully understand why, as it was all new to me, but if it felt anything like the pain I'd already experienced, then it was going to be a long three days.

"As for you, Omega Kari, I do not tolerate self-harm of any kind in this sector, and your behavior will be corrected. You will eat. Starvation is not an option." He took a step away but paused at the door.

I hadn't moved from my spot, terrified that he might add to my punishment.

"Alpha Kazek will be hungry when he's finished the challenge, and I don't mean for food. So prepare yourself, Omega. He'll be demanding and ruthless, and he'll require complete obedience." With that ominous proclamation, he left.

It took me several minutes to lift my focus away from the floor, my heart in my stomach.

When I finally glanced upward, it was to find Kari in her human form, gazing at me with pity in her eyes.

That alone said everything about my pending fate.

Three days of separation agony followed by a brutal claiming.

I can survive this, I told myself. *There's no alternative.*

Alpha Kazek hadn't destroyed me during estrus, even at

his most brutal points. He sure as hell wouldn't shatter me now.

But the physical act wasn't what scared me.

No. It was the anticipation thrumming through my blood, the desire to be consumed completely and entirely. I *wanted* him to dominate me. And worse, I wanted it to be done publicly.

Mine, my wolf agreed, her existence a constant presence in my mind.

I shivered at the thought, my body betraying my need as slick pooled between my thighs.

Only, the Alpha I desired for satisfaction didn't come.

And that was when I realized the real horror of my situation.

My soul craved her mate, while my body *needed* him. Yet I was trapped here, away from the very male I desired. That was the true agony. My real punishment.

I closed my eyes on a groan, Ludvig's name a curse in my mind.

"Perhaps it'll dissuade you from future reckless activity," he'd said.

"Bastard," I hissed, curling into a ball once more. "You fucking bastard."

I swore I heard him chuckle from the shadows. It was all probably just a figment of my imagination, but it made me hate him even more.

He'd just sentenced me to three days of anguish.

All because I'd boarded a plane to seek refuge in his territory.

Well, perhaps not just that. I'd not exactly been all that respectful to him. And he was right—I hadn't apologized. But how could I feel remorse for saving my own life? What did he expect me to do? Call first?

I growled in annoyance, the sound vibrating along my spinal cord to the top of my rump. A bad idea because it reverberated lower, to a tender area that longed to be stroked.

Kazek had addicted me to his cock.

Fucking Alpha.

Damn Omega genes!

I squirmed in annoyance, trying to find a comfortable

position on the bed of grass below me, the room's forest-like surroundings pulling me back to my senses.

My wolf agreed to come forward, white fur dotting my arms and legs on impulse as I engaged the shift in an attempt to heal myself. Only, I wasn't sure exactly what required alleviation. I wasn't wounded, just *owned*.

I snorted, the sound deepened by my snout, and I clawed my way out of the clothes I'd failed to remove. Then I sniffed them. *Kazek. Mmm.* I shredded the fabric to my heart's content, creating a bed of cotton on the earthy floor. *Perfect.* I curled up inside it, longing for the familiarity of his warmth, and pushed away all my reservations. Everything felt right again.

Home.

I'm home.

Except the male I desired was missing, my makeshift nest not quite right without him.

A howl escaped my throat, causing my ears to perk up as the male I yearned for responded in kind. I cocked my head to the side, listening to the much deeper reverberation and allowing it to soothe me momentarily.

He wasn't here, but I could hear him. And for now, that would be enough.

CHAPTER NINETEEN

KAZEK

I PACED THE FIELD FOR THE MILLIONTH TIME, my focus on the Alpha at the edge. If he didn't call time soon, I was going to lunge at him and rip his fucking throat out. Maker be damned.

This had been the longest three damn days of my entire life. Winter's howls had dimmed into cries, her need chafing every inch of my fur. I'd remained in wolf form because I preferred the enhanced senses, which came with my ability to scent her.

Ludvig had her locked up in the tower, and from what I could tell, she hadn't left the outdoor room that tied the two holding areas together. Her wolf could at least hear mine, probably smell me, too. And while it prolonged our agony, it also soothed us.

This hold over me and my mind was exactly why I didn't

want a mate. Winter weighed on my heart and soul, my desire to protect her and take her mounting with each passing second.

I growled at Ludvig, letting him know my patience had reached the end of my very long rope. My punishment was over. I'd won. Not even Joel had come back for a second challenge.

Wolves in animal and human form lined the perimeter, waiting for the end.

They knew what would come next.

A very public claiming.

My paws tore a path over the earth as my pacing sped up. I needed my mate, and I needed her right fucking now.

Three days of awaiting a challenge that never arrived had left me without an outlet for my violence. Defeating Joel and the other two idiots on the first day hadn't been enough. I needed more blood. Someone to chew on. Something to *destroy*.

All for her.

To prove my worth.

Yet no one bothered to try, and that pissed me off. It served as some sort of fucked-up compliment that I didn't want to acknowledge.

All the wolves watching me now saw me as an Alpha worthy of my prize.

I wanted at least one of them to try to knock me from my throne, but no one did. Not after Joel fell.

I growled at them. Snarled. Tried to provoke anyone to step forward.

They didn't.

The cowards were too afraid. Too damn *respectful*.

What happened to those who questioned my human birth? How about the Alphas who despised my position as Second in Norse Sector? Where were they now?

I whipped around, searching the field and finding those who once questioned my status. None of them would meet my gaze.

Because they saw me as worthy.

They accepted my claim.

Well, good. Because it was already done.

Now where the hell is she? I wondered, swinging around to find Ludvig.

He wore a bored expression, but I sensed the pride lurking beneath. He liked that no one dared to challenge me. If I didn't have all this aggression built up inside me in preparation, I might like it, too. But I really needed an outlet, someone to—

My nose twitched, everything coming to a pause around me. *There*, I thought, focusing on the perfume swirling in the air. *Mine.*

He didn't stand in my way as I prowled forward, searching for the source of all my pent-up *need*. Her intoxicating scent led me by my snout, drawing me closer with each step.

A gorgeous female wolf walked along the periphery of the field, her obsidian eyes familiar. I froze at the sight of her, momentarily stunned by the beauty of her all-white coat. She seemed just as taken with my own fur, which was a solid black that complimented my inner chaos.

I took another step toward her, a growl coming from my throat as I demanded she submit by returning to her human form so I could properly take her. It was the kind of growl I could deepen to *force* her transition, but I gave her the option to transform on her own first.

She didn't.

Instead, she turned tail and ran in the opposite direction.

I snarled at her back, displeased by her clear disobedience.

"Apparently, she's going to make you work for it," Ludvig commented, humor in his tone. "Go get her."

I didn't need his permission or his comment to follow the instinct to chase. I'd already started running before he finished, my inner wolf furious that Winter thought to flee.

Three fucking days I'd spent in this field, defending her honor, and she rewarded me by running? I'd spank her ass raw for this. Then fuck it because I could. Leave her a writhing mess of need without a climax. Take her repeatedly while never giving her my seed in the place she longed for it most.

Yes.

That was how I would handle this once I caught the little

minx who thought she could outrun me.

I'd howled for her when she cried out for me. I'd reassured her every step of the way. How dare she tempt me into a chase. I expected immediate submission, splayed thighs filled with slick, waiting for my cock to slice into her.

Not this.

Not a jaunt through the damn woods.

Where the fuck was she even going? She'd left the main square, heading away from the docks and toward the snow-laden mountains beyond. Did she intend to hide behind a tree? I growled. I'd take her up against that perceived barrier instead.

Hiding was not an option.

She would fucking heel.

I followed her path upward, then sideways, then upward again. She was a fast little thing, purposely squeezing through trees my larger body couldn't accommodate. Respect trickled through my mind with each curve in her trail, my wolf pleased that she knew how to flee. It might come in handy later against enemies.

But to use her skills to escape me was not acceptable.

I growled after her, grunting when she responded with a soft whine.

If my noises upset her, she'd be in for a rude awakening when I got my paws on her.

She switched direction again, this time causing my eyebrows to rise as I recognized her intention.

The little wolf was leading me back to my cabin.

To her makeshift nest.

Something inside me twisted in understanding.

She wasn't rejecting me or my claim. She was *playing*. Winter wanted me to chase her back to her nest, to devour her in the comfort of familiar surroundings.

Oh, the wolves back in the main square would be disappointed by that.

Hmm. A new sequence of events unfolded in my mind as I finally caught up to her about a hundred yards from the cabin. I nipped at her heels, causing her to stumble into the snow. I pounced on her, holding her down with my much larger form, and growled again.

Last chance, I was telling her. Because if she didn't shift back right now, I'd make her.

A low sound left her throat, one that implied defeat, as she began the process of transitioning back into her human form. I hovered over her while she transitioned, my wolf immediately protective of her vulnerable position.

She shivered, her human skin not appreciating the blanket of frozen earth beneath her.

Winter averted her black eyes away from mine as she showed her neck, submitting to me entirely.

I pressed my snout to the tender skin and gave her a tentative lick with my tongue. She didn't move, her breath shallow with idle fear.

Good.

She should be afraid.

She'd challenged my predator side with that little stunt.

I licked her again, a soft growl coming from my chest as I acknowledged that she should also be proud.

So fast, my wolf praised. *Expert maneuverability.*

Yes, a fine mate indeed.

I nipped the tender area of her throat, then slowly moved off of her to begin my own shift. She didn't try to run or even move, her eyes remaining downcast and submissive the entire time.

Finally.

I rolled my neck to loosen my stiff muscles, my human form protesting my prolonged four-legged state. It would pass in a moment.

My limbs shook, my torso flexing as spikes of agony shot through my bloodstream. The transition never felt quite right, perhaps because I hadn't been born a wolf. I wasn't sure, but the sensation dissipated after a few moments, leaving me rejuvenated and ready to play with my mate.

She still hadn't moved, pleasing me greatly.

I scooped her up into my arms and purred for her. She melted into me, her nose pressing into my chest as she inhaled deeply. Her reaction caused me to purr louder, my inner wolf approving of her clear surrender.

However… "You shouldn't have run, little one," I said, my voice gravelly and deeper than normal. "Now I have to fill you with my cum and parade you around the village afterward."

"You were going to do that anyway." Her words were a breath against my hot skin, her nose trailing along my collarbone. I could barely feel the snow beneath my feet or the wood planks as I entered the cabin. All my senses belonged to the beauty in my arms. I needed her in a way I'd never experienced before.

This would be rough. Harsh. Maybe even violent.

My savage desires battled in my mind, debating how best to fuck her first. This wasn't like her estrus where I took her out of duty. This experience was for me and my wolf.

I dropped her on the bed and prowled toward her. She parted her thighs for me, allowing me an uninhibited view of her soft, pink, wet flesh. I took a long lick, adoring the taste of her arousal on my tongue, and pressed my palm to her belly to keep her in place as I repeated the action.

"*Fuck*," I muttered, my cock hard as a rock already.

She groaned in response, her slick decorating her pretty pussy, preparing for my entry.

"You're not going to fight me?" I questioned, surprised she made this so easy after providing such an exquisite chase.

Winter swallowed, her dark irises meeting mine. "Do you want me to?"

An interesting response. I considered her inquiry for a long moment before saying, "Yes."

"Okay." She didn't hesitate, her nails flying forward and meeting my arm to rake down my flesh. I hissed, the sensation unexpected in a good way.

She repeated the action on my neck, causing me to jerk back in surprise. Winter used the moment to wiggle out from beneath me and roll off the mattress to her feet.

I growled, annoyed by the distance between us.

Her thighs clenched in response, more of her delicious slick saturating the air. Omegas were programmed to respond to the Alpha's mating call, their bodies readying themselves for sex in every way.

I used that to my advantage, growling again as I moved

toward her.

She visibly winced, her stomach muscles clenching with the action.

"What's wrong, Omega? Am I making you ache for me?" I purposely infused a rumble into my tone, enjoying the way it made her squirm.

And then I lunged for her.

She ducked faster than I anticipated, rolling across the bed to the other side in a deft move that impressed me thoroughly. My wolf both smirked and snarled, proud and annoyed at the same time.

"I told you to fight me, not evade me," I pointed out while I considered my next play.

"We all have different methods. This is mine."

"To run?"

She lifted a delicate shoulder, drawing my focus to the nearly healed claiming mark on her neck. I needed to fix that with my teeth. The ambrosia of her blood called to me, reminding me what it tasted like during her estrus.

Again, my wolf encouraged.

But first, I needed to catch her once more.

I faked a lunge across the bed, only to dart around the foot of it to grab her. She narrowly escaped my attempt, her quick feet taking her backward into the mouth of my bathroom.

"That's a dead end," I informed her.

"Then I guess you'd better come get me," she replied, a taunt in her tone that excited me immensely.

I darted forward, intending to snag her hips, but her nails raked across my chest and cheek. Growling, I grasped her nape, tugging her into me and wincing as her knee connected with my upper thigh, narrowly missing my groin. I released her on instinct, my cock not pleased.

"Fuck, Winter."

She ignored me, her defense mechanisms coming on in full force as she demonstrated years of training with her kicks and hits while I did my best to subdue her without actual harm.

I'd wanted her to fight.

And fight she did.

Impressively.

Boldly.

And with a lot more precision than I ever could have anticipated.

Whoever had trained her had done an amazing job.

"Enough." I caught her punch, whirling her around into my chest, and clamped my opposite arm around her waist. She kicked backward, forcing me to lift her into the air. "*Enough*," I repeated.

Yet whatever button I'd triggered wasn't turning off, and Winter continued trying to take me down. She didn't stand a chance, which only seemed to make her more desperate as she screamed and writhed and used those deadly nails to draw blood across any part of my skin she could access.

"Stop," I demanded, bending her over the bed and collecting her arms behind her back.

It was like she couldn't hear me, her rage continuing as she attempted to escape an impossible hold. If she wasn't careful, her antics would disjoint her shoulders.

I grasped her forearms beneath one palm, pressing them against her spine, and kicked her legs apart.

"You're mine, Winter." And it was damn time she acknowledged it.

"Fuck you!" she screamed, her beautiful neck arched as she struggled to lift her upper body off the bed.

"That's exactly what I'm going to do," I replied darkly, angling myself over her and finding her hot entrance. She kicked her lower limbs in response, still fighting me. I grabbed her hip with my free hand, holding her exactly where I wanted her. "Stay."

She snarled something unintelligible, causing me to fold over her, fully trapping her beneath my much larger form.

"Oh, darling, disobedient little Omega," I murmured against her ear. "You're *mine*."

Heat flooded my veins, driving me forward with a speed much harsher than I'd originally intended and eliciting a guttural sound from her throat as I forced her to accept every inch inside her tight little channel.

"God, you feel amazing," I praised, sliding out and back

in with the same power as before.

She shook beneath my hands, both from the shock of my entry and her impending orgasm. I could feel her walls squeezing around me, begging for me, urging me to drive in even harder. And so I did, claiming her savagely the way I craved, the way we both required.

My name fell from her mouth on a rasp of sound, her lungs not working fast enough to provide her with a voice.

I lifted away from her back, using the ground beneath my feet for leverage as I increased my speed, surging deeper into her and drawing more of those hypnotic sounds from her lips.

She gasped.

Screamed.

Begged me to stop.

And demanded more.

All within the span of minutes, her chants on repeat.

I chased my pleasure inside her, my knot forming at the base and shooting upward to find its home within her tight sheath. She cried out beneath me, the force of my orgasm shoving her into oblivion with me.

Winter cursed me.

Sobbed.

Moaned.

And eventually deflated, her shoulders shaking as she caught her breath from the explosion of lust and emotions riddling her petite frame.

I released her arms and kissed her shoulder. "We're nowhere near done," I warned her.

She swallowed and nodded her acceptance, her face pressed into the mattress to hide her tears.

I gently worked my arm beneath her belly while my opposite hand remained on her hip to keep us glued together. She didn't fight me as I guided us both more firmly onto the bed and spooned her from behind, my knot still throbbing inside her in a pulsing orgasm that satisfied my inner beast.

"Are you okay?" I asked softly, my lips trailing along her neck to the place where I desired to claim her again.

She nodded once more.

"Use words," I said, needing to hear her voice.

"I'm okay," she whispered.

"You wouldn't stop fighting me."

"It's what you needed."

I blinked, surprised by her comment. She was right. I needed to dominate her completely, and the only way to do that was through a real battle of wills.

"How did you know?" I wondered out loud. She'd been the one to ask if I wanted her to fight me. Then she'd continued even after I told her to stop, which had only excited me more.

"Because my wolf needed you to win," she admitted, her voice soft.

Ah, now I understood. "That's why you ran. To test your mate."

She nodded. "I sensed your aggression and gave you what you needed. What *we* needed."

I nuzzled her throat, enthralled with her all over again. This female was perfect. "You're my ideal mate," I told her softly, my lips sealing over her claim mark. "And I want everyone to know you're mine."

CHAPTER TWENTY

WINTER

I WAS ON FIRE FROM KAZEK'S TOUCH. His hands were everywhere, his fingers dipping into my sex to gather our mixed fluids and bringing them upward to saturate my body in our mixed scent.

He'd started this ritual as soon as his knot released me, his focus resolute.

First, he'd painted my lips, my tongue, and forced me to swallow to coat my throat.

Then he'd moved on to my breasts and my belly.

Followed by my arms.

And now he'd begun the process of coating my legs.

"We need more," he said, his voice a low growl that caused my thighs to clench with want. He slid his fingers inside again, collecting my slick and sliding downward at a new angle. "Flip over onto your stomach."

I knew better than to deny him.

The man had disappeared into his wolf, his inner beast driving all his actions once more.

"Beautiful," he praised, his palms squeezing my ass before parting it to reveal the place he desired to claim next. His thumb pressed inward, forcing me to accommodate him. I vaguely remembered him doing this during my estrus, my mind so consumed by sex I hadn't been able to feel the pain of his entry.

But I would feel every inch of it now.

Gods, my female parts still ached from his brutal penetration before. If he took my ass like that, I wouldn't be able to sit all night, or likely tomorrow, either.

"Shh," he murmured, his opposite hand petting my spine. "I'll take care of you, baby."

I squirmed, this connection between us leaving me decidedly uncomfortable. He read me as well as I read him, perhaps even better. I just instinctively knew what he needed, and vice versa, our bodies and souls married in a way my mind couldn't comprehend.

He placed a kiss between my shoulder blades, the action surprisingly tender and contradicted by his fingers sliding inside me. At least he'd chosen to prepare me for his entry, unlike with my pussy. I'd felt ripped in two when he'd penetrated me. The burn and ache had quickly given way to pleasure, but those initial few seconds had *hurt*.

Kazek added another finger as he licked a path up my spine to nibble the back of my neck.

"You smell amazing, Winter." His warm breath made me shiver, the sensation traveling down to my nipples and tightening them with want. He grinned against my skin as my lower body clenched, creating more slick and permeating the air with my desire.

His free hand slipped beneath me, his thumb finding my clit and circling it once before his fingers slipped downward into my entrance. He rumbled in approval, his touch against my rump quickening as he readied me for his claim.

I whimpered when he slipped out of me, missing the feel of him while also fearing what would come next. "Up on your hands and knees, baby."

The endearment cascaded warmth over my skin, encouraging me to comply despite my shaking limbs. He gently nipped the back of my neck once more, then nuzzled the claiming mark on my shoulder.

"I'm going to bite you again," he warned.

"I know."

"Good." He positioned himself at my front entrance and slid inside on a hiss. "So tight and hot. I could seriously live inside you, princess."

I didn't reply, because part of me wanted him to. And that part couldn't be trusted to speak right now.

Kazek pumped in and out a few times before pulling out and moving backward to my other hole. I braced myself for the pain, my fingers digging into the bedding as he pushed forward just an inch to breach my entrance.

He folded himself over me, pressing his chest to my back as his hand went to the bed beside mine. His opposite palm found my hip, holding me steady. "It's going to hurt," he said, his lips against my spine. "But I promise to make it feel good."

"I trust you." The words slipped from my mouth from that place I'd muted before, the one that adored him and would do anything he asked, including let him live inside my pussy if he so desired.

I suspected my wolf had something to do with that little voice.

He didn't move or speak for so long that I wondered if I'd upset him.

Then he pressed another of those tender kisses to the back of my neck and thrust forward. I cried out, my elbows bending and causing me to fall forward, only to be caught by his palm against my stomach. He'd moved it from my hip, using it to hold me against him.

I expected to lose him to the rut, just like before, but he remained still as he allowed me a moment to get used to his size.

How the hell had I liked this during my heat cycle?

Because right now, it *burned,* and not in a good way.

He nuzzled my throat, his purr invading my senses. My

muscles relaxed in response, my wolf soothed by the familiar sound of her mate. "That's it," he encouraged, the rumble a caress against my back. "You can take me, Winter. I know you can."

I wasn't sure what he meant until he started to move again. Only then did I realize he hadn't entered me fully, his Alpha dick way too big for my much smaller form. "Kazek…"

"It's okay," he promised. "You took me in your heat and enjoyed it. I'll make sure you do now, too."

I didn't believe him.

This was an entirely different situation because my mind was fully engaged. He couldn't just switch it off like my estrus did. The heat cycle was designed to accommodate a rutting Alpha. Hence the mental shutdown. But right now—

I jolted as he did something to my clit.

A flick.

Followed by his thumb applying subtle pressure and moving in a sensual circle that had my knees threatening to buckle beneath me. His touch created a firestorm in my belly that spread through my veins, leaving me trembling uncontrollably.

Magic, I thought. *This male is full of magic.*

Even his lips resembled flames against my skin, each kiss feeling like a brand that singed me to my very soul and stoked the inferno within me. This time his name escaped me on a moan, his movements increasing subtly and turning that burn into a beautiful ache.

Yet his thrusts created an emptiness between my legs that caused me to whine. He wasn't fucking me where I wanted him. His knot wasn't brushing the place deep inside that I craved. I protested on a groan, my mounting orgasm lacking the connection I needed.

He fucked me harder, as if to make up for the lack of sensation in my other channel. It didn't help. I only ached for him more.

"Kazek," I whimpered, my head falling forward on an orgasm that did little to dispel the maelstrom churning in my abdomen.

His pleasure followed mine, spurts of cum bathing my

insides from the wrong direction.

There was no knot, my ass not built to accommodate it.

His forehead fell to my shoulder, his body shaking with ecstasy. "I need more," he growled. "I need your cunt."

I moaned in approval, then cried out as he left me completely. My skin pebbled with goose bumps from the cool air, my ears perking up at the sound of water running. Maybe he intended for us to fuck in the shower?

My forehead hit the mattress with the thought, my body refusing to move. I needed at least five minutes before I could stand. Maybe longer.

I shut my eyes and focused on my breathing, the fire mounting to deafening heights in my bloodstream. "Kazek," I whispered. "Carry me."

If he heard me, he didn't acknowledge me, but he did return, his warmth a welcome blanket of familiarity that had me picking up my head enough to watch his approach. He was wet, his cock shiny and angry with need.

Suddenly I felt very similar to that raging purple head. "You washed me off of you?"

He arched a brow, saying nothing in reply.

I forced myself up on my knees and dug my nails into his chest to hold on for balance. "You did, didn't you?" I scratched down his abdomen to his groin and bent to sniff him. A hiss left my throat, my wolf livid at the unacceptable scent. "Fix it. Fix it now."

His lips curled into a feral smile. "Oh, I intend to, Omega." He pushed me backward onto the bed and settled between my thighs, his arousal prodding mine as he went onto his elbows on either side of my head. "You'll be dripping with my cum when I'm through with you."

"And you'll be covered in my slick."

The wolf gazed down me. "Damn right I will." He entered me slowly, drawing out the moment. I raked my nails down his back, wanting him to move faster, but he remained completely in control, his eyes holding mine as he slid in inch by inch.

"More."

"No."

I growled.

He growled back, causing my pussy to flutter with *need*.

"*Please*," I begged.

"No." He dropped his head to my neck, his teeth sealing over his claiming bite and clamping down to draw blood.

I screamed, arching into him, only to be pinned down by his hips as he thrust all the way inside and remained there.

My fingers dug into his shoulders, making him bleed and leaving little crescent moons behind that deeply satisfied my wolf.

His tongue laved the wound on my shoulder, his mouth dotted with red as he pulled back. The sight made me jealous. So I lifted up as far as I could and licked the marks I left on his shoulders.

He watched me carefully, a thousand thoughts flying through his blue-black irises.

Then, ever so slowly, he pressed his lips to mine.

I startled beneath him, shocked by the foreign sensation of his kiss. We'd fucked several times but hadn't done this. And the way he proceeded told me he didn't do this often, if ever. It wasn't that he didn't excel at it—I was pretty sure Kazek could do anything he put his mind to—it was the way he watched me with wonder while he kissed me.

He pulled back, his eyes aflame with emotion.

I stared at him.

He stared at me.

Then his mouth crashed down on mine, and he devoured me with the strength of an Alpha lost to his rut.

Only, he didn't fuck me with the same ferocity. Instead, his hips were slow, his cock sliding in and out in a hypnotic manner that he eventually matched with his tongue.

I lost myself to him in that moment.

Every part of me was officially owned by him, including my heart. And all I could do was hold on for the ride.

It went on for minutes, or maybe hours, his lips and tongue claiming mine just as his cock took my body.

I came on a wave of heat and bliss.

Peaked again with shudders that rocked me to my core.

Climaxed on a scream I swore could be heard all the way

in Winter Sector.

And eventually fell off a cliff of oblivion with his knot deep inside me.

We lost time, just like with my estrus. He fed me our mingled arousal, then kissed me to share in the taste. He had me suck him clean and rub my face in his groin before he returned the favor in kind, bathing himself in our shared ecstasy.

My hair was a knotted mess.

My body covered in the evidence of our lovemaking and fucking. There were bruises, bite marks, scratches, and fluids that should have disgusted me but didn't.

And that was exactly how we left his cabin.

Holding hands.

Our mating clear for the world.

Each step drawing us closer to the festivities of Norse Sector.

Each stride emboldening my faith in him even more.

Alpha Kazek was mine. And tonight, he would make sure everyone knew I was his.

CHAPTER TWENTY-ONE

KAZEK

HOWLS GRACED THE NIGHT AIR as we approached the main square in Norse Sector, masculine growls of approval reverberating against my senses.

Winter stood naked beside me without shame, her gorgeous pale skin illuminated by the moon overhead. My wolf purred with contentment, approving of her scent and filthy state.

"You look beautiful," I whispered against her ear. "I love that you're mine."

She smiled and moved into my arms, her nose pressing against my pectoral as she sought my comfort. I increased the vibration in my chest for her and kissed the top of her head while meeting Ludvig's gaze.

He dipped his chin in clear endorsement, as did every Alpha who approached to give their blessings on the union.

They didn't speak, just sniffed the air and nodded in respect and acknowledgment.

My mate remained locked in my embrace, her face pressed to my skin as if trying to inhale my essence. She wasn't afraid. Just content. Her post-orgasmic glow a sight that supremely delighted my wolf.

I made her look like that.

I painted her in my scent.

I fucked her into beautiful submission.

And I loved every damn minute of it.

"Does Winter Sector follow this ritual?" I asked her softly, referring to the act of wolves sniffing and nodding their approval.

"No, but matings such as this are rare," she whispered into my skin. "We don't frequently welcome new members."

"What about Enrique?" He wasn't from Winter Sector originally.

Alana approached, her lips quirking upward at the corners. She didn't speak, but her expression told me she was happy for me.

Winter either didn't notice her or didn't care. She remained calm and content in my arms, her body melting into mine.

Alana winked and strutted off, her acceptance clear and paving the way for the next wolf in line. *Joel*. He begrudgingly inclined his head but otherwise didn't react.

More Alphas presented themselves. Those with Omegas arrived as a pair, welcoming Winter in a similar fashion.

Then the Betas.

The ritual lasted about thirty minutes, every member of Norse Sector approaching and welcoming her into the pack with the customary head bob. A few went as far as to bow.

At one point, Winter turned around to watch, her back pressed to my front. I rested my chin on her head and kept my arms wrapped around her. It was all so natural. So right. I'd been a fool to think I never wanted this. Winter completed me in a way no one else ever had, and I adored her all the more for it.

Mick was the last one to approach us, his expression strained as he acknowledged our mating. I frowned at him and reached out to grab his shoulder, but he gave me a shake of his head as if to say, *Not now.*

I knew better than to push him, so I went back to holding Winter and instead arched a brow at Ludvig as he approached from the sidelines. "Go get ready for the midnight barbecue. You'll understand then."

Ah, it has something to do with the slave Omega's introduction, I translated. That Omega appeared to be putting him through the wringer. He'd only visited me once on the field in the last three days. Normally, I couldn't get him to fuck off. Now he was practically nonexistent.

"We'll see you in an hour," I replied before dropping my lips to Winter's ear. "Come with me, princess."

She let me lead her out of the clearing, her dreamy state from our fucking still firmly in place. I'd seen Mila in a daze similar to this once. She'd draped herself over Ludvig's lap in his office, making it impossible for him to attend a meeting. He'd shamelessly tasked me with taking the call on his behalf, his amusement at his mate's state palpable.

I hadn't understood his reaction that day.

But I did now.

She remained pressed into my side down the freshly shoveled path, mounds of snow on either side. I wrapped my arm around her and smiled as she snuggled into me on a sigh, her feet seeming to move on autopilot.

My cabin was too far away, so I took her to my condo instead. She didn't seem to notice, even as we stepped into the elevator and were whisked upward to one of the higher floors—a level I owned entirely. Ludvig also lived in this building, as did Mick.

She blinked a little at the modern surroundings, her gaze dropping to my marble floors and plush carpet as we walked toward my master suite.

Her nose crinkled a little at the scents.

The bed and bedding were all new. Ludvig had them replaced for me while I was awaiting a challenge. He'd also taken the liberty of having my place cleaned thoroughly. When he'd told me about it yesterday, I'd grunted in annoyance. Mostly because I'd been irritated by the separation. When I saw him later, I'd have to thank him for the foresight. Had I brought Winter up here to the previous conditions, she would have smelled Alana in my sheets and lost her shit.

I rarely used this location, preferring my cabin. However, for tonight's intents and purposes, it would be faster to shower here.

"This way," I murmured, pressing my palm to her lower back and directing her into my walk-in shower. She glanced around, taking in the brown stones and glass walls. Her focus went to my massive closet at the back, then to the double doors that led back into my bedroom and the four-poster bed.

"Why are we here?" she asked, her voice still holding that dreamy quality.

I gently moved her backward until she touched the glass, then reached over to turn on the water and gave the showerhead my backside. Cold water bit into my skin, my larger form protecting my Omega from the icy chill of the spray.

Her dark eyes slid up to mine, confusion mingling with heat in their depths.

I smiled and bent to press my forehead to hers. "This is my place when I stay in town. We're here because it's closer than my cabin and we're not done with the festivities yet."

"We're not?"

I shook my head, my hands finding her hips. "No. Norse Sector enjoys a good celebration. It'll run all night until sunrise."

She shivered. "Like celebrations in Winter Sector?"

I grunted. "No. Nothing like that foul Queen of Mirrors has created." I pressed my lips to her ear. "Ours involve chocolate and wine."

"Ch-chocolate?" she repeated, her palms flattening against my abdomen.

"Mmm," I murmured, drawing my nose across her cheek. "Norse Sector enjoys sweets."

"Winter Sector can't afford them," she whispered.

Yes. Winter Sector was among some of the poorer wolf territories in this world. Their primary resource was fish and ice up in the Arctic Circle. Well, and Beta pussy. But I discounted that infamous "resource." If we returned to take Winter's throne, that'd be the first industry I'd dismantle.

Using my grip on her hips, I guided us backward beneath the warmer water and allowed it to begin the process of cleansing our skin. Winter tilted her head back and opened her mouth, drinking the fresh substance and trembling as it worked down her throat.

"Are you hungry?" I asked, realizing that I'd failed to feed her properly after sex. I didn't even know if she'd eaten in the last few days.

She nodded, then opened her mouth for more water.

I sighed. "I should have fed you."

"You did," she murmured, her dark eyes opening and meeting my gaze with a devilish twinkle. "You fed me very well."

I grunted. "I meant food."

"I know," she replied, her lips curling into a sassy little grin that made me want to kiss her. "The blond Alpha brought me meat while I was in wolf form. I meant I was hungry for *you*."

A rumble sounded in my chest, my wolf appeased by her flirtatious response and her devious smile. But I also wanted to know who fed her so I could properly thank the Alpha later. "Ludvig gave you food?"

She shook her head. "No. The blond who attended the engagement ceremony with you."

"Mick." He really was a decent wolf.

"Is that his name?" she asked, tilting her head forward to dampen her hair. "He seems okay, but Kari doesn't like him."

"Kari?" I repeated.

"Mm-hmm." She nodded. "The Omega that Bariloche Sector sent to be Enrique's mistress."

Ah, the slave Omega. "Do you know her well?"

"Not really, no." Winter's lips slid downward. "She's not a fan of Alpha males."

"I imagine she wouldn't be," I replied. "They turned her into a slave for their knot."

Winter paused, her shoulders going rigid. "Will Ludvig do the same?"

"I don't know," I admitted. "She's the property of Norse Sector now. As Sector Alpha, he'll decide what's best for her."

She didn't appreciate that reply. Her expression no longer held that dreamy quality but one tinged with anger. *My feisty female is coming out to play.*

"Tell me your thoughts," I encouraged her.

"You won't like them." The little growl in her tone amused me.

"Tell me them anyway."

She swallowed, then boldly met my gaze. "Perhaps Alpha Ludvig should talk to her before he determines what's best for her. Unless all he cares about is her body, in which case, he's no better than Alpha Vanessa."

Oh, I was glad she said that to me and not to Ludvig directly. He would not have taken kindly to the accusation.

"Perhaps you should wait to pass judgment until after you hear his verdict," I countered. "Alphas are charged with protecting the weak. It's not an easy burden, little one." I wrapped my palm around the back of her neck. "That's why I haven't decided what I want to do with your Winter Sector throne yet. Taking on all those lives is a hefty requirement. I'm not sure I want that responsibility."

Her gaze narrowed, and I distracted whatever she wanted to say by turning her away from me. "Grab the shampoo," I told her.

She complied, but her stiff movements told me she wasn't pleased.

I drew my fingers through her hair, brushing out the tangles caused by our intense fucking. She slowly melted into me, letting me take care of her and worship her the way she deserved. I conditioned her strands, then took the soap and slowly caressed every inch of her until she resembled a liquid puddle before me.

I loved how she responded to my touch. It emboldened my claim and made me feel worthy of adoring her.

Her forehead rested against my chest while I washed my own hair. Then I handed her the soap and let her explore my body to her heart's content. She hummed in approval as my cock responded to her strokes and brushes down my abdomen. "Keep looking at me like that, sweetheart, and I'll make you wash me with your mouth."

She glanced up at me from her knees, an enchantress plotting her seduction. Her tongue inched forward to touch the head of my cock, eliciting a deep groan from my throat. Damn, this female was going to destroy me. We didn't have time. I told Ludvig we'd return in an hour, and at least thirty minutes had already passed.

"Feed me," she whispered against my hard flesh. "Please."

"*Fuck*," I growled, my fingers already weaving through her hair to guide her forward.

She wasted no time in parting her plump lips and fulfilling the fantasy I'd crafted in my mind a week ago about her alluring mouth. She'd tasted me several times during her estrus, her talent definitely honed by someone else in her past. Yet, this felt different. More intimate. More *right*. I liked her being aware and wanting to do this, to watch her take control in her own sensual way.

Heat spiked through my insides at the feel of her velvety tongue stroking my shaft, her mouth applying pressure in all the right places.

Complete and utter perfection.

My muscles clenched in appreciation, my back blocking the water to keep Winter from drowning. Not that she seemed to be paying attention to anything other than my dick in her mouth. She was too busy turning me into her next meal.

Mmm, I adored this dance with control. She wanted to devour me, to push me off the edge. I could see it in her eyes as she gazed up at me. My little Omega desired to top from the bottom.

It was never going to happen.

But I'd reward her with the sustenance she craved.

Then I'd knot her to oblivion and back.

Because fuck the celebration party. Her pretty mouth wrapped around my cock was far more important than a damn chocolate fountain.

Her eyes smiled as if she could hear my thoughts, and she sucked me harder. My thighs flexed, the inferno burning hotter and hotter inside.

"Just like that, Winter," I encouraged her, my voice a low growl.

Her throat vibrated as she swallowed my head, taking me deeper and deeper with each pull of her addictive mouth.

"Fuck." That word was becoming a favorite of mine in her presence.

She didn't back down, her lips moving in a hypnotic pattern I couldn't stop watching. Her pupils flared as she took me even further, causing my fingers to tighten in her hair as my body reacted to her sinful move.

"Swallow, baby," I demanded, my pleasure exploding down her slender throat. "Every drop."

The command wasn't needed. She practically drank from me, her face flushed with excitement as I provided her with the taste she craved.

God, how did I ever want to live without an Omega mate?

Watching her now drew me into another state of being I never knew existed. This little wolf was all mine. And she *liked* it.

I picked her up off the stone floor and grinned as she released a sound of protest. She didn't like me removing my cock from her mouth. I quickly fixed the problem by sliding into her slick heat and wrapping her legs around my waist.

Her groan of approval went right to my groin, my knot throbbing for her.

"Hold on, sweetheart," I murmured.

She grabbed my shoulders, her nails biting down as I pressed her back against the wall.

I didn't give her a moment to comment on how she wanted to be taken. I decided for us both, and her howls of ecstasy told me I'd chosen correctly.

Hard.

Fast.

Urgent.

A claiming on top of a claiming. A way to thank her for sucking me off while also tying us together in a way only Alphas and Omegas could bond.

She screamed into my mouth, her tongue dueling with mine as rapturous ripples took us both under to that dark place where we lost time.

This female was a fucking drug.

I couldn't get enough.

Even as my knot pulsated inside her, releasing even more of my seed deep into her womb, all I could think about was taking her again.

"You've destroyed me," I admitted on a whisper, my forehead pressed to hers. "I don't even know who I am with you."

She trembled at my words, her breaths sharp and quick from the ferocity of our mating.

"I…" She inhaled to try again. "I want you to"—another pause to bring in more air—"to be my king."

That wasn't at all what I expected her to say after our experience, but I also wasn't surprised. I sighed against her mouth and lifted my head to meet her heavy-lidded gaze. "I'm not sure I can do that, Winter."

"Why not?" she asked, her voice an adorable rasp that indicated I'd done my job well. My wolf preened in response while I considered her question. She deserved an honest answer. Some Alphas might just tell her not to worry her pretty little head, but I wasn't like that. I preferred a partner, similar to the way Ludvig and Mila worked together.

Which meant I needed to confide in my mate.

Explain my choices. My background. Tell her *who* I was and how I'd come to be that person.

I nodded, deciding a longer conversation was in order.

This, too, was more important than a party.

I needed to satisfy my Omega's mind, just like I did her body.

"All right." I turned off the water and carried her to my bed, not caring at all about the puddle I created along the way. Our bodies were still glued together, so I lay on my back while she straddled my hips.

Her palms went to my chest, her brow furrowed. "All right?" she repeated.

"Yes. All right, as in I'll tell you why I can't commit yet to Winter Sector." I propped my head up on the pillows behind me, then reached up to cup her cheek and drew my thumb along her swollen lips. "I've never been a leader. Nor have I ever desired to lead. I worked alone as a human, and I still do now. It's my preference."

She tilted her head to the side. "Why?"

"Because I court death, sweetheart. It's easier to face that alone."

"I don't understand."

My lips curled. "I know. To do that, I need to tell you about my life before I became a wolf. Back when they called me the Huntsman."

CHAPTER TWENTY-TWO

WINTER

KAZEK'S HISTORY PAINTED A PICTURE in my head underlined in red.

He wasn't just lethal, but savage.

A hit man for hire.

A rogue assassin.

They called him *the Huntsman* because that was literally his job—to hunt men. Bad men. All over the globe during a time when wolves were a secret.

He gazed down at me with his head propped up on his hand. After his knot subsided, he'd flipped me over and licked me clean, then kissed me with a passion that still hummed through my veins. His actions were that of a lover, not a killer, but the predator danced in his sinful gaze. Kazek might have been born as a mortal, but the male inside was all wolf.

"You killed an Alpha as a human," I said, drawing us back

to the discussion we were having before he devoured me.

He nodded. "It was a freelance assignment sponsored by a government organization that couldn't seem to track the guy with their own teams. So they sent it through the freelance channels, and as I've always enjoyed a good challenge and this one suited, I picked it up."

"Which is how you met Ludvig." That'd been the part he started talking about when his knot had released me.

"Yeah. Unbeknownst to me, Ludvig had challenged my mark due to a territory dispute. I killed the guy before Ludvig could carry out his sentence. Needless to say, he was pissed. I just saw him as a witness who needed to be removed, only the fucker moved faster than humanly possible and nearly ripped my heart out of my chest." He chuckled and shook his head.

Kazek definitely didn't view life-and-death situations in a typical manner.

Actually, nothing he did seemed *typical*.

Including how he treated me.

"What stopped him from finishing the kill?" I wondered out loud.

Kazek's lips twitched. "I told him I was thankful to fall to a worthy opponent. He was both stunned at my arrogance and shocked at how calmly I delivered the verdict of my impending death. I passed out before he could finish, then woke up later in a lab. The doctor was supposed to help me heal. He chose to interpret that requirement a little differently than intended, and I became an Alpha wolf in the process."

My eyes widened. "That's how you became a shifter?"

"Yep. A happy little accident." He shrugged one shoulder. "Ludvig recruited me to work for him shortly after that. I've been his main enforcer ever since."

"And you don't see that as a leadership position because you prefer to work alone," I said, translating everything he'd told me so far. "You understand dealing in terms of death, but not life."

His pupils flickered, his wolf reacting to my words. "Yes." He blinked. "I rarely sleep in this bed. Do you know why?"

Yes. "You prefer the solitude of your cabin." It was clear in the lived-in appearance of his home versus this much colder condo. "You're not a pack animal, but a lone wolf." He'd made that clear when he took me back to his bed and mated me without consulting anyone else. He was a male who did what he wanted when he wanted it. But that behavior was exactly what made him an Alpha.

All dominant wolves chose to command.

All Alphas claimed Omegas on their own terms.

"Alphas are meant to lead," I said out loud. "But you can choose your own method."

"Not all Alphas want to lead. Including me."

"It doesn't matter what you want. Alphas are born into the responsibility of protecting others. To not do so defies the purpose of your existence."

His eyebrows rose. "That's the equivalent of saying Omegas only exist to take the knot."

I snorted. "Most Alphas do say that." Or at least, that was what I'd been raised to understand. My experience with Alphas was rather limited.

"Do you want me to be most Alphas?" Kazek asked, a dangerous edge to his tone. "Fuck you as my obedient little Omega slave and give you a nest of my offspring?"

I shivered at the image, some dark part of me whispering *yes* to his questions.

His gaze narrowed. "Is that what you want?" he pressed, his free hand going to my throat as he moved over me. "Do you want me to use you, Winter? Fuck you into oblivion? Knot you whenever the need strikes?" His hips met mine, my legs automatically parting to accommodate him.

I whimpered at his words, hating the weakness stirring inside me. He was threatening me. I could see it in his gaze, the savage intent behind his words. One confirmation from me and he'd tie me to his bed. And some treacherous voice in my head wanted me to let him.

It would be so much easier to rely on him, to forget myself and just become his Omega.

Pleasure for days.

Grooming pups.

Living a life inside my nest, waiting for my Alpha to return and play.

175

"Fuck, Winter," he whispered, some of the darkness leaving his expression as he pressed his forehead to mine. "Is that what you want from me?"

Was it? *Yes. No.* "I don't know."

His lips tasted mine. Sweet. Chaste. Gentle. Not at all what I expected from him. "I like your fight, Winter."

He captured one of my hands and pulled it over my head.

"Most Alphas would desire to break your disobedient habits," he murmured.

He caught my opposite wrist and brought it up to join the other, effectively caging me beneath him.

"But I would grow bored with a compliant mate." He drew his lips across my cheek to my ear. "I need a challenge. It makes the reward so much sweeter." He nibbled my neck and rolled off me.

I gasped at the loss of his heat.

He chuckled and shook his head. "You're an insatiable little thing, but we're already late. Let's go to the festivities. We'll discuss my lack of leadership desires later." His dark irises captured mine once more. "Take tonight to think about what you want from me, Winter."

I frowned as he turned away, my heart beating wildly in my chest.

How had we gone from discussions of taking back my kingdom to me not knowing what I wanted from him? *Because he just provided an alternative*, that dark voice whispered in my head.

"What would life be like for us if we stayed in Norse Sector?" I asked, feeling dazed by even the consideration of remaining here. I'd escaped with the hope of finding help. But I never thought beyond that moment or how exactly I planned to implement that assistance.

To take back Winter Sector.

To reclaim my throne.

To kill Vanessa.

But most of those notions were recent, derived by realizing how horribly the Queen of Mirrors had played me.

What if I just let her win and remained here? What would that mean for me and Kazek? What would it do to my protective seven?

"Come to the party with me and find out," Kazek replied as he placed a box on the bed. "Your name's on here. I believe the dress inside is a gift from Omega Mila, Ludvig's mate." He said the name with a fondness that irked me.

Kazek must have noticed, because he grinned. "Your possessiveness intrigues me." He prowled over me to place a kiss against my mouth. I bit his lip in response, irritated by his comment. "Mmm, there's my fighter."

He licked his way inside, his tongue dominating mine in a way that left me shaking beneath him once more.

How was it possible for someone to control my body so expertly? A single touch lit me on fire. One kiss destroyed my ability to process thought.

When he pulled away and told me to put on the dress, I did. And it wasn't until he finished running a comb through my hair that reality started to drift back into my mind.

"You're like a drug," I rasped, my throat working on a swallow.

He chuckled and nibbled the pulse point at my neck, his teeth sending a jolt of longing down my spine to the apex between my thighs. I squirmed, the silk of the gown whispering over my skin in response.

"You look beautiful," he said against my ear, his chest pressed to my back. At some point, he'd put on a pair of black slacks and a dress shirt. Our appearance in his floor-to-ceiling mirror was elegant, even with the dazed glimmer in my gaze.

"Why do I feel like I'm dreaming?"

"It's the mating haze," he explained. "Or a human would probably say you've lost yourself in subspace."

"Subspace?" I repeated.

"Where a submissive goes during sex."

I frowned. "We're not having sex."

"Unfortunately, no." He smiled at me in the mirror, his arms coming around my waist in a backward hug. "It's what humans from my world would liken it to. But we're wolves. We don't need sex to acquire certain sensations."

"You're not affected," I pointed out as I melted into his chest. His soft shirt tickled my spine, keeping me warm in the otherwise flimsy gown. It was solid black, with an open back and a deep V-neck. The skirt slit up both my legs to midthigh, making it one of the sexiest outfits I'd ever worn.

Vanessa would have a freaking meltdown if she saw me right now. She preferred me mostly covered. Only the Queen of Mirrors could wear erotic apparel such as this.

Kazek pressed his growing erection into my rump. "Oh, I'm affected, sweet beauty. Trust me."

"But you're not dazed."

"No. Only Omegas experience that part of the mating high. I suspect it's left over from your incomplete estrous cycle. You should have been in heat for a week, not four days." He pressed his lips to my temple and released me to place the comb back on the counter. I hadn't even realized he still held it.

He returned a moment later with a pair of heels. "It seems Mila thought of everything."

Rather than hand them to me, he knelt and slid them onto my feet, his deft fingers buckling the straps along my ankles. He ran his fingers up my legs as he stood, the jet-black fabric parting for him along the way.

"Knowing you're naked under this is going to drive me crazy," he admitted softly.

"I was naked for the ceremony," I pointed out.

"And drenched in the afterglow of sex with me." He wrapped his palm around the back of my neck to pull me into him. "Now you're dressed in silk and on display for the world to admire. It's going to take significant control not to fuck you in front of them all." He gifted me with a quick kiss and a wolfish smile. "I might not experience the mating high, but I'm drowning in possessive urges, baby."

My belly did a little flip. "I feel possessive, too."

"I know." His lips curled. "You growled when I mentioned Ludvig's mate."

"I did?"

He nodded, his gaze bright with amusement. "Yes. And I liked it."

My cheeks heated at the confirmation of my reaction and the way he praised me for it. This mating thing was a whole new way of life. I just had to figure out how to properly navigate it.

"Let's go," he said.

All the modern furnishings of his condo passed by in a blur as he escorted me out into the hallway to the elevator in the middle. I'd read about so many of these furnishings, but it was entirely different to witness them.

My stomach lurched from the elevator motion but quickly subsided once Kazek guided me outside. The moon shone overhead, the lack of lighting in the territory allowing it a beautiful glow that appeased my wolf. Winter Sector was similar, our moon always a bright ball in the starry night.

We wandered along the paved paths, snow glistening across the landscapes of colored buildings. When we passed the empty town square, I frowned. "We're not meeting here?"

"No. We have a warmer venue for large gatherings." His palm burned against my lower back, his stride long and sure beside me. "I imagine Ludvig will want to announce us when we arrive."

That made sense. Vanessa always required to be announced when entering an event. It was always "Alpha Vanessa, Queen of Mirrors." She even wore my mother's crown.

My hands fisted at my sides.

She doesn't deserve that crown.

But I couldn't take it back from her without Kazek's help. Not because I feared her strength—there were other ways to take down an arrogant Alpha female—but because I couldn't go to Winter Sector without him. The last three days showed me what would happen if we were parted, and we hadn't even been that far away from each other.

Which meant I needed him to willingly accompany me.

However, he didn't want to lead. That'd be a problem because the sector would require a new leader without Vanessa. And if we didn't take up the mantle, someone else would.

I couldn't allow that to happen to my kingdom.

I also couldn't stay here and allow Vanessa to continue to rule.

My feet stopped moving, causing Kazek to falter midstep and turn toward me with an arched brow. We were outside a massive building decorated in glass and colorful siding. Voices and low music reverberated from inside, suggesting this was our intended destination.

"Winter?" my mate prompted, his expression exuding patience and a hint of concern. I idly wondered if that was a new emotion for him.

Kazek struck me as the type who rarely felt emotion for anything or anyone. However, he clearly cared for me. I knew it was just the bond forcing him to feel, but that didn't stop the little tingle of warmth from stirring inside my heart. This dangerous, lethal Alpha had chosen me. Claimed me. And was, in his own way, respecting me, too.

Which was what gave me the courage to tell him, "I want my kingdom back."

CHAPTER TWENTY-THREE

KAZEK

WINTER'S WORDS WERE A DAGGER to my heart. Even after everything I'd shared with her, she still wanted me to take on the responsibility of her former home.

Every action carried consequences.

Mating her required me to acknowledge the baggage that came with her. A good Alpha would take back the throne and claim her birthright. But I never professed to be good. In fact, I considered myself quite the opposite.

"I'm a lone wolf," I reminded her. "I don't want to lead." It was hard enough having her rely on me. An entire kingdom? No, thanks.

"You told me to tell you what I want. So I am. I want Vanessa to pay for what she's done. I want to protect my people. I want to live out my legacy as Queen of Winter Sector. And I want you to become king."

Such a heavy proclamation.

"You're asking a lot of me."

She nodded. "I know. But Alphas are made to shoulder the burden."

"And Omegas are made to take the knot," I tossed back at her, annoyed by this argument. We already went through this song and dance. If she wanted to live by societal expectations, then it would go both ways.

"Yes. And I've taken your knot several times this week. Now it's your turn to do your job." The fire in her gaze both turned me on and infuriated me.

"I saved your life, Omega. I claimed you in front of my sector. Don't push me for more. Not right now."

"You act as though that was a hardship. We both know you enjoyed it. Now that I'm asking you to do something hard, you're balking at my request."

Both my eyebrows shot upward. "Are you trying to provoke me into a fight?"

"No. I'm trying to make you understand that what I'm asking you to do is the right thing to do. Vanessa can't be allowed full access to my throne. We need to remove her."

"You mean I need to remove her." I dropped my hand from Winter's lower back and stepped away from her. "Don't sugarcoat it, sweetheart. You want me to go in and destroy the Sector Alpha, then take over and lead. That's a tall order."

"It's your duty."

"Then do your duty and remove that dress and bend over."

"No." She folded her arms and glared at me. "I've done my part for a week. It's your turn to do yours."

I gaped at her. "Did you just deny me?"

"Yes. And I will continue to deny you until you do your job."

Oh, she was playing with fire. I grabbed the back of her neck and tugged her to me. "One growl and you'll be putty in my hands."

She didn't back down. "Force me and I'll start hating you."

"It won't matter as long as your body welcomes me," I replied, my free hand sliding up her leg to grab her pussy.

"You want to play by societal rules? Then this is mine." I slipped two fingers into her damp heat and nearly smiled when her pupils flared. "I'll knot you day and night. Force you to go on your knees and lick me clean. And leave you alone in your nest while your stomach grows from my seed. Is that what you want?"

"If it means you'll take over Winter Sector and lead, then yes. That's what I want."

Fuck! "You don't get to tell me what to do or how to do it, Omega," I seethed. "I can chain you to a bed here in Norse Sector and fuck you whenever I damn well please instead. And there is nothing you can do about it."

This bratty streak needed to end. I'd tried the conversational route. I'd opened up to her about my past in a way I hadn't with anyone else. And still she was pushing me.

"You. Are. Not. In. Charge." I thrust my fingers into her slick cunt with each word against her lips. "I own you, Winter. Not the other way around."

She said nothing, her gaze boldly holding mine. But I caught the slight wobble of her lower lip. The only hint of defeat rioting in her mind.

So damn stubborn.

So regal.

So fucking beautiful it hurt.

I wanted a fighter, and she was proving with each passing second to be exactly the kind of female I craved. And that stiffness in her spine only made me desire her more.

I could threaten all day to make her a pet and bend her will to mine, but it wasn't what I wanted. Not from a life partner.

Yet I couldn't allow her to control the situation or try to manipulate me by denying me access to her body. That sort of impudence didn't work for me. It was childish and counterproductive.

She could absolutely say no.

But to do so for the sole purpose of pissing me off was not okay.

I pressed my mouth to hers and winced when she bit down on my lower lip. "You're provoking me in all the wrong ways, sweetheart," I warned as I walked her backward into the wall of the building.

"I want my kingdom back," she repeated. "If you're too scared to own the position you claimed, then give me to another Alpha who isn't afraid."

I growled. "Careful, Winter."

"Or what? You'll rape me?" She laughed without humor. "Do it. Break me, Alpha. I'd prefer a shattered mental state over being aware and knowing my kingdom is suffering because my mate isn't Alpha enough to lead them."

It took significant effort not to fucking throttle her.

I removed my fingers from her heat, deciding a punishment orgasm wasn't enough.

She needed to be reprimanded in an entirely different way for her disrespect.

After everything I'd done for her, she chose now—*here*—to lash out at me?

Un-fucking-acceptable.

I threaded my fingers through her hair while my opposite palm squeezed her throat just enough to assert dominance. "You're very lucky no one has heard this little outburst, Winter. Because then I'd be forced to reprimand you publicly. I strongly suggest you behave for the next hour inside. Maybe it'll convince me to discipline you less harshly afterward."

"Will that make you feel more Alpha?" she countered, her chin notching upward.

"Winter—"

"Will it help lessen the burden of knowing you've failed me and my people?" she interjected. "To dominate the Omega you already own?"

I growled, my wolf furious at her continued disobedience. "If this is your way of convincing me to do your bidding, it's not working."

"Because I'm pointing out your weaknesses?"

"No. Because you're being fucking disrespectful to the Alpha who saved your damn life. I've done everything in my power this week to help you, and you're acting like an ungrateful little brat." I released her, livid and striving for control.

Maybe she needed another time-out. The one Ludvig had

184

subjected her to clearly wasn't enough.

Fuck, she'd spoiled an otherwise beautiful evening.

I paced, uncertain of what to do next.

I couldn't bring her into the gathering in this mood. The Alphas in there would eat her alive and expect me to keep her in line. Part of me just wanted to let them do it for me. She'd hate it—having other males' hands on her. I'd hate it, too, but obviously my dominance wasn't enough for her.

Hell, if she wanted to experience the others, to test their mettle and see if one of them was more Alpha, then so fucking be it.

I turned away from her without a word.

I didn't trust myself to speak.

"Kazek," Ludvig called, halting me after only ten feet or so.

Slowly, I faced him and noted the concern in his expression. Had he overheard Winter's little tantrum? She seemed to be wondering the same thing, her eyes falling to the ground as she immediately submitted to his presence.

A growl caught in my throat at the act.

How dare she submit to him and not to me.

"Omega Winter wants another Alpha," I told Ludvig, furious. "Someone who *isn't afraid*. Feel free to pass her around and introduce her to the others. We'll see how she feels about her fate afterward."

I ignored her flinch and turned again, only to be stopped by Ludvig's bark of sound.

Glancing over my shoulder, I arched a brow. "What?"

"I didn't come out here to handle your domestic dispute. Vanessa just sent through a broadcast that you both need to see. I suggest you get your Omega in line, then join us in the entertainment hall." He rotated on his heel and dismissed us both.

A broadcast? Awesome. Just what I fucking needed.

"K-Kazek," Winter stammered, her focus still on the ground. "I-I don't want another Alpha."

I snorted. "I don't care about your desires right now, Omega."

She reached for me when I walked by her. I stepped away,

185

not interested in her touch or her words.

"Follow me or don't," I said, stalking off after Ludvig. If she misbehaved in front of the crowd, I'd deal with it appropriately. For her sake, I hope she cooperated.

Sweet scents assaulted my nostrils as I entered the great room. Tables dotted the massive entertaining space, all boasting an array of desserts and wine. Norse Sector loved to bake, chocolate being one of our specialties. Ludvig had it all imported from various territories around the world.

Normally, I enjoyed taste-testing all the cakes.

Tonight, not so much.

I just wanted to hear the broadcast and leave.

Winter's hand brushed my lower back as she came to stand behind me. When I didn't immediately move away, she took that as an invitation to get closer. Part of me wanted to snarl at her and tell her to fuck off, but the growing interest around us held me hostage.

Shit. I had no idea what to do with her. The notion of other Alphas coming near her had my wolf raging in my head, but she'd insulted my pride. I understood her goal, just not how she went about achieving it.

She inferred that I was weak for not wanting to lead.

She claimed to want a worthier wolf, one who wasn't *afraid.*

She'd pissed all over our bond, implying she'd only slept with me out of duty and now expected me to repay the favor.

Just reiterating her words in my head made me see red. I could barely focus on my surroundings, didn't notice Ludvig approaching me with a stern expression, and failed to reply to whatever the fuck he'd just said. Something about the broadcast.

"Play it," I said, wanting to get it over with.

Winter's nails dug into my shirt, causing me to flinch away from her.

Ludvig frowned. "That's not handling it," he muttered under his breath.

I merely looked at him and repeated, "Play it."

He lifted a shoulder. "Your funeral."

Yeah, my funeral. Whatever. I welcomed whatever challenge

this video provided.

The room quieted as Ludvig cued the media to roll for everyone in Norse Sector. It was a broadcast meant for every X-Clan sector in the world. Which meant the Queen of Mirrors wanted everyone to hear whatever the fuck she had to say. I had no doubt it was about Winter.

Static electricity rolled over my skin as Vanessa's porcelain features appeared at various points in the room from projector screens secured in various gadgets—such as our watches. I'd left mine back at the cabin, so I watched the one hovering over Ludvig's wrist.

Vanessa appeared all dolled up for the occasion, her red lips painted to perfection. Most would consider her a beautiful woman, but I caught the black-widow villain lurking in her dark eyes. I'd never cared for her, and I knew Ludvig felt similarly.

"X-Clan nation, I come to you with solemn news from Winter Sector. The sole Frost family heir has gone missing." She paused for dramatic effect, a misty sheen taking over her irises, causing me to roll my eyes.

Winter moved to my side, distracting me momentarily with the defeated curve of her shoulders. I refused to give in to the urge to comfort her and instead took a step away from her, not wishing to align with the female who outright admitted her lack of respect for my claim.

My distance only seemed to wound her more, her lower lip giving a telltale wobble.

I ignored her in favor of the screen, where Vanessa feigned a sigh.

"I've spent the last seven days trying to locate her and have come to two possible conclusions. Either someone took her the night of the engagement festivities benevolently hosted by the great Betas of Winter Sector, or…" She took another of those breaths, her features icing over in the process. "Or Snow Frost deliberately deserted our beloved sector."

Winter stopped breathing.

Several eyes in the room zeroed in on her location to stare, and I waited with them to see her reaction.

Twin splotches of red graced her cheeks, but she didn't

otherwise react apart from stealing a sharp inhale when Vanessa continued.

"The purpose of this announcement is to let everyone know that Winter Sector will be conducting an international search for our princess. Should we find that she was taken against her will, justice will be sought. Should we find that she deserted us all, Winter Sector will decide her fate. And anyone who is known to have helped her will be punished in accordance with Winter Sector law. If you know anything, step forward now. Otherwise, my security teams will be in touch. End transmission."

Silence.

I shared a look with Ludvig before glancing at Winter once more.

She wanted to be in charge of her fate; now was the time. I'd spent the better part of a week helping her. As far as I was concerned, she could help herself now.

Maybe that made me an asshole.

I preferred to think of it as the ideal punishment instead.

Folding my arms, I waited for her to speak.

She cleared her throat and tried once, then twice, but her voice appeared to be failing her.

"What the hell is wrong with you?" Alana hissed under her breath, the Alpha female seeming to appear out of thin air beside me. "She's your mate, Kaz."

Winter glanced at us. She was close enough to hear the words. A flare of her nostrils told me she didn't appreciate Alana standing beside me. Probably because I'd brushed off Winter's attempts to touch me yet allowed Alana to essentially whisper in my ear and touch my shoulder in the process.

Ludvig cleared his throat and arched a brow at me. "Alpha Kazek?"

A muscle ticked in my jaw.

Right. It seemed everyone was going to force me to lead.

I had half a mind to leave and not look back. This whole addressing-the-sector bullshit wasn't my thing. But if I walked out now, Winter would be left to fight for herself, and they'd likely vote to ship her back. Without the respect and support of her Norse Sector mate—*me*—she'd be perceived as an outsider.

While I was angry with her, I couldn't in good conscience subject her to such a fate.

So I cleared my throat and told them the tale of how Snow Frost became Winter. There were growls of disapproval when I mentioned the suppressants and a few more growls when I covered the plot for her death. However, by the end, they were silent, their anger palpable.

I awaited their judgment without looking at Winter.

For her part, she remained silent, giving me all the control of her fate and mine. At least she had enough faith in me to tell the truth on her behalf.

"Are there any questions or motions?" Ludvig asked, shattering the stillness of the room.

More silence, shocking the hell out of me. Not one person wanted to hand us over to Vanessa? That essentially incriminated every single member of Norse Sector, as they were technically hiding Winter's presence from the Queen of Mirrors.

"We acknowledged her as part of our pack," a male voice spoke up from the back of the room. *Joel.* "That makes Winter ours. I report to you as Alpha, Ludvig. Not the Alpha of Winter Sector."

Several murmurs of agreement followed.

"The Queen of Mirrors should pay for threatening the life of an Omega, let alone one with such a strong legacy." That came from Alana. As a fellow Alpha female, she had a lot of choice words to say about Vanessa over the years, particularly regarding her penchant for keeping all the male Omegas to herself.

Approval radiated from the crowd, more voices speaking up above the rest, all of them echoing Joel's and Alana's comments.

Some even called for war.

Ludvig eventually lifted his hand to calm the room, his expression unreadable. But Mila stood beside him, beaming with pride. She always had her Alpha's back, the duo making a formidable team.

I wanted that for me and Winter, but she stood several feet

away looking alone as ever. And still, I couldn't go to her, my earlier fury still very present in my mind.

"The decision on how to handle Winter Sector will be left up to Alpha Kazek, as is his right as Winter's mate."

I watched Winter for her reaction. She gave none, her gaze on the ground in a defeated manner that ate at my insides. This obedient stillness wasn't what I desired from her. There had to be some sort of middle ground where she exuded strength in a respectful manner. I just had no idea how to encourage that.

"Excellent," Ludvig continued after several rounds of nods waved around the room. "I'm pleased we are all in agreement on Alpha Kazek's right to decide, as well as how to proceed in regard to Winter remaining in Norse Sector. Particularly because I've just been notified by Vanessa that Alpha Enrique will be paying us a visit tomorrow to discuss Snow Frost's whereabouts."

My head whipped upward to meet his gaze. "What?"

"Yes, it seems he also wants to debate the ownership rights for Omega Kari," Ludvig added.

"Over my dead body," Mick snapped, eliciting gasps from the crowd. He stood in a suit on the edge of the throng. Alone.

I frowned. *I thought he was supposed to introduce Kari tonight to the pack.*

"As Omega Kari clearly has no wish to join Norse Sector, Alpha Enrique is within his rights to negotiate for her release," Ludvig said, his voice cold and underlined in dominance. "I am not accustomed to forcing Omegas to remain in my territory when they wish to leave."

Mick cursed, his anger palpable, but he intelligently kept his mouth shut. He had no claim on the Omega, particularly as she couldn't mate him. Her sterilization altered her estrus, making it impossible to deliver a claiming bite.

"How do you wish to proceed?" Ludvig asked me. "You'll need to be part of the meeting, and killing him will be frowned upon by Bariloche Sector and Winter Sector."

I grunted. Like I gave a fuck about the other sectors. But I did care about the way Winter had started shaking at the mention of Enrique's impending arrival. Did she think I might hand her over? Not a chance in hell that would happen.

"When is he expected to arrive?" I asked.

"In fifteen hours."

Considering it was well after midnight, that meant he intended to meet for dinner. "I'll have a response to you on how I want to handle the situation by twelve hundred hours."

Ludvig dipped his chin, accepting my need to think this through. "Understood."

I looked at Winter. "Let's go." I wasn't in the mood to stand around and socialize. She could properly meet the pack later.

I didn't wait for her to reply.

I just left.

It was up to her to follow.

CHAPTER TWENTY-FOUR

WINTER

MY BLOOD RAN COLD AT KAZEK'S DISMISSAL. He walked with a briskness, not once acknowledging my presence. Yet he had to know I was behind him.

I didn't know what to say or where to start.

I owed him an apology for pushing, but I wasn't sure I could voice it appropriately because I stood by my proclamation. Minus, maybe, the "other mate" part. I could admit now that I took it too far.

"Feel free to pass her around and introduce her to the others. We'll see how she feels about her fate afterward."

Kazek's comment to Ludvig played through my thoughts, drizzling ice along my skin. He couldn't have meant that, right?

I swallowed. *Yeah. Yeah, he could.*

I'd gone about it the wrong way, my mouth running before

I considered the meaning of my words or how they would be perceived. His reluctance had set me off.

Kazek was an Alpha with leadership potential. I saw it in the way he handled the crowd tonight, yet he seemed completely oblivious of his power. I suspected his human upbringing had something to do with it. Our society forced him to work that much harder for respect as a wolf, but he'd clearly earned that status in his pack. How he didn't see it was beyond me.

I wanted to push him, to make him understand the importance of his role in my life, and I'd gone about it the wrong way.

Except he was the one who'd asked what I wanted. It wasn't my fault he disliked my response.

His shoulders remained rigid as we reached his cabin door. I longed to brush my fingers down his spine, to relax him, but he'd denied my touch tonight. That had hurt more than I could admit. He'd stood beside another female, his former lover, instead of staying by my side. Rather than feel anger at his stance, I'd felt rejected, which was somehow worse.

I deserved it after some of the things I'd said to him. However, that didn't make my feelings on the topic any less true.

Kazek was an Alpha. His kind was meant to lead. And I needed him to own that position.

He disappeared into his bathroom, the doors open behind him. I leaned against the bedroom wall, my heart in my throat. "I—"

"Don't," he said from the cavern of his closet, tucked beyond his bathing area.

Don't what? I wondered. *Don't apologize? Don't talk?*

He returned with a pair of boxer shorts and a white shirt. Rather than hand them to me, he tossed them toward the nest. "Go to bed. I'm going for a run."

"What?" I turned after him, unnerved by his cold tone and equally frigid movements. "Kazek—"

"Alpha," he corrected sharply. "I'm not in the mood to knot you tonight, Omega. So go sleep in your nest. I'll return when I feel like fucking you again."

My lips parted, his fury a whiplash against my senses. The male who had held me hours ago and told me all about his past was lost to this mask of anger. I didn't know what to say or how to react. An apology formed and died on my lips as he ripped his shirt off and kicked off his black shoes.

Ripples of muscles danced before my eyes, his tattooed arm reflecting a series of patterns in the light that drew me to the strength beneath his skin. I wanted to lick him. To claim him. To mark him as mine and remove this negative cloud hanging over our heads. But he wouldn't even look at me.

Dismissed. That was what his body language said. He'd dismissed me.

I needed to say something. Do something. Apologize. Beg. I wasn't sure which, but I couldn't just let him walk away from me in this state. Despite being angry with me, he'd stood up for me tonight. Eventually, anyway. He'd considered not saying a word. I'd *felt* it in his hesitation. But he'd supported me in the end, just like an Alpha mate should. I owed him my gratitude and an explanation.

"Kazek, plea—"

He growled, the sound sending me backward a few steps. "I've done my part as *Alpha* tonight," he snapped over his shoulder. "Now do your job as an Omega and fucking obey my commands. Do not call me by my given name—that's not your right."

I gaped at him and he glowered back at me.

"You're the one who wanted to play by societal standards, Omega. So go the fuck to sleep. I'll see you again when I feel like knotting." He slammed the bedroom door shut behind him, effectively ending the conversation.

A chill skated down my spine.

He's just mad, I told myself. *You pushed him too far.*

I shouldn't have said anything.

Kazek was an Alpha. They made decisions on their own time. Control mattered to them. I'd insulted his pride by insinuating he wasn't Alpha enough to lead. And I never should have suggested he let another male take me.

He'd just made me so angry with his stubborn reactions. How couldn't he see the destiny laid out before him?

While I recognized he'd only claimed me to save my life, I'd thought he understood the repercussions of that decision now. My birthright complicated things. I wasn't just a random Omega but the heir to Winter Sector's throne.

What if he never wants to go back? I wondered. *What if he demands we stay here?*

Another chill slipped over me, followed by an assault of mental visions of my kingdom suffering flicking through my mind.

Staying here wasn't an option.

I just had to convince Kazek to do the right thing, which, I thought, was him leading. But maybe... maybe I needed him to let me go instead.

My wolf balked at the notion, unwilling to consider such an idea. However, leadership required sacrifice. If saving my people required me to live in discomfort over a frayed bond, then I would.

Vanessa couldn't be allowed to remain in charge.

Someone needed to take her down.

And if Kazek wouldn't do it, then I had no choice but to do it myself. Somehow.

Dropping my dress to the floor, I slid into the nest and wrapped myself in the blankets that smelled like Kazek. His scent did little to comfort me, my heart fracturing inside.

Hopefully, my mate would return in the morning.

If not, I'd start making plans.

I had to.

It was my only option.

CHAPTER TWENTY-FIVE

KAZEK

I TRIED TO RUN, but I couldn't seem to go more than a hundred yards away from my cabin. Leaving Winter unprotected went against my wolf's nature, his stubbornness easily defeating my fury.

So I lay under a tree and slept with one eye open all night.

By sunrise, I still couldn't face her. I didn't trust my temper. Males had died at my hand for insulting me less than she had last night.

It was her threat to find a worthier male that really did me in. The rest, I could stomach. She wanted her kingdom back and needed an Alpha to lead at her side. I understood that. Her delivery, however, sucked. It didn't motivate me so much as piss me off, and I wasn't ready to get back into it with her. Not with Enrique's pending arrival.

With a sigh, I stood and stretched out my front legs, then

my back, and shook the snow off my coat.

As talking to her was out of the question right now, there was only one thing I could do.

I trotted up to the wraparound porch and turned back into my human form, then used my human fingers to key in a code on the pad beside the door. Electricity whirred around me, locking down the interior.

Winter would be pissed, but at least she'd be safe. We'd hash out the details later.

Shifting back into wolf form, I ran back to my condo for a quick shower and to change into something presentable for my meeting with Ludvig. By the time I arrived, I still didn't have a solid plan, and he read it on my face the second I stepped through the door in my slacks and button-down shirt.

"You're new to this, so I'm going to offer you some advice that I suggest you don't ignore" was his greeting as I sat in the chair across from him. "Letting fights fester between you and your mate will only worsen the outcome. It doesn't matter what else is happening in the world; she should always be your priority."

"She is my priority," I argued as I rested my ankle over my opposite knee. "I'm here to talk about how to handle Enrique, which involves her safety."

Ludvig sighed. "You know that's not what I mean."

I stared at him.

He stared back.

"She'll be fine."

"Will she?" he countered. "She seemed fairly broken last night when you stood beside your former lover rather than at her side." He arched a brow. "Was that meant to be a punishment? Because I'd say it worked, and Winter behaved admirably as a result."

"Alana came up to me."

"And you chose to remain beside her rather than show solidarity with your mate. Even Alana noticed your misstep."

I snorted, recalling how Alana pushed me to speak up on behalf of my mate. "Winter challenged my opinion on leadership and told me to find her another mate who isn't afraid to be an Alpha." Those weren't her exact words, but the point was roughly the same. "Forgive me for being pissed at her approach."

"Maybe they were the words you needed to hear," he suggested. "She's embraced her Omega side without much of a fight, despite years of believing herself a Beta. Meanwhile, you're too stubborn to realize your potential. She's within her rights to push you forward."

"Not in the way she did last night."

He dipped his chin. "Perhaps, but that's a learning discussion for you both. Something you've denied her by sleeping outside last night."

I arched a brow. "Are you spying on me now?"

"No. I don't need to. You walked in here with the expression of a male who hasn't slept well in a week, which tells me you didn't indulge your mating instinct and share a bed with your Omega last night. And I know you wouldn't leave her unguarded. Hell, she's probably locked up in your cabin right now."

My jaw clenched. I really hated how well he read me.

"Yeah, that's what I thought." He regarded me for a long moment, and I sensed him weighing his options on what to say next. "Look, I'm not going to tell you how to handle your female or the opportunity before you. We both know you're too stubborn to listen to me anyway."

I suppressed a retort and instead invited him to continue speaking, as I knew from experience he wasn't finished.

"However…"

And there it is, I thought. *Lecture time from Alpha Ludvig.*

"I suggest you consider the events of the last week and what they actually mean. You often think shifters are judging you for your human origins. But have you ever considered that it's actually you passing judgment on yourself?" He cocked an eyebrow with the question. "Norse Sector respects you a hell of a lot more than you realize. I think it's time you learn to respect yourself. Maybe then you'll finally realize your potential. And I think you'll owe your little Omega a debt of gratitude as a result."

"She implied that I'm afraid."

"Because you're acting afraid," he retorted. "And don't

fucking deny it. The idea of leading Winter Sector terrifies you. All that responsibility for anyone other than yourself, it's a daunting task. You have the knowledge and history to own it. The question becomes, will you allow yourself to seek that potential or squander it away behind a wall of selfishness?"

"Are you trying to piss me off?" I asked, my knuckles turning white from squeezing the arms of the chair.

"You walked in here pissed off, Kazek," he tossed back at me. "I'm just telling you the words you need to hear. Which, I imagine, is what your Omega was trying to do last night. Did she insult you? Probably. But was that a good reason to shun her at a time when she needed your protection and confidence? If you think the pack didn't notice, you're wrong."

I knew they noticed. I just hadn't cared because it wasn't their fucking business. At least, that'd been my narrative at the time. Looking back through his point of view, I could see the error in my judgment.

Winter had looked so small with her shoulders hunched, her lower lip wobbling as she fought to keep herself in line. All the while, I'd stood aside with an aloofness that had to sting.

Because she'd wounded my pride. She hadn't stopped pushing me. I wasn't used to that from anyone, let alone a female mate.

When anyone questioned my status or decisions in the past, I handled it by showing my strength and proving them wrong. Some were even punished with death.

But I couldn't react that way to Winter.

Mostly because, deep down, her words rang true.

"Winter Sector could do a lot better than me as a leader," I said out loud, flinching with how weak that phrase sounded coming from my lips.

"I agree," Ludvig replied, shocking the hell out of me.

"Fuck you."

He smirked. "Do you think I was a perfect leader when I took over Norse Sector? I sure as hell didn't want the position, but you forced me into it by killing the previous pack master."

"You were going to kill him anyway."

"Yes. On my own terms. But an arrogant jackass forced my hand." He glared pointedly at me.

"So, what? This is my ultimate punishment for taking the job over a century ago?"

"No. It's my way of saying that shit happens and things don't always play out the way we want, but we deal with the hand fate gives us and prove all the fuckers who doubt us wrong. So go prove me wrong and take the Winter Sector mantle. Be the leader they deserve."

"And if I don't want to?" I demanded, aware I sounded like a whiny little dick. Winter would surely have some choice words for me right about now.

"Then I'm going to call you a pansy-ass motherfucker who lacks the balls to see a project through. You bit Snow Frost. You claimed her. Now fucking deal with the consequences and stop bitching about them."

There was the Ludvig we all loved to hate. "You're a shitty mentor," I informed him.

He grunted. "I never wanted to be a mentor."

"Yet here you sit," I pointed out, gesturing at him.

"Because I did my job as an Alpha," he countered. "Now do yours and tell me how the hell we're going to handle Enrique when he arrives."

"I vote we kill him," I said flippantly. The annoyance in Ludvig's gaze told me he wasn't amused by my suggestion at all. I'd clearly struck a nerve, probably when I didn't stand by Winter's side. Which, I could acknowledge now, was a major fuckup. So yeah, I owed her an apology. And probably a lot of other things right about now.

Having a mate was fucking exhausting.

"Stop feeling sorry for yourself and be the Alpha I know you are inside," Ludvig snapped.

"You're lucky I like you," I muttered, my wolf rioting through my thoughts and demanding he pay in blood for that remark.

"You'd submit," Ludvig replied. "Barely. But you'd submit."

I considered the outcome of a fight between us, calculated each move I knew he would make, and slowly shook my head.

"No. I don't think I would."

He held my gaze, and I stared at him without blinking, the tension between us palpable.

"This is why you need your own sector," he said after a long, intense beat. "A decade ago, you would have conceded."

"Maybe," I admitted. Only because I saw no reason to fight him. However, right now, I felt a little bit like punching him in the fucking face.

"You would have," he repeated, certain. "Not because you feared me. Not because you would have actually lost. But because you liked it here and wanted to stay. That was always our dynamic—you served as my Second out of loyalty and not having anything better to do. That changed when you bit Snow Frost."

"I'm still loyal to you," I vowed.

"Yeah, but that's not what I'm pointing out, is it?" His tone dared me to deny it, and I couldn't.

He was right.

I had something—a new responsibility—that pulled my focus away from Norse Sector.

There was nothing else to discuss about my future. We both knew what I had to do. It was up to me to accept my fate, not him. No point in dwelling on it.

I lifted my ankle away from my knee and leaned forward to balance my forearms on my thighs. "Alpha Enrique conspired with the Queen of Mirrors to have Snow Frost killed. That crime would be punishable by Winter Sector law, but not Norse Sector law. Unless he knew she was an Omega."

Ludvig visibly relaxed at my change in topic, seemingly pleased that I'd finally gotten down to business. "Do you think he did?"

I shook my head. "No."

There was no way he knew. No Alpha male in his right mind would pass up a mating opportunity with an Omega heiress. It also went against the grain to harm one so precious.

Omegas were revered by X-Clan wolves. Killing one was unacceptable in every circumstance.

"I imagine he'll be livid to learn Vanessa tried to use him

to commit an international crime," I added. "We should give him an opportunity to react. That's how we'll learn the truth of the situation."

"You want to present your mate to him."

"I do, but after he's settled." I wanted an opportunity to watch him first and test his aggression levels. It would help me determine the likelihood of a challenge. I wasn't well rested and needed to be for an Alpha like Enrique. I also wanted an opportunity to work things out with Winter before facing him.

"Fair," Ludvig replied. "I'll have the guest quarters made up for him. We'll use the discussions on Kari as a reason to keep him overnight."

My lips twisted to the side. "Mick isn't going to like that."

"I'm aware. But this is his mess to sort. I'll set the stage, and he can perform however he sees fit."

Another teaching opportunity. "For an Alpha who claims he didn't want to lead, you certainly are good at arranging situations for your wolves to learn from," I pointed out conversationally.

"Makes me wonder what kind of Sector Alpha you'll turn into," he replied. "Anything else in terms of your desired plan?"

"We should entertain him with dinner. Distract him. It'll help me see what kind of mood he's in." As an Alpha whose betrothed had run away, I imagined he was probably furious. But I wanted to test the limits of that fury with a few word games. "Kari should attend, too. Maybe seeing the male who intended to keep her as a slave will help Mick's case."

Ludvig smiled. "See? You're following the playbook already. You'll make an excellent Sector Alpha."

I narrowed my gaze. "I haven't accepted the position yet."

His gaze twinkled as he looked at me. "On the contrary, Kazek. You accepted the job a week ago. You're just catching up on all the paperwork now."

I didn't bother replying to that.

Nor did he wait for a reply.

Instead, he opened a drawer and retrieved an envelope that he passed across the dark wood expanse of his desk. "I found this in the holding suite upstairs. I suspect it fell off of Winter when she shifted into her wolf form."

I peeked inside and noted the glint of silver. "Her necklace."

"It belonged to her mother," Ludvig replied, his expression morphing just enough to warn me of some sentimental value behind the comment. "I imagine she'll want it back."

"Yes. She was adamant that you see it." I frowned. "Any idea why?"

He stared at the desk and nodded slowly. "Yeah. I know why." His eyes slowly lifted to mine, a storm of emotions in his gaze. "I gave Sofie that necklace on her sixteenth birthday. But I doubt Winter is aware of that. So whoever told her to wear it knew who gave Sofie that paw print."

"You gave Sofie a necklace?" I asked, shocked. "How did Mila feel about that?"

He swallowed, his blue eyes flickering with a hint of the past. "Mila selected the charm," he said softly, his lips lifting into a sad smile. "The whole thing was actually her idea."

"What aren't you telling me?" I asked, feeling like I'd missed some secret piece of the puzzle.

And the look he gave me now confirmed it. "Why do you think I sent you to visit Winter Sector, Kazek? The invitation was for me and Mila, but I didn't trust myself to attend."

I frowned at him. "You sent me and Mick to scope out the festivities for foul play."

He nodded. "Yes. Because I don't trust the Queen of Mirrors."

"You think she killed Sofie and Einar Frost," I translated.

"Yes," he repeated. "I do."

"And you didn't trust yourself not to punish her for it."

He dipped his chin once more.

"Why?" I asked. "Alphas war over power all the time. Sure, Vanessa went about it in a cowardly manner, but why would you want to punish her for it and not the many other assholes who lead around the world?"

"Because the other assholes didn't kill my little sister," he replied, his words coated in ice. "So whoever gave Winter that necklace to wear knows who I am to Sofie. It's the only reason he or she would feel confident enough to put her on one of our planes and send her here."

"Sofie Frost was your sister?" I couldn't contain the shock in my voice. "How the hell didn't I know that?"

He smiled sadly. "We all have our secrets, Kazek. This is one of mine. Prove to me you're worthy, and maybe I'll tell you the story someday. For now, figure out who gave her the necklace. That person is clearly an ally."

CHAPTER TWENTY-SIX

WINTER

WHAT. THE. FUCK?

All the windows and doors were locked. I'd tried every single one multiple times and nothing. The latches falling into place were what woke me up from a fitful sleep. I hadn't understood what they were until it was too late, and now I was trapped in this cabin that smelled like sex with Kazek.

I growled, low and meaningful.

He couldn't keep me here, not with Enrique arriving soon. Winter Sector was my home. The edict Vanessa gave the people pertained to me. I did not agree to be hidden away like some secret burden. Maybe he thought he was protecting me, but this felt more like a punishment.

"You're the one who wanted to play by societal standards, Omega. So go the fuck to sleep. I'll see you again when I feel like knotting."

I shivered at the memory of his words, my stomach

LEXI C. FOSS

cramping with the realization that he really meant them.

Did that mean he planned to help Winter Sector? Or keep me here like some bad secret while Vanessa continued to rule?

There was no way to know his intentions without talking to him.

And that clearly didn't seem to be a thought on his mind.

I muttered a curse and took a shower, attempting to pass the time.

By three in the afternoon, he still hadn't returned. I tried to recall what time Ludvig said Enrique was scheduled to arrive, but last night's events created a puzzle in my mind that I couldn't sort. My fight with Kazek sat firmly at the front, my annoyance with him mounting with each passing minute.

Yes. I'd acted poorly and said some things without thinking them through. But that didn't mean he could just lock me up in a time-out. Not with my kingdom on the line.

Winter Sector was my responsibility.

The announcement pertained to me and my disappearance.

Hiding wasn't an option.

I needed to face Vanessa and reclaim my throne. Show everyone what she'd done to me and finally determine the truth about how my parents really died. Because I suspected without a doubt that she'd killed them. I just needed to prove it. And I couldn't do that while locked away in a cabin waiting for my stubborn mate to return.

He'd more than made his stance clear regarding leadership. He wanted nothing to do with the position of supporting my kingdom. Fine. Then I'd have to do it without him.

It would hurt. I'd hate being apart from him. But leadership required sacrifice, and this would be mine.

I hunted through his things, searching for my knives and the phone I'd brought with me. It was past time I called Doc; I just needed to find my things.

Come on. Come on. Come on.

It has to be here somewhere.

I turned over the living area, the bedroom, the kitchen, and both bathrooms. Opened every drawer. Searched in every closet. Looked under sinks, in cabinets, beneath cushions, and even tried to find loose floorboards that might hold pockets of hidden items.

Nothing.

And that damn clock was still clicking down my fate with no sign of Kazek.

"Gah!" I sat back on my heels, naked, furious, and feeling as though my execution were imminent. I had to do something. I couldn't just wait. "There has to be a way out."

I switched my focus to searching for exits.

The doors and windows were out.

Except for the small window in the bathroom that doubled as a vent.

I considered the size compared to my width and pushed it as wide as I could. A glance outside showed it led to snow.

It was too narrow for me to fit through, but if I pried apart the metal rim and removed the window itself, I might be able to make it work.

"Wait…" I opened the door beneath the sink and eyed the pipe.

Kazek was going to kill me for this, but I didn't care. He'd locked me up in this fucking cabin, and I was tired of waiting.

I went to my knees and yanked on the pipe as hard as I could, flinching at the agonized sound it gave me in response.

Again.

Harder.

More.

Sweat dripped from my brow as I angled my body to add my legs for leverage. With my bare feet against the back of the cabinet beneath the sink, I wrapped my fingers around the pipe again and yanked.

I fell backward as the piece came apart, giving me a solid metal object to use against the—

My eyebrows flew upward. "Oh!" Another idea smacked me in the face, and I cursed my stupidity. I didn't need to go through the damn bathroom window; I could use this to bust one of the other, larger ones. "Idiot."

I considered my options and chose the one in the living area that dropped into a pile of snow outside. "Perfect," I praised myself, then worked on finding something to wear. As much as I might prefer my fur for this, I couldn't speak in wolf form and needed clothes for this.

All of Kazek's clothes were too big, but I found a pair of jogging shorts with a drawstring waist and a T-shirt. Wool socks covered my feet. Not the most practical for snow, but I'd walked naked through it yesterday and survived just fine.

"All right," I murmured, eyeing the window once more. "Now or never."

My mate would already be furious about the sink, so I might as well go through with this crazy plan now. Not that I really had one. I wanted a phone to call Doc. Then I'd go from there.

The glass shattered with a blaring sound that pierced my ears.

"Shit." The asshole had an alarm in place. I should have expected that.

Well, too damn bad.

He'd have to catch me.

I jumped through the window, narrowly avoiding the glass, and took off toward the sector perimeter.

This was definitely one of those *I should have thought it through a little better* moments, but at this point, I couldn't turn back. He'd locked me in a damn cabin like some sort of child in time-out. My behavior now probably deserved that type of response, but pointing out his flaws? Not so much.

I'm a dead wolf. Yep. Total dead wolf.
Why did I do this again?
For my kingdom.
Right.
Run. Run. Run.
I have no idea where the hell I am.

I did a circle, scenting the air as a current of energy swept over my skin.

Not Kazek, but something else.

The rumble of electricity caused the hairs along my exposed arms to stand on end and my neck to prickle with unease.

Wind stirred all around me, the leaves fluttering in the unnatural gust.

Aircraft, I recognized. *Enrique. I must be close to the airfield.*

I trailed the source through the trees and paused at the sight of the ocean beyond. It was beautiful and dark blue, the setting sun a pale globe on the horizon.

The entire day had passed me by, not that the sun remained out for long during this time of year. Shaking my head to clear it, I continued toward the energy source and found myself approaching the plane from a backward path.

This was a really bad idea.

But I couldn't stop moving.

Not when I scented Grum's cologne on the wind.

I started to run toward it, needing my seven now more than ever.

Are they all okay?

Did Vanessa hurt any of them?

She would have held Doc responsible for my disappearance, his job as my primary guard coming into question. I hadn't considered that at all when he sent me away, had been too caught up in all the revelations of the last week to think beyond my mating bond and what it meant to even ponder the others.

I'm selfish, I realized. *I put myself before them all.*

I never should have gotten on that plane. I should have stayed back and fought. There was nothing I could do about the past, but I could change the future. I still had a chance to do the right thing.

I just wished I knew what that was.

Except I knew what it wasn't. Sitting in a cabin waiting for others to act on my behalf didn't suit. I'd never been the type to let others fight my battles. I'd wanted a partner to take on Vanessa with me, not a mate to handle it all for me.

But he didn't want to lead.

Which left me to follow my rightful path on my own.

Shirking my duties for a mating bond was never an option. If it meant I had to live in agony every day to secure my kingdom, then I would.

Vanessa had to pay for what she'd done.

Once my people found out, they'd remove her. I just had to return home and give them a statement. Point out her black heart. And hope they all had my back.

It was a horrible plan, but what else could I do? Kazek didn't want to lead. Ludvig hadn't seemed interested at all in helping me. Thus, nothing had really changed since my arrival. I was still just as alone as I was the night of my engagement party.

No. I was even more alone. I didn't even have my seven.

But Grum was here. I could smell him.

I ran faster along the coast, searching out his familiar scent, and nearly wept with relief upon finding him standing in the center of a tarmac.

Until I realized who else stood with him.

Enrique.

Kazek, Ludvig, and Alana were waiting on the sidelines, their expressions morphing from stoic to shocked upon seeing me in the field.

Then Grum and Enrique turned slowly in unison, their lips parting in disbelief.

I ignored everyone except Grum.

His shoulders tightened, his brow coming down as he sniffed the air.

I didn't think.

I ran right for him.

And then froze when Enrique stepped into my path, blocking my view of Grum and the Norse Sector Alphas behind him.

"Snow?" Enrique spoke my name like he couldn't believe it was me. His nose twitched, my scent clearly not what it was before, yet his eyes told his brain who stood before him. And that caused a myriad of emotions to fly over his features.

Annoyance.

Sadness.

Shock.

More grief.

And an unexpected glimmer of relief, like he was glad to see I was okay.

I probably imagined that last part.

"What are you doing here? Are you okay?" he asked, causing me to blink.

That was not at all how I expected him to react. I anticipated yelling, perhaps even violence, not his genuine concern.

"I, uh…" I paused to clear my suddenly dry throat, the words I wanted to say disappearing into a fog of uncertainty.

Kazek darted to my side, his arm around my shoulders in an instant as he tried to move me behind him. I wasn't sure how he moved that fast. Maybe I'd lost a second to own my stupidity, but I swore he stood a good fifty feet away a second ago.

His manhandling brought me out of my stupor, and I dodged diagonally to get away from him.

"No," I said as he faced me with a thunderous expression. *Yeah, I'm totally a dead wolf.* But that didn't stop me from returning his look with one of my own. "This is my mess. Let me speak."

A muscle ticked in his jaw, his teeth clenched so hard I was shocked he didn't chip a canine. "Your mess," he repeated, his voice low and gravelly. "And who do you think is going to have to clean it up?"

"Me," I told him. "I understand that now. I've come to do what I need to do."

"And what the hell is that exactly?" he demanded.

"Turning myself in," I replied, taking a step to my right to meet Enrique's dark gaze.

I didn't give Kazek a chance to interject. My mouth was already moving.

"I overheard your conversation with Alpha Vanessa the night before our engagement party where you discussed knotting me to death. So I plotted my escape and snuck on board the Norse Sector jet the following night. This was without anyone's knowledge, including Alpha Kazek's."

I took a deep breath and plunged ahead, not wanting to risk someone interrupting me.

"The strength pills Vanessa provided me with were actually suppressants, something I didn't know, and when I failed to take them, I went into estrus. Alpha Kazek saved my life. For that, I owe him my gratitude and respect. But it was done without him acknowledging or accepting my familial destiny. I relieve him of his obligations, and I'm ready to return home to face the consequences of my actions."

Knowing full well the kingdom is going to fry Vanessa alive when they realize she hid my identity from them all, I added to myself. *Hopefully*.

I took a step toward Enrique, my head bowing in a gesture of respect. He was my superior as an Alpha, and my intended jailer. It felt right to acknowledge his higher-ranking position.

"This has nothing to do with Norse Sector," I added, my voice taking on a gruff note thanks to my closing throat. "This was all me. So take me home and let the formalities commence."

Silence.

I swallowed, uncertain of how to proceed. This had all been a spur-of-the-moment decision on my part, one I couldn't bring myself to regret. It was the right response. Alpha Kazek shouldn't have to fight the battle on my behalf. No one should. It was mine to navigate and win. That was the piece I'd missed from the very beginning.

Running was the coward's way out.

I should have faced Vanessa head-on and taken her down my own way—through revelations and truth.

Fear had driven my reactions. Just as pride drove my decisions today. Well, pride with a sprinkling of stupidity. Because Kazek's resulting anger created a heat wave at my back that had my wolf wanting to cower in submission. But I couldn't.

He didn't want to save Winter Sector.

That left me to stand up for them.

The back of Enrique's knuckles whispered across my jaw, drawing a warning growl from the Alpha behind me.

"I acknowledge your claim, Kazek," Enrique said in a low tone. "I don't intend to fight you for her. I'm just in awe at missing something so obvious." His body angle changed, allowing me to see Grum once again. "Did you know?"

"Doc suspected it," Grum admitted. "None of us ever understood how Einar and Sofie had produced a Beta heir. It's customary in our kingdom for the type to be revealed on the progeny's first birthday. Snow's parents died before we reached that date."

"Thus, Vanessa made the announcement instead," Enrique inferred.

"Yes," Grum confirmed. "She used it to her advantage by promising the kingdom she would raise Snow for leadership, despite her Beta tendencies. She also suggested the birth was a result of being surrounded by Betas."

Enrique scoffed at that. "And these strength pills were prescribed by her?"

Grum nodded. "Yes."

"Fucking bitch," Enrique cursed, causing me to jump backward into the masculine wall of hot steel behind me. Kazek immediately locked his arms around my waist, holding me against him. I knew better than to melt into him, despite my wolf's inclination to do just that. My mate was holding me hostage, not offering comfort.

"My feelings exactly, sir," Grum murmured.

Enrique blew out a breath, his palm wrapping around the back of his neck. "Fuck. I don't even know where to start. I need a fucking drink."

"We can oblige you with that," Ludvig offered. He and Alana hadn't moved from the sidelines. "I suspect we have a great deal to discuss."

Enrique nodded. "Yeah. I imagine my fate very much rests in your hands right about now, too."

"Not mine, but Kazek's," Ludvig corrected. "Assassinating an Omega is a punishable offense."

"I'm aware." Enrique pulled a gun out from behind his back and tossed it into the snow. "I have two more blades in my boots."

"You can keep them," Kazek said. "I prefer fair fights."

"Then don't visit Bariloche Sector," Enrique muttered. "We're not known for playing by the rules."

Kazek stilled against me. "I suggest you try, or you'll find out what happens when I work outside the law."

Enrique dipped his head in acknowledgment. "I'm not going to fight you."

"We'll see," Kazek replied.

Enrique gave a sad shake of his head. "No, we won't." His

213

near-black eyes met mine, sadness lurking in their depths. "I didn't know, Snow. I realize that changes nothing, but I honestly didn't know."

"Yet you were fine killing me as a Beta," I whispered, more to myself than to him.

Sadness etched itself into his brow. "You only overheard part of the conversation, not the intentions of my mind, Snow White." He took a step backward and shifted his attention upward before I could reply. "I'll cooperate. Just tell me what you want me to do."

"Go with Ludvig," Kazek said, not missing a beat. "I'll be along in a bit. My mate and I are long overdue for an obedience discussion."

CHAPTER TWENTY-SEVEN

KAZEK

WINTER SHIVERED AGAINST ME as the others left the
field. The only one who glanced back at us was the Beta who'd
arrived with Enrique. I hadn't caught his name, Winter
appearing before any formal introductions could occur, but I
didn't like the way he looked at her. A protective flare lurked
in his gaze, one that shouldn't exist.

Mine, I told him with a glare. If he tried to test me on that
claim, I'd serve him his balls for dinner.

He finally turned away, the message seemingly received.
For now. I would have to ask Winter for his name later. After
we finished a much-needed conversation about what the fuck
she was thinking.

My wrist had buzzed with the notice of a disturbance at
my cabin. One flick of my thumb had brought up the
communication screen, the image showcasing Winter

escaping out the window. I'd cursed and started toward her, only to be held back by Enrique's arrival. Then she'd shown up and destroyed my entire plan.

Ludvig had gifted me a knowing glance, one that'd said, *Should have talked to her, Kaz.*

Yeah, a little too late for that.

Winter had already taken her fate into her hands by that point.

Fury vibrated through me as I considered how to handle this situation. She fucked up. Yet so did I.

Leaving her cooped up in the cabin without a single word after our fight had been a mistake. I realized that the moment she attempted to relieve me of my obligations. Those words had hurt and pissed me off at the same time. She had no authority to make such a regal claim, nor was it the right move. It set us further apart and painted me as a nitwit who refused to lead.

Which was exactly how she saw me after our fight last night.

I could own that part of the issue, but she needed to realize how her rash behavior impacted our mating. She presented a divided front, similar to what I'd done last night, yet I hadn't left her in the dark. I'd stuck by her. Unlike what she'd just tried to do to me.

She'd offered herself up on a platter to be taken home without any regard to what could happen to her. Did she think Vanessa would just give her the throne? Allow her a ceremonious reentry into the sector?

My female had clearly lost her fucking mind.

Because I'd left her unattended for too long.

And she had no idea what I'd planned to do.

I closed my eyes and strove for patience, reminding myself that I shared the blame in this entire mess. What we needed to do was fix it, and quickly. I just had no idea how.

"Kaz—" Winter abruptly stopped speaking and cleared her throat. "Alpha, I'm… I didn't know what else to do."

I flinched at her using my title rather than my name, which, of course, was my own doing. My temper had gotten the better of me, and she'd paid for it dearly.

I pressed my nose to her hair and inhaled deeply, the scent of my shampoo calming my nerves. She smelled like she belonged to me, she wore my clothes, and she submitted in my arms, and all those actions pleased my raging wolf.

"It's my kingdom," she continued in a whisper. "I've been selfish staying here. They're all at risk and I've… I can't stay here. I have to… Vanessa needs to be taken down. I'm the only one who can do it."

"How?" I asked against her hair. "How do you plan to take her down?"

"B-by exposing the truth," she stammered.

I sighed and shook my head. "That's a noble outlook but implies you expect Vanessa to play by the rules. And I think she's more than proven herself incapable of following any sort of guideline."

Her shoulders slumped. "There's no other option."

I snorted. "So you intended to risk yourself and our bond on a mission you knew would likely fail?"

"What else was I supposed to do?" The demand of her question was lost to her softer tone, her body trembling against mine. "Just wait in the cabin for you to knot me again? Fully embrace my Omega needs and forget my duties? Become a doll for you to fuck instead of becoming the queen my parents meant for me to be?"

She sounded broken by the end, as if she truly expected that to be her life. And I supposed my earlier comments were somewhat to blame for her assumptions.

"Fuck, Winter," I breathed, most of my ire drifting away on the gentle breeze coming in from the sea. "I was angry last night about your approach and—"

"I shouldn't have pushed you," she interjected. "I'm grateful you saved me, but it was done without thought of what it actually meant, and it's not fair of me to expect you to just accept my baggage. I get that now. I'm sorry."

I spun her in my arms, tired of talking to the back of her head. "Don't interrupt me again," I told her. Not necessarily harshly, but sternly, because this communication thing wasn't going to work if she wouldn't listen to me. Not that I had a lot of room to talk after last night's performance, but we were living in the present, not the past.

Winter swallowed, her eyes immediately falling to my chest. "Sorry," she whispered.

I gripped her chin and tugged her gaze back up to mine and hated the fear I saw lurking in her depths. "I'm not going to hurt you."

"I wouldn't hold it against you if you did." Such quiet words, but they filled me with anger for an entirely different reason.

"When I punish you—and I will—it'll be the kind of pain you enjoy, not the kind that leaves you fearing me. Remember the other day? When I bent you over my knee?" I arched a brow, waiting for her reply.

Twin spots of pink graced her pale cheeks. "Y-yes."

"That's how I prefer to punish you," I informed her, my touch drawing up her jaw to palm the side of her face. "I'm not Vanessa or Enrique." She twisted her lips to the side, causing both my eyebrows to shoot up. "You don't believe me?"

"N-no," she replied, causing me to release her in shock. "No, that's not…" She cleared her throat. "Enrique never hurt me," she rushed to say. "Well, okay, he sort of did during the engagement party, but it wasn't lasting pain. And I think he only did it to appease Vanessa. Because she would have punished me had he not demonstrated his dominance. He sent me away early, too, instead of making me dance more, which was what Vanessa wanted."

I stared at her and considered Enrique's behavior upon arrival. He hadn't shown an ounce of aggression toward Winter or me. If anything, he seemed remorseful. I suspected it was a result of his pending sentence—he knew his life was forfeit—but maybe he genuinely felt guilty for what had been done to Winter.

We'd debate that later.

There were more important items to discuss right now.

"Okay. Let's start over," I suggested, pulling her back into my arms with one palm against the base of her spine and the other clasping the back of her neck. "First of all, your plan of surrender is a bad one. There's no way in hell I'm letting you go back to Winter Sector alone."

She stiffened, her shoulders locking into place. Yet she smartly remained quiet.

"I told you leadership doesn't come naturally to me, Winter," I continued. "I provided a thorough explanation as to my reservations, but I never gave you an outright refusal. You pushed me when I requested time for consideration. Then you pissed all over our bond by essentially denouncing me to Enrique and requesting he deliver you to the Alpha female who tried to kill you."

"I-I didn't denounce you."

"You did," I corrected. "You told him you relieved me of my duties, which you can't do."

"You don't want them."

"You're right. I don't," I agreed, then squeezed the back of her neck to force her to hold my gaze. "But that doesn't mean I don't intend to take them on. That's what you're failing to understand, Winter. I'm a stubborn asshole. I don't make decisions lightly. You tried to push, which only makes me fight back that much harder. But never once did I tell you I *wouldn't* do it. I just said I didn't want to do it. Those are two entirely different phrases."

Her brow furrowed. "I don't want to force you."

"Then don't," I replied, my thumb brushing her pulse. "Let me force myself instead." I drew her closer and pressed my lips to hers. "I know what I have to do, Winter. But I'm not jumping into something out of obligation alone. You need to let me think through every angle. That's who I am. That's how I process decisions."

She nodded slowly, her sable irises holding mine. "I'm sorry."

"I know you are," I replied, kissing her again, this time with a whisper of my own apology behind the movement.

Neither of us had signed up for this. Yet Ludvig was right; Winter had done a decent job of embracing her Omega side despite being raised as a Beta. Well, at least until the showdown on the airfield. That had been all regal Beta, not the behavior of a claimed Omega.

"Don't ever denounce me again," I told her. "And don't

ever put yourself in danger like that again."

I didn't give her a chance to acknowledge my demands, my mouth already claiming hers. There were things I wanted to say that I didn't know how to convey, like how terrified I'd felt when she put herself in danger and how much I wanted to throttle her for acting so brazenly without regard to her own safety.

My kiss was a punishment in and of itself, my tongue lashing hers in reprimand for all the choices that pissed me off. Each punctuation soothed the violence brewing inside me, calming my fire and stoking another in its place.

Oh, I wanted to punish her.

To color her ass pink with my palm.

Fuck her into oblivion and force her to remain there until I finished planting myself inside her very soul.

But we didn't have time.

So I settled my desires through my mouth, dominating her with my palm wrapped around the back of her neck and allowing her to feel my power and command in each touch and savage lick.

She melted into me, her wolf submitting to my every whim.

There would be no more arguing.

No more sparring.

Just an obedient mate succumbing to her Alpha's will.

A purr reverberated in my chest, causing Winter to nearly sag against me in relief. Whatever misgivings she had about our bond seemed to seep out of her, replaced by a content, humming little wolf. Her dark eyes held a drowsy appeal as I pulled back to study her, that special place only an Omega could disappear to.

I smiled at her and nuzzled her nose. "I'm still going to punish you, baby."

"I know," she said dreamily.

"Come on. As much as I enjoy seeing you in my clothes, there's an outfit Mila picked out for you to wear to dinner tonight. It's back at my condo."

"Dinner?"

"Yes. The activity I was going to take you to after I met

with Enrique to feel out his aggression levels," I replied, giving her a look. "I had a plan, Winter. You ruined it." Not that it really mattered now. Enrique was going to find out about her Omega status regardless of how things went down. She'd just accelerated my timeline. Thankfully, the Alpha didn't seem keen on challenging me.

"Sorry," she whispered, that word appearing to be her favorite today.

I pressed my lips to her cheek. "I'm sorry, too." Pretty sure I'd never said those words out loud to anyone. Ever. "I think we both have some learning to do in regard to communication," I added, the words foreign on my tongue.

My hurdle would be harder to overcome. I worked alone for a reason, but mating implied I now had to consider someone else in my decisions. And sometimes, I'd need her input as well.

"I… I'm also sorry about your, uh, cabin," she said as we started walking.

"I can fix a window."

"And the sink," she mumbled, causing me to pause midstep.

"My sink?"

"Uh, um, the pipe…?" It came out like a question.

I stared at her in confusion for a moment, then pieced it all together. "You used a pipe to take out the window."

She nodded stiffly.

"I see." I resumed our path toward my condo, my mind formulating all the ways to properly reprimand my mate for her behavior today. Letting her get away with all this bullshit would weaken my stance as her Alpha.

Although, I couldn't go too hard on her, not with my wolf beaming in pride at her resourcefulness. She'd also stood up for what she believed in, something I'd admired even while being livid at her for not thinking the plan through.

Hmm, I needed to do something that would remind her who was in charge while also conveying my pleasure at her demonstration of strength.

My lips curled as I thought of the perfect correction method.

Poor Winter.

She wouldn't know what to do when I finished with her.

And I couldn't wait to hear her beg.

CHAPTER TWENTY-EIGHT

WINTER

THE METAL OBJECT BUZZED between my thighs, causing me to jump beside Kazek in the elevator. He smirked and I gasped. "*That's* what that does?"

I'd asked him the purpose when he'd slid the item inside me before drawing up my lace panties. He'd merely said, "Don't remove that without my permission." So I'd held the two-sided beaded-like item inside, my inner muscles contracting to keep it from falling out. I didn't want to disappoint him. Not again. But as the buzzing increased, I wondered if I'd be able to obey his order all evening.

"Alpha," I breathed, my back meeting the cold mirrored wall behind me as I fought for something to hold on to.

Kazek stepped into my space, his suit-clad form blocking my view of everything except his powerful body.

"These are the rules for tonight," he said, his gaze

capturing mine. "No coming without my permission. No removing the Ben Wa balls. No moaning. No crying out. No reacting at all beyond your scent and slick. That means I expect you to carry on conversations all night in your usual eloquent fashion. Obey me, and I'll reward you. Disobey me, and, well, I don't suggest it."

I whimpered at the realization of what he intended to do to me. I never should have agreed to let him put that thing inside me. Not that there'd been much choice. He'd unwrapped the box and taken out the toy before I could read the purpose of the contents. I should have known it would do something like this.

"Also, I like hearing you call me Alpha, so that's how you'll continue to address me tonight." His lips went to my ear as the pulsating increased. "You've already earned yourself quite the punishment, Winter. Don't make it worse on yourself by ignoring my commands."

He licked my thundering pulse and stepped back just as the metal slats parted to reveal our destination. I was practically panting behind him, my thighs slicked with need. *Everyone* would be able to smell my arousal. It would make conversation with other Alphas difficult, something I suspected was the point. Kazek wanted to remind me whom I belonged to and force me to beg him for comfort.

In front of the entire damn party—a dinner party.

Everyone stood around with drinks in their hands, their focus falling to me as Kazek guided me out of the elevator with a palm pressed to my bare lower back. The black silk fabric hugged my curves, leaving me braless and exposed for the crowd.

I nearly groaned in embarrassment, knowing my nipples were tight buds of agony thanks to the incessant thrumming inside my pussy. Kazek hadn't turned the damn thing off but left it on the same level, stirring my intrigue and maintaining it with a rhythmic throb.

Grum gave me a look filled with concern, while Enrique narrowed his gaze.

Kazek approached them with an easy grin, his wolf clearly pleased with his choice in punishment method.

I wanted to throttle him.

Well, no. That wasn't true. I wanted to fuck him. *Then* throttle him.

He must have sensed my annoyance, because the thrumming increased, causing me to flinch and bite back a moan.

That would feel amazing against my clit, I thought, an image of Kazek using it on me there appearing behind my eyes. *Yes, please.*

"Alpha Enrique, my apologies for the interruption before. The matter has since been corrected." Kazek's thumb brushed my spine, telling me his opposite hand was controlling the vibration inside me. He had his fingers tucked into the pocket of his black slacks, confirming my assumption. "I believe you're familiar with my mate's former identity, but allow me to introduce you to her chosen one. She now goes by Winter Flor, Omega of Norse Sector and future Queen of Winter Sector."

I glanced at him, surprised by the latter half of that introduction. He merely arched a brow as if daring me to deny it.

My cheeks heated slightly in the confidence in his tone and expression.

Okay.

I no longer wanted to throttle him. Now I wanted to kiss him. And then fuck him.

Which meant I needed to play by his rules, and that included making conversation. I forced a smile and said, "Yes. My name is no longer Snow Frost. She died when she went into estrus and was reborn Winter Flor, mate to Alpha Kazek Flor."

The vibration decreased, Kazek's approval clear in the way he held me closer and kissed the top of my head. "I don't believe we've met, Beta," he said, focusing on Grum. "I'm guessing you're part of the royal guard?"

"I'm the lead weapons expert in Winter Sector," Grum replied, his silver-blue eyes finding mine. I knew what he wanted to know.

Have you told him about the seven? he was asking me.

No, I attempted to tell him with a slight shake of my head.

He didn't seem to care for that response. It showed a lack of trust, which was an accurate assessment. His attention returned to Kazek. "My name is Grum."

"Grum," Kazek repeated, his body stilling beside mine. "Winter's mentioned you."

I frowned. *When did I...? Oh. Oh, shit!* I'd brought him up after refusing to wear Alana's clothes. My palm immediately went to Kazek's abdomen as if I could hold him back, and he replied by amping up the vibration inside me. My knees nearly buckled from the onslaught of sensation, a moan inching up my throat, only to be swallowed down by sheer will alone.

I curled my hand against him, my nails snagging on the fabric of his jacket.

This was unfair on so many levels right now.

Grum glanced at me with concern, while Enrique took a step back. My arousal had to be taunting him. Unmated Alphas were programmed to respond to Omega pheromones, and Kazek was worsening my scent with his trickery below.

A punishment, I realized, my lips parting at the knowledge that had escaped me earlier. This wasn't just about me but about Enrique as well. He'd be forced to endure my scent as the only unmated Alpha in the room, and if he reacted to me in any way, Kazek could issue a challenge.

I glanced at Kazek in shock, but he was too busy staring Grum down and measuring up the male he perceived as potential competition for my affection.

I wrapped my arms around Kazek in a show of solidarity, my legs wobbling from the pleasurable onslaught occurring between my thighs.

There was no way I'd last all night in this state.

Follow the rules, I coached myself. *No moaning. No crying out. No removing the devilish technology. No... Ohhhh, that feels good. Mmm...*

I pressed my nose into Kazek's chest, a groan stilling against my lips.

Everyone knew. I could feel their eyes on me, could sense Kazek's growing amusement, and hated him a little for embarrassing me in this manner.

226

But I understood the purpose.

He wanted me to experience the helplessness he did on the airfield, just in a more sensual, seductive way.

Devious mate, I thought at him as I met his wicked gaze.

At least I'd captured his attention.

The buzzing subsided as he gifted me a kiss meant to entice me while also delivering a message to our audience regarding his claim. "Mmm, you smell delectable, Winter," he whispered, his nose drawing across my cheek to my ear. "I can't wait to eat you later."

I shivered, a fresh wave of slick saturating my lace panties. Pretty soon, it'd be dribbling down my legs. Good thing my dress's skirt went to the floor. Of course, the slit up my left limb would provide Kazek with all the access he required to touch me intimately during dinner.

Enrique cleared his throat, his expression strained. "I'm glad you were able to save her when I couldn't."

Kazek shifted, placing me at his side once more, and wrapped his arm around my lower back. I leaned into him but kept my hands to myself. With the heat wave riding my system, I didn't trust myself not to grab him inappropriately. Or worse, go to my knees and beg him to fuck me in front of everyone.

At least the vibrations had ceased.

For now.

That didn't stop me from clenching my thighs together in an attempt to find friction. Kazek's little toy had left me craving him in a manner that reminded me of estrus. My mind continued to play through all the ways he could relieve my aching need, each visual causing my belly to flip with intrigue.

This is bad.

Very bad.

"Tell me, *Grum*." Kazek uttered the name like a disease. "Who's Doc? You mentioned he suspected Winter might not be a Beta. Why didn't he do anything about it?"

Grum folded his arms, his expression bored. "He tried but couldn't find any evidence of tampering."

"The 'strength pills' weren't a clue?" Kazek pressed, arching a brow.

"Winter Sector is a Beta colony. Strength pills are a common substance among the wolves to help empower our defenses against Alphas. Suppressants, however, are not available or even discussed. It never would have crossed our minds that Snow, I mean, *Winter*, was ingesting them." Grum shrugged. "I have no idea where Vanessa was even getting them."

"From the Bariloche Sector Alpha," Enrique muttered. "That's my guess, anyway."

Kazek gave him a look. "And why is that your guess?"

"Vanessa and Carlos are close friends. That's why the engagement request for Snow went to Bariloche Sector. Carlos offered it to his council, and when no one volunteered to take a Beta bride, I stepped forward."

I flinched at the image of his council rejecting me on the basis of being a Beta. Of course, all the Alphas would want to hold out for an Omega mate.

"Bet they're going to regret their decision soon," Kazek drawled.

Enrique grunted. "Several will challenge you, yeah."

Kazek smiled. "Good. I've never been a fan of Carlos or his pet Alphas."

Enrique didn't react negatively to the statement. He merely stared at Kazek with a bored expression. "Why do you think I offered to leave?"

"I thought Kari was your payment. She came from Bariloche Sector, yes? As a gift?"

Some of Enrique's facade cracked, his eyes giving away just enough to pique my curiosity. Was that why he agreed to wed me? So he could have the Omega as his personal slave? I knew he intended to take her as a mistress, but didn't realize he already knew her. Was Enrique why she feared Alphas?

Enrique started to answer, only to be cut off by the arrival of the female in question. The blond Alpha—Mick—entered with her. He had his arm around her lower back, his lips near her ear as he whispered something that had her trembling.

Her fear overwhelmed my nostrils, causing me to flinch at the acrid stench.

What did she expect to happen?

Enrique made a noise that had Kazek tensing beside me. And then Kari's head flew upward.

The terror in her eyes melted into stark relief as she met Enrique's gaze, her blue eyes filling with tears.

"What the fuck have you done to her?" Enrique demanded, taking a step forward.

Mick pushed Kari behind him in a protective move that made Enrique growl.

"I wouldn't suggest it," Kazek said conversationally. "Technically, I won Omega Kari. So I'll be forced to intervene, and, well, I already have several reasons for wanting to kill you. Adding another might just tip me over the edge."

Enrique glared at him. "This isn't a game."

"It's not?" Kazek sounded affronted. "You mean you didn't conspire to kill Beta Snow so the Queen of Mirrors could take the throne without interference? And you didn't plan to become her king? I mean, I imagine that's what was in it for you, anyway. Feel free to correct my assessment."

"Conspiring, yes. But that doesn't mean I intended to follow through on her plan. Which, obviously, I can't prove. However, as to what I wanted, the answer is in this room." His focus went to Mick. "Tell me she's okay."

"I don't need to tell you shit," Mick replied.

"I'm okay," Kari said, her voice holding a notable quiver. "You shouldn't be here."

"Neither should you," Enrique muttered, running his fingers through his hair.

"It seems we have a lot to discuss," Ludvig mused, his stance relaxed. "And I sense there's a story here that I would be most interested in hearing. Shall we hear it over dinner?"

Kazek drew his thumb up and down my spine, causing heat to scatter across my skin. His little device had left me ultrasensitive, the fire still brewing inside my lower belly and just waiting for him to stoke it higher.

Something told me he intended to melt me alive.

And his words confirmed it as he murmured, "I do enjoy a good tale. Sounds like my kind of appetizer." I jumped as he flicked the vibrations back to life. "Allow me to escort you to your seat, Winter." His palm went to the bottom of my spine, his fingers brushing my ass.

Oh, this is going to be a long night.

CHAPTER TWENTY-NINE

KAZEK

WINTER SQUIRMED BESIDE ME, her eyes glazing over. She'd stopped listening to the conversation some time ago.

I scooped another bite off my plate and brought it to her lips. She opened, accepting my offering, then chewed on autopilot, just like she had with everything else I fed her. All her focus was on the pleasure buzzing between her legs.

Everyone in the room knew what I was doing. They could hear the reverberation coming from her cunt as well as scent her responding arousal.

Enrique sat across from us, the tendons of his neck pulsing with growing aggression. Still, he'd told us his story with admirable patience, his concern for Kari becoming clearer with each passing second.

Mick appeared ready to commit murder by the end, his knuckles white from clasping his silverware so harshly.

Ludvig, however, looked unsurprised by the tale. Given his age and experience, I supposed he wouldn't be shocked by Kari's maltreatment, or that of her sister.

"You chose to wed Winter in an effort to save Kari from her fate," I surmised. "Admirable."

Enrique snorted. "I didn't do it to be *admirable*. I did it to save her, only to have her ripped from my grasp after I thought I'd finally won."

Which explained his angry pacing the night of his engagement party.

I thought he'd wanted to fuck the little Omega. An adequate assessment under normal circumstances, but nothing about Enrique's tale could be considered *normal*.

"Well, as you can see, we've treated her a little differently from her father," I drawled.

Kari flinched at my statement, her dislike of me calling the Alpha of Bariloche Sector her *father* palpable. But he birthed her, so the designation was appropriate. That he'd failed his duty of protecting his progeny was an entirely different matter.

Well, *failed* was putting it lightly.

He'd fucking destroyed his children.

The prick deserved a sentence far worse than death for his insane antics.

"We should confer with the Alpha of Andorra Sector. I think he might be able to assist us in reverse engineering whatever Carlos did to her," Ludvig said, all business. "I'll give him a call when we're done here."

"Reverse engineering?" Kari repeated in a whisper.

Mick stretched his arm out across the back of her chair and brushed his fingers along her shoulder. She didn't shrink away from him. If anything, she seemed to calm at his touch.

Interesting. Last I'd heard, they were constantly bickering. It seemed they'd bonded, at least on some level.

"Let's see what my brother has to say, then go from there," Mick suggested to her softly, a slight purr radiating from his chest. "Ander has the best team of physicians and researchers in the world. If anyone can help you, it's him."

Poor female, I thought, pitying the pain she had to be in from

232

whatever the fuck her father had done to her insides. All because he didn't want her to be able to take a mate.

It seemed Carlos didn't like competition. When Kari's older sister took a mate—Enrique's twin brother—Carlos killed the poor bastard and broke his Omega daughter in the process. Then he altered Kari to keep her from being able to conceive. And if that wasn't bad enough, he turned her into a fuck toy for his personal guard to pass around.

There were humane ways to prevent pregnancy among wolves. Alpha and Omega pairings did it all the time.

But Carlos had gone for the most torturous method possible.

The asshole was exactly the kind of male I enjoyed killing. Alas, I had other priorities on my plate. Including the dazed Omega beside me. I'd left the vibrations on a low level, enough to tease her without forcing her over the edge. Thus, she was riding the edge of an orgasm that refused to crest, similar to how she'd feel during estrus without an Alpha cock to satisfy her. Only not as impactful because she wasn't a puddle of weeping need yet.

I didn't intend to let it go that far, just long enough to prove a point.

Which was where we were now.

I picked up my wine and sipped it while considering my next play.

The others all understood my intentions here. Winter had acted without recourse, superseded my authority in front of the pack, and put herself in serious danger as a result. I couldn't let that stand without correction.

Some might have favored a more violent approach.

I preferred my method of bringing her to her literal knees by reminding her of our dynamic.

We were slaves to our bond. Her need for pleasure directly correlated to my desire to knot her. I'd been hard for the last hour, anticipating the moment I could bend her over and bathe in her sweet heat.

The difference between us was my ability to focus and carry on a serious conversation while aroused.

If one of the wolves at the table addressed her now, she'd

be an incoherent mess. The vibrations were partly to blame, but mostly it was her yearning to submit to her mate. Some intrinsic part of her knew she'd acted poorly and wanted to be corrected as a result.

Omegas naturally craved their Alpha's approval. And Winter knew she hadn't earned mine. If anything, she'd lost it completely, and now her wolf longed to fix the balance.

I set my wine down and leaned into my mate. "Excuse yourself to the bathroom," I whispered in her ear, low enough for no one else to hear. Not that they would be surprised by anything I said at this point.

Winter shuddered but did as she was told, her dress molded to her fine ass as she searched out the restroom hallway off the corner of the restaurant.

Norse Sector had a few social areas for dining, most of them used for situations like this where Ludvig wanted to entertain a foreign dignitary. Other wolves used the makeshift restaurants for smaller celebrations or gatherings as well. Those in the kitchen profession just moved locations as requested. In this case, Ludvig had borrowed his own team of chefs for the occasion.

The conversation at the table shifted to a discussion on the infamous Alpha of Bariloche Sector, with Mick driving the questions about Carlos's esteemed Alpha Guard. Enrique appeared content with providing unlimited information, which worked for me. As long as he proved useful, I'd allow him to live.

Grum, however, remained on my "kill consideration" list.

So far, he'd provided nothing of import other than to piss me off with his insignificant existence. Knowing he'd fucked my mate didn't improve my opinion of him.

I held the Beta's gaze as I excused myself from the table, letting him see the hunger in my stare meant for the female he'd never have the privilege of touching again. "I'll be back in a bit," I said, not caring if anyone heard me.

Grum frowned, his disapproval evident.

Good.

This would punish him, too. His excuse about not knowing anything about suppressants pissed me off. If he, or this Doc asshole, had suspected foul play, they should have acted. As far as I was concerned, they were all worthless.

I smirked at him, then turned to follow the delectable scent of my Omega.

Mmm, beautiful. The Ben Wa balls had done exactly what I wanted. I increased the volume of their intensity as I approached the bathroom and smiled at the gasp she released through the door.

Technically, not a moan or a cry, so I allowed it.

She fell to her knees as I pushed through the threshold, her arms wrapping around my thigh. "Please, Alpha," she whispered, her face pressing to my groin. "*Please* let me come."

I ran my fingers through her dark hair. She looked amazing like this—submitting, begging me to please her, and rubbing herself all over my erection as if she couldn't stand another moment without my cock inside her.

"Are you on fire, Winter?" I asked her softly. "Do you feel as though you're about to explode?"

"Yes," she hissed, her cheek pressing into my zipper and rubbing against me like an Omega in heat.

I continued to draw my fingers through her soft strands, my touch purposely light and not nearly enough for her. "Does it remind you of your estrus, baby?"

She nodded, a whimper falling from her lips as she pressed her nose to my dress pants and inhaled deeply. "Knot me, Alpha. *Please.*"

"Hmm," I hummed, slipping my touch to the back of her neck to grasp her nape. "How did you plan to handle your first estrus without me?" I used my opposite hand to increase the sensation between her thighs.

She pressed her mouth to my trousers and released a sound against the fabric. It sounded rather close to a scream mingled with a moan, but I decided not to punish her for it. She was suffering enough.

"Did you think about that, baby?" I asked her, my grip tightening. "Did you think about how you'd handle your estrus without me? Because it would be a lot worse than this. You'd be in pain, screaming for anyone to knot you. All those

Betas would try and fail. And then what, Winter? What would you do? Let them rip you apart? Make me feel your death from thousands of miles away?"

Her nails dug into my thighs, her shoulders shaking. "No," she whispered.

"No what, baby?" I slid my palm up to take a fistful of her hair and yanked her head back to study her beautiful face.

Her pupils were full-blown, overtaking her dark irises, causing her eyes to resemble black, hungry orbs. But I caught the understanding in her expression, the stark fear of what I was telling her about the fate she'd chosen for herself and for me.

"It would have killed me to feel that, Winter. To know you were too far away for me to help you, and to know exactly how you were being harmed."

I knelt before her, which still left me towering over her smaller frame, but I could hold her more easily. She immediately grabbed my shoulders, her body pressing to mine to convey her need for me. But I held her back, my fingers tangled with her hair while my opposite palm went to her hip.

"The pain you feel right now, that orgasm your body continues to refuse you, would be multiplied by a million during estrus. You'd lose yourself to that desire and let anyone and anything fuck you, all the while craving only one knot. *Mine.*" I pressed my lips to hers in a chaste kiss meant to tease. "Do you understand our bond, sweetheart? How it ties us together in every way?"

She nodded, her arms encircling my neck as she clung to me like her lifeline. "Mine," she said on an exhale.

"Yours," I agreed, releasing her hip to find my remote. I flicked off the vibrations, my mouth still resting near hers. "Stand up and give me your panties, Winter."

She swallowed and used my shoulders for support to do as I requested. I held on to her hips while she bent to remove the lace between her legs. She trembled wildly but managed to handle the task with a grace I admired.

I took the garment from her fingers and slid it into my pocket, then said, "Now you can remove the Ben Wa balls. But don't come."

"Yes, Alpha." She closed her eyes and glided her fingers downward over her swollen lips, into the slick heaven created for my knot. Winter quivered as she pulled on the metal beads, drawing them out of her and presenting them for my view.

"Lick them clean for me, baby."

Her eyelids rose to display enchanting orbs of ebony. She held my gaze and did exactly what I demanded, her lips and tongue seducing me without even trying. Fuck, I wanted her to do that to my cock.

Later, I told myself. Winter deserved my devotion and thorough attention after her behavior tonight. She'd done exactly what I wanted, and I intended to reward her properly for it.

"Mmm, that looks good, sweetheart," I praised. "Now lift your skirt for me so I can enjoy my dessert."

She panted in anticipation, her nipples protruding sharply through her thin silk dress as she bunched the fabric up to her hips. With my hands on her hips, I guided her back into the door, wanting her to have something to lean on.

"Try not to fall," I said.

"Am I…?" She pulled in a harsh breath to finish her question. "Am I allowed to come, Alpha?"

Fuck, I adored her. She'd taken all my rules and memorized them gloriously.

I wouldn't just lick her to completion now; I'd give her the knot I knew she needed, too. And I'd hold her until she was ready to move again afterward, even if it required hours in this tiny one-stall bathroom. At least it was clean and elegantly furnished.

"You can come, scream, and moan, Winter," I told her. "Don't hold back. I want everyone in this damn sector to hear me claiming you. Understand?"

"Yes." Her head fell back against the door. "Thank you, Alpha."

I rumbled in my throat, pleased with her reactions, and sealed my mouth over her clit.

My name fell from her lips, and while I hadn't given her permission to call me Kazek, I didn't correct or reprimand her. I'd ordered her to inform the pack who owned her, and she'd done precisely that.

She came almost immediately, her body shaking from the needed climax rocking her core. I devoured her, driving her pleasure onward, sending her tumbling into a second peak within minutes of her first one, and licking her thoroughly as she came down from the torturous high.

Winter had released one hand from her dress, her fingers locked in my hair as she clenched and held on while I continued my pleasurable onslaught.

I vowed to continue making her come until she begged me to stop, or demanded more.

And I did.

I suckled her sensitive bud, slipped my fingers inside her to massage that spot deep within which made her legs shake, and drove her over the cliff.

Again.

And again.

And again.

She practically sang my name in response, mingling curses and pleas and whimpers in between.

"Stop" turned into "More" and later became "Too much." Then she started to cry, her pussy clamping down on my fingers and rejecting me from her womb.

"Knot," she whispered, tears streaking her cheeks even as another orgasm crested inside her. "Please, Alpha. I need your knot."

I nibbled her swollen nub, not hard, just enough to still her mounting rapture. Mostly because I knew another climax would send her to the floor.

She was finally ready for her mate.

Anything else wouldn't do.

"I want you to remember this, Winter," I said as I stood to tower over her. "Remember how you feel right now. How empty you are despite all your ecstasy. Because that's what life would be without me. Without *us*."

"P-please don't..." Her lower lip trembled. "P-please don't leave me like this, Alpha."

I cupped her jaw and kissed her slowly, allowing her to taste herself on my tongue. "It would be the ultimate punishment, wouldn't it?" I whispered. "Leaving you unfulfilled. Walking away and leaving you behind to fend for yourself. Responding to my duty in the other room instead of seeing to your needs and putting you—*us*—first."

She began to quiver for an entirely different reason, her fear of me doing just that ricocheting through her, causing her tears to renew in full force.

As I said, it would serve as the ultimate reprimand.

It was what she deserved for her earlier act of defiance.

Yet she'd done so well respecting me tonight and doing exactly what I asked.

And *that* was why I chose to go easy on her.

"I'm sorry," she whispered, her palms falling from my shoulders as she nearly crumpled to the ground at my feet.

But I caught her hip with my free hand and held her against me. "I know," I replied against her ear. "Now free me from my slacks."

She practically melted with relief. It'd be easier to send her to her knees to finish me off, but I wasn't that cruel.

Well, at least not with her.

I slid my touch back into her hair, toying with her silky strands as she deftly unbuckled my belt, popped open the button on my dress pants, and pulled down the zipper. I hadn't bothered with boxers, aware of what I intended to do this evening, so my cock fell into her eager hands.

She stroked me without asking permission.

I growled in response, mostly in approval, but with a hint of a reminder on who controlled whom.

Her forehead began to fall forward in a show of submission, but my grip on her hair held her back. I didn't give her a chance to apologize or speak, my mouth claiming hers in a harsh kiss meant to dominate.

She opened for me.

Allowed me to devour her the way I craved.

And waited for me to make the next move.

I never knew kissing could be so fucking erotic. It'd never been high on my activity list, as I'd always preferred to get right down to it. But Winter changed everything. She made me want to go slow, to memorize each and every moment, and to ensure her comfort before taking anything to the next step.

Which was exactly what I did now.

I eased her into the experience, demanding control at first and gently, slowly, allowing her preferences to shine in the process.

She enjoyed fluid movements, ones where my tongue stroked and danced sensually with hers.

Winter wanted passion.

She required my emotions.

Desired me to give her everything and more.

So I did. With each sensual possession of my mouth, I gave in to her methods and allowed her access to all of me. My feelings, including my anger at her for trying to leave me today. My alarm over almost losing her. My acceptance of our fate, as well as my aversion to leadership and subsequent understanding of the need for it.

And most importantly, I allowed her to sense my adoration for her. My devotion. My promise to always protect her. My vow to stand by her side. My full acknowledgment of our bond and what it meant.

Now she wept for an entirely different reason, my strong little mate overwhelmed by everything I told her with my mouth while never uttering a word.

I palmed her ass and lifted her in the air, then pinned her hips against the door with my own. Her legs went around my waist for balance as my cock found her entrance with unerring rightness and slid home inside her.

She arched into me on a gasp, her tears falling even faster as I took her in the manner we both craved.

This wasn't about pain or pleasure but about *need*.

My wolf demanded I stake my claim, and her wolf required I knot her thoroughly.

Our mouths grew hungrier against one another, her tongue a benediction against my own. I'd never felt for anyone like I did in this moment. So much intense possessiveness, so much completion. It was as if I wouldn't be able to breathe without her, as if I'd only just begun to live because of her.

I drilled the emotions home inside her, aware that I was probably bruising her from the potency of my thrusts and acknowledging that she required *more*.

"Winter," I breathed, lost to her.

This whole exercise had been about control, my need to own her entirely, and yet, I'd never felt so unrestrained in my entire life.

Our mating mastered us both, brought me to my figurative knees, and demanded I succumb.

And I did.

To her.

To *us*.

To the moment.

She moaned, her walls clenching tightly around me in indication of her growing euphoria. "Give it to me," I ordered. "Scream, Winter. Scream my name."

"Kazek!" She fell apart on a sound I would forever remember in my darkest dreams, and always attempt to re-create.

Pure ecstasy.

No pain.

Just completeness.

We were finally on the same level of understanding, our minds matching that of our souls and forcing our bond to a whole new plane of existence.

My knot exploded out of me, causing me to howl in agony-filled pleasure, my wolf fully at the helm. I stopped thinking. I reacted. And I bit Winter all over again, in the same place I'd tasted her days before.

She shrieked and tumbled into oblivion, her wolf giving in to mine without a fight.

It felt like a brand-new mating, our bodies joining in an even stronger union than before. I knew that wasn't possible or logical, but nothing between us seemed to be driven by reason. It was all underlined in magic. A fucked-up fairy tale. My own happily ever after.

I released her neck and held her with a passion I didn't know I possessed. And she clung to me right back, her legs shaking, her breath coming in pants.

"Thank you," she whispered. "Thank you, Alpha."

"Kazek," I corrected her, needing to hear my name from her sweet lips.

"Kazek," she repeated softly. "Thank you, Kazek."

I kissed her softly and lowered us both to the floor with my back propped against the door and her straddling my hips while my seed continued to spill inside her.

Silence fell over us.

A contentment.

A clear path.

Our futures marrying one another for eternity.

I didn't care who remained in the dining area, didn't care if they were all waiting for us to reemerge, this moment too powerful and meaningful for me to cut short.

Winter seemed to feel the same way, her forehead resting against my shoulder as her fingers played over the buttons on my jacket and shirt.

Such a beautiful mate.

So perfect.

I brushed her hair over her shoulder and admired my mark. *Mine.*

She seemed to sense my thoughts, because she hummed in what sounded like agreement, the content little sound doing all sorts of things to my insides.

"I'm yours, Winter Flor," I said softly, a purr resonating in my chest. "Always. You run, I chase. That's our dance. Remember that next time you try to leave me."

She hummed again, the noise seeming to be the only one she could make in her post-orgasmic state.

I accepted it as a response.

Mostly because I felt her assurance through the bond.

I'm yours, too, she was saying. *Always.*

CHAPTER THIRTY

WINTER

KAZEK HELPED ME FIX MY DRESS, his fingers running over the black silk with expert ease and smoothing out the wrinkles in all the right places. His seed dampened my thighs, my panties lost to one of his pockets. He didn't let me wash off, nor did he bother to clean up himself as he tucked his cock back into his pants.

Everyone had heard us already. There was no point in hiding what happened here. I also didn't want to shy away from his claim. He belonged to me and I belonged to him.

As if sensing the direction of my thoughts, Kazek lowered his lips to his claiming mark and placed a kiss against my neck. "Are you all right, Winter?" he whispered.

I nodded slowly. "Yes."

"Good." He brushed his mouth against my temple and moved behind me. I didn't understand why until my necklace appeared in his hand. "I meant to put this back on you earlier but forgot." He drew it across my skin and clasped the metal at my nape. "Ludvig said you left this in the holding suite."

I touched the paw print charm while studying my reflection in the mirror. "I forgot about it," I admitted. "Did he tell you about it?"

Kazek met my gaze in the glass. "Yes."

I waited for more, but he didn't elaborate. I turned in Kazek's arms and pressed my palms to his chest. "What did he say?"

"You really don't know?"

"Know what?"

His hands went to my hips, the hold possessive and very welcome. "Alpha Ludvig is your uncle."

My eyebrows shot upward. "*What?*"

"Yeah, you definitely didn't know," he murmured, amusement underlining his tone. "It was news to me, too. Shall we go ask him about it?"

I couldn't take in enough air to provide a response.

My uncle? I blinked. *How?*

What had Doc said? Something about Ludvig recognizing the necklace. He'd been certain it would convince the Norse Sector Alpha to help me. Which meant Doc knew. Did Grum?

I spun around toward the door, Kazek right behind me. He didn't tell me to stop or remind me of my place, his nearness a dominant, supporting presence at my back.

And somehow that only made me fall for him that much harder. Because he allowed me to be who I needed to be when it counted and reminded me of my place when I required the lesson.

Marching onto that airfield without a proper plan had been a huge mistake. I acknowledged that, just as he admitted that keeping me locked up without an update had been wrong. Sort of, anyway. He'd definitely alluded to the shortcoming.

Regardless, communication wasn't our strength. We needed to work on that realm of the relationship and would, but right now, I needed answers.

"Did you know?" I asked as soon as we arrived at the table.

Everyone had moved on to dessert cocktails, their gazes drifting to me as I interrupted whatever they'd been discussing.

But I only had eyes for Grum. "Did you know?" I repeated.

He stared at me. "Know what?"

"That Ludvig is my uncle," I replied through my teeth.

Grum didn't even hesitate. "Yes."

"All of you?" I pressed.

"Yes, Princess. We all knew."

"We?" Kazek repeated.

But I already knew whom Grum meant. *My protective seven.*

"Who is 'we'?" Kazek demanded when Grum ignored him.

"I don't report to you, Alpha," he replied, his focus still on me. "My loyalty lies with Princess Snow. Always."

Kazek growled, the sound a violent vibration against my back. "Careful, Beta."

Grum finally looked away from me and focused on the angry male at my back. "I respect that you're her mate, Alpha Kazek. But I swore an oath to the Frost family dynasty, and I won't break it."

Silence.

Grum couldn't explain more, his vow one of protective silence.

But I wasn't subjected to the same rules.

The seven existed to serve me and my familial line. Kazek had joined my dynasty as my mate, and it seemed Ludvig was related by blood. I assumed he was my mother's brother, because my father's family had been wiped out during the reformation of society a hundred years ago. It was how he became King of Winter Sector.

His mate, Mila, would be considered family as well. Same with his son Mick—a relationship I discerned over dinner. I also learned that everyone else referred to him as Sven, not Mick.

That left Kari and Enrique as the two outsiders in the room.

"What oath?" Kazek asked, turning me in his arms.

"What's he talking about, Winter?"

I lost myself in his dark irises, allowed his strength to overwhelm my misgivings, and whispered, "He's part of my seven." If Enrique reported any of this back to Vanessa, my Beta circle would be in jeopardy. They could handle themselves, but the Queen of Mirrors clearly didn't play fair.

"Snow," Grum cautioned.

I shook my head. "Everyone in this room is technically family, Grum. Except for two, and I trust Alpha Kazek to keep them in line as needed." Maybe not Kari, but I didn't really know whom she could talk to. Enrique was the only real threat, and his fate already rested in the palms of my mate's hands.

Kazek palmed my cheek, his expression warm. "Tell me about your seven."

"My protective seven," I replied, clearing my throat. "They're the ones who taught me how to fight. They raised me in secret without Vanessa's knowledge, their loyalty always being to my bloodline and not to hers. They're the ones who helped me escape on the plane. Their identities are only known by me and those in the seven, and they all have powerful positions in the kingdom."

"That's why you volunteered to come with me," Enrique said. I turned to find him gaping at Grum. "You knew she was here and intended to protect her."

"Yes." Grum wasn't one to lie or elaborate. He merely confirmed the detail and returned his focus to me, waiting to see what else I would reveal.

"The seven were created during the reformation to protect the last heir of the Frost family line—my father. They're an elite team of Betas who, as I said, all maintain valuable stations in Winter Sector. Grum is the sector weapons expert. Doc is the head of my security detail. And there are five others, whom I won't reveal. They all come together to protect the Frost bloodline as required."

"We swore a blood oath to Einar Frost and later to his mate, Sofie Frost," Grum confirmed.

"That's great," Kazek said, not sounding at all impressed. "How old are you, Winter? Twenty? Twenty-one?"

I frowned. That seemed like the sort of thing he should already know, but I supposed we hadn't really reviewed the basics. "Twenty-one."

"Twenty-one," he repeated. "Wow. You all had two decades to figure out that she was an Omega. I get the whole suppressant thing being an abnormality for you all, but there had to be other signs."

"I didn't know," Enrique pointed out. "And there were situations where I should have noticed."

I flinched at his not-so-subtle way of saying we'd been somewhat intimate.

Kazek growled, stepping forward, but I jumped in front of him. "He never came close to knotting me," I told him, my hands on his shoulders. "Only you, Alpha."

His orbs blazed as he looked down at me. "And what about Grum?"

"I eased her transition in preparation for her wedding night. It was more medical than anything and was nothing like the show you just put on in the bathroom," Grum replied, the sound of his chair sliding over wood echoing around his words.

I winced at the way he described our experience. He wasn't wrong in his depiction, but I didn't enjoy hearing the summary out loud.

"If you wish to discipline me for something that happened before you claimed her, Alpha, then that's your choice," Grum continued, the sound of his boots reverberating behind me. "But remember that you would be disabling one of Snow's protectors in the process. And trust me when I say you could both use loyal support right about now."

"Loyal support," Kazek scoffed. "She nearly died the night she landed in Norse Sector because her estrus kicked in with suppressants still soiling her veins. My claim saved her life. What did you do?"

"I helped raise her, taught her how to defend herself, and protected her to the best of my abilities, all under the queen's nose. I know the palace inside and out, understand the motivations of the wolves, and most importantly, I maintain all the weapons vaults. Even the ones Queen Vanessa doesn't know about."

Kazek took his measure once more. "You're telling me why you're useful to me."

"Yes," Grum confirmed, always matter of fact and to the point.

"Elaborate," Kazek demanded. "Convince me to let you live for touching what's mine."

I curled myself into Kazek's chest, trying to plead with him through touch, and sensed Grum coming to stand right behind me. He might be a Beta wolf, but he had the heart of an Alpha. He would face his punishment head-on, even if he didn't agree with the purpose for it.

"Kazek," I whispered, a soft plea in my voice. *He's my brother. Please don't kill him*, I wanted to say. But I knew better than to interfere too severely. Alphas were possessive creatures. Grum had touched me. Just that knowledge was enough to drive Kazek to commit murder, similar to how I'd reacted to Alana's presence in Ludvig's office.

"Shh, little one," Kazek replied. "I want to hear your *protector* defend himself."

Grum's calm energy warmed me from behind, suggesting he held a casual stance. He rarely let threats faze him, even from a lethal assassin. If it were Doc, he'd go toe to toe and argue. But with Kazek, he seemed to be evaluating his place and choosing his words.

Always so wise, my Grum, I thought.

"You need me, Alpha," he said bluntly. "So beat me if you have to, but remember my value, particularly to Snow. The seven made a mistake on the suppressants. However, that doesn't erase two decades of constantly saving her life. There have been other plots against her. We've thwarted all of them without anyone knowing, including Snow."

I blinked at that. "What?" I tried to look at him, but Kazek's arms wrapped around my shoulders, keeping me pressed against his chest.

"What threats?" Kazek asked.

Grum began to list each one as if he read the incidents straight from some confidential document that existed only in his brain. My mind reeled with questions as he spoke.

Someone tried to drown me when I was five?
That's why I fell off that ledge as a teenager?
When did I sleep for a week? Why can't I remember that?

The others were all threats that had never reached me, such as a basket full of poisonous apples—my favorite fruit.

"How many people have tried to kill me?" I asked breathlessly at the end, shocked.

"Several," Grum replied. "Mostly rogue wolves from outside the kingdom, and unfortunately, only two were left alive to speak. They referred to the benefactor as the *Old Witch*. They'd never met the person, just accepted the bounty offered."

"Did you track the bounties?" Kazek asked.

"We tried, but they continued to disappear without a trace. Which indicates there is more than one party involved in the assassination attempts."

"That's what she meant," Enrique interjected, his tone dark and deep. "Vanessa once referred to Snow as a 'problem she'd been trying to fix for years without much progress.' She then spent thirty minutes praising me for being the right Alpha for the job, saying she should have known a fellow Alpha of standing would be the correct route, not poorly fed mutts. I had no idea what she was talking about. Now I know."

I shivered, the conversation surreal. Knowing Vanessa conspired to have me killed by Enrique's hand had hurt and pissed me off. Realizing he wasn't the first person she hired to take me out, however, wasn't just infuriating but also alarming.

"Why didn't you tell me?" I asked, cutting off whatever was being said around me. I faced Grum so he would understand the question was meant for him. Kazek allowed it but wrapped his arms around me in a clearly possessive manner. "Why did you keep me in the dark?"

"To protect you," he replied. "Without evidence, we couldn't implicate Vanessa, and Doc worried you might go to her by accident. So we taught you how to fight and defend yourself instead. It's why we trained you as hard as we did."

"Oh." That made sense. It wasn't until the last year or so

that I really started to feel uneasy around Vanessa. As a child, I often looked to her as a maternal figure and always sought to please her despite it seeming to be impossible.

"What happened to the two that were left alive?" Kazek asked, shifting the conversation back to the list of attempted claims on my life.

Grum met Kazek's gaze over my shoulder, his silver-blue eyes glimmering with satisfaction. "They're living in a hole, half-starved. Doc thought we might need them at some point for a future trial." Grum lifted one shoulder. "He's a logical sort. Likes to plan long-term."

"Where the hell are you keeping them?" Enrique asked.

"In a safe location that the Queen of Mirrors will never visit," Grum replied vaguely.

Kazek remained silent behind me for a long moment, but I felt the approval radiating off him as his muscles relaxed. "You're right. You're very useful to me, Beta."

"I thought you might see it that way," Grum replied.

"Mmm," Kazek hummed in agreement. "But if you ever touch my mate again in any way other than to save her life, I'll flay you alive and force you to eat your own balls. Understood?"

Grum gazed at me and tilted his head to the side. "My oath is to Snow Frost. If that's her wish, then I can agree."

"Hugs are allowed." I glanced back over my shoulder at my mate. "He's like a brother to me."

"A brother who has been inside you," Kazek retorted with a low growl in his throat.

"I tolerated Alpha Alana." *Barely.* "You'll tolerate Beta Grum."

He studied me, his dark irises glowing with a convoluted mixture of annoyance and pride. But eventually, he dipped his chin in acceptance. "All right, Omega. Brief hugs are allowed."

My lips curled at his negotiated terms. "Okay."

"Okay," Kazek repeated, pressing a kiss to my temple, our deal struck.

I turned around to find everyone gaping at us.

Well, everyone except Mila and Ludvig. They both wore

matching expressions of approval. Alphas rarely conceded to their Omegas, especially not in public, but we'd already established that almost everyone in this room was family in some way.

"You'll do," Grum said, a hint of respect in his voice as he addressed Kazek.

My mate cocked a brow. "Was there ever any question?"

"Yes. About a thousand of them," Grum replied, then turned to take his seat again. "Now, are we going to talk about taking down the Queen of Mirrors or continue to posture? Because I'm fucking tired of bowing to that bitch."

My lips parted in shock at his bold statement. He only spoke like that around the other seven. To address Kazek that way indicated my mate had won his favor. Warmth blossomed inside me at the thought. I liked that he accepted Kazek as mine. It meant he respected my decision. Not that I'd had much of a choice, but that was neither here nor there.

Queen Vanessa had put me in a difficult position.

She was to blame for my lack of a choice, not Kazek.

My mate grunted, but a flicker of a smile played over his lips. "Don't worry, Beta. You'll be bowing to me and Winter very soon."

Grum conceded with a nod. "Then I imagine you have a plan."

"Actually, I do," Kazek replied, his focus falling to Enrique. "And it all starts with you."

CHAPTER THIRTY-ONE

WINTER

MY STOMACH PROTESTED as the plane descended. "I'll never get used to this sensation," I breathed, my knuckles turning white from clutching the armrests so tightly.

Kazek laid his palm over my hand, his thumb stroking my wrist as he stared out the window. "We won't fly often," he murmured. "I promise."

"Good." Because this sucked and I never wanted to experience it again.

I closed my eyes, inhaled through my nose, and exhaled slowly through my mouth. It was the only thing that seemed to calm my rioting insides.

A jolt rocked my body as the wheels touched the ground, the uneven surface below us rumbling with the speed of our landing. We'd chosen a location about sixty miles outside of Winter Sector, not wanting to appear on any radars or be heard approaching.

According to Grum's last message, he'd disabled the aerial surveillance scanners about an hour ago. It'd been his primary objective upon returning to Winter Sector. Meanwhile, Enrique's task was to distract Queen Vanessa with the news of my death. As he hadn't provided an update yet, we were left with no choice but to assume he was busy doing his job.

Kazek rolled his neck beside me, his energy humming around me in a heady wave of Alpha and dominance. He'd never once suggested I stay behind at Norse Sector, his plan of attack always involving me. I'd thanked him properly for that last night but had the urge to do so again right now. His presence was intoxicating, especially when he radiated control. And it was practically vibrating from him now as he assessed our surroundings through the windows.

"I can smell your interest," he mused, his hand still on mine and squeezing gently. "We'll revisit it once I've worked off some of this aggression." He released me, unbuckled himself, and stood. "The vibrations of our landing disturbed the Infected. There are at least three nests in the distance on my side."

"I see two on mine," Alana replied as she ruffled through a bag on the floor. Like me, she wore black pants, black boots, and a black sweater.

Kazek was adorned in similar attire, except he also sported a pair of leather gloves.

He grabbed a case from the overhead compartment and dropped it at my feet as I released my seat belt. "Pick a weapon, princess. It's time for you to show me what you can do."

"Is there a bow in here?" I wondered out loud as I tugged on the zipper. My lips curled in delight at finding one right on top, with a quiver full of arrows resting beside it. I stared up at my mate adoringly. "Thank you."

He winked. "I want to see why they call you Winter's Arrow. I hope you're ready."

Aside from my stomach still acclimating to our landing, I felt prepared enough. I slid the quiver over my shoulder and paused at the perfect fit. My eyebrow inched upward as I met

Kazek's knowing gaze.

He leaned down to brush his lips against my ear. "Consider it a gift," he whispered, then kissed my cheek. "Now let's go test your aim."

Mick snorted as he entered the main cabin from the cockpit. "Are you going to toss her into a nest if she fails to meet your standards, Kaz? Because that was a fun weekend." His light blue irises flicked to me. "He's a shitty teacher, by the way."

"You threw him into a nest?" I asked, shocked.

Kazek lifted a shoulder. "He needed more practice."

"Yeah, because I missed one kill opportunity," Mick drawled. "Dick."

"You've never missed any since, have you?" Kazek countered, giving him a look. When Mick didn't reply, my mate grinned. "Yeah, that's what I thought."

"Are you two going to flirt all night or get down to business?" Alana held a massive machine gun in one hand and a pistol in the other. "Or shall I let you two fuck it out while I go handle the Infected outside?"

Mick grunted. "Yeah, whatever. I didn't fly you all here just to sit on this damn plane. Let's go put these assholes out of their misery."

"There's a toast I can agree to," Kazek said, twirling a knife before settling it into his belt. He had a gun on each side as well and bent to retrieve a third for his hand. "Let's go start the party." He glanced my way. "You're with me, Winter."

"Forever," I replied automatically, earning me a grin from my mate.

"Forever," he agreed, dragging me in for a kiss. "I can't wait to see you use that bow, baby." He nibbled my lower lip and released me. "Aim for their necks to sever the heads. Then we'll take care of the brain stem with a bullet."

"I know how to kill an Infected, Kazek," I told him. "A well-placed arrow through the mouth does the trick."

He seemed impressed with the knowledge. "You've hunted Infected before?"

"How do you think I perfected my aim?" I countered. Grum and the twins had often taken me into the woods for target practice. The Infected couldn't pass the zombie virus onto X-Clan wolves, but they could still bite and feed off our flesh, which made them a nuisance that required frequent eradication. They were drawn to our body heat, traveling night and day up to our sector for a potential snack.

I used to feel bad about killing them, but there was no cure. So, really, putting them down was a mercy. Their humanity died when they changed into mindless flesh-eaters.

Kazek grinned. "All right, Winter's Arrow. Paint the snow red."

"Now you're talking," Alana said, unlatching the door. "I'll take north."

"I've got south," Mick informed us.

"Since there's just water to the west, we'll take the east," Kazek replied, letting Mick and Alana leave first. "Find a perch and do your thing, Winter."

I nodded and followed him outside into the bitter cold. It bit into my skin through the sweater and pants, but my adrenaline moved me forward.

Tromsø used to be a cultural hub.

Now it resembled a dead zone.

The inhabitants were all Infected, as the humans who survived the initial purge had fled to die in the mountains. It all occurred before my time, but the seven had told me stories about what happened.

This entire region had been wiped out.

The closest known human sector was midway between here and Oslo.

Which was why the Infected came for Winter Sector instead. They were desperate to eat. Fortunately, that made them slower and easier to pick off.

Kazek crouched low, his focus on the moving mass before us. He'd fallen into predator mode. I could see it in the lethal lines of his body and the precision of his steps. He lifted his arm and fired three shots in sequence, taking down the first row of Infected. "Stop watching me and get to work," he demanded while releasing two more bullets. "Now, Winter."

Mmm, I enjoyed my bossy mate. Particularly like this.

However, I had something to prove to him.

He hadn't admitted it out loud, but this entire landing exercise was meant as a test. We could have put the plane down in an empty field upstream, yet he'd chosen the airfield on the edge of the city instead, knowing it would draw out the Infected.

And he'd done it because he wanted to make sure I could handle myself before we snuck into Winter Sector.

Why else would he bring a bow for me?

All right, Alpha, I thought, readying my bow. He'd mentioned a perch. I didn't need one. Close-range shooting was a specialty of mine.

I released an arrow on an exhale, nailing an Infected approaching from the side. Then I sent a second one into his buddy. Both were precise shots through the mouth, severing the brain stem in one go.

It'd taken me years to perfect that aim. Now, the motion came naturally. I rolled around, catching the glimmer of the moon and searching for those notorious glowing red eyes in the dark.

That was what made hunting Infected easy—wolf eyes shined yellow in the moonlight. That included shifters in human form. Always yellow.

The Infected, however, gleamed red.

I released a series of arrows into the dark, each one nailing my target.

Living in the Arctic Circle forced me to learn how to hunt in the night hours, particularly during the colder months.

I used it to my advantage now, falling into a rhythm as I took down Infected after Infected. Kazek was right on my heels, his gun loud and annoying to my wolf's ears. But I forced myself to ignore him and the sounds ricocheting around me and homed in on the enemy.

An Infected had bitten me once.

It wasn't a pleasant experience, and it'd left a nasty bruise on my leg that took forever to heal, even with my shifter genetics at play.

Never again.

Minutes passed.

Infected died.

Howls and screams on the wind were the music of the night, the crisp white snow discolored by morbid remains. I was vaguely aware of Mick and Alana crushing skulls to finish the job in their quadrants, my eyes searching the area for more targets.

But between the four of us, we'd successfully taken down the nests surrounding the airfield. There'd be more in the city. Although, we wouldn't be staying long enough to take them down.

Kazek had brought additional transport in the cargo hold of the plane.

Which was how I knew this had all been a test, because we could have gotten into that vehicle and plowed through the Infected. Yet he'd wanted to fight them.

I faced him with my bow at my side and arched a brow. "So. Did I pass, Alpha?"

His lips curled. "Oh, yeah. You passed." He wrapped his palm around the back of my neck and yanked me to him, his tongue demanding against mine. I clutched his sweater with my free hand, holding on for dear life as he devoured me in the sea of violence surrounding us.

My heart thudded wildly, my adrenaline fueling me forward and exciting me even more. I pressed into him, eager for his touch, his adoration, his everything. And he gave it to me with his mouth.

"You're beautiful, my little warrior princess," he whispered. "I'm very impressed."

"I don't need to worry about being dropped in a nest?" I asked, referring to Mick's comment earlier.

Kazek smirked. "No. You just have to worry about Winter Sector now."

Yes. And the wicked queen on my throne. "I want to put an arrow through her head."

"Good," he replied, brushing another kiss against my lips. "Then let's go refill your quiver."

"Why does that sound like a euphemism for sex?" I wondered out loud as he led me back to the plane.

"Because you're addicted to my knot, Omega."

I nodded solemnly. "It's true, Alpha. I am."

He laughed and slapped me on the ass. "Stop trying to seduce me. We have work to do."

"It's not my fault you're addicted to me," I tossed back at him, purposely reusing his term.

His gaze ran over me in a heated wave of molten arousal. "I beg to differ, Winter."

My cheeks warmed at the hungry way he looked at me. Then he tapped me on the rump again and sent me up the stairs to where Mick and Alana were waiting.

"I'm phoning in an update to Ludvig," Mick informed us. "Have you heard from Enrique yet?"

"No," Kazek replied, his palm on my lower back as he guided me toward the weapon bags. "But I don't anticipate he'll have what we need for at least another hour or so. If we don't hear anything by twenty-three hundred, I'll be concerned."

Enrique had the hardest task of all of us—convincing Vanessa I was dead. Kazek had offered him the role as a way of turning over a new leaf. If Enrique succeeded, my mate would let him live. If the Alpha failed, well, his fate remained to be seen.

Given how angry Enrique had been at Vanessa for trying to use him as a pawn, I expected him to follow through with the task. But there was more to it than just persuading her to believe he'd killed me. And that was the part I worried about.

"I'll let Ludvig know." Mick brought up a screen above his wrist and headed toward the cargo section of the plane. "Be ready to move in five."

Kazek smirked at his back. "Yes, Alpha."

Mick flipped him off and disappeared into the back.

"Man, that Omega is riding him hard," Alana muttered.

"Or he wishes she was," Kazek replied as he started going through the supply bags. "Sending her to Andorra Sector makes sense. Ander's researchers will take care of her."

"They're not the ones who turned you, right?" I asked, thinking of his story about how he became a wolf. The *researcher* had used Ludvig's blood to experiment on Kazek to "heal" him, and it'd caused my mate to shift into a wolf as a result. It was why Kazek considered Ludvig his creator.

That'd freaked me out a little when I learned Ludvig was my uncle. I'd asked if that made Kazek and me cousins, but then Ludvig had explained his true relation to my mother. He wasn't a brother by blood; rather, his parents had taken her in as their own after she was orphaned during the revolution years.

It'd been a secret because most wolves didn't take in strays, and that was what my mother would have been considered even with her Omega traits. She would have been auctioned off to an Alpha for her upbringing and an eventual mating.

Ludvig's mother couldn't bear the thought of that happening to an innocent girl, so they kept her hidden. At least until my father sniffed her out. And then they mated.

It was nice to have insight into how my parents met. Given everything I knew about them, it'd been a happy union, and Ludvig had confirmed it with his story.

Kazek snorted. "No. I killed the bastard who turned me into his own little experiment. Then I took out the rest of his associates for good measure."

"I remember that." Alana sounded amused. "Ludvig was torn between killing you and turning you into his personal enforcer."

"I think he's still torn on that decision most days," Kazek admitted as he filled my quiver with more arrows.

"Then it's a good thing you're about to become the Alpha of Winter Sector." Alana glanced at me as she said it, her expression radiating approval. As much as I wanted to hate the female, she was sort of growing on me. *Sort of* being the operative words there.

"You planning to take up my job as Second?" Kazek asked her.

"Maybe." She considered us both. "Or maybe I'll stick around Winter Sector for a bit, help you both get settled."

Kazek straightened. "You want to be my Second?"

Alana lifted a shoulder. "If the job is open, maybe."

Kazek stared at her, then glanced at me. "We'll have to discuss it."

I adored my mate a little more in that moment. Rather than make the decision as the Alpha, he agreed to let me provide input. Perhaps it was because of his history with Alana. Regardless, I appreciated the token of respect and kissed his cheek to show my gratitude for the gesture.

"Of course," Alana agreed, her blue eyes glittering with approval. "I'm not ready to accept yet anyway. We need to take down a certain Alpha bitch first."

Yes, I thought. *One step at a time.*

"We need to get to the rendezvous point," I murmured. Grum had promised to send one of my seven to meet us.

I really hoped it wasn't one of the twins.

They'd hate Kazek on sight.

CHAPTER THIRTY-TWO

KAZEK

"YOU'RE PACING," I murmured, watching Winter walk back and forth along the tree line. Her antsy behavior had started when we arrived at the meeting point, her short legs eating up the snow-laden earth with admirable agility.

"They should be here by now," she replied. "Something's wrong."

"We're early," I reminded her softly. "It's fine."

She shook her head. "No. I can feel it. Something isn't right."

I pushed away from the car and stepped into her path. "Winter." I cupped her cheek and forced her to look at me. "What are your instincts saying?"

"That we need to go to Winter Sector," she whispered. "Right now."

I nodded. "Then we'll go."

"What?" She seemed startled. "Just like that?"

"Just like that," I replied. "I've been doing this a long time, sweetheart. If your gut is telling us to move, then we need to move."

She swallowed and slowly nodded. "Yes. I don't know why or how, I just… We can't wait until dawn."

"Okay." I whistled for Alana and Mick to return to the vehicle from their perimeter sweep.

They jogged out in wolf form, one big and black like me, the other a brown-and-white one that rivaled me in size. I focused on the latter—Mick.

"Winter says something's not right, so we're going to move in early," I told him. "Do you want to run ahead and scout?"

He snorted in affirmation and took off into the woods.

"I need you in sniper form," I told Alana. She was wicked with a gun but even better at long range.

She responded by walking to the back of the four-by-four and beginning her shift back into human form.

"Plan B it is," I mused, checking my weapons.

"I'm sorry. It's just—"

"I don't need an elaboration, Winter. I trust you." I pulled her in and kissed her forehead. "The Special Forces taught me to always have a backup plan. That's why we have several. So we'll move on to plan B and reevaluate once we get closer. Okay?"

She nodded again, her dark irises flaring with relief.

I understood. Trust took time.

We were still getting to know one another, discovering our boundaries and learning how the other person operated, but I had no doubt in my mind that this female was made for me. Particularly after her display with the bow. Winter had moved with the grace and precision of a well-trained recruit. I'd thoroughly enjoy continuing her education in the lethal arts after all this was through.

"Ready," Alana announced, her black pants and matching sweater in place. There were at least a dozen weapons hidden throughout her outfit, all in secret pockets that she favored for sharp objects. I'd learned all about that the first time we ever sparred. The bitch had stabbed me twice before I'd taken over the fight and subdued her.

She really would make an excellent Second.

But only if Winter was comfortable with it. Given how I felt about her keeping Grum on as a guard, I wouldn't be surprised if she told me to fuck off with the request. However, maybe we could work something out.

"All right," I said, taking stock of our weapons. "They're going to smell us approaching, so we need to go in fast and hard. Take down the sentries Grum mentioned and go in through the clearing like we originally planned. If the queen—"

A foreign scent in the night had my focus shifting to the east.

Intruder.

The hairs along my arms stood on end at the unknown threat, my nostrils flaring to identify the wolf type.

Beta.

"Wait," Winter said, her palm against my abdomen as she looked toward the forest.

I shared a glance with Alana before focusing on my mate, my breath stilling in my chest at the intensity in her features. She seemed to be aware of something I couldn't sense. This was her territory—her home—so I'd yield to an extent and *wait*, as she requested.

My wolf paced inside, eager to protect, vigilant of every angle within my vision. I knew Alana had my back. However, my instincts flared red. I didn't appreciate the secretive approach.

Which was why I growled when I sensed movement nearby. *Too close to my female,* my wolf raged. I couldn't see the intruder, but I *felt* his presence. "Show yourself," I demanded.

"It's okay." Winter stepped closer to me as if to hold me back. "It's one of my seven."

A pale wolf jumped down from a fucking tree to land not ten feet in front of us. Alana cursed in surprise while my eyebrows shot upward.

"How the hell did you do that?" I demanded.

I'd scoured the woods for any and all signs of approach,

and I didn't sense this guy until a few seconds before he pounced. I hadn't even thought to check the fucking tree branches.

He was like a damn cat.

The wolf sniffed the air, his head tilting to the side as he examined Winter. She crouched before him, causing my animal to rise to the surface. "Winter…"

"It's Opy," she murmured, reaching out to scratch the massive Beta behind the ears. "He's a perimeter scout and one of my protectors." He headbutted her hand and glowered up at me, his disapproval evident.

"Careful," I growled at him, locking gazes. "That's my mate you're rubbing all over, Beta." I wrapped a possessive arm around her, pulling her back against me. "*Mine.*"

The Beta smartly looked away.

"Good boy," I said, unable to help the derogatory nickname.

Alana snorted.

And Opy—what kind of name was that, anyway?—shifted into his hulking human form. He was almost as tall as me, and broad-shouldered, too. What the hell did they feed the Betas in this sector?

"We don't have time for posturing, Alpha," Opy said by way of greeting. "The queen has called for an emergency ceremony. She's assembling everyone in the sector right now."

"That must be the urgency I feel," Winter whispered. "She's radiating displeasure."

Opy dipped his chin in confirmation. "Leep sent me because I'm the fastest, but he's waiting at the city's perimeter with clothes for you to change into. We're hoping it'll help mask your scent enough to allow you to get close without detection."

That jelled with the original plan. "Is she calling everyone into the main hall?" I asked.

The Beta met my gaze. "Yes."

I nodded. "All right." I picked up the weapon bags and handed Winter her bow and quiver. "It's earlier than we anticipated, but we can roll with this. Lead the way, Beta."

He replied by returning to his wolf form and trotting off on silent paws.

I shared another glance with Alana. She seemed as impressed as I did by the male protector. His agility and grace were at odds with his size, and the way he glanced back at Winter to check on her while we walked told me he took her safety seriously. Good. Anyone who put my mate's life first was an asset I wouldn't ignore.

We met two more of those *assets* at the border in the form of identical twins with shaggy brown hair and gray eyes. Winter seemed able to tell them apart, perhaps because of their varying attire, but I couldn't say, because they appeared the same to me. Both lankier, tall, definitely Betas, and reeking of fish.

"Here you go, Snow," one of them murmured, handing her a pair of black jeans and a matching turtleneck.

"Thanks, Ez," she replied.

The other twin was called Leep. Seemed a fitting match to Opy, I supposed.

Alana appeared as amused by their names as I did but refrained from commenting.

The three of us changed into the foul-smelling dark clothes, my nose curling in protest. "You must have been responsible for the outfit Winter wore on the plane," I muttered.

"Worked, didn't it?" That came from Leep.

"Yeah. It did," I admitted. "But only because I thought Winter's scent was in my head, not real."

She glanced at me. "What?"

"Yeah, I thought you were a fantasy," I told her. "I started to hunt you down that night before all the drama with Omega Kari. So I thought your scent had followed me home as a taunt."

Her dark gaze glittered from the moonlight sprinkling in through the fir trees. "You tried to follow me?"

I wrapped an arm around her waist, pulling her closer and ignoring the stench engulfing us both. "Are you telling me all that disrespectful banter earlier in the evening wasn't actually flirting? Because I certainly took it as an invitation to play with you."

"You were going to punish me."

"I was going to fuck your disobedient mouth, yes." I pressed my lips to her ear. "I think we both know how much you would have enjoyed it, baby."

She shivered against me, and the twins cleared their throats in unison.

My eyes slid sideways to find them scowling at me. Not the looks of jealous men so much as brothers angry at the treatment of their little sister. I'd allow the annoyance, but I sure as shit wouldn't apologize for it.

"Yeah, I've wanted to kill him before, too. But I don't recommend trying." Mick sauntered up to us, naked from his shift, and grabbed the remaining clothes. "Kazek'll own you in seconds, then toss you into a zombie nest just to watch you fight your way home. He's a real prick like that."

"You're never going to get over Stockholm, are you?" I asked him.

Mick grunted as he pulled on a pair of dark pants. "Actually, I was talking about Copenhagen, but thanks for the reminder." He looked at the twins. "As I said, he's a prick."

As it was true, I didn't feel the need to correct him and instead focused on my mate. I cupped her cheek and studied her facial features. "Are you ready?"

"Yes." She didn't hesitate, not even a blink. "I want my throne ba—"

The shuffling of feet cut her off. I drew my gun, as did Alana and Mick. However, the others merely watched the tree line, clearly recognizing the scent.

Another Beta with olive skin and black hair parted the trees with several quick strides, his expression telling me we had a problem before he started to speak.

"What is it, Happa?" one of the twins asked, clearly sensing the unease, just like the rest of us.

The newcomer paused to catch his breath, his forehead dotted with sweat. "It's Doc," he announced on an exhale.

"What about him?" Opy demanded. He'd changed back into human form and had donned a pair of jeans but nothing else.

"Vanessa has Doc," Happa said. "And she's planning to execute him before the sector for failing to protect Snow."

Winter went rigid. "*What?*"

The four Betas shared a grim look before Opy said, "She's had him in custody since the night of your disappearance. She blames him for losing track of you. We have no idea what state he's in."

"Why didn't Grum tell me?" she demanded, my fierce little warrior on full display.

They all glanced at each other again, then Leep cleared his throat. "I can't speak for him, but I'm guessing he felt you had a lot going on with your, uh, new arrangements and all that."

I snorted. "She's handling her 'new arrangements' just fine."

"He should have told me." Winter didn't sound whiny so much as pissed, and damn if that didn't intrigue my wolf a little. "Have you heard from Enrique?" she asked me.

I shook my head. "Not yet." And at this point, I suspected we wouldn't be hearing from him at all.

The fucker better not have let us down. That sob story he told us about his brother had convinced me to put faith in him, but only a little. Alphas were dominant creatures. At the end of the day, we all looked out for our own best interests.

And Enrique's sole interest was himself.

"Then we just need to hope he got what we needed. I won't let Doc be punished for something that isn't true." Her tone and expression dared me to argue with her.

Instead, I cupped her cheek and pressed my forehead to hers. "I'm with you, Winter. But remember what we talked about. I need to be the one to challenge Vanessa." It was part of the Alpha hierarchy and the way things were done in our world.

Winter's bloodline declared her Queen of Winter Sector, and I was now the rightful king as her mate. That made it my duty to take down the Alpha female standing in the way of my throne. As strong as Winter might be, she couldn't take Vanessa down. I had to do it.

She laid her palm over my hand. "I know."

"We'll still try to take her down your way, but you need to

let me drive this," I pressed. "All right?"

I was putting a lot of faith in her to cooperate here. She couldn't allow her emotions to drive her. We had to work together as a team, which required her to trust my leadership.

Essentially, we were even on the responsibility score—I needed to be able to rely on her to keep it together, and she needed to have confidence in my ability to dethrone Vanessa like we'd planned.

Her obsidian irises gleamed as she nodded, giving me the reassurance we both desired. "Okay."

"Good." I kissed her softly and pulled back. "Then let's go."

CHAPTER THIRTY-THREE

KAZEK

THE TENSION IN THE ROOM irritated my wolf. Everyone had assembled in the entertainment hall of the palace, their focus on the throne at the front of the room. There was only one this time, unlike the three that'd been up there the night of the engagement party.

That alone made a statement and had the crowd whispering rumors throughout the room.

I stood in the back, taking advantage of the shadows, with Opy beside me.

Winter had agreed to stay back, just outside the room, to await my signal.

We had several plans to accommodate the myriad of possible routes this could go, but none of them had factored in a potential execution. I'd be exchanging words with Grum later about him not giving us a heads-up on Doc's incarceration. That was an item we needed to be aware of prior to arriving. But I'd improvise to appease Winter.

A few Betas glanced toward the shadows where I lurked, their noses curling at the foul stench permeating the air. Opy had put on a sweatshirt of similar origin, adding to the aroma and further masking my Alpha scent. The other members of Winter's seven had done the same, their goal to ensure her Omega perfume couldn't be sensed by anyone on the palace grounds.

It had worked.

We'd wandered through the trees and onto the partially paved paths of Winter Sector, her hat and scarf covering most of her features. Mick, Alana, and I had worn similar accessories, while the members of Winter's seven allowed their identities to be known to help cover any conspicuousness about our group. To the average observer, we just appeared bundled for the chilly weather on our way to a meeting.

Time continued to tick by, causing my jaw to tick along with it.

I suspected this was all part of Vanessa's show, as she liked to draw out the moment and prolong the anticipation. Yet a twinge of unease pricked at the back of my mind.

Rash actions weren't the way to go. We needed Vanessa to incriminate herself in front of the sector. It was the only method that would ensure her downfall.

And yet, that tickle of suspicion nagged at me.

I checked my watch subtly, searching for any updates from Enrique or Grum.

Nothing.

I shook my head. "Something's off," I muttered, glancing around the crowd, searching for the source of my agitation. As I told Winter earlier, I trusted my gut. It was how I'd stayed alive for so long.

"She always does this" was Opy's gruff reply.

I nodded because I already suspected that. But that didn't explain the churning in my abdomen.

"Can you distract the guards?" I asked, gesturing to Tweedledee and Tweedledum by the door we'd entered through moments ago. "I need to make a quick call." My technology would be immediately noticeable, as the wolves in this sector didn't possess gadgets like the one on my wrist.

Ludvig had provided a set to Grum and Enrique, which they were supposed to use for communication. Clearly, that hadn't gone as planned.

What if Vanessa found them? I wondered. I'd trusted Enrique's and Grum's abilities to hide the devices, but maybe she'd outsmarted them.

If that was the case, we had a serious problem.

Opy rolled his neck and sauntered off without a word.

Apparently, that was his way of accepting my mission.

Because he walked right up to one of the guards and punched him in the face.

Chaos ensued with his unexpected attack, wolves all turning their focus to the now raging Beta guard as he demanded Opy explain himself. It seemed his communication skills were nonexistent all around, because he just punched the guy again.

If I wasn't concerned about Vanessa's antics, I would have been deeply amused.

Instead, I focused on my watch, brought up a screen, and quickly selected Mick's comm. He buzzed to life in my ear, the pieces all having been inserted before we left Norse Sector.

"You feel it?" he asked by way of greeting.

"Yeah. Budapest?" I asked softly, referring to a training exercise we'd completed a few years ago that nearly killed us both.

"Yeah. Total trap," he agreed. Which was exactly how that mission went down. We'd landed in the center of a massive Infected nest without realizing it, all because we'd followed a stray Ash Wolf without considering every potential outcome.

Fucking stupid decision, that was.

Definitely not making a similar one tonight.

"Winter okay?" I asked. Mick and Alana were guarding her in a secret corridor that bordered the entertainment hall's walls. Leep and Ez were with them as well. Happa had run off to hunt down Grum and the final member of the seven.

"No," Mick muttered, replying to my inquiry about my mate. "She feels it, too."

She didn't have a watch, because we didn't have one on hand that was small enough for her wrist. I also wanted to have one programmed to her DNA so it shifted with her wolf, like mine did. The ones I gave to Grum and Enrique were old technology—their functions similar to the cell phones from my youth, just in watch form.

I palmed the back of my neck and glanced at Opy's distraction by the doorway. He'd taken on both guards now, and his grin said he was enjoying the task of kicking their asses.

Maybe the wolf would grow on me after all.

"I don't like this," Mick continued in my ear. "We should have heard from Enrique by now."

I agreed. Even just a short message to indicate his success. That we hadn't received anything told me—

A sharp snap crackled through the line, causing me to wince. "Mick?"

Silence.

"Shit," I cursed and started toward the door.

Only to freeze as Vanessa entered with a flourish. She grabbed Opy by the scruff of his neck, dragging him through the makeshift aisle created by the crowd.

Enrique walked behind her, his hand holding the lead of a metal chain that connected to a bald Beta's neck. The Alpha didn't look my way, his focus on the queen ahead of him.

It all happened in a blur of motion, the hairs along my arms standing on end.

Silence fell across the crowd, their fear a drug for my wolf. I wanted them to submit, to see me as their leader and Alpha, but their focus was on the bitch ascending the steps to her throne.

Wrong, I thought. *My throne.*

However, I remained quiet, watchful, wondering what she would do next.

She'd done something to interfere with the radio signals. That was the only explanation for Mick being cut off mid-conversation. She'd entered too soon afterward to indicate any foul play, and the bond confirmed that my mate was fine.

Which left me to focus on the infamous Queen of Mirrors.

She took her seat with a flourish, her claws digging into Opy's nape as she forced him to kneel between her legs.

My jaw ticked at the degrading position.

"You dare attack my guards?" she growled, blood trickling from the wound her nails created against his skin. "And *what* is that foul smell?"

"I came straight from my perimeter sweep, my queen."

"And you swam through the muck on your way here?" She sounded disgusted. I couldn't blame her on that front. The stench was atrocious, but it worked to hide our presence.

"I ran along the coastline and made a misstep," he explained.

She snarled at that response and shoved him away from her. "Worthless mutt. Stay there until I'm ready to deal with you."

"Yes, my queen," he replied, taking a position of submission on the floor.

The shock from the audience indicated this wasn't her usual approach, perhaps because she'd been on her best behavior for two decades while raising their princess. It seemed they were about to see the real Alpha Vanessa, now that she thought her reign was infallible.

Maybe Enrique did his job after all. He seemed as stoic as ever, standing a few feet to her right with the Beta on his knees beside him. Nothing about his stance gave him away, and his expression exuded a boredom I admired.

I really hope you came through, I thought at him. Not that he could hear me. Probably for the best because the brutal image that followed my mental comment would have likely made him blanch. But that would become his fate if he betrayed us. As it was, the bastard was lucky to be alive.

"Now," Vanessa said, her bloodied nails drumming a repetitive pattern against the arm of her throne. "I've brought you all here for several reasons. The first is to inform you that Princess Snow Frost is dead."

Well, she didn't waste any time getting to the point. Nor did she bother to soften that blow for her constituents.

Gasps went through the crowd, a general aura of dismay covering the wolves of Winter Sector. Vanessa allowed them their moment, her expression one of false sympathy. I caught the slight twist to her lips, revealing the smirk that lay beneath her mask of empathy. The Betas were too caught up in their distress to notice.

She eventually told them to quiet, her hand waving through the air in a motion that required their focus. "Yes. I'm as distraught as the rest of you, truly. But I have found the culprits responsible for her demise, which is the purpose of tonight's emergency congregation."

Culprits? I repeated to myself, frowning. *What game are you playing now, wicked queen?*

"Video footage from the airfield reveals that seven of our own forced Snow Frost to leave on a jet for Norse Sector, which is where she was later killed by Alpha Kazek for trespassing without permission. I intend to hold the seven individuals responsible for their duplicitous behavior, then seek charges against Alpha Kazek for wrongful cause of death."

I almost snorted at her clever ploy. Enrique was supposed to take the blame for killing Winter to win favor with the queen, but it seemed he'd contrived a different story. I'd allow it, assuming it worked in our favor. He knew Vanessa better than I did, so perhaps he'd read the situation differently.

Hmm, we'd see if his version achieved the same outcome.

For his sake, I hoped it would. Or he'd be meeting the end of one of my daggers. Repeatedly. No quick death for him.

Same with the Alpha bitch sitting on my throne.

"Block the doors," Vanessa snapped at her guards.

I cocked a brow as the Beta minions marched to fulfill her orders, sealing off all the exits. That would be a bit of a problem for the show I planned to put on next, but we'd get to that in a moment. I needed Vanessa to say a few more words first, then I'd hand her a death sentence she could choke on.

The queen surveyed the crowd, her focus missing me entirely as I remained in the shadows at the back of the room. I supposed that was one benefit to using candlelight to illuminate the room. It provided a medieval ambience, one I intended to improve drastically to meet the modern times once I took over. Because unlike Vanessa, I had resources at my disposal to help improve the Winter Sector grounds, starting with installing some fucking electricity.

"Where are you?" Vanessa mused. "I know the identities of all seven. You can't hide from me now. Two of your brothers are on this platform. Where are the other five?"

Winter's seven.

How did the queen find footage of her escape? There were no cameras here, and the security sucked. Was she lying? Had someone talked out of line? I didn't even know who Winter's seven were, so there was no way Enrique told Vanessa.

Maybe someone saw them that night, but why wait a week to come forward with that information?

"Where are your conspirators, Doc? We're missing Ez, Leep, Happa, Grum, and Bash."

Whispers broke out through the room, the names stirring unrest amongst the crowd.

Enrique yanked on the metal chain. "Your queen just asked you a question. Answer her, Beta."

"Fuck you," Doc replied, spitting on the ground.

Vanessa laughed, the sound maniacal and chilling.

I didn't like where this was heading. She'd just outed my mate's protection circle. Perhaps unknowingly, but it didn't feel that way.

Had someone provided her with information? The way Winter spoke about her seven, it sounded as if no one knew except her and the Betas involved. Had one of them betrayed her?

Grum, perhaps?

He hadn't checked in since his initial landing, and he'd withheld Doc's capture from us.

Yet I'd seen the way he looked at Winter, his protective adoration a shield of brotherly affection. Their history infuriated me, but I could accept it. He clearly understood my claim, and from what I'd seen, he'd respected it.

So it wasn't him.

And I doubted it was any of the others I'd met tonight.

Which only left Bash, the final name I'd not been familiar with until Vanessa had uttered it out loud.

I added his name to my potential kill list.

A hiss from the stage drew my focus back to the infuriated queen. She had her silver stiletto heel pressed against Doc's groin while Enrique held him in place with the lead around the Beta's neck. It forced him to kneel before the sadistic bitch as she drove her foot into his manhood.

The audience reacted in gasps of protest and dismay, again suggesting this wasn't their queen's typical performance.

"He needs a trial!" someone shouted. I glanced at the shorter male who'd voiced his opinion, and took in the anger vibrating across his wide shoulders. He could be useful.

"I want to see the video," another voice said, the owner lost to the middle of the room.

"Me, too," a wolf agreed from the opposite side of the entertainment hall.

"This isn't right," a petite female Beta announced from the front lines.

Questions and protests rained through the room, each one increasing my respect for this sector more and more. They clearly valued a form of democracy. I could work with that to an extent.

"Where's the proof?"

"Has he admitted guilt?"

"Why would they send her to Norse Sector?"

"Are we sure she's dead?"

"What evidence is there to support your claim?"

"Why is he in chains?"

"What—"

"Enough!" Vanessa roared, her attention shifted away from Doc and centering on the wolves before her. "*I* am Alpha here. *I* am the law. You will *bow*."

She accompanied her words with an impressive howl that bounced off the stone walls and brought several Betas to their knees in a blink. Those who refused were stared down until they submitted, her growls ferocious and dominating.

Whimpers echoed, a few underlined with curses, and I couldn't help but smile at her little tantrum. "A true leader earns respect from her domain through actions and leading by example. I'm not sure your methodology would be well received by other Sector Alphas."

Vanessa's gaze flew to my position in the shadows. "Show yourself," she demanded.

"Why? So you can attempt to make me kneel?" I tsked as I stepped into the light. "That's not going to happen, sweetheart."

A chorus of confusion swept through the crowd, my name an obscenity on the wind. That would soon change. Or I hoped it would.

"How dare you show your face here after killing our princess," Vanessa seethed, her act right on point. I almost applauded her for the performance. It truly was remarkable.

"Snow Frost?" I asked, tilting my head. "Now that's an interesting accusation."

"Seize him!" she ordered.

"I wouldn't," I replied, cautioning her approaching guards. "It's not her command you answer to, but mine. And I don't take kindly to challenges in my own territory."

The Betas who had stood to act on her behalf paused in confusion.

Well, at least I couldn't fault their intelligence.

"You fools," she hissed. "He's just posturing. Take him down!"

"Why don't you try to take me down instead?" I suggested, waving off her Betas once more. "It's my throne you seem to have claimed as your own, after all. And I'm not particularly fond of what you've done with the place. The decorating is, well, a little dated, don't you think?"

I had my hands in my pockets as I started forward, aware of every wolf in the room and their focus on me.

"The wolf who killed Snow Frost walks among you, and you do nothing?" Vanessa infused so much disapproval and disbelief in her statement that she deserved a fucking standing ovation for her effort. But my palms couldn't be bothered to clap. All I really wanted to do was wrap my fingers around her neck and squeeze.

"Did I kill Snow Frost?" I asked her. "Or did I save her?"

That question seemed to earn me even more attention from the room, which was exactly what I wanted. "Winter?" I called, knowing my voice would carry to her wolf ears behind the wall. "Would you care to provide an opinion on the matter?"

CHAPTER THIRTY-FOUR

WINTER

GRUM NODDED AT ME. "Go. Distract her."

I swallowed and fixed the waist of the dress he'd given me to wear. It wasn't my usual attire for Vanessa's ceremonies but one my mother had worn as queen. He'd shown up about ten minutes ago with it, saying I needed to look the part. And now I did, save the quiver of arrows affixed to my back. That part was new, but he and the others had approved of the enhancement.

Mick handed me my bow. "We'll work on setting up the feed Enrique gave Grum, but it's going to take more time. Your fucking mate jumped the gun."

"He wouldn't have jumped the gun had someone not cut off our feeds unexpectedly," Alana replied, her gaze narrowing at Bash.

The Beta merely lifted a shoulder. "How was I to know he

had comms on? I was trying to ensure that Vanessa couldn't broadcast to the other sectors."

"Well, had you—"

"You're stalling." Vanessa's voice interrupted Alana's reply, the chill in her tone sending ice down my spine even through the stone wall. "I don't know why you're here, Alpha Kazek, but I'm going to enjoy killing you for the intrusion. You've committed three killable offenses. First, you stole an Omega slave who didn't belong to you. Second, you killed our beloved princess. And third, you've arrived uninvited, which is an indication of war and a potential threat to my position as Sector Alpha."

"Wrong on all accounts," Kazek drawled. "First, I won Omega Kari after you offered her as bait to the room. Second, I haven't killed anyone. Third, you're not Sector Alpha. I am."

"Go," Grum repeated, his hand on my lower back providing a nudge down the corridor.

I dipped my chin and started my journey to the exit, which would put me in the massive palace hallway that led to the entertainment hall doors.

With each step toward the exit, my natural Omega scent rose and permeated the air. The others had all fogged my presence with their soiled outfits, but I'd be noticeable very soon without them. I just had to reach Kazek's side before Vanessa sensed my presence.

I heard her roar through the walls, the foundations of the castle shaking from the reverberation of an irate Alpha. "*Excuse me?* Is that a direct challenge?"

"I don't need to challenge you, Queen of Mirrors," he drawled.

His words shivered across my skin as I entered the hallway that had given her that nickname. The walls were covered with mirrors in this part of the castle, all because she enjoyed admiring herself as she walked.

"As I said," Kazek continued, "I'm already Sector Alpha, at least according to Winter Sector rules."

"What rules?" Vanessa demanded as I reached the main doors.

I pushed them open, causing everyone to shift toward the

sound and approaching Omega scent. "The one that says my mate is king," I informed her, my spine straight as I stepped through the threshold and into the firelight.

Sounds of astonishment met my entry.

Kazek didn't face me, his focus on Vanessa. My heels clacked over the gray marble as I approached him, intending to stand at his side.

I held Vanessa's narrowed gaze the entire way, refusing to bow to her "regal" presence. There was only one Alpha I'd kneel for in this room—my mate.

"As the daughter of Einar and Sofie Frost, I am the rightful heir to the throne. And Alpha Kazek is my bonded mate, making him the rightful king." My arm brushed his as I halted beside him. "Your services in Winter Sector are no longer required, Alpha Vanessa."

Kazek snorted beside me. "Is it considered a service to hide an Omega's true nature from everyone, including herself, through the art of administering supplements disguised as strength pills?"

A shock wave went through the crowd, murmurs of surprise gracing the air.

"I would refer to that as a crime," Alpha Enrique spoke up, his voice deep and carrying through the room. "Similar to recruiting an Alpha from another sector to take a Beta as a bride, knowing full well she was actually an Omega."

"Don't forget the request to knot her to death," Kazek reminded him, eliciting more gasps from the wolves.

"Oh, I'll never forget that task," Enrique replied. "In fact, I think it'll haunt me for the rest of my life."

"Good." Kazek pressed his palm to my exposed lower back and bent his head toward me. "You look gorgeous, by the way, *mate*."

He hadn't even glanced at me, but maybe he could see me in his peripheral vision. Actually, knowing Kazek, that was definitely how he caught a glimpse of my dress, because nothing seemed to pass by him without notice.

"Thank you, Alpha," I murmured, purposely using his designation as a sign of respect.

He brushed his lips against my temple, then righted

himself. "Alpha Vanessa, Queen of Mirrors, I charge you with the murder of Snow Frost, Beta of Winter Sector."

I leaned into him, supporting his decision.

Vanessa, however, didn't. She laughed and shook her head. "That's an outrageous charge, Alpha Kazek, considering Snow Frost is standing beside you, alive and well. As to everything else—"

"Snow Frost died the night she became an Omega," I interjected.

Vanessa hissed in response, hating that someone she considered to be beneath her standing dared to interrupt her. But I wasn't done.

"My bloodline is Frost royalty. And I am now Omega Winter Flor of Norse Sector, mate of Kazek Flor, and entitled Queen of Winter Sector." I allowed that proclamation to settle, ensuring she understood the gravity of what I was saying. "You stand upon my stage as an imposter, and I will not bow to you, *Queen of Mirrors.*"

"You dare speak to me that way after everything I've done for you?"

"I do." I thrummed the string on my bow idly. "Your suppressants nearly killed me. You conspired with Alpha Enrique to have me killed. And you assassinated my parents."

Everyone in the room could have heard a pin drop after that final accusation.

And then Vanessa laughed, a deep, callous sound that reminded me of claws screeching against glass. Kazek's thumb drew a warning circle against my lower back. I couldn't say how I knew that was his intention, just that I felt it in the very precise way his nail moved along my skin.

Be ready, he was saying. We both knew she wouldn't accept this fate lying down. She was an Alpha, and she'd been planning this for too long to fail now.

"Such outlandish claims," Vanessa said, shaking her head. "Who gave you the strength pills, Snow? What proof do you have of this supposed assassination? And do you really think I'd ever ask Enrique to kill you? He's lying, just like he lied to me about you being dead." She glowered at him on that last part.

"I never lied. Snow Frost is dead. She's now Winter Flor." He lifted a shoulder. "As for the rest, well, Winter Sector is already gathered for a trial. Perhaps it should be yours rather than Beta Doc's?"

Her stature turned regal. "His trial and execution are forthcoming."

"On what grounds?" I demanded. "Doc has done nothing but protect me since my youth, something I can't say about you. I do not condone his trial or his execution."

"And you believe that's your call?" she asked, her dark eyebrow inching upward.

"I do," I replied, aware of Kazek vibrating approval beside me. He liked seeing me take back my kingdom and exude my rightful place. And for that, I fell for him just a little bit more.

"Well." Vanessa smiled, and the wickedness in that look had my stomach churning with foreboding. "I disagree."

Her hand moved so quickly that I didn't catch the motion until the claws glistened in the light.

"No!" I shouted as she went for Doc's chest, her intent clear.

I reacted on instinct, an arrow falling into my grasp, lining up with my bow, and sailing through the air with a precision that would have made Doc proud.

But I wasn't fast enough.

Blood spilled across the stage, Vanessa's claws slicing into Doc and creating a roar of protest from the room.

My arrow pierced her shoulder, rendering her arm useless. She shrieked in response, just as Doc's body fell forward, the chain around his neck all that held him upright.

Enrique released him and focused on the raging queen, his fist connecting with her jaw just as she turned on him and started to fight.

It all happened in a blink, the entertainment hall going from tense to chaos in half a heartbeat.

I lined up my bow, arrow ready, but I couldn't get a shot, the Betas of Winter Sector moving around and disrupting my ability to aim.

Vanessa needed to pay.

She'd nearly ripped the heart out of my protector, her

hands drenched in his lifeblood as she tried to take down Alpha Enrique.

Opy jumped away from the stage, disappearing into the crowd, and I screamed in frustration.

Then a howl sounded beside me that caused my knees to buckle.

I fell to the ground beneath the overwhelming dominance of my mate, my wolf cowering at the fury in his tone. A whimper left my lips, one that was echoed by several of the Betas collapsing around me.

Kazek released a second, harsher growling bellow that brought tears to my eyes. This was an Alpha exuding his command and demanding the pack heel before him. I curled into the smallest ball imaginable, unable to withstand such superiority.

I was an Omega.

The bottom of the food chain.

Incapable of ever comparing or competing with such authority.

I would never even try. I could scarcely breathe at the moment.

Silence followed, the terror in the audience sweeping a chill across my skin and dotting goose pebbles up and down my arms.

"I am Alpha of this territory," Kazek announced into the stark stillness. "King of Winter Sector."

I nodded, agreeing with him for the sake of survival. Furious Alphas weren't meant to be—

Warmth stroked my hair, freezing me inside. "Stand," he said, his tone gentler yet underlined with steel.

I trembled, unable to comply. My lips parted to explain, but there wasn't enough oxygen in my lungs to utter a single word.

Oh, this was bad. Ignoring an Alpha's command was a death sentence. Especially one so angry, so full of reprimand.

I tried again and failed.

A tear fell from my eye, a part of me hating myself for being unable to react beyond this abject horror shredding my insides. I'd never felt this way before, not even at Vanessa's angriest moments.

But Kazek wasn't Vanessa.

No.

He was all Alpha. A true leader. A male destined to be king.

"Winter." My name from his lips felt like a kiss against my soul.

And then he began to purr.

My limbs shook in reaction, the rumble from his chest reviving my ability to move. It shot through my bloodstream in a heated caress, unlocking me from my bow and providing me with the strength I needed to lift my head.

He held out his hand for me, his eyes capturing mine. "Join me, my queen. Please."

His purr intensified, surrounding me in a cloud of comfort that erased my unease, leaving me refreshed and sturdier than before. I clutched my bow with one palm and extended my other to accept his assistance.

He guided me to my feet, his hand remaining in mine while his opposite one went to my cheek. "Breathe," he whispered, his dark irises flaring with power.

I inhaled on his command. Then exhaled slowly.

"Better?" he asked.

I nodded. "Yes."

"Good." He pressed a sweet kiss to my lips, then drew his thumb across my mouth. "Walk with me, Queen of Winter Sector."

His words vibrated through me, my heart skipping a beat at the realization of what he'd just done. He'd taken control of the pack with two bellows, their submission prevalent all throughout the room.

Not a single soul stood within the crowd.

Even Enrique had bowed his head, though I suspected that was more out of respect than out of need. He didn't want to challenge for the territory, and his posture showed that.

Vanessa, however, stood beside him, her body vibrating in fury. Yet she seemed unable to move, as if Kazek had cast a spell over her, freezing her on the stage.

It was something about his aura, the dominance radiating

off him in harsh waves of electricity that forced everyone to submit. Including the other Alphas.

Kazek brought my wrist up to his mouth to nibble my pulse as we approached the main stage. It was a simple gesture but indicated his claim in a sensual manner. My wolf hummed inside in approval, reveling in the music vibrating inside his chest.

His purr.

For me.

His mate.

It was all that kept me moving, his inner beast still very much in charge. "You stand upon *my* stage, attempting to possess *my* throne, and issue punishment to *my* people without proper authority." The words were calmly stated, yet his aura pulsated with aggression. "Kneel, *Queen of Mirrors*."

"Never," she managed to say through gritted teeth.

Kazek smiled and brought my hand up to his lips once more. "Mmm, you hear that, my queen? She refuses to acknowledge us as her betters." He spoke against my skin, his pleasant rumble lacing through his voice. "What do you want to do about that?"

"Put her on trial," I said, remembering our original intention. It hadn't gone entirely to plan, but there was still time. And, according to Grum, we had everyone we needed to convict her properly.

"Trial," Kazek repeated. "Similar to the trial she gave Doc?"

I winced, reality spinning a dark whisper inside my mind, reminding me of her sin and what had led up to this moment. Kazek's purr had distracted me, clouding my judgment and drawing me into a false sense of peace that shouldn't exist.

"Doc," I whispered, my heart breaking for the male who had protected me all my life. The leader of my seven. My savior.

Kazek caught my jaw and tilted my head in a way I didn't want it to angle, forcing me to take in the gruesome scene of my massacred mentor. "Look at him," Kazek said, his vibrations growing louder. "Really look at him, Winter."

I didn't want to, didn't understand why he was doing this

to me, forcing me to face the violence of…

Wait.

My gaze narrowed, then my eyebrows lifted in surprise at the subtle movement on the ground. I almost missed it, but then I heard the shaky exhale come from Doc's lips. "He's breathing."

"Yes," Kazek replied, releasing my chin. "Your arrow saved his life. Barely. But he'll survive."

I nearly collapsed in relief, but Kazek's palm went to my lower back to apply subtle pressure, forcing me to remain upright. His touch served as a reminder that we needed to present a strong united front. He'd allowed me my emotional moment, and now he wanted me to show some teeth. I sensed that in our bond and in the way his thumb stroked my spine.

"She needs a real trial," I said. "Only a coward delivers punishment without a conviction."

She snarled at me. "You ungrateful little—"

Kazek growled sharply, cutting her off with his dominant flare. "You will speak when I tell you to speak."

"You're not—"

The sound that left Kazek's mouth had my knees wobbling all over again, stirring whines and whimpers from the Betas in the crowd, and drew a retaliatory howl from Vanessa.

She lunged and Kazek reacted, the two of them becoming a ball of fists and animalistic war cries. It all happened so fast, my mate's fist slamming into Vanessa's jaw as she fought to drag her nails across his face. But he was too fast, too Alpha, for her to stand a chance.

"Submit," he demanded.

"Never!"

Splatters of blood flew across the stage, causing Kazek to snarl and shove Vanessa to the ground beneath him, the sound of her skull hitting the ground a victorious crack that vibrated through the air.

She roared in fury, her wolf threatening to take over her, but a demanding rumble from Kazek forbade her from shifting.

So much power.

It had my knees going weak all over again.

Enrique grabbed me and pushed me behind him in a surprisingly protective maneuver, but I didn't want to hide.

This bitch just attacked my mate.

She'd taken my throne.

Tried to have me killed on multiple occasions.

Denied me my Omega birthright for two decades.

And she'd killed my parents.

Grum had proof, a recording of her admitting it to Enrique. I'd intended to play it for the sector, to show them all the truth about their queen, but as I took in their stances now, I realized they already knew.

Maybe they'd always known.

Maybe I'd been the one oblivious to her true nature.

She rarely let me out, claiming to be protecting me, but that was all a lie. Vanessa had hidden me to keep me separated from my people, to isolate me as their future queen, and to deny me the opportunity of getting to know my sector.

It was all so clear now in my head, the reason for all of her decisions, her treatment, and her plans. This wasn't just about killing me.

Vanessa had kept me weak so I wouldn't consider myself worthy of the kingdom.

But my seven had held me together in ways she never knew, and then Kazek provided me with the platform I required to stand on.

He was the final piece of my life puzzle, the player on the board I never knew I needed.

Together, we were the true King and Queen of Winter Sector.

Vanessa never stood a chance.

She was unworthy. Vile. A creature not even deserving of a trial.

I stepped out from behind Enrique, my bow already drawing back with an arrow that had fallen gracefully into my hand.

Kazek had her pinned, his teeth bared in a feral snarl even while she thrashed beneath him, refusing to submit.

But it didn't matter.

He'd clearly won even before the sparring match had begun.

Everyone in the sector bowed to him now, not to Vanessa.

"Vanessa, Queen of Mirrors, you're hereby dismissed from your duty to the Frost family and Winter Sector," I said, my voice miraculously steady. Adrenaline thundered through my veins, my heart pumping in overdrive as she glowered my way.

I released the arrow, the aim spot-on, hitting her directly between the eyes.

Her red-painted lips had parted in surprise upon impact, giving her a morbidly fascinating appeal, one I studied for a long moment before walking through the audience toward the main entrance to the entertainment hall.

No one tried to stop me.

No one asked my intentions.

They all merely watched, including my mate, as I left the room and entered the infamous hallway of mirrors.

I chose the glass toward the end of the hallway and released the arrow from a safe distance. The mirror shattered on impact, as did all the rest as I shot arrow after arrow into every single one, destroying her prized creation.

Then I found the longest piece with a jagged edge among the ample debris, picked it up, and carried it back into the room.

Kazek had left Vanessa on the ground and now stood with his elbow resting idly on top of the throne. Pride glimmered in his expression, his wolf pleased with my decision.

Because he knew what I intended to do.

I suspected Enrique knew, too. He'd taken on a submissive pose near the side of the stage, deferring to Kazek in the way he should. I ignored him as I passed him, my focus lowering to the fallen Alpha on the stage with my arrow protruding from between her eyes. She'd removed the one from her shoulder, which had allowed her to start healing, but blood still oozed from the contusion on her head.

She wasn't dead. Not quite. There was only one way to ensure she never drew another breath.

I needed her heart to stop beating.

Indefinitely.

By cutting off the flow and making it impossible for her to regenerate.

Because wolves who lost too much blood consistently couldn't heal.

"Alpha Vanessa has committed several acts of violence against the Frost dynasty, including being responsible for the deaths of Einar and Sofie Frost. As is my right as the sole heir, I deliver unto her a punishment befitting the crime." I knelt beside her, my hands steady as I positioned the jagged glass at her throat.

And began to saw.

A blade would have been more efficient—it also wouldn't have cut into my own hands—but I needed this to be painful for us both. I needed to *bleed*. It was the only way I knew how to grieve.

Grum hadn't told me the specifics, but he'd grimly confirmed my suspicions regarding the deaths of my parents.

Vanessa had admitted it. Gleefully, too, from what he'd confessed.

She needed to pay.

To feel each stab of agony as I sliced open her neck to sever her head.

It's what she deserves.

With each prolonged swipe against her flesh, I thought of all the ways she'd hurt me throughout the years.

"I'm not inferior," I told her. "I'm not a weakling. I'm not your burden. I'm not a bargaining chip to be wedded off. I'm not someone you just kill and throw away like trash. I'm Queen of Winter Sector, as is my birthright, and you, Vanessa, are *dead* to me."

On and on it went, my eyes blurring with rage and pent-up frustration.

I hated her.

I loathed how she made me crave her affection and approval over the years.

I despised how she'd stolen two decades of my life.

She killed my parents.

Stole my kingdom.

Damned me to *hell*.

And I returned the favor with each... fucking... *slice*.

Die.

Die.

Die.

I couldn't even see what I was doing, the blood coating my vision in a wave of watery red.

It was then that I realized I was crying.

A scream ripped from my throat, and Kazek was there, his palm on my back and his opposite hand falling to the top of mine. "You're almost done," he whispered into my ear. "Finish her."

I nodded, bit back a yelp, and did exactly as he said. My fingers screamed in agony, my own skin shredded from the effort I'd put into sawing off her head. But there it was, lying in its gory glory with my arrow proudly embedded in her skull.

Dead.

She's dead.

I collapsed backward onto my heels, Kazek's body a shield at my side as he pried the bloody glass from my hand. Then he bent to lick the deepest wound, his eyes holding mine the entire time. It was strangely erotic, a new kind of claim, and I felt my heart explode with new, raw emotion.

This male had let me deliver my edict without any interference. He'd given me my moment of much-needed revenge while having my back each step of the way. And he'd just allowed me to rise as queen.

I went up onto my knees again and kissed him with every ounce of feeling I possessed. I was essentially confessing my love with my tongue. He wrapped a palm around my nape, holding me to him as he responded in kind, the words not required. Because I sensed his love for me in return.

Mine, my wolf sighed.

Yours, his replied.

We couldn't hear each other's thoughts, but the bond told us everything we needed to know.

This was real. Our mating had secured our fate. We were forever bound to each other, and this kingdom belonged to us equally.

"You were magnificent, my queen," he whispered against my mouth. "Fucking magnificent."

I smiled, my heart rate slowly returning to normal. "I had help from an equally magnificent king."

"That's what mates are for," he replied, pulling back enough to smile down at me. "Now I think we need to address our sector."

"Yes," I agreed. "There's a recording they need to hear."

He nodded. "Then let's play it for them."

CHAPTER THIRTY-FIVE

KAZEK

"CONGRATULATIONS, ENRIQUE. You get to live," I informed him after dismissing the Betas back to their homes.

It'd taken some time to calm them all down after playing the audio that sealed Vanessa's guilt, but Winter had managed it with admirable ease. Even covered in blood and grime, she resembled a queen they could respect, and I adored her all the more for it.

Enrique snorted. "Not sure your Betas are okay with that decision."

I lifted a shoulder. "Your fate was never up to them, but to me." And a good thing, too. He'd played the part of asshole on that recording a little too well. But I couldn't fault him for doing a superior job of trapping the queen.

"There's just one thing I don't get," he'd said. "You knew she was an Omega. So how did you plan for me to knot her to death? As an

Omega, she could accept my knot."

Vanessa had laughed, the maniacal sound grating on my every last nerve.

And then she'd uttered the words that'd put the nail through her coffin.

"How do you think Einar Frost killed Sofie Frost?" Another of those cackles followed her question. "You should have seen his face when he realized his knot had killed her. I'm sure she'd screamed for him to stop, but you know how Alphas are when they lose themselves to the rut. Especially when doped up on a hallucinogenic."

"He took hallucinogenics?" Enrique sounded shocked, just as he should. Hallucinogenics were dangerous to wolves. Particularly Alphas.

"As you know, Carlos uses them all the time in Bariloche Sector. I just asked to borrow a little. He always did favor me as his youngest sibling."

Their familial relation was well known but not something I'd considered relevant to the situation. How wrong I'd been on that front. It seemed she'd used her brother quite a bit to help her take over Winter Sector. The question was, did Carlos know? I suspected he did and that he didn't care.

Enrique had fallen silent for a moment after her admission. Then he provided the missing piece of the puzzle, one that had sent a shock through my system and caused Winter to tremble against me.

"You borrowed the old serum, too. The one he uses to punish disobedient Omegas, to make them tighter."

Vanessa chuckled, her glee palpable. "Of course I did, and I had another dose for Snow that I guess won't be needed."

"But that doesn't kill Omegas."

"It does when you give them more than recommended. I also induced Sofie's estrus, which caused Einar to go into the rut, while on a strong hallucinogen. Not a great combination for Sofie."

She paused to let that sink in, then thoughtfully added, "Did you know the Bariloche serum has a different effect on male Omegas? It makes them unable to come. Prolongs the pleasure for me, though. Even more so when I stimulate them."

Alana's expression had been positively murderous during that section of the tape. Which explained why she'd gone directly to Vanessa's quarters afterward, seeking out the male

Omegas who had clearly been tortured by their mistress. As she hadn't returned, I suspected she was helping them heal in the only way an Alpha could. She'd never force herself on them, but she would assist in any way they allowed.

"So Einar killed his mate," Enrique had replied after several beats of silence. "But how did he die?"

"Oh, he was quite distracted when he realized what he'd done. Let's just say I offered to walk and talk with him, and he tripped over some rocks. There are some dangerous cliffs on the edge of this sector. I don't suggest wandering around out there unless you know where to properly step."

"You made it look like he committed suicide."

"I did. And who could blame him after the way Sofie died? We all know it's an Alpha's primary job to protect his or her mate. Why do you think I've not mated any of my Omegas? I don't want the baggage."

Enrique had snorted and then praised her for the job well done, claiming to be impressed. Then she'd returned the favor by thanking him for taking care of her "royal brat" problem.

"Shall we go deliver the good news to Winter Sector?" she'd asked, sounding positively gleeful by the prospect. *"We'll kill the Beta guard in charge of her protection for fun. He's been useless to me anyway and refusing to corroborate Jackal's claims about them helping her escape."*

That'd been the part where we'd learned there was no footage, just a Beta with a loyalty problem. Opy had delivered the Beta to me before I even had a chance to ask. Suddenly, his willingness to attack the guards earlier had made sense— because Jackal was one of them. I'd offered Opy the chance to finish the job of taking the rat to task, and the Beta had obliged with a joy I admired.

Jackal's head now rested beside that of his dead queen.

A fitting demise, in my opinion.

Which left me one loose end to tie up. Enrique. He'd proven himself useful tonight, and he'd made his lack of interest in leadership clear. But that didn't mean I trusted him to hang around.

"I need to tend to my mate," I said to him now from my seat upon the throne. Winter was in my lap, her head against my chest as she listened to my purr. "Don't leave Winter

Sector. I want to talk to you again tomorrow." Technically, it would be later today given the late hour.

Enrique dipped his head in acknowledgment.

"Good," Mick said, narrowing his gaze at the other male. "You can come with me because I have questions."

I shook my head as they left, amused by Mick's obsession over Omega Kari. "They're not even mated," I said. And I was pretty sure they hadn't even fucked yet either.

"She can't mate in her current condition," Winter replied, her voice soft. "But you wanted me before I even knew I was an Omega. Isn't that why you tried to follow me after I left the party?"

"I wanted to fuck you and your smart mouth."

My mate scoffed at that. "Such a romantic."

"I'm not romantic."

"Clearly." She lifted her head to look at me. "But you wanted me as a Beta. Not an Omega. Maybe he wants her despite her inability to mate."

I considered her point of view and slowly nodded. "It's possible. I did really want to fuck you."

"You still do," she pointed out, her saucy little rump rubbing across my groin in a provocative manner.

I smiled. "Yes. I definitely still do. But we really need to bathe."

Her lips pinched to the side. "You may not enjoy the process here as much as back in Norse Sector."

I nearly groaned at what she meant, the dismal firelight around us reminding me of the lack of proper utilities in this sector. "I guess we'll need to do something to warm up the water."

She didn't seem to mind the fish stench clinging to my clothes as she rubbed her cheek against my torso, perhaps because she could smell the skin beneath. Or maybe it was my purr subduing her reactions.

The information on the recording had upset her. She'd not outwardly allowed the others to see it, but I'd felt it through the bond. The deep rumble in my chest was all I could offer her as comfort, and it seemed to be working.

I lifted her as I stood, cradling her against me as a groom

would his bride on a wedding night, and walked through the now empty entertainment hall. "Direct me to your quarters, mate."

She did in a soft tone, her energy seeming to wilt with every passing moment.

I admired her handiwork in the hallway of mirrors, my lips curling at the destruction. When I'd first arrived, this corridor had reminded me of the famous corridor in the Palace of Versailles. I imagined that was Vanessa's intent when she'd re-created it. The original was grander but had been destroyed during the rise of the Infected.

I wondered how Winter would prefer to redecorate the corridors after they were swept clean of glass.

It'd be one of our many necessary conversations, the first being a discussion on proper heating and electricity. The summer months in this region provided ample sunlight that could be used to replenish energy reserves. We just needed the technology installed to handle it, something I'd work on immediately with Ludvig and his son Ander.

I pushed through the door Winter indicated as her own and paused at the entrance of her gold-adorned quarters. It was befitting her station, surprising me. Given Vanessa's treatment, I'd half expected Winter to live in the dungeon.

"These are my mother's old quarters," she explained softly. "My seven ensured my claim through methods of advisement. Vanessa thought she had the loyalty of all the Betas. She didn't."

I set her on her feet. "More points in their favor."

Her lips curled. "They've done their best." But as she said the words, her brow began to crinkle. "Except, I don't understand how anyone bought Vanessa's story about my parents. How could anyone believe my father killed my mother? And then himself? Suicide is nearly impossible for a wolf."

I hooked my thumbs under the straps of her silky dress and drew them down her arms. The fabric pooled around her waist before falling to the floor, leaving her naked except for a pair of heels.

Beautiful, I thought, indulging in the view for half a beat before focusing on her concern.

"Emotions can blind a person's perception," I explained. I pulled the filthy sweater over my head and tossed it into a corner of the room.

"But Omegas can take a knot," she replied. "Especially during estrus."

I unbuttoned my pants and pushed the fabric down my legs, eager to remove the foul material. "Yes. But it's not unheard of for an Alpha to accidentally kill an Omega when lost to the rut. Not all Alphas are created equal in terms of their ability to remain in control." I palmed her cheek and drew my thumb over her plump lower lip. "Omegas are much smaller than us, and while your bodies are meant to accept ours, that doesn't mean you can survive all the power we have to give."

She shivered in response, her pupils flaring.

I drew her into my chest, wrapping my arms around her.

"That's why trust is so important," I whispered into her ear. "Omegas trust Alphas to take care of them, to listen to the cues through the bond, and to act accordingly. Unfortunately, not all Alphas are honorable. And not all of us are good at controlling our mating instincts."

I kissed her forehead before going to my knees in front of her and taking one delicate ankle into my hands to unbuckle and remove her shoe. She watched me, her tongue sneaking out to dampen her lips. "But my father was honorable," she replied slowly. "The Betas of Winter Sector knew that, yet they believed he rutted her to death anyway."

"As I said, emotions distort perception. They were grieving and following the lead of an Alpha they thought they could trust. But you said your seven always suspected something wasn't right, and after the show tonight, I'm certain they weren't alone in that intuition. Did you see how fast they changed allegiances? That's not the response of a loyal pack."

"Your howl called to them."

I shook my head. "No, sweetheart. *You* called to them." I finished removing her other shoe and stood, then lifted her into my arms again. "They submitted to me, but they bowed to you. I watched it happen while you executed Vanessa. No one protested. All they did was admire your handiwork and gaze upon you in astute approval. You're their queen, Winter."

"And you're their king." She pressed her palm to my cheek, her gaze locking with mine. "You're their *Alpha* king."

"Because I was chosen by their queen." I might have mated her in a dizzying cloud of lust and need, but Winter had accepted me at some point along the way, and her people had recognized that tonight.

"You're mine," she said, her fingers sliding into my hair to draw me down for a kiss. I allowed her to lead for a moment, knowing it was what she needed. She sighed in content when she finished, her dark eyes glazed with arousal. "I'm ready to heat up the water now."

I smiled down at her. "Good. Because I'm ready to devour you, my queen."

"Promise?"

"Always."

CHAPTER THIRTY-SIX

WINTER

"THERE," I said, pointing to the center of the wall of the corridor.

Opy picked up the framed painting to place it right where I requested. Grum stood beside me, nodding. "Good choice."

"Better than a mirror?" I joked.

"Abso-fucking-lutely. If I never see my reflection again, I'll be glad."

My lips twitched in amusement. "But it's such a nice reflection."

"Careful, don't let your Alpha hear you complimenting me. He already wants to cut off my balls." He spoke the words in a mock whisper, earning a grunt from Kazek down the hall.

"Trust me, I want to do a lot more than just cut them off, Beta," he drawled. The wink he sent me said he was mostly joking. Sort of. He returned to his conversation on his digital screen, but he never really took his attention away from me. Kazek always seemed in tune with my location, even when we weren't in the same room.

"What about this one?" Happa asked, holding up a portrait of my father. "Next to Sofie, or across the hall?"

"Next to Sofie," I replied in unison with Doc.

He'd fully healed, thanks to his wolf genetics. Vanessa had almost ripped out his heart, another surefire way for a shifter to die. Fortunately, my arrow had stopped her. Now he stood in the hallway with his hands tucked into his trousers, his focus on the images of my parents decorating the improved ambience of the castle interior.

We had a lot of work to do, but everyone seemed eager to help. Kazek had disbanded the Beta brothels on his first day as king, something I'd approved of, and was now busy trying to figure out what tasks to assign everyone. His contacts in Norse Sector and Andorra Sector were coming in handy already, their technology leagues ahead of ours.

It would take time to restructure the sector. Luckily, we were heading into the spring months, which would grant us ample hours of sunlight to work through the summer.

"They'd be proud of you," Doc said softly, coming to stand on my other side. "I just wish they were here to see it."

"They're here," I promised, smiling as Opy used a tool to ensure the paintings were both balanced against the wall. I pressed a palm over my heart and looked up at the leader of my seven. "I carry them in my heart."

His black eyes gleamed. "You remind me so much of your mother, Snow." He kissed the top of my head as a pair of strong arms wrapped around my middle, pulling me backward and away from Doc and Grum.

"She prefers Winter," Kazek reminded him, a subtle growl in his tone. It didn't matter how many times I told him my seven were like family to me; he still didn't enjoy them showing me affection.

I understood because I'd want to rip Alana apart if she touched him. Thankfully, she had her hands full with the Omega males right now. She also hadn't shown a single interest in my mate even before that, so I allowed her presence to continue in Winter Sector. However, I knew the second I asked Kazek to remove her, he would.

That knowledge was good enough for me.

"Yes. Winter," Doc agreed. "Our Winter's Arrow."

I smiled. "Trained by the best." Kazek coughed at that, so I amended my statement. "Trained by the best Beta team in Winter Sector, I mean."

He squeezed me tighter and rested his chin on top of my head. "They did well." My mate's version of a compliment made my heart flutter in response.

Everything felt right for the first time that I could remember.

The aura of relief was palpable, causing me to realize that we'd all lived beneath a cloud of tyranny without even realizing it. Vanessa had purposely limited everyone's ability to improve, something Kazek had already started undoing by bringing in his contacts from other sectors.

"I need to get back to the weapons room to review the upgraded security system," Grum said. "Thanks for the facelift," he added, glancing at Kazek.

"It was needed," he replied.

"I know." Grum gave a wave and left, Opy following him without a word.

Doc walked up to stroke the edges of my father's painting, his expression full of memories. "Good to have you back, sir," he whispered before focusing on Kazek. "You have big shoes to fill, Alpha. Wear them well."

"Winter will ensure that I do." Kazek hugged me from behind as he said it, and Doc dipped his head in approval before taking his leave.

I studied my parents for a long moment, pleased with my decision to place them here at the entrance of the main hall. Everyone needed to see them and remember them and respect their legacy.

For too many years, there'd been this fog of unrest due to the fact that many believed my father had lost control and ended my mother's life in addition to his own. Now they knew the truth. Despite the horror of the story, I was deeply pleased that we all had closure on the topic.

"My parents were good leaders," I said, more to myself than to Kazek. "I want to ensure their legacy is never forgotten."

"And we will," Kazek promised. "Every day." He gently turned me in his arms, his expression soft as he studied me. "You'll teach me how to be a better Alpha to our people."

"You don't need my guidance," I told him, cupping his cheek with my much smaller hand. "You're already leading."

"Because of you," he said. "I'm doing all of this—for you."

I shook my head. "You're doing all of this because it's the right thing to do."

"No, Winter. It's always been for you, and always will be for you." He kissed me, his lips firm and dominant against mine. I submitted as I always did with him, my body melting on instinct, but a buzzing on his wrist interrupted the moment. "Mmm, one moment. I've been expecting this call."

I didn't understand what he meant until he brought up the screen over his watch and a tan male with long black hair populated the screen. "Alpha Carlos," Kazek greeted with a falsely jovial note in his voice. "Did you receive my gift?"

"I did," the other male replied gruffly. He glanced at me through the screen. "Is this your new mate?"

"Yes. Omega Winter Flor, Queen of Winter Sector," Kazek informed him. "She helped me put the gift together for you."

"I see," Alpha Carlos replied, his expression exuding his displeasure at the situation. "Do you commonly allow your mate to attend calls with other sector leaders, Alpha Kazek?"

"Well, I'm still rather new to this. Ask me again in a year and I'll let you know." His flippant reply earned him a scowl from the other male.

"You won't last long in your position, mutt."

"Is that a direct challenge?" Kazek countered, arching a brow.

"Not from me, but you'll be hearing from others soon."

"Ah, a threat, then," Kazek drawled. "My favorite."

Carlos wasn't amused. "There are protocols in place for a reason." The topic switch confirmed the reason for his call.

"Your sister tried to kill my mate on countless occasions. I didn't require protocol to end her life. But if you would prefer I send a copy of that recorded confession to all the Sector Alphas, I'm happy to do so."

"Who's threatening who in this scenario?"

"Oh, I'm the one threatening you," Kazek clarified. "Retaliate and I'll destroy you and your penchant for drugs."

Carlos snorted. "You can try."

Kazek grinned. "I would do more than try."

The Alpha fell silent on the other end of the line, his jaw ticking visibly on the screen. "Bariloche Sector does not wish to challenge you at this time. The death of Alpha Vanessa is accepted and forgiven."

The line went dead before Kazek could reply.

My mate chuckled and shook his head. "Well, that's about what I expected."

"Do you think he means it?" I asked. "That he's going to just accept his sister's death?"

"He cares more about himself than about his sister, and that recording Enrique captured for us implicates Alpha Carlos in the deaths of your parents. He may not have administered the drugs, but he supplied them. There are several sectors that would stop trading with him if they knew how deep his depravity really goes."

"Are you going to tell them?" I wondered out loud.

He shook his head. "No. I'm keeping it as a wild card for now. It'll help me maneuver the political arena as a new Sector Alpha. But if he so much as steps one toe out of line, I'll share the recording with the entire world."

I nodded, agreeing with his decision. "You've given Ludvig a copy, right?"

"Yes, and Ander Cain," Kazek replied. "Carlos isn't naive. He'll know we have backup outlets if needed. We're safe from his retribution. He has his own sector to worry about."

"And we have ours," I said, waving down the hall.

"We do." He smiled and pulled me close. "And we have each other."

"Forever."

"Forever," he agreed, pressing his mouth to mine. "And

maybe one day we'll have a pup or two as well."

I warmed at the idea, an image of Kazek holding our child populating in my mind. "I think I'd like that."

"Yeah?"

I bobbed my head. "Yeah. But maybe not yet. We have a lot to do here first."

"Then I'll talk to Ludvig about procuring some birth control before your next cycle." He brushed his lips against mine. "We'll just practice in the interim."

"Like maybe right now?"

He scooped me up into his arms in response. Except he didn't head for our chambers but for the entertainment hall.

"Kazek?"

"The thrones arrived today," he said as he pushed through the main doors. "It seems fitting considering they're in the place we first met."

"Someone might interrupt us."

"Not if they value their life," he replied, nibbling my lower lip. "I'm going to sit, then you're going to straddle me and ride me until we're both satisfied. Afterward, I'm going to take you again because I can. And then, if I'm pleased with the performance, I'll lick you clean and worship you like the queen you are."

I was panting by the time he finished, my thighs slick with need beneath my dress. "Yes," I whispered. "Yes."

He chuckled darkly, his lips ghosting over mine. "I love you, Winter Flor."

My heart skipped a beat in my chest. He'd not said those words out loud, but I'd felt them floating between us for what felt like forever. "I love you, too, Kazek Flor."

"Kiss me," he demanded.

"Knot me," I countered.

"Oh, little mate." He settled onto the throne and rearranged me to straddle his thighs, just as he'd promised. "I'm going to knot you until you beg me to stop."

"I welcome that challenge."

"Good. Now get to work and undress."

"Always an Alpha," I teased even as I complied. It was pretty easy to just lift the dress over my head and drop it to the ground.

"Always *your* Alpha," he corrected, his eyes running over me with dark interest. "Just as you're forever mine."

I pulled my hair to one side to reveal the mark on my neck that would never fully heal, the one that confirmed his claim to the world. "Yours," I agreed.

"Yours," he repeated, yanking me down for a kiss that seared my insides.

It took only seconds for him to free his cock, and another handful of breaths before he was seated inside me, angling his hips upward, driving the momentum, and owning me in a way no one else ever would.

The throne more than accommodated us both.

And it seemed fitting, just as he'd said, that he took me in the same spot where we originally met.

Only now I was a queen and riding my king, straight into our own personal version of a happily ever after.

Together forever.

United as one.

The King and Queen of Winter Sector.

Kazek and Winter Flor.

EPILOGUE

SVEN

I PACED THE HALLS of Andorra Sector's primary hospital facility, my mind already made up.

There wasn't another option. Alpha Carlos had to pay for what he'd done. He couldn't be allowed to take another breath. He was a monster of the worst kind, an Alpha without an ounce of remorse, and he'd nearly killed his own daughter.

My intended mate.

Oh, she didn't agree. She'd fight me every step of the way. But she couldn't deny the pull between us.

Kari was mine. I'd known from the moment I laid eyes on her in that cage, her golden hair a beacon in the firelight.

And Alpha Carlos had tried to destroy her.

I pulled up my screen, dialing the one person I knew would understand. Well, the one male who would have my back, anyway.

My father wanted me to take a more worthy Omega, one without all the baggage. My wolf disagreed. Kari belonged to me, which made it my responsibility to see this through.

Kazek answered my call with a chuckle, his Omega sprawled out beside him in their nest. "This had better be important," he said by way of greeting.

Winter blushed and burrowed into the sheets, her skin covered by the mountain of fabric. It'd been a few weeks since I last spoke to Kaz, and from the looks of things, his mate was about to enter another estrus.

My chest squeezed with a hint of jealousy. *Will Kari ever act like that with me?* The female seemed to hate me more than like me, even though I'd done everything in my power to help her these last few months.

"Mick?" Kaz prompted, arching a brow.

I cleared my throat, preparing what I needed to say. "I just called to let you know I'm on my way to Bariloche Sector."

All signs of amusement died in his expression. "*What?*"

"Alpha Carlos can't be allowed to live for what he's done. I'm going to challenge him and kill him." There wasn't much else left to say. Kaz would consider this a suicide mission, as would my father, but I couldn't stand down. Not after what Kari just went through. "I leave tomorrow. I thought you'd want to know."

"Whoa, hold on, wait. You can't just waltz into Bariloche Sector and challenge the Sector Alpha. You'll never get past the borders."

"I already have that part figured out." Because Enrique was going to help me. His feelings for Kari had become abundantly clear when I learned about his connection to her sister. She'd mated his twin. Which had somehow linked him to the girl—an Omega who was still very much alive and tormented daily. He'd wanted to rescue Kari with the hope of going back to save her sister as well.

I'd give him the opportunity.

And kill Carlos in the process.

"Enrique is going to help you," Kaz said, realizing the path of my thoughts in that uncanny way of his. "Have you lost your fucking mind?"

A beat passed between us, drawing a deep sigh from my chest. I met and held his gaze, my resolve inflexible.

Then I said the only thing I could.

The only thing he'd understand.

"No, Kaz. I finally found my fucking heart."

SVEN AND KARI'S STORY CONTINUES IN BARILOCHE SECTOR...

Life is a series of prisons.
And in the end, there's only death.

Kari Zamora

My father enslaved me. Ruined me. Sold me. Left me to suffer. Until he rescued me.

Alpha Sven Mickelson of Norse Sector claims to be my savior, to want me to live, and vows to protect me. But I know Alphas can't be trusted. All he wants is my mating bond. To own me. To make me his.

No one cares what I want. But they will.

Because I have a plan.
One no one will see coming.
And by the time they realize I'm gone, it'll be too late to chase me.

Sven Mickelson

My destiny is to lead. To own. To possess. I'm an Alpha of significant birthright, and I'm ready to claim what's mine. Except she continues to deny me.

Omega Kari is broken. Destroyed. A female shredded apart by those she trusted most. And I'm the only one who can piece her back together. If she lets me.

She thinks I'm blind to her conniving ways, but I sense the fighter lurking beneath her fur. I'm daring her to come out to play. Because when she does, I'll finally be able to stake my claim.

So go on, then, little wolf.
Try to run.
I won't be far behind.
And together, we'll burn Bariloche Sector to the ground.

ABOUT THE AUTHOR

USA Today Bestselling Author Lexi C. Foss is a writer lost in the IT world. She lives in Atlanta, Georgia, with her husband and their furry children. When not writing, she's busy crossing items off her travel bucket list. Many of the places she's visited can be seen in her writing, including the mythical world of Hydria, which is based on Hydra in the Greek islands. She's quirky, consumes way too much coffee, and loves to swim. Cheers!

Printed in Great Britain
by Amazon